CHIRAL JUSTICE

ALSO BY LL RICHMAN

The Biogenesis War Series

The Chiral Agent

The Chiral Protocol

Chiral Justice

Chiral Agent/Chiral Conspiracy audiobook set

Chiral Protocol/Ambush in the Sargon Straits audio set

The Biogenesis War Files: The Early Years

Operation Cobalt

Ambush in the Sargon Straits

The Chiral Conspiracy

— BOOK 3 —
THE BIOGENESIS WAR

CHIRAL JUSTICE

LL RICHMAN

CONTENTS

Power works by division, influence by multiplication.
Power, in other words, is a zero-sum game:
the more you share, the less you have.
Influence is a non-zero-sum game:
the more you share, the more you have.

~Rabbi Lord Jonathan Sacks

PART ONE: DISCOVERY

TURNING THE ASSET

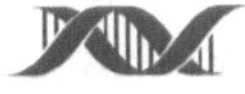

PREMIER'S BRIEFING, STATE ASSEMBLY HOUSE
CENTRAL PREFECTURE, ERIDU
AKKADIAN EMPIRE (ALPHA CENTAURI A)

THE PRISONER'S HEAD hung forward, his restraints the only thing keeping him from collapsing into the slick of bodily fluids pooling at his feet. The lone patch of illumination was centered on the chair, yet something about the recording suggested a cavernous space extending into the darkness beyond.

Che Josza wasn't watching the holographically projected image; he was watching the man riveted to the frozen scene before him. Asher Dent, the new Akkadian premier.

"This is the Alliance's vice chief of Joint Operations?" asked Dent.

Che nodded. "Yes. Harris Carlisle."

The premier flashed him an approving look. "Excellent."

Asher Dent had made good use of the political fallout from a failed bioterror attack on the Coalition of Worlds' Defense Summit eighteen months earlier. Having been one of its targeted victims, he was the only Akkadian that the settled worlds knew was uninvolved with the attempt to decimate the intelligence community.

Dent had used that political currency to trade his seat as the Coalition's Minority Leader for the reins of the Akkadian Empire. The botched operation by the previous administration had provided the leverage needed to 'retire' the aging premier and lay the blame at his heir-apparent's feet.

It hadn't mattered that the premier's daughter had no prior knowledge of the failed attack. Asher Dent had an ironclad alibi; he would have died with all the rest had the viral agent not been neutralized in time.

With Dent at the helm, Akkadia enjoyed an unexpected leniency within the Coalition. Sanctions held against the Empire by other star nations were relaxed, tariffs lowered.

If they only knew, Che thought. *They have exchanged a sleeping fox for a ravenous wolf.*

Che's own appointment to the ministry had been whirlwind—and utterly undeserved. Had Asher Dent known the truth behind Che's own involvement in the bioterror attack, Che was certain he'd be resting with his ancestors now, instead of serving as Minister of State Security.

The previous minister—his superior, Rin Zhou Enlai—had been convicted of crimes against the state, and subsequently been made to disappear. She yet lived, but Che wondered if she wouldn't rather have been gifted an honorable death.

"How long before he breaks?"

The premier's question pulled Che back to the present. He glanced over to see if Dent had noticed his wandering attention, but the man's focus was entirely on the prisoner that Che's senior interrogator had recently acquired.

"I was told a single session secured his cooperation," Che replied.

Dent frowned at him. "Truly? That is... a surprise. Although..." The premier's fingers drummed a soft pattern on the table's surface as his attention returned to the man on the screen, "I would expect no less from the Tèzhŏng."

The Tèzhŏng was the elite intelligence branch of Akkadia's

state army. It had been Che's responsibility once upon a time to train these warriors, to forge them into the ultimate weapons of the State. Part of him wished for those days, simpler times with a singular goal, when the weight of duty was a much easier burden to bear.

But his words betrayed none of these thoughts, his voice calm and measured as he spoke. "You'll soon see why. It's evident the man never had any form of resistance training."

Dent's lip curled in a sneer of distaste. "Yet another reason our citizen soldiers are superior. The militaries of other star nations cannot compare."

"I'm not certain we should judge all of the Geminate Navy by this measuring stick," Che cautioned, thinking of the men and women they had encountered eighteen months ago inside the Hawking Habitat.

He inclined his head toward the holoscreen. "Carlisle may have served in their military, but he is no warrior. It is to our benefit that he managed to rise to the rank of general, but he is clearly a career bureaucrat, not a soldier. He cares more for recognition than respect. These political ambitions were what led us to choose him over other targets."

Dent shot him a look. "That just serves to prove our military superiority. He never would have made it to that position here on Eridu. Resistance training is mandatory for our soldiers. We both know this. You were the leader of the Junxun; I was one of your students."

Che lifted his coffee in wordless acknowledgment. "One of the best."

The recording began to play, though it was difficult to tell. The man being turned into an Akkadian agent remained slumped in his chair, pasty skin glowing in the harsh light. Carlisle was in his mid-fifties, with the telltale softening of a man who'd spent recent years behind a desk.

Footsteps sounded over the feed, echoing off the bare metal walls of the empty warehouse. A pair of boots stopped short of visual range, their toes just touching the pool of light surrounding the subject.

The man didn't stir.

"You know, I've always thought it strange how something as basic as clothing can so easily be used against a prisoner," Dent mused as he continued to watch the screen with rapt absorption. "Yet, time and again, I've seen how the simple act of stripping someone naked ends up being the chink in their armor."

"That's a fitting metaphor," Che agreed. "That thin layer of fabric is a sort of emotional shield. Removing it renders the subject bare in more ways than the obvious."

A sharp slapping sound broke through the conversation. Che saw a short leather crop in the hand of the agent in charge, and watched the restrained man flinch when it met her bare palm.

"So, General Carlisle." The woman addressed the man, her face hidden from the holorecorder's field of view. "Are you ready to cooperate now?"

The prisoner lifted his head, and Che saw blood dripping from the man's nose. He worked his mouth, and Che knew the man was gently probing his broken front teeth with his tongue.

He winced, then nodded once.

Che saw the agent lean forward, light haloing the back of her head.

"I can't hear you, sir. Will you cooperate?"

"Yessss." The word was hissed, pain-filled, as cold air slid over the tooth's jagged remains, firing the exposed nerves.

The woman gestured one of her men forward. The soldier crouched beside Carlisle and attached electrodes to the man. The prisoner jerked in his restraints, panicking. Promises of fealty quickly devolved to epithets, and then pleas for clemency.

Che looked away. He knew what would come next; he'd performed the same interrogation himself countless times as he'd risen through the ranks. Agents like these did the work for him now, removing him from the process and providing a thin film of deniability on the off chance they were discovered.

He used to find satisfaction in the hands-on brutality of the work. There was a gritty immediacy to it all that he could still vividly recall. The blood dripping from the man's face, mixed with the piss that he'd just voided, would give the air in the room a sour, slightly metallic smell, Che knew.

Now, it sickened him.

This next phase wasn't calculated to break the man; that had already been accomplished. It would serve to guarantee his compliance. The psychological effects of this particular brand of torture, targeting his most vulnerable core, would sear an important lesson into the man's brain. Memory of this event would serve as a reminder of the consequences he could expect, should he ever entertain the thought of refusing his handlers.

Actions like this were necessary, for once an asset was restored to his position behind enemy lines, the individual invariably fell into a false sense of security. The man would receive one final round of torture, conducted in his own office one week from now, specifically to disabuse him of that falsehood.

The interrogation team cleared the pool of light, and a stream of water hit the prisoner, hosing him down. In the next moment, Carlisle's body arched as an electrical stimulus poured into it. The military-grade carbyne nanofloss augmentation that ran through his skeleton served as an excellent conductor; the man's face twisted in a rictus of pain.

Blood foamed at Carlisle's mouth as he began to seize. From the corner of his eye, Che saw Dent lean forward, despite the fact that the drama playing out before them had occurred several hours earlier.

"Don't lose him," the premier growled, and Che heard Dent's words echoed by the agent on the other end.

Once released from the current, Carlisle slumped forward. The feed ended as operatives cut him loose and then dragged his unconscious form away.

"That session ended an hour ago. Carlisle has already been treated by medical," said Che as he shut off the recording and turned to face his premier. "He'll be returned from his 'vacation' this evening, and will resume his duties with the Geminate Alliance tomorrow."

"Very good. How long after that before we enact Obelus?" the premier asked. He stood, signaling to Che that his time was up.

Che followed the man's lead. "It shouldn't be long. Our people are moving into position now."

Dent nodded and started for the door, but then came to a stop at the minister's next words.

"Carlisle isn't the holdup. It's Clint Janus."

The premier turned, his expression icy with displeasure. "I understood he'd successfully cloned a working proof of concept. I was told that our assets inside the Alliance made the swap a few days ago, and that the clone is already in position."

"He is—or rather, he was." Che worked hard to keep his expression blank. "Janus has allowed the pawn to slip its leash."

A STRANGER'S PLEA

The Hill – Fine Dining District
Downtown Montpelier, Ceriba

MICAH CASE PAUSED in the middle of the crowded Montpelier district known as The Hill and inhaled deeply as a savory smell teased at his nose. The dark-haired Shadow Recon pilot looked around, but pinpointing the origin of the mouth-watering aroma was an impossible feat. He was literally surrounded by bistros and curry houses, marisquerías and trattorias.

The dining district, located in a town just south of the capital city of St. Clair Township, was a popular destination, as evidenced by the crush of people flowing past him.

He inhaled once more, and his stomach growled. That earned him a light elbow jab from his companion.

"Don't they feed you up on that base, Captain?"

The warmth of her voice danced through his mind, a bright glow dispelling the darkness that had sunk its claws into his soul at the end of his last mission.

He'd brought *Wraith* in hot, both Nina and Will laying covering fire for the special forces team they'd been sent in to retrieve. The sight of two bodybags carried by the remaining four members of SRU Team Six was an image that would be forever seared into his brain.

When return fire spat back from the cargo bay of the derelict space station, he'd slewed the ship, bringing it in on a crab to give his gunner and crew chief better targeting solutions.

At the time, Micah'd been engaged in a battle of his own. The smugglers had launched two technicals—improvised fighting vessels—at them. Still, he'd managed to keep one eye on the team's approach.

He'd seen the flash, called out a warning over the combat net, but it was too little, too late. The frag grenade took out Tank, the team's EOD and lead breacher—or maybe he'd launched himself toward it to shield the others, Micah couldn't tell. Regardless, it ripped the man apart.

Six inserted. Three retrieved.

Unacceptable.

A hand tapped him on the sleeve. The memories retreated as he looked down, his blue eyes meeting laughing green ones.

"Ahoy the ship. You with me, flyboy?" Samantha Travis tugged lightly on his arm, silently encouraging him to resume their stroll.

"Sorry. Just..." His words faded.

He felt Sam squeeze his arm briefly in silent understanding before giving him another gentle nudge. Micah took the hint and began maneuvering them once more through the dinnertime crowd. He made an effort to shake his morbid thoughts, to stay in the present with the woman who held his heart.

His stomach growled once more, eliciting a soft chuckle from Sam. "I'll take that as a no," she said.

"As a—?" He abruptly recalled her earlier question. "I guess it would depend on your definition of the word 'feed'."

He forced a quick smile, working to inject a lightheartedness he didn't yet feel into his tone.

"There's food... and then there's *food*. You know what I

mean?" He spun his finger to indicate the various eateries. "Trust me; what the Navy serves and what I'm smelling here? No contest."

She cast a critical eye around as if considering his words.

"I can't believe you just reduced the best Montpelier has to offer to a four-letter word." She arched a mocking brow at him. "There's a reason this area's known as Restaurant Row. This isn't *food*, you heathen. It's culinary artistry."

"Watch it, wiseass."

Sam bumped her hip against his as he snaked a hand around her waist.

"That's *Doctor* Wiseass to you."

Micah felt the chill in his soul retreat a little bit, Sam's warmth holding the shadows at bay. He decided it felt good to be planetside, with her by his side.

He looked over just as the last rays from the white dwarf lit Sam's hair, the strands glinting gold in the waning light. He resisted the urge to tuck an errant strand behind her ear.

Instead, he tugged her closer. She settled comfortably against him as they meandered through the small borough, the murmur of voices from the crowded street washing over them. The sounds mingled with the chirping of the birds flitting through the trees at a nearby park.

The setting was peaceful, idyllic. Everything he needed right now.

They'd both been busy of late. He'd been tasked to fly special forces teams in and out of the Badlands, while she'd been wrapped up in a time-sensitive chiral experiment. The moment he'd been cut loose, he'd pinged Sam to see if she could get away for the evening.

He was glad she'd accepted.

A small street vendor cart filled with shawarma caught his eye, the meat's juices making quiet sizzling sounds as spatters of the liquid dripped onto the searing hot plate below.

Reaching for Sam's elbow, he pulled her to a stop. "Come on."

He nudged her toward the street vendor and extended a token, silently pointing to one of the skewers of meat.

"We're on our way to dinner. You'll ruin your appetite," she scolded.

The vendor smiled and handed it over, despite Sam's protest.

Micah lifted one eyebrow as he regarded her. "Woman, have you seen me eat? Besides, our reservations aren't for another hour. We'll be lucky if I survive that long."

Sam rolled her eyes, but didn't refuse the skewer of meat he held out to her, pulling the topmost piece off and popping it past her lips.

Mouth full, she switched to a more private method of communication. *{Sometimes, I find myself forgetting that none of this food will sustain your chiral body.}*

Micah shot her a sardonic look. *{I don't. Can't afford to.}*

When he saw her stricken expression, he saluted her with his skewer and sent a reassuring smile.

{It does come with a few perks, you know. I can't get sick... and I can eat all I want and not have to worry about packing on the pounds.} To illustrate his point, he tossed a piece of the spicy meat into his mouth.

The smells hadn't done it justice; the savory flavor that coated his tongue was sheer heaven. Sam agreed, if the sounds she was making were any indication.

He inclined his head toward the nearby park. "Come on. Let's get out of the crowd and go enjoy these in peace."

The park incorporated the same tasteful architectural lines as The Hill. Surrounded by a colonnade, its entrance was a graceful, arched trellis, tumbling with a waterfall of colorful flowers. A park bench sat just inside, and he angled toward it, their entry briefly interrupting the birdsong.

"How's work coming along?" he asked, sparing Sam a glance once they'd settled onto the bench.

She popped another piece of meat into her mouth and chewed thoughtfully, waggling a flattened palm back and forth before letting it drop.

{Eh. We're taking it slow, trying different methodologies as we work our way up from simple organisms. Creating quantum-entangled chiral clones of complex, multi-celled organisms like a Trichoplax is much more involved than when I was working with molecular compounds.}

{A trick-o-what?} Micah slid the last chunk of meat off his skewer with some regret, wishing he'd purchased more than one.

Sam sent him an image of something that looked a bit like a disk-shaped blob with fuzzy tendrils as she licked the juices from her fingers.

{A simple sea animal. It only has six cell types, which is why we chose it.} She brushed her hair from her face with the back of her hand as a light breeze stirred her short, blonde locks. *{By comparison, your basic fruit fly has fifty cell types. Humans have hundreds.}*

Micah grunted as he processed her words. He wadded up the napkin he'd used to wipe his fingers, and then looked around for a recycling receptacle. "Someone needs to uninvent those things."

{What? Chiral clones?}

"No. Fruit Flies."

That earned him a laugh. She dropped her napkin-wrapped skewer into his waiting hand, and rose to follow as he walked toward the exit.

{Sometimes the quantum entanglement between the two chirally-paired mirror organisms is complete,} she continued. *{But sometimes, it's not there at all.}*

The puzzlement in her tone had him glancing sharply at her as they reentered the flow of the crowd.

He considered his words carefully before responding, keeping their conversation a mental one, more for security reasons than efficiency, now that they'd finished their snack.

{It's… difficult to wrap my head around how slowly you're progressing when I think about—}

She cut in, her words scathing.

{About what that sorry excuse for a chief scientist did to you back on deGrasse? I suppose you could say he 'got lucky' when he chirally cloned Jonathan and brought you into this universe. But the fact remains he experimented on you without permission.}

She turned to face him, heedless of the press of the crowd, her eyes snapping.

{That was more than unethical. It broke every rule in the book. There's no possible way to precisely duplicate the methods he used. We may have his research notes, but his lab perished when deGrasse blew up, and we lost a lot in that explosion.}

She turned and resumed walking.

{I won't pretend the mental connection you and Jonathan share due to your quantum entanglement isn't unique and worth studying,} she added. *{But we sure as hell aren't going to skip the important interim steps to get there, like he did. And as a reminder, we're doing it so we can better understand and assist you, **not** so we can make more of you.}*

He pulled her to a stop, laid his hands on her shoulders, and turned her to face him. "I know that, Sam. I'd never think otherwise."

She stared back for a beat, and then her gaze softened. She tucked her hand through his arm, and they resumed walking. "Thanks. What he did was horrid," she added in a soft voice, "but I can't say I'm sorry, when it brought me you."

They walked in silence for a while.

A small cluster of swantail flitters erupted from a nearby bush as they passed, catching his attention. The colorful butterflies were native to his home planet of Beryl; they brought back warm memories of family picnics from when he was a child.

"I didn't know you had these on Ceriba," he said, craning his neck to follow their flight.

"What, the flitters?" Sam followed his gaze. "I remember a newsnet cast about it several years back. They migrate in large swarms, don't they?"

"Yeah, it's called a kaleidoscope, I think. The southern migration's a pretty big deal back home."

Sam made a noise of agreement. "Well, if I remember correctly, they were having some trouble with the pollinators here on Ceriba, so the conservatory decided to introduce them into the ecosystem to help balance it a bit better."

The flitters disappeared behind one of the buildings, and Micah turned his attention back to the street. "Reminds me of home."

He saw Sam slide a glance his way. "You don't talk about your homeworld much."

Micah hesitated, and then lifted his shoulder in a half shrug. "Jonathan and I don't go back as much as we used to prior to Luyten's Star. Kind of awkward, not being able to tell them there are two of us now."

"Understandable," she murmured after a moment.

Micah's mouth tipped up into a wry grin. "When Mom complains about us not visiting, we blame your uncle. Since the... incident... at Luyten's Star coincided with the creation of Task Force Blue, he makes a convenient scapegoat."

Sam laughed. "Fair enough."

The clink of glass and the murmur of patrons reached Micah's ears as they passed by an open-air café. The chatter reminded him of the two people who would be joining them at their destination.

"Hey, you sure you're okay with Thad and Ell joining us for dinner?" he asked Sam. "He kind of invited himself along tonight."

Thaddeus Severance was the commander of Task Force Blue, and an imposing man. A former active-duty Marine turned special forces soldier, Thad could make hardened veterans quail in their boots.

Despite his foreboding aura, the warrior had a quick wit and a ready smile that flashed white against his ebony face for those he counted as friend, and that included Micah. He trusted Thad to have his six, no matter what, when, or where.

Ell—Elodie Cyr—was a bit harder to read, but no less trustworthy despite that fact. She'd been a sniper on Thad's team for many years, until an injury forced her down a different career path. Now a special agent for the Navy's Criminal Investigation Command, Ell had been instrumental in the takedown of the Akkadian terrorists that had targeted the Defense Summit on Hawking eighteen months ago.

A dimple formed in Sam's cheek at Micah's mention of Thad and Ell.

"I think Mister Tall, Dark, and Dangerous might have a thing for...." Sam's voice trailed off as she sought the words to describe the woman Thad was bringing along with him.

"Small, silent, and deadly?"

Micah's comment earned him another ripple of laughter.

"Accurate." She lifted a finger, one eye narrowing in contemplation. "Elodie Cyr is one scary lady when she wants to be."

"Never known a sniper who wasn't a bit scary. Boone's the same way," he reminded her.

Sam dropped her finger, tilting her head at his mention of the task force's sniper. She shot him an appraising look. "True. I'm sure you've known your share of them, too. You flew recon on missions for how many years before the task force was commissioned?"

Micah smiled, but didn't comment.

After a beat, she let it go, and he silently thanked her for it. Some things he was cleared to discuss with her; others, he was not.

As the white dwarf gave up its last light and sank behind a mountain range in the distance, Micah drew Sam closer, noticing her shivering in the breeze.

After a few more steps, she came to a stop, pointing across the busy street. "There it is."

Micah spotted a marquee hanging above an establishment's entrance and read the name off the tasteful, holographically-extruded sign. "The Rieger. Never heard of it."

"It's fairly new. Someone back at the CID told me we needed to try their signature Hanna cocktails."

"Cocktails? You mean, like, sweet drinks with tiny umbrellas?" He shook his head. "Nah. Think I'll leave those fancy things to you ladies."

Sam rolled her eyes. "Got news for you, Micah Case. A Hanna cocktail's what they used to call a 'man's drink,' made from liquors the Reiger's owners distill themselves."

He didn't miss the heavy sarcasm she laid on the phrase 'man's drink,' and a grin tugged at his lips. "Oh yeah? Now you're talking."

Sam ignored him as she began to tick them off. "There's the Sage Advice, the Smokin' Choke, the Settle Down, and my favorite, Cortez the Killer. Mezcal, tequila, mango, a healthy dose of habanero, and a little bit of lime." She shot him a look he knew better than to cross. "That sound like a girly drink to you?"

He held up his hands. "Ma'am, no, ma'am."

They waited with the crowd for traffic to clear and then crossed the street. Just as they stepped up onto the sidewalk, Micah heard someone shout his name.

"Captain Case!"

Micah turned, and the crowd parted just enough for him to see a man rapidly approaching. He tensed, reaching out instinctively to his mirror twin.

Brother...

Trouble? The response came instantly, the connection as clear as if his other self were standing beside him instead of at his post, up at the base.

Don't know. Do we know who this is?

He sent Jonathan a mental image of the man as he jolted to a stop before them. The stranger was young, of average height and looked vaguely familiar. He seemed unusually anxious, his eyes shifting left and right as if seeking danger in those milling about.

"Captain Case," the man repeated, stepping close and

lowering his voice. "Doctor Travis. You have to help. Please, you're the only ones who can."

Sam's eyes widened, and she inhaled sharply at the stranger's use of her name. *{How does he know who we—}*

Her words cut off abruptly as a bloody trail grazed the man's forehead.

The stranger's body jerked in reaction, and he staggered back a step, bumping into the people nearest him. A woman turned, her irritation over being jostled morphing into horror as two more holes silently appeared, one in his abdomen, the final one near his heart.

She screamed and quickly backed away as he fell to the ground. "He's been shot! Somebody help!"

Cries of *"Shooter!"* and *"Run!"* mingled with the press of bodies as people nearby panicked, stampeding to get away from the unseen threat.

Micah grabbed Sam and shoved her against the recessed alcove of the restaurant's entrance, urging her into a crouch.

"Stay down!" he yelled over the shouts of the crowd. At the same time, he initiated a combat net, the mental connection snapping into place. *{Shots fired, downtown Montpelier!}*

His words were sent simultaneously to all the members of Task Force Blue.

{We're two blocks out. Ell's going high.} Thad's mental voice sliced through Micah's mind.

{I need a visual,} the former sniper's voice cut in, slightly breathless. *{Can you give me access to your optics?}*

In lieu of response, Micah patched Ell into his wire.

{Good. Let me see the vic.}

Micah set his eyes on the young man bleeding out, three meters away. *{He was facing us. It was odd, not the standard two to the chest, one to the head.}* He added, *{If I didn't know better, I'd say this was done by an amateur, but from some distance away.}*

{Reverse angle of street,} Ell instructed. *{Just a quick look, and then get back under cover.}*

Based on the placement of the shots, Micah had a good idea of the shooter's location. From where he crouched over Sam, he let his gaze sweep the street, his eyes darting from rooftop to rooftop, looking for the shooter—but he saw nothing.

{Got it. Thanks.}

Thad's voice returned, barking out a quick, *{Sitrep!}*

Sam tried to rise to get to the fallen stranger, but Micah pulled her back, forcing her to remain still.

"Don't move," he ground out, when she resisted his hand.

"Micah, I don't think there's a shooter. Not one here locally, at least."

"Holes don't just mysteriously drill themselves into a person's head and chest," he countered.

"They could, under certain conditions."

Her words made no sense, but in the heat of the moment, Micah didn't try to parse their meaning.

He continued to cover Sam with his own body as he relayed what he could see of the street in staccato bursts of information. Something about what she'd said snagged his attention, though, and he found his gaze returning to the downed man.

She's right. We didn't hear any gunshots.

The fallen man was, surprisingly, still alive, though Micah could see the life draining from him by the second. So could Sam, and she redoubled her efforts to get free, her doctor's instincts and medical training demanding she go to him and treat his wounds.

When the man met Micah's eyes, he gasped a word that speared Micah with a cold terror.

"Chiral." Then his gaze sought Sam's with a pleading intensity. "Prisoner." He took a shuddering breath, blood bubbling from between his lips. "Stop them...."

The man's eyes glazed over, fixed in the distance.

"Dammit, Micah, let me *go*." Sam elbowed him in the solar plexus, attempting once more to get to the fatally wounded man. "Micah, I'm telling you, the only danger is to that poor man!"

"Want to elaborate on that a bit, *cher*?"

Sam jerked as a deep bass rumble sounded above them. Thad had arrived.

An ebony hand reached down; Sam grasped it, and the Marine pulled her to her feet. Micah saw an icon flash over his wire and realized Thad had added Sam to the team's combat channel.

{Ell doesn't think anyone's out there. She's checked out the most likely spots, but the single microdrone we had between us isn't showing any residual IR heat signature.}

Sam shot Micah an impatient look and moved toward the man lying on the sidewalk, three meters away. *{Told you so. I need to get to him before someone tries to steal his body or alter the evidence.}*

{She has a point.} Thad slanted a meaningful look at the once-empty street. After several minutes had passed without additional bullets fired, a few brave souls were beginning to stir, morbid curiosity overcoming their fear. Some were on an intercept with the body.

If they wanted to keep a lid on this incident, they'd have to move fast.

One look at Sam's expression suggested she was on her own communications network. If Micah had to guess, it was with people back at the CID.

Thad moved to follow Sam. "We need to keep everyone back. Damn, I hate that we're out here with no gear."

Micah felt much the same. This was supposed to be a night off; no one had kitted up for that.

Ell showed up, and something unspoken passed between her and Thad. The former sniper nodded and then stepped forward to flash her NCIC special agent's badge at those in the restaurant, assuring them that things were under control.

{Local LEOs are going to be all over this, and that's pissin' me off, hoss,} the Marine admitted as he lifted a hand and shot a warning look at an especially bold bystander. *{You say he*

mentioned you by name?}

"Yeah," Micah replied. "Me and Sam both."

Sam looked up from her cursory exam. Her eyes slid to the people standing in a loose semicircle around them before returning to him and Thad. "I need to get the body into stasis. I've contacted Admiral Toland, and she's dispatched a critical care team; they're on their way."

He nodded. "Copy that."

Admiral Amara Toland was the officer in charge of the Navy's chiral project, based at the CID's main offices here in Montpelier.

It wasn't long before Micah heard a shuttle coming in on a fast intercept. As it came to a stop, medical personnel spilled out, two of them pushing a stasis pod between them.

Seconds later, the strobe of flashing lights signaled the arrival of two police cruisers converging on the street. Thad waved Ell toward them.

{That badge of hers is coming in handy tonight,} Micah commented.

Thad grunted as he stopped another curiosity-seeker from trying to get a better look at the victim. *{By the time this wraps up, I'm going to owe that woman a lot more than a nice dinner.}*

The medics stopped in front of Sam, and she beckoned impatiently to one of them. He handed her the medical bracer he had tucked under one arm. Shoving her hand into the gauntlet, Sam's fingers danced over its controls as she brought the unit to life.

The medics staffing the stasis pod bent to lift the body, but she snapped a quick command, halting them so she could conduct her exam. The pod hummed softly, hovering between them while the two medics waited.

Sam's gauntleted hand traveled from the entry wound in the man's forehead to the ones in his chest, the bracer cataloguing each injury as she went. She ended the exam by placing her hand against the man's neck. After a second, she nodded and motioned the medics forward.

They lifted the body into the unit and sealed the lid. Micah could just make out a faint blue glow emanating from the pod when the unit cycled on, signaling the body had entered stasis.

The crowd that had stuck around to gawk dissipated quickly once the body had been removed.

As the medics piled back into the shuttle and Sam retraced her steps back to them, Thad motioned Micah closer.

"What in hell went down here?" he asked in a low voice.

Micah scrubbed a hand through his hair. "Damned if I know. We'd just crossed the street when the man ran up to us. He called us by name, but before he could say anything else, he was shot. That's about it—except projectiles that cause wounds like his usually travel fast. We should have heard a sonic crack, and we didn't."

Thad nodded. "That tracks with what Ell found—or rather, *didn't* find. No evidence of a shooter."

"If there was no shooter, then how'd he die?" Micah didn't try to hide the skepticism in his voice.

"I can think of one way." Sam's gaze was troubled, and Micah could see her mind working, analyzing. "Right before he died, the man said something... something that might explain it."

"What was it, *cher*?"

She looked Thad in the eye. "Chiral."

OBELUS

JOINT OPERATIONS COMMAND HEADQUARTERS
PARLIAMENT HILL
ST. CLAIR TOWNSHIP, CERIBA

TWENTY KILOMETERS AWAY, in Joint Operations Command Headquarters, General Harris Carlisle whipped his head around angrily at the sound of his office door opening.

"Dammit, I *said* no interrup—"

The words clogged in his throat as he caught sight of the person standing in the open doorway.

Jackknifing from his chair, he stumbled back, hitting the credenza that lined the wall. The papers he'd been reading scattered on the floor as they fell from nerveless fingers.

They should have been stopped at the entrance; security was tight at Joint Operations Command, just as tight as it was up the hill, at Parliament House itself. And yet here they stood.

Remembered pain caused his heart to race, panic welling. Carlisle felt his hand tremble, and he shoved the betraying limb deep into his pocket, his other supporting him against the wooden sideboard.

"I'm gratified to see you haven't forgotten me, General," the woman said as she glided to a stop in front of his desk.

The two men with her rounded the obstacle, coming to stand on either side of him. His knees threatened to give way as mental pictures began to replay in his mind.

A dark chamber. His body, stripped bare. Cold, hard metal— and pain, so much pain.

"What do you want?" he rasped, his eyes shifting rapidly between them, prey frozen in place by an apex predator.

"I warned you. There is no place you can retreat where we cannot reach." She smiled, and it was a cold thing.

A quick nod to the man on her left brought the glint of steel as the man raised his fisted hand. Carlisle's eyes caught with sick fascination on the set of molded metal rings the man wore. He recognized the fist-load weapon for what it was: a simple device to concentrate the force of a strike, inflicting maximum damage to tissue and bone.

As the man advanced, Carlisle was unable to tear his eyes away from it.

"Call this... a refresher," the woman continued. "A reminder that your life belongs to Akkadia now, and you serve at the pleasure of Obelus."

Carlisle ripped his terror-filled gaze from the advancing threat and over to the woman. He began to shake his head, slowly at first, then with increasing vehemence. "Not necessary. I told you I'd comply."

The woman's eyes grew intense. "We are here to ensure that you do."

She motioned to the other man. He spun Carlisle around, securing his arms behind his back. The general felt something cold hiss against his neck, and the embedded wire in his head instantly muted. He scrabbled after it mentally, but his connection to the Joint Operations network had been severed.

The man in front of him drew his fist back, and then powered it forward in an explosive jab.

Agony exploded along Carlisle's ribcage, and he realized whatever they'd injected him with was also blocking his medical nano. He should have felt a measure of relief almost immediately after the blow landed; instead, the pain bloomed and intensified as the man's fists pummeled him again and again.

They worked him over with silent efficiency, the blows carefully placed to remain unseen.

Finally, they were done. The man holding him released him, and Carlisle sagged to the carpeted floor, his breaths coming in shallow gasps.

A shadow loomed, the woman's voice sounding in his ear.

"Now, listen carefully, and I will tell you about your first assignment...."

DEBRIEF

The Hill – Fine Dining District
Downtown Montpelier, Ceriba

Despite Ell stepping in to claim the incident as an NCIC investigation, it took another hour before the Montpelier police cut Micah and Sam loose.

Sam couldn't shake the sense of unease she felt when the CID transport carrying the dead body began to pull away from the restaurant. She turned to where Micah and Thad stood quietly conversing a few meters away. Just beyond them, she could see Ell talking quietly with local authorities. It looked like the NCIC agent was close to wrapping things up.

Sam looked back at the transport as she stepped close to Micah. Its taillights flashed brightly as the vehicle braked at the end of the street. On impulse, she pinged the driver.

{Hold up, I'm coming with you.}

The driver sent his assent, and she saw the ambulance-sized vehicle pull over to the side of the street.

She turned back to Micah and Thad. "I have a feeling about this. I know they want to question me about what I saw, but I don't really want to let that stasis pod out of my sight."

Thad shot her an approving look. "No worries, *cher*. We'll handle it."

Sam gave Thad a quick smile and reached out to squeeze Micah's hand. "Raincheck on dinner?"

Micah's return smile was lopsided. "Plan on it."

She jogged toward the end of the street where the transport awaited. Murmuring her thanks to the medic who opened the passenger door, Sam slid into the small space just behind the front seats.

She glanced through the pass-through window at the stasis pod they'd loaded into the back as the driver took off once again, reassured by the steady glow of the blue ES field. She checked her chronometer; they should be at the center within ten minutes, easily.

With a relieved breath, she sat back in her seat.

* * *

The deep rumble of a ship-to-surface shuttle sounded, drawing Micah's attention away from the round of handshakes that meant they were free to go.

{Shuttle's here,} he called out unnecessarily.

{Caught that, ami.*}*

Thad turned toward the waiting ship, Micah falling into step next to him. Behind them, Ell promised to send the officers a copy of the final report.

Micah exchanged a hooded look with Thad. *{That ought to be an interesting bit of fiction.}*

Quick footsteps sounded on the pavement behind them. When Ell caught up to them, she slid Micah a glance.

{That's what probies are for, Captain,} she deadpanned.

Micah's lips twitched in amusement as she swept past and stepped up into the shuttle's open hatch.

{Glad I'm not a probie, then,} he said, following her inside.

Micah wished he'd been able to talk Sam into coming along with them, but he couldn't fault her for wanting to accompany the medics to the CID. At least the trip back up to the base would be a quick one.

He spotted Boone waiting for them as the shuttle slipped into the task force's hangar. Beside him stood Asha, the team's medic. Boone lifted a chin in greeting as they piled out of the ship.

"Heard you had an exciting evening," Asha said as he, Ell, and Thad neared.

Thad grunted. "You could say that."

Boone lifted a brow and exchanged a look with Ell, but refrained from commenting as they all piled into the lift.

The smell of greasy pizza assaulted Micah's nose, and his stomach chose that moment to remind him he'd missed dinner.

"Sounds like someone's hungry," observed Boone with a laugh as the lift began to rise.

Micah shot him a sour look. "Having someone chase you down and die right in front of you has a way of messing with dinner plans."

"Come on, then." Thad jerked his chin in the direction of the team's bullpen when the lift doors opened. "The colonel had Hyer order in. There should be plenty to go around."

Asha sent him a scowl. "You sure about that, sir? Have you seen how much that woman eats? I have no idea where she puts it all."

An alarmed look crossed Boone's face. Thad's laugh boomed out when the sniper bolted for the operations center, ostensibly to try to rescue some of the food from Hyer's hands.

"Asha's right," he called over his shoulder. "Better hustle if you want anything."

The medic groaned and broke into a jog, following after him.

Chief Warrant Katie Hyer's metabolism was legendary. The fact she could eat anything she wanted and not gain a pound was a sore spot with the rest of the women on the team—and some of the men.

Micah spotted her the moment the doors to the bullpen slid open. Tall and with a shock of blue fuzz atop her head, Hyer was hard to miss.

She was young, still in her twenties, and a natural-born pilot. Her life on the mining platforms had also given her plenty of experience with the mechanics of a ship.

Gabriel Alvarez, the task force's second-in-command, had seen this ability firsthand and recruited her to the unit. Her unique skillset meant she'd been tapped to cross-train as both flight engineer and pilot for the team.

A quick glance around told Micah that most of the headquarters element and the rest of the team had been pulled together for this debrief.

Gabe lifted his head in greeting and waved him over, but another rumble in his gut sent Micah in a different direction. At his quick hand motion toward the table, heavily laden with food, Gabe nodded his understanding as Micah diverted to load up a plate.

He'd just grabbed a seat and popped the seal on a water bottle when the head of the Special Reconnaissance Unit appeared in the doorway.

"Tell me what we know." Colonel Tala Valenti cut directly to the topic as her hands came to rest on the back of the empty seat at the head of the table.

Hyer waved one pizza-laden hand. "Well, some dude just dropped dead right in front of Micah." Her gaze remained fixed on the string of gooey cheese dripping off the side as she looped it expertly around a finger and then popped it into her mouth.

She froze when Valenti's dry voice cut in.

"Other than that."

Katie lowered the pizza, shot Gabe an apologetic look, and then turned to the colonel. In a much more subdued voice, she said, "Sorry, Colonel. Guess that was stating the obvious."

{*Always a good idea to remember who cuts our paychecks, Chief.*} Gabe's mental tone held mild reproof.

Katie was renowned for her tendency to say whatever was on her mind. She just put it all out there, with no filter. The team didn't care, but Gabe had been working with her to try to curb that tendency whenever the brass stopped by.

Colonel Valenti looked around at those assembled. "Well? As the chief said, a man dropped dead in front of Captain Case. I want to know why." Her expressionless gaze lingered on Katie for another moment before her eyes landed on Micah. "Captain?" she invited.

Micah wished once more that Sam had accompanied them.

He shook his head, his eyes defocusing as he transported himself back mentally to the minutes just before the man had called his name. "Not a lot to tell, really. Doctor Travis and I were crossing the street in downtown Montpelier when I heard someone shout my name."

Valenti's stare bored into him. "He called you by name."

"Yes. Sam, too. Before he had a chance to say anything else, he was shot. Or at least, he gave a really good impression of someone who'd been shot," he amended.

Valenti's eyes cut to Thad's. "Severance?"

The big Marine frowned, his eyes wandering to Ell as he thought. "It looked like he'd taken a head shot, and then two more, center mass. He was dead when I arrived."

"What kind of shot?"

Thad squinted. "Sure gave a fine impression of a 6.8 mm round, burned through his skull. Problem is, there was no evidence of a bullet anywhere we could find."

"We," Valenti repeated. She swiveled, her attention now on Ell. "You were there as well."

"I was. We were a few minutes behind Captain Case, so we weren't there to see the incident when it happened." Ell's mouth turned down in an unhappy line. "I had a single standard NCIC-issue crime scene drone with me. It scanned the most likely spots a shooter would have used."

"Conclusion?"

Ell shook her head. "No weapon residue. No lingering heat signature."

The colonel turned to Micah. "I find it interesting that

Doctor Travis insisted there was no shooter. How could she possibly know this?"

"Beyond the fact there was no sonic crack that accompanied the bullet?" Micah shook his head. "I didn't get a chance to ask before she left to follow the body to the CID."

"What *exactly* did the man say to you before he expired?"

Micah thought back to the incident. "Just four words. 'Chiral,' 'prisoner,' and 'stop them'."

Gabe's voice was thoughtful. "Was he saying someone was involved in a chiral study and holding someone prisoner? A scientist, maybe, like the situation with Sam?"

"And is it really safe to assume that, by 'stop them,' he means the Akkadians?" Katie interjected. "What about drug cartels, or even other star nations?"

Asha stirred. "Last we knew, Akkadia was in a similar position as we are, working with viral organisms and chemical compounds. Should we consider they may have cut corners and upped their game? Could *he* have been chiral?" Then she shook her head. "But he wasn't a prisoner."

Jonathan sat up suddenly, and Micah felt his twin's gaze land on him. "Or maybe he was, and he escaped. Maybe the Akkadians did to him what Stinton did to us, and cloned him."

"Omigod!" Katie exclaimed, her hand flying to her mouth. Her eyes were wide as they swung from Jonathan to Micah and then back again.

"Katie?" Gabe prompted.

That was enough to jolt the chief warrant out of her headspace.

"Remember what the doc told us about the viral weapon they'd created on that secret base? They managed to entangle them. They used the chiral version as the trigger, and when they altered it, the non-chiral version became altered, too, in the exact same way. What if...."

She swallowed hard, and a sick look came over her face. "What if they've managed to achieve the same thing with living creatures?"

A shadow of impatience crossed Valenti's face. "We already know that's possible." She gestured to Micah and Jonathan. "That's nothing new to us."

"Yes, but they're different." Hyer waved her hand between the two men. "When Jonathan was injured on Leavitt Station, Micah wasn't."

Micah rubbed his chest, recalling the moment Jonathan had been stabbed. "I might not have been injured, but I sure as hell felt it," he reminded them.

Gabe sat up straighter. "So, let's consider this for a moment. We know the machine Stinton used on Case was destroyed when deGrasse blew up. Not only that, Stinton himself had no idea he'd successfully accomplished what he'd set out to do—chirally clone a person."

He shook his head, stopping himself. "No, wait. It was more than that. Even if he found out, he would've had no idea *how* his chiral clones finally became viable, because it was Sam's intervention that did it. Nothing of her actions would have been included in the research the Akkadians stole from Stinton, correct?"

"True," Katie admitted. "But then eighteen months ago, Sam told them that chiral pairs could be entangled."

"She didn't know she was telling them," Micah began, and Thad waved him off.

"We know that, hoss. She thought she was telling an Alliance colonel that. One who'd been read into the program, remember?"

"What are you suggesting, Chief?" Valenti asked, her gaze on Hyer.

Katie licked her lips nervously. "Well, they have all of Stinton's early research—or at least, we're going on the assumption they do, because Janus stole it and sent it to Akkadia, right?"

There were nods all around.

Clint Janus had been Stinton's right-hand man. They also suspected the biochemist was behind the destruction of the deGrasse research torus, but there was no proof, so he'd walked free. After Akkadia's recent attempt to decimate the intelligence community, Janus had mysteriously disappeared.

"If he defected to Akkadia like we think he did, and he has access both to Stinton's research *and* the research Sam did on entangling viral pairs… what if he combined the two?"

The room fell silent as they contemplated Hyer's words.

"Are you suggesting that he's cloning humans, and that they're somehow more entangled than Micah and Jonathan are?" Valenti asked.

Katie nodded. "If their entanglement works like Sam's viruses do, then they could have killed this guy from a distance."

"You may be onto something, Chief," a new voice cut in.

Micah looked up to see Admiral Toland enter. The woman didn't look happy about the news she was about to share.

Her gaze landed briefly on Micah before shifting over to Jonathan as she pulled up a seat and joined them. "You're suggesting they're entangled in the same way we've been entangling viruses at the CID. Where if you alter one in a chiral pair, the other is automatically altered in the same way?"

Katie nodded.

"But that doesn't happen with us," protested Micah, waving his hand between himself and Jonathan.

"True," the admiral allowed, "but that's more a case of you two being *imperfectly* entangled in the first place."

"Anyone else realize she just made a pun? A case for Case?" Katie clamped her mouth shut at a look from Valenti. "Come on. Everyone was thinking it," she muttered under her breath.

Jonathan's half laugh broke the tense silence.

"What do you mean by imperfectly entangled?" Micah asked.

Toland looked thoughtfully between the two men. "You aren't absolute, perfect chiral copies of each other. Stinton made minor tweaks. Why he did it, we'll never know; maybe it was just a desire to easily tell you two apart. But there's no denying that Jonathan is left-handed, and Micah isn't. Your hair is parted on opposite sides, as well.

"The point is, those subtle irregularities have nothing whatsoever to do with mirror-molecular structure. It's possible that's why Micah felt Jonathan's pain, but the injuries did not physically manifest."

Valenti pursed her lips. "You're suggesting someone had this man's twin in custody, and shot him… and our victim ended up with the same bullet holes as a result?"

Toland nodded, but her expression was uncertain as well. "It's what we *suspect*," she clarified. Her face turned grim. "We'd like to be able to confirm this with a greater degree of confidence, but that's going to be a bit difficult. The body's disappeared."

THEFT

En route to the CID
Montpelier, Ceriba

SAM SPENT THE greater part of the trip back to the CID fighting the impulse to constantly check the stasis pod. She wasn't entirely sure what caused her unease, but finally, a kilometer from the center, she gave in to the need to physically inspect it.

Setting her bracer down on the bench beside her, she twisted, reaching through the window toward the unit's control panel. Its palmpad was just out of reach, so she turned around fully, bracing her knees on the bench so that she could shove her head through the opening.

"Everything okay back there?" the driver asked.

"Fine," she called back over her shoulder. "Just running a quick check."

She stretched out a hand, leaning deeper into the back of the transport until her fingers grazed the unit's palmpad.

The physical connection was necessary, since the pod was programmed to accept only those security tokens within the CID's database.

She must have accidentally nudged her bracer in her efforts, because she felt it move by her knee, and then heard a soft *thunk* as it tumbled onto the transport's floor.

Sam ignored it. Focusing her attention on the pod, she ordered it to perform a stasis field status check. Once satisfied the unit was operable, she turned back around and bent down to pick up the bracer.

That action saved her life.

The high-pitched whine of energy weapons sliced through the air over her head, spearing into the vehicle's interior and turning surprised shouts into screams of agony. From where she crouched, Sam could see the driver's lifeless body slump over the controls as the transport veered sharply left.

A large *crump!* sounded and they lurched to a stop. This was followed by a second explosion at the rear of the vehicle, which blew the aft doors from their hinges.

Sam sent out an emergency ping to the CID's security team, keeping her face pressed to the ambulance's floor, praying no one would see her. But as the ringing in her ears began to clear, she heard feet pounding toward the vehicle.

A jacket belonging to one of the now-dead medics had been tossed on the bench seat beside her. She pulled it down on top of her, hoping desperately it would conceal her presence, crowded as she was into the confines of a space not usually meant to carry people.

How the hell did someone plan an attack so quickly?

Whoever was attacking them had likely been in pursuit of the man, even as he approached them outside the Rieger.

Easy enough to know where this transport's headed. The CID logo on the side of this thing is hard to miss. It wouldn't have been hard to ping ahead for backup.

She felt the whole conveyance rock as their attackers hopped in beside the stasis unit and began muscling it out the back. Voices cursed when they realized the pod was security locked and they'd have to physically carry the thing.

Sam didn't speak Aka'a, the Akkadian native tongue, but the liquid syllables were easily recognizable.

There was a scraping sound as they pulled and tugged, and then grunts followed as the intruders hoisted the unit between them. Their footsteps faded as they retreated with their prize as quickly as they could.

Evidently, it wasn't fast enough to please their ringleader.

Sam heard a low, gruff voice rasp out an urgent, "Move it, move it, move it!"

She blew out a silent, relieved breath when it appeared that they were more focused on retrieving the pod than they were on checking for survivors—or witnesses.

Cautiously, she began to ease her way toward the passenger door. From the sound of retreating footsteps, that side of the transport was hidden from the raiders' view. If she could crawl out and get a quick look at the thieves before they got too far away, then maybe she could ID them.

Her eyes widened when she heard the shouted command, "Okay, blow it!"

Slamming her palm against the door's controls, she hissed a soft "*Dammit!*" when it slid open several centimeters and then stopped.

The impact must have bent its frame.

Heart slamming in her chest, she crammed both hands into the opening and pushed, her panic lending her strength.

It worked.

She shoved her way between door and frame, falling onto the pavement in her haste. She heard the sound of sirens approaching in the distance as she scrambled to her feet, and looked around wildly for cover; there was little to be found, save for the low wall bordering the office park that the ambulance had rammed into after the driver had been shot.

She raced for it, legs pumping. The explosion followed fast on her heels, the leading shockwave lifting her and sending her body cartwheeling through the air. Shrapnel from the shredded ambulance overtook her, superheated air searing her lungs.

She barely registered the wall as her body slammed into it. She lost consciousness before her body hit the ground.

* * *

The bullpen erupted with exclamations of disbelief at Toland's news.

Micah lurched to his feet, hands pressing against the table's surface as the food he'd just eaten threatened to come back up.

"Sam," he said hoarsely. "Sam... she was with them, in the transport—"

The admiral nodded, her expression sympathetic. "I know. She managed to get out an SOS to the center's security, but they couldn't get to her before the attackers blew the transport."

Micah stumbled back. Thad was suddenly there beside him, but he ignored him, gaze locked with the admiral's.

"Is she...."

He couldn't finish the sentence.

She shook her head. "She's incredibly lucky. She was on the opposite side of the transport from the people who hijacked it. I didn't wait around to get the whole story from security. Once I saw she was stable, I left to come up here."

Micah shrugged off Thad's hand. "I need to get down there," he insisted, but Toland held up a hand.

"She has some burns, and took some shrapnel. They're working on her now." Toland shook her head. "I'm honestly not sure how she managed to escape; whoever did this shot and killed the medics in the cab of the ambulance before they lit it up."

Thad's hand was back on Micah's shoulder, squeezing.

"I should—"

Toland interrupted him. "There's nothing you can do right now, Captain. Addy Moran's treating her; let the doctor do her job. I also posted guards outside medical. Don't worry, Sam's in good hands."

Gabe sent Micah a reassuring look. "She's right. No one's going to get past Addy. When it comes to her patients, that woman's a pitbull."

Valenti pressed both palms onto the table. Leaning forward, her eyes swept the group. "This attack makes it even more critical that we figure out what happened tonight."

She turned to Micah's twin. "Jonathan, contact that analyst of yours at the NSA. Get her to run a report of any suspected Akkadian activity on Ceriba."

Her gaze swiveled to Gabe. "Alvarez, assume the chief's theory is right. Trace Janus's movements up to the point he disappeared; see if you can pinpoint potential moles by the people he interacted with the most."

The two men nodded and pushed away from the table.

"We'll need someone to interview the doctor when she wakes up, find out what she recalls—anything that can help us trace these people," Valenti continued, and she turned to face Micah.

Something moved behind the hardened colonel's eyes, and though her tone remained as curt and dispassionate as ever, her words had him closing his eyes in relief.

"Go on. Get your ass down there."

NARROW MISS

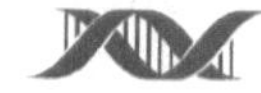

Ministry of State Security
Eridu, Akkadia

"The chiral clone has been dealt with."

The woman who spoke blended so seamlessly into the office's wood paneling, Che Josza could hardly see her. He pushed his chair away from Rin Zhou's desk and stood, his gaze searching.

"How?"

Dacina stepped forward into the light, banked anger in her eyes. "Janus had the original dragged from his cell, and then shot the man himself."

Che felt anger well at the doctor's audacity.

He rounded the desk and stopped in front of her. "And the clone?"

"Dead, as a result."

He clenched his jaw. "That call was not his to make."

She inclined her head but said nothing.

He began to pace, and she maintained a watchful silence, her head turning to follow him.

Ordinarily a man acutely aware of his surroundings, Che

passed the priceless antiques and real wood, pre-colonization furniture Rin Zhou had collected without really seeing them. He came to a stop in front of the sitting area the former minister had used for ritual coffee.

Abruptly, he realized he had yet to extend the same offer to the generals under his own command.

Staring unseeingly down at the low table surrounded by piles of pillows, he asked, "What about the body?"

He heard a soft exhale.

"Janus had no plans in place to handle cleanup."

Che jerked his head around at that.

The Dagger's eyes snapped with a rare display of annoyance, yet when she spoke, her voice was as measured and emotionless as ever.

"I dispatched a team to handle it. The transport carrying the body had an unfortunate accident, and in the confusion, our people took it."

She hesitated, the movement so slight it was almost unnoticeable, but for Dacina, it was the equivalent to a shout.

"There's more," he guessed.

"Reports from the agents who were following him say that the subject made contact with Micah Case and Samantha Travis. Words were exchanged before he perished. This, I believe, is what set Janus off in the first place."

A headache began to form behind Che's eyes. He gripped the bridge of his nose, pinching hard as he drew in a calming breath. "What idiot gave Janus secured access to the agents assigned to monitor the clone? Don't answer that; it was rhetorical."

He caught her eye. "Do they have any idea who that young man was —or that he was chiral?"

He resumed his pacing, and he saw the beads woven into her brown braids glint as she turned her head to follow his progress.

"Unknown, but we must assume so."

Irritation flared. Che took a calming breath and focused on

counting the steps from the low table to the sweep of clearsteel windows.

Thirteen. Fourteen. I will strangle Clint Janus with my bare hands....

Weariness settled suddenly upon him.

Che turned to face her once more. "Thank you for handling this. You have done well."

She inclined her head. "There is... one more thing. Three hours after your debrief on Carlisle, the doctor arrived for a private audience with the premier."

This surprised Che. Janus's work fell under the auspices of State Security; if Asher Dent had questions on Obelus's progress, protocol dictated he should have asked Che.

The first stirrings of unease shafted through him.

"Janus is supposed to be kept off-grid and away from Alliance spies," he said after a moment's consideration. "That's why we built the lab thirty meters below ground, inside our most heavily-guarded prison in the heart of the wastelands."

The Shar-Kali Correctional Facility, Akkadia's maximum security prison, was located where the Hohen Savannah met the Aksu Desert. It was the ideal way to ensure both Dent's plans for Obelus and its associated research remained secure.

Dacina's lips firmed, but she held her counsel.

"Do you know why Dent called him in?" Che pressed.

"I do not. They met behind closed doors."

The glint of determination in her eyes told him she was up to something.

It was clear that the Dagger did not like to be denied.

"I do not know... *yet*," she clarified. "Though I can think of only one reason why he would do such a thing."

Che could, too.

He nodded. "Whatever it is Dent wants from the doctor, it's something he does not want his ministry to know about. It could be for deniability."

Something moved behind Dacina's eyes. It was cold and deadly, and caused a chill to race down Che's spine, despite the fact that it was not directed toward him.

"Or it could be that he is plotting against his own people," she countered. "I will find out."

Che had no doubt that she would.

"I applaud your initiative in shadowing Janus," he said finally. "That was a wise move. But proceed with caution; Dent is not a man to be underestimated."

Dacina inclined her head. "Neither am I."

* * *

Up the hill from the State Security building, Asher Dent stood, staring out his office window, considering the information he'd garnered from Clint Janus.

Just past Eridu's main space elevator, he could make out Akkadia's sister star, Zoser, so close it was visible during daylight hours. The star formerly named Rigel Kentaurus was at periastron right now. At night, it turned Eridu's blackest sky into a dusk-like twilight.

The vista didn't even register in Asher's mind. His memories were drawing a different set of images inside his head.

With a mental command to the room's systems, he turned the window's thermoplastic carbon fiber surface from transparent to reflective.

He smoothed his business suit as he studied his visage, seeking weaknesses his enemies might exploit. The man staring back at him was tall and athletically trim, with penetrating, dark eyes, and hair that held a natural wave. A flick to the cuff of his suit triggered a command that had its intelligent weave refreshing its crisp lines.

He nodded in satisfaction at his reflection: Asher Dent, eldest son of a man who had once controlled State Security, now the most powerful man on Eridu... and soon to be the most powerful man in the settled worlds.

He had no doubt that last would come someday. He'd accept nothing less than total space superiority for Akkadia.

He'd worked hard to become Minority Leader, his position won by being the most aggressive, charismatic, and ruthlessly calculating leader in the Coalition of Federated Worlds. His meteoric rise had taken some politicians in the Sol, Alpha Centauri, and Proxima systems by surprise.

Not those who knew him.

Not those who had known his sire.

Asher fisted his right hand reflexively as he recalled the rigors of his childhood. His father, who had been head of Akkadian State Security before Rin Zhou Enlai had betrayed him, had forced Asher to cut off his little finger as penance for poor performance when he was eight. Another training failure had him severing his ring finger at age eleven.

He'd been seventeen when he'd been bound by honor to slice off his hand at the wrist. That act had been particularly difficult, as his father had insisted it be done with a traditional blade instead of a plasma one. The leverage he'd needed to achieve to ensure a swift, clean stroke had been… challenging.

None but the elite inner circle of Akkadian State Security had been aware of this grisly practice, for his father always had Asher's hand repaired. Sometimes this occurred hours later, sometimes days, but it always happened before the son of the most feared military leader on their planet returned to the public eye.

By the time Asher was twenty-one, he'd been on his third cloned hand.

He consciously unclenched his fist as he smothered a surge of impatience. His upbringing had taught him the importance of singular focus, to demand excellence from himself and those who owed him their allegiance.

For his vision to succeed, it required strict adherence to the plan. That's where Clint Janus came in. The biochemist would become the means by which Dent would guarantee absolute control over every man and woman who reported to him.

Once that was in place, betrayal would become an impossible thing—and Project Obelus would be unstoppable.

INTERCEPTION

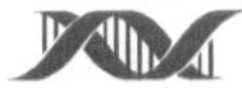

Montpelier, Ceriba
Geminate Alliance (Procyon System)

THE SNOW-CAPPED mountains of Beryl's Teter Range were covered in half a meter of fresh powder, and Raphael Garza's twin daughters were eager to tear into it.

His wife, on the other hand, was too busy wringing her hands.

"They'll be fine," the Alliance's newly appointed prime minister assured her for the fifth time, as they sat down to breakfast in their vacation condo. "They've had their lessons, and the slopes are covered with spotters in case someone gets into trouble."

The look she shot him was unconvinced.

"I've ordered half my protection detail to follow them." His eyes twinkled with rare humor. "You know what an old maid Ramirez is. If he has anything to say about it, not a hair on their heads will be out of place."

Jackie coughed in derision, but she nodded reluctantly. Even she knew the truth of his statement. "Okay, then." She sighed, bringing her cup of tea to her lips and sipping contemplatively.

"I suppose I could bundle up and go out there, too...."

Her offer surprised Raphael. She had never been very sports-minded.

I'd give just about anything to be able to switch places with her, he thought with sudden envy.

For the prime minister of the Geminate Alliance, vacation was a thing in name only. He'd not been able to carve out more than half a day of skiing on this trip, thanks to work.

As if conjured by his thoughts, one of Garza's newest staff members popped his head around the corner. "Sorry to interrupt, sir. Ma'am." Ed nodded politely to Jackie. "We're going to have to pull you away from the slopes for a bit. Something's come up."

Jackie made a disappointed sound, and Raphael shot her an apologetic look. "Sorry about this, love. Hang on. Let me check and see if it's something I can get out of."

He connected his wire to the encrypted government partition that Parliament had set him up with when the governor-general had first appointed him to the position, but oddly, he found no record of any pending meetings, other than the ones he'd already scheduled prior to his departure.

Ed shifted, drawing Garza's attention. "Sorry, sir, you won't find this one on the net." He handed over a blank white sheet.

Physical memos were almost unheard of in a world that relied upon digital traffic sent via implanted evanescent wires. They were employed only when there existed a need for extreme security.

Unfortunately for Garza, the running of a star nation was one such job where this level of security was a prerequisite.

The bioplas sheet was keyed to his biosignature and could only be read when his security token accessed it. As he took it from the man's hands, Garza's own personal identification token performed a handshake with the security nanofiber embedded in the page, revealing the contents of the classified memo.

His eyes skimmed the document, and a sense of resignation

filtered through him. This was one meeting he could not shunt off until after he returned to Parliament House on Ceriba.

He shot his wife an apologetic look as his thumbprint once more secured the paper from intruders who might seek to read it.

"We'll have your husband back to you as soon as we can, ma'am." Ed smiled, but something about it felt off to Garza. "You won't even know he's gone."

The words struck the prime minister as odd, and yet, there was nothing menacing about them.

He'd recall that odd turn of phrase in a few hours, when the universe as he knew it turned sideways.

Two protective detail agents stood waiting in the condo's foyer. They were unfamiliar to him, and Garza wondered if Parliament had contracted with local officials here on Beryl to fill in during his much-needed holiday.

He hadn't taken a vacation in three years—a fact his wife had made sure he couldn't forget, especially considering their daughters were just about to turn five.

It was Ed who had suggested the trip to Sirius, pointing out that this particular lodge, nestled at the foot of the Teter Range, was a very defensible structure, and one that the Protective Services team had recently vetted for the governor-general's own trip with her family last year.

Beryl was known for its magnificent mountain ranges, and its skiing was the best in the Alliance, bar none. It hadn't taken much of a suggestion for Garza to agree to make this the family's destination.

Another plus had been the remoteness of the location. Wireless network access was nonexistent at the base of the mountains, against which the lodges and condos were nestled. It was spotty at best on the slopes, and what bandwidth existed was reserved for the exclusive use of the rescue teams that patrolled the mountain range.

This had been one of the Teter's major selling points, in Garza's opinion. The thought that he could be out of commission for a week, truly on his own, without the burden of office weighing him down, had been too appealing to ignore.

His wife had been a bit less enthused with the idea, but the shopping the small resort town offered and the plethora of artisans and craftsmen selling their wares had drawn her like a moth to a flame. Once on site, she'd admitted to him in a private moment after they'd retired one evening that this was one of the best vacations they'd ever had. It had done wonders for their marriage, too.

But now this.

Well, at least I had three decent days without interruption, he thought resignedly with a last glance back toward the kitchen table, where his wife still sat. *That has to count for something.*

"Sir, we're ready for you," one of the detail said, opening the door and motioning with his hand.

Garza nodded and followed the man outside, pulling his jacket around him and adjusting its internal temperature controls to ward off the worst of the winter chill.

Outside, at the entrance to the row of condos, sat an armored, unmarked vehicle. Three men strode ahead of him, leading the way, as three more took up their positions to the side and behind. His assistant walked beside him.

Garza glanced over at the young man. "Anything you can tell me about this?"

Ed shook his head, then gave a tilt of his chin to indicate the vehicle. "The general will be able to tell you more than I can, sir."

Garza stopped and turned to stare at his aide. "The general?" His voice was tinged with surprise. "Is this more serious than you led me to believe?"

The detail up ahead came to a stop, the first man's expression one of barely masked impatience.

"Sir, we're on a bit of a schedule. If you would, please," he urged, and turned to resume his walk.

Garza blinked rapidly in startlement as he followed in the man's wake.

It wasn't that he demanded respect; it was that he'd become used to a certain amount of it, simply because his status seemed to require it, despite his protests.

But this man, this leader of his protection detail, seemed singularly *unimpressed* with the prime minister's title. More than that, the man's attitude bordered on *hostile*; it struck warning bells deep in the back of Garza's mind. Something was off here, and yet he couldn't put a finger on what or why.

Before he sussed out what it was that bothered him, they'd arrived at the transport, and the detail spread out in the familiar watchful positions they took each time he embarked or disembarked. His mind settled at seeing the routine reassert itself.

It shouldn't have.

Ed stepped up beside the vehicle, rapped once on the frame of its door, and then stepped aside.

"You aren't coming with us?" Garza asked, surprised.

Ed shook his head, an odd smile ghosting along his lips. "I'm too junior, sir. Besides, I'm needed here. I'll see to your family personally, sir. You have my word."

Something in the way the man worded that phrase resurrected the unease he'd felt earlier, but then he shook his head and dismissed the errant thought when he heard a familiar and unwelcome voice call his name.

General Carlisle was the last person he'd expected to see in the transport. The general was a three-star, and one of those men whose personal ambition eclipsed what was best for the star nation's military.

Garza had come up through the Geminate Marines himself, once upon a time. He'd seen men like this, had been unfortunate enough to serve under a few.

Most of the men and women who served in the Alliance Navy had his utmost respect. They were individuals who fought, bled, and were willing to give their lives in service to and protection of the Geminate star nation.

Carlisle, on the other hand, seemed to only be concerned

with what it took to get his next star, his decisions and actions based more on how it would impact his social and political standing, rather than what was best for those in his charge.

Men like Carlisle had the mind of an administrator, not a warrior. As such, they didn't lead by example. Instead, they led those who reported to them by demanding the respect due to the rank, and not the man.

Garza had heard through the rumor mill that Carlisle had been promoted out of active duty and benched behind a desk. Something about his career trajectory suggested they were angling to position him in a place where he would do the least harm. Not exactly a stellar recommendation.

All this flashed through Garza's mind in an instant as he bent to peer into the transport. He schooled his expression to neutrality as he greeted the other man.

"General, what's going on here?"

Rather than answer, Carlisle gestured him inside.

With one last glance at the protection detail surrounding the transport, Garza ducked his head and slid inside.

Carlisle nodded to the assistant to close the door, sealing them in.

Garza noticed immediately that the faint signal his wire had alerted him to, one he expected was encrypted and for the use of the protection detail, cut out the instant the door shut.

The car is armored, and... jamming?

He turned to the general, his suspicions flaring once more. "What's going on?" he repeated.

The general smiled. "Well, I'd like to say nothing bad, but I think by now you've figured out that we have a problem on our hands. The Alliance has been infiltrated at the highest levels— by Akkadia."

Garza straightened. "You have proof of this?"

Carlisle nodded and then grimaced. "I do. Firsthand, you might say."

"Why come directly to me?" Garza frowned. "You know as well as I do that this is highly irregular. I assume our first step was to take this up the chain of command? Was the chief of Joint Operations informed? What about Duncan Cutter?"

The general shook his head, a slight smile playing about his face. "No need to involve the NSA—or anyone else, for that matter."

Anger began to stir in the prime minister at the man's attitude. "I disagree, General. Admiral Wake should have been the first person you notified. The command chain is there for a reason—"

"And I *bypassed* it for a reason." Carlisle's expression was smug. "Right about now, your newest staff member is informing your wife that you won't be returning to the lodge this evening as planned. You'll be back in a few days, though, from what I've been told—in some shape or form."

Garza stiffened, and he reached instinctively for a sidearm he hadn't carried in decades, his military career long past. The threat to him, to his family, was clear in the general's tone.

"Who turned you?" he demanded.

He reached for the door, but froze when Carlisle shoved the barrel of a pulse pistol in his face. The general shook his head. "I wouldn't if I were you, Prime Minister."

Garza stilled, his eyes narrowing as he debated whether to make an attempt anyway, if only to alert the men and women standing guard outside that something was amiss.

Carlisle must have seen it in his eyes; the man began to chuckle.

"Won't do you any good. Those new men and women you picked up when you arrived on Beryl?" He shook his head. "Not local Sirian law enforcement."

Garza clenched his jaw, his body coiled as he tried to gauge if he could trigger the door open before Carlisle got off his shot. Even if there were traitors in the midst of his detail, he still had a duty to the Alliance.

"I can see you're not entirely convinced. Think of it this way: those men and women loyal to you are looking outward for threats, not among their own ranks. They'll be cut down before they have a chance to respond."

Garza realized the truth of the man's words, and yet his duty to his people overrode his need to prevent the loss of life.

He looked down as if in defeat, and then lunged for the door.

The general discharged his pistol, which, at close range, caused agony to rip through the prime minister. Still, his fingers latched onto the door's controls, and it slid open. He heard startled exclamations and the exchange of gunfire just as Carlisle fired a second blast that sent him careening into oblivion.

* * *

He awoke in a strange, utilitarian room. A man, tall and blond, stood with his back to him.

Garza scanned the room through slitted eyes, careful to remain motionless as he assessed the situation. It had been a long time since he'd served as a Marine, but his training resurfaced, kinetic muscle memory flooding back effortlessly as he regulated his breathing to simulate unconsciousness.

Once a Marine, always a Marine.

He recalled the adage with a brief flare of inner humor.

...Even if you've just been appointed the Alliance's newest prime minister. Okay, Garza, what are you going to do about your situation now, old man?

He surreptitiously tested his body's readiness. His captors had been foolish—or perhaps overconfident—to not restrain him, treating him as the politician he was, and forgetting the warrior he used to be.

He glanced once more over at the only other person in the room. There was something familiar about him, and Garza wondered where he'd seen the man before.

Prior to his recent appointment as prime minister, he'd been serving as a retired three-star general, assigned to the Parliamentary Intelligence Commission. Potential enemies, high-value targets, and persons of interest were constantly being brought to the Commission's attention. If this man was one of them, the Alliance Navy might already be searching for him.

He instructed his body to remain still as the man turned to face him, and he continued his study as the other man approached.

The light green eyes set into the man's narrow face were cold and calculating. They were also familiar.

And then it clicked.

Aw, shit. Clint Janus.

This was the biochemist, formerly of deGrasse Research Torus, who had disappeared so suddenly after the thwarted viral attack against the intelligence community on Hawking Habitat.

Though it claimed to be a privately held company, the intelligence community suspected differently. All indications pointed to Brower being an Akkadian-owned and run agency. That meant that anyone in its employ was also suspect.

When Clint Janus went missing shortly after the Hawking incident, speculation was the man had officially flipped sides and openly joined the Akkadians. It had come as no real surprise to anyone who had been following him—and it didn't surprise Garza to see him here now.

Guess that means I'm in a tighter spot than I thought....

He saw no indication Janus was armed, so he tensed, readying himself to overpower the man and force him to assist in an escape. But then a voice sounded in his head.

Don't.

Garza paused, wary, and confirmed his wire was still offline, the mental pathway he used to access it cut off. The claustrophobic feeling his probing evoked was sure indication that someone had applied a ziptie, or the Akkadian equivalent.

Since the voice hadn't come from over any network connection, he dismissed it, chalking it up to an aftereffect of the sedation.

He readied himself to take Janus down once more.

Don't, the voice sounded again, this time more insistent.

Garza froze, indecision warring inside him on whether to respond.

It doesn't matter. I can sense your thoughts. You don't have to respond for me to know what you're thinking or how you're feeling.

Who are you? he ventured after a long moment.

The mental voice laughed, the sound harsh and bitter. *Not sure you'd believe me if I told you.*

The ensuing silence drew out long enough for Garza to consider taking on Janus once more, but then the voice was back.

This time, it was cautious, carrying the kind of tone Garza had always associated with the delivery of bad news.

Do you recall Duncan Cutter's briefing, the same day as the swearing-in ceremony?

The prime minister was startled by the question. *That's classified.*

The other voice made a sound of derision. *You think? He gave a 'state of the star nation' update, where you were read into what really happened around Luyten's Star. Stinton's illicit research. The results that came from it. Akkadia's attempt to steal it....*

The voice paused briefly, and when it resumed, there was a tenor to it that caused the hair on the back of Garza's neck to rise.

The existence of Jonathan and Micah Case.

The voice again fell silent for several long moments.

Garza ignored Clint Janus as the man ran several diagnostic tools over him, muttering to himself at the results of the readings. Distantly, he registered that the biochemist was referring to brain wave activity and the unusual way in which it was spiking.

The voice returned.

You're aware of the special... bond... that the captains share? Chiral entanglement?

Garza felt a chill wrap around his heart as the meaning behind the strange voice in his head, combined with the words Janus uttered, crashed together in his mind, and their implications sank in.

No. It... it can't be.

A sense of grim resignation flooded into him from the other's mental presence.

Believe me, I wish it weren't true. But it is.

How?

They haven't exactly been forthcoming. See what you can get out of the asshole hovering over you. By the way, the guy's a real prick.

Garza almost chuckled aloud at that.

Now, he realized that the mental voice held the same flavor as his own inner dialogue, which chilled him all the more.

If this is true....

It is.

Then Janus created you while I was unconscious. How long was I out?

It was several moments before he got a response.

I... don't quite know how to tell you this, the voice began, *but we're no longer above Beryl. I can't tell you how sorry I am to be the one to break this to you, but I guess it's better if it comes from me... We're on an Akkadian space station in the Alpha Centauri system. And you're not....*

Not what?

The voice let out a long, gusty mental sigh. *Well, Garza, my man, you read the after-action report from Valenti. Did you catch Thad Severance's initial reference to Captain Case—both versions—when he first saw them?*

*Oh... **shit**.*

Yes. Hello, 2.0.

Garza's mind faltered, forcefully rejecting what the voice implied.

No. That can't be. I have eighty fucking years of memories. I remember my sixth birthday party, for star's sake. No one can duplicate that.

You mean the time Beth asked you to watch over her drink so no bugs got in it, and instead, you caught a fly and stuck it inside?

I'm sure I told someon—

No, you didn't. Dammit. **We** *didn't. We've never told anyone about that.*

Garza shook his head. *This can't be. I'd know. Surely, I'd feel it somehow. I don't feel any different. I'm me. I mean, I should know if I'm not the original, right?*

He cast about for a reasonable explanation. *This has to be some sort of Akkadian manipulation.*

How?

I don't know. Maybe they've perfected some way to scan memories and share them. You couldn't know any of that, otherwise.

Unless I'm right.

The mental words landed heavily inside his head, its owner as bowed by the weight of them as Garza himself felt. He could feel the gravity as the voice continued.

According to what the assholes holding us prisoner have said, there are a few very simple tests that should prove beyond a doubt which one of us is the chiral clone.

That word, the word Garza had been avoiding, sliced through him like jagged shards of glass, and he reeled as the certainty in the other voice hooked its claws deep into him.

His sense of self shifted, teetering on its axis, and he sucked in a sharp, steadying breath.

"Good, you're awake." Janus's face swam into view over him. "Get up. We have a lot to do to prep you for your assignment, and very little time in which to do it."

When Garza remained on his back, the other man's expression twisted into a snarl.

Janus brought a pulsed, directed energy weapon up and aimed it, point-blank, at Garza's face. "While it's true that we need you alive, there are many, many different states of 'alive' that you can be in and still be of use to us. I'm a biochemist and a medical doctor. Believe me when I say I know several that are particularly unpleasant. Now... Get. *Up.*"

CABINET APPOINTMENTS

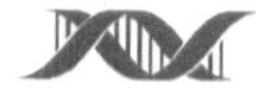

NATIONAL SECURITY AGENCY
ST. CLAIR TOWNSHIP, CERIBA

One week later....

DUNCAN CUTTER WAS flipping through the major news outlets covering the prime minister's press release when the rapid thud of footsteps sounded outside his office. He heard his protective detail confront the person, and suppressed a flare of annoyance at the precautions that came with his position.

Most of the time, Duncan had trained himself to ignore his keepers. He'd known when he accepted the role of national security director that he would be surrounded by a cadre of agents. These people were determined to insert themselves as human shields between him and any perceived threat, at the least provocation.

He hated it. Although he understood its necessity, sometimes the feeling of being smothered threatened to overwhelm him.

An alert flashed over his wire, notifying him of a priority incoming message from Harper, his senior analyst. He brought it up on his optical overlay.

The note was brief, but its contents had him pushing away from his desk—just as Assistant Director Sullivan stuck his head around the corner.

"Did you hear? The news conference...."

Duncan nodded in response, purposely withholding the report he'd just received.

Oblivious to the very different concern that now held Duncan's attention, Sullivan ran an agitated hand through his hair, his mind entirely on the clusterfuck that had just been announced by Garza's press secretary.

"How in the hell could we have read Garza so wrong?"

Duncan rose. "I don't know."

Shoving his hands into his pockets, Duncan walked over to a bank of windows that looked out on the NSA's inner courtyard. After a moment, he glanced back at the assistant director. The other man's expression was troubled.

Sullivan adjusted the cuffs of his suit, and then adjusted them again, a mindless habit Duncan knew to be the man's tell.

What is it, really, that has you so upset?

The thought bounced around in Cutter's head, yet nothing showed on his face.

Sullivan gestured almost helplessly. "Appointing Jamieson as secretary of defense? Garza knows the woman's been running her mouth for years about the number of Navy ships deployed outsystem. She's going to decimate their ranks."

He paused and then added darkly, "That is, unless the new treasury secretary he just appointed beats her to it by cutting the military's funding."

Duncan's lips thinned into a straight line as he regarded Sullivan. "I agree. Both of those choices are very out of character for Garza."

He motioned to the far wall, where a holoscreen displayed headshots of various news commentators standing on the steps of Parliament House. The audio was muted, but a ticker scrolled beneath the image, headlining the breaking story.

Already, the news outlets had rounded up experts, and they

were busy pontificating over this very unexpected turn of events.

Sullivan's gaze fixed on the holoscreen, but then snapped back to Duncan when he spoke once more.

"It wasn't Garza who announced the appointments, though. It was the parliamentary press secretary, correct?"

At Sullivan's nod, Duncan drew in a breath. "Well, then. Let's make certain of our sources before anything else. I suppose it's remotely possible they could have erred in their content."

Sullivan shot him a sardonic look. "You don't believe that, and neither do I."

Duncan's mouth twisted in a slight grimace. "No, you're right. But I'd rather believe that than think I've so completely misjudged the man. We've had numerous conversations. Not once did Garza indicate he's anything but completely supportive of our need to maintain strong borders and protect the jump gates."

"So what do you intend to do? Confront him?"

Duncan reared his head back, startled at Sullivan's brash proposal. "Of course not. But it wouldn't hurt to ask for confirmation."

Sullivan nodded reluctantly, and then heaved a sigh. "I suppose I could do that."

Duncan gave the AD a slight smile. "I would appreciate it."

He stood there, waiting for the other man to take the hint that Duncan intended for him to do it *now*.

Sullivan startled, and then jerked a nod. With a murmur of apology, he left.

For the first time in a long while, Duncan Cutter voluntarily shut his door. Engaging an added layer of secured encryption that he rarely felt it necessary to invoke, he reached mentally for the file Harper had sent before Sullivan barged in. He skimmed it quickly once more—an easy thing to do, as the entire report was made up of only three lines.

Prime Minister Garza being held in Akkadian maximum-security prison. AD Sullivan suspected of collusion. Proceed with caution.

Duncan's gaze landed thoughtfully on the door Sullivan had recently exited before he reached out to the analyst who had sent him the alert.

{*Harper, I need you to sit on this information you just sent me,*} he instructed without preamble, as the woman accepted the ping on her end. {*Gather everything you can on it, but be sure it remains untraceable. I'll set up a meeting with Valenti. I think we need Task Force Blue on this.*}

The analyst's voice sounded both determined and a bit anxious. {*I thought you might say that. I've already erased all evidence of the report, and taken steps to have the agent's handler reassigned. From here on out, everything will come directly to me.*}

{*Excellent. Good work.*}

CELLMATES

Shar-Kali Correctional Facility
and Reeducation Center
Aksu Desert

THE ORIGINAL RAPHAEL Garza was dressed in prison coveralls, hands bound before him by magnetic cuffs he had no hope of breaking. The place where he was being held was both a prison and a research facility. Though he had a pretty good idea he was on Eridu, he had no real way of confirming it.

His latest round of testing and interrogation complete, Raphael was being marched back to his cell, down a starkly lit hallway buried deep inside a prison that, if he had to guess, was somewhere in Akkadian space. He was acutely aware of the two guards marching behind him, their booted feet echoing off the dirty ceramacrete floor, and the third, who held his upper arm in a bruising grip.

The guards were utterly unnecessary. The patch of skin behind his left ear was raw from the number of times that Akkadian shackles—their equivalent of a ziptie—had been applied since his capture. The subjugation nanopackage that made him both deaf and blind to network comms also controlled the nanofloss lattice reinforcing his musculoskeletal system. All they had to do to render him helpless was activate it.

The spot between his shoulder blades itched in reaction to the weapons trained on him, and he understood this was the real reason he had an escort: it was an intimidation play, pure and simple.

He suppressed the irrational urge to laugh at the absurdity of the situation, and the humor fled as quickly as it came.

How in the ever-loving stars will I be rescued if the Alliance doesn't even realize I'm missing?

The one person the ziptie could not confound was the man inside his head. Though Raphael's question had been rhetorical and not directed at anyone in particular, the man whose thoughts he shared responded.

Don't give up. We can never give up. There has to be a way.

Garza 2.0's mental tone was groggy, and Raphael realized his own thoughts must have dragged his other self from his sleep.

He suppressed a surge of jealousy at the thought of another man in his bed with his wife, and then extinguished it.

He wasn't fast enough.

You know it's not like that. I've told Jackie I needed to stay on at Parliament House for the next few weeks, to buy us some time.

They drew to a stop in front of the holding cell he'd called home since his arrival, but Raphael hardly noticed.

How did your keepers respond to that?

2.0 laughed bitterly. *They reminded me that keeping my distance doesn't make her or the girls any safer.*

Raphael brought his teeth down on the inside of his cheek to keep himself from growling in rage. It wouldn't help his mirror twin to add his own anguish to that which his other self already felt.

The door to his prison parted. He saw his cellmate look up, her movement arrested by the sound of the doors swishing open.

The two guards took up position on the other side of the hallway, their weapons trained on him, as the third guard made a production of working the device attached to his sleeve.

Garza felt a small mental pop of displacement, and sighed inaudibly in relief as the nano subjugation released its hold on him. It didn't make much difference, since the cell itself was a Faraday cage, effectively sequestering all inside. But it sure felt far less constraining.

*Not all **that** effective. It doesn't block our connection.*

That's something I hope they never find out. Gotta admit, I'll take the Faraday cage over a ziptie any day, he replied. *Remember how Jackson used to describe it?*

When he'd been active duty, one of the Marines under his command had likened it to the difference between sex with a condom versus going bare.

Inside his head, 2.0 chuckled. *Yeah, I remember having to scour through the history records to learn what in the hell a condom was.*

Raphael smiled at the memory. He'd been half amused, half shocked at the primitive method of birth control used by his ancestors.

You have to admit, it was an apt description, he replied.
That it was.

The guard's eyes flickered over to the woman standing at the back of the cell before returning to him. With a wordless grunt, he stepped back and palmed the door shut.

Raphael felt his twin's mind retreat back into sleep now that 2.0 knew he was back safely in his cell—though 'safe' was a relative term.

He looked up as his cellmate spoke.

"Well, Mister Prime Minister. You don't look... how do you say it? Any the worse for wear?"

He lifted a brow in polite disbelief as he considered her.

The former minister of state security, the vaulted Rin Zhou

Enlai herself, fallen from grace nearly a year and a half earlier when her off-the-books bid to decimate the intelligence community among the settled worlds in one masterful stroke fell short.

"You really expect me to believe you care what condition I'm in?" He favored her with a quizzical look.

Rin Zhou shrugged, then lifted a graceful hand and gestured about her. "If you haven't noticed, we've fallen into similar circumstances. As far as why...." A second shrug accompanied the first. "Why not? There is little else here to entertain."

A harsh laugh escaped him. "Entertain," he repeated. "What an odd choice of words."

"You appear to be physically unharmed by your interrogation," Rin Zhou pressed, her head tilting in an oddly birdlike motion. "Unless the wounds they inflicted were internal? Yet you weren't moving with discomfort, and I fail to see the purpose behind an injury, if not to create discomfort."

The prime minister shook his head. "Our beliefs differ on that quite a bit, I would imagine. The Alliance's position on torture and interrogation is clear. We don't condone it. Ever. In any form," he said flatly.

It was Rin Zhou's turn to raise a brow. "So, you take the moral high ground? Your words are accusation. You find yourself better than us, judging Akkadia for its ways. I wonder, Mister Garza, if you had to endure the hardships my people have, if you would find yourself so comfortable on that moral high ground. We do what we need to do, what we *must*, in order to survive."

Raphael dismissed her words with a tired wave of his hand. This was an old argument, though they'd only been cellmates for a little more than a week.

She abandoned the topic in favor of returning to her previous line of questioning. "What did they want this time?"

He gave her a hard look. "I repeat, why do you care?"

He stepped up to the nearest wall and began to run his hand over it, tracing its contours once more.

"They likely have surveillance on us, you know," she said conversationally. "If I were in charge, I certainly would have."

"You *were* in charge; you should know."

She inclined her head, accepting his truth.

"Is this your angle, then?" he murmured. "Are you trying to get back into their favor by chatting me up? Possibly getting me to reveal things to you in an unguarded moment that I would not to those who interrogate me?"

Shrewd eyes met his. "Would it work?"

He gave her a flat stare, and she chuckled softly, nodding.

"I thought as much. Very well, then. If you do not wish to speak of what you know, then I shall speak of what I know."

This was new.

Garza pushed away from the wall and moved to the cot assigned to him. He sank down onto its threadbare blanket, resting his forearms on his knees before silently motioning for her to continue.

Rin Zhou looked up to one corner of the room and made an odd sign with her hand. Turning back to him, her gaze acquired an intensity it hadn't had before. "I still have friends within the ranks, and they sneak me information from time to time. They have also allowed me access to a bit of equipment prisoners don't ordinarily have access to."

She held out her fisted hand, rotated it, and then uncurled her fingers. On her palm rested a small unit that Raphael instantly recognized.

"You have a jammer?"

Her fingers wrapped around it once more, and it disappeared somewhere into the robes she wore.

"They would kill me if they found it. In showing it to you, I have placed my life in your hands."

Garza barked a short laugh. "Of what use is this to me?"

Rin Zhou gave him a pointed stare. "Doubtless, I am responsible for many deaths among your people. You could turn me in, see it as a sort of recompense... though, one life for many is not much of a balance."

He lowered his chin, acknowledging her words, but didn't speak.

"I am in here because I opposed Asher Dent as premier. My actions were taken with one goal in mind, and that was to protect the late premier's daughter, to ensure her ascension to the position she had been groomed for since birth." She paused and tilted her head, considering. "It was my loyalty that convicted me, one might say."

Raphael knew all this. She had to know he'd been briefed on the role she played in that near disaster on Hawking. She had little hope of garnering his sympathy.

"By all accounts, Asher Dent is behaving in a much more civilized way than the premier you backed," he retorted. "Tensions between your people and the rest of the settled worlds have been the lowest in recent memory."

"You know that is but a smokescreen," she scoffed. "Your presence here proves that."

He lost his patience. "Look, I know ritual is very important to you and your people, and you love nothing more than to drag things out, but I'm in no mood for it. Just say what you want to say."

Rin Zhou leaned forward and let out a breath. "I help you, you help me."

Raphael motioned for her to go on.

"I know what Janus has done to you. I know your chiral clone has been returned to Ceriba and is even now being forced to do Dent's bidding."

He fought to keep his surprise to himself. "Do you know his endgame?"

Rin Zhou's eyes shuttered. If she knew, she apparently wasn't willing to share.

"I can help you escape. In return, I want your help to depose Dent."

"Why? So you can rule instead?"

For the first time since they'd been thrust together, Rin Zhou's words sounded without artifice, her words unguarded.

"Believe me, Mister Garza. I pose a much smaller risk to the Alliance than that man does. And an even smaller risk to the settled worlds."

Her words gave him pause. It seemed she held a critical piece of information regarding Dent's intentions; something so grave, she was willing to treat with an adversary to stop him.

"Dent is one man. You think he poses a threat to every star nation in the Coalition?"

She stared at him, her expression frank. "Raphael, I *know* he does. And we need to stop him at all costs."

HURRY UP AND WAIT

THE WEEK FOLLOWING the mysterious man's death passed with interminable slowness for Task Force Blue. Valenti instructed them to remain close and to be prepared to deploy at a moment's notice. As the days went on, Gabriel Alvarez saw that the constant state of readiness was beginning to wear on the team and flight crew alike.

After Hyer's attitude set Boone off for the third time in as many days, out of desperation, Gabe reached out to Major Snell, the officer in charge of the stealth combat aviators.

{What can I do for you, Alvarez?} asked the Shadow Recon leader.

{I have a bunch of people up here ready to tear each other's heads off. You wouldn't have any drills you could manufacture to help the crew burn off a bit of steam, by chance, would you?}

Snell's mental laugh was droll. *{Valenti's SI contacted me a week ago and told me the colonel was putting you on call. That causing a little bit of tension, is it?}*

{A bit, yeah. So her SI contacted you, huh? The one she calls Takeko?}

{That's the one.}

Gabe must have made a mental noise that gave away his discomfort, because Snell chuckled.

{I know; I'm still getting used to that thing in her head, too.} There was a brief pause, and then Snell asked, *{Still no orders, eh?}*

{No, sir. Looking forward to the time when that comes, I can tell you that much,} was Gabe's heartfelt response.

{I'll just bet you are. Actually, this is perfect timing. Shadow Recon just took control of that new vessel Cutter commissioned for you people.}

{That thing finally arrived?}

Gabe was surprised. He'd been hearing for a year and a half about the mysterious spacecraft that the Geminate Navy had commissioned from Siderius Aerospace, a vessel designed specifically for TF Blue. It had taken on the tenor of an urban legend among the team; no one really thought the ship would ever show up.

{It did,} Snell confirmed. *{It's everything we'd been told to expect. And the folks from Siderius are almost done with the refit that'll give* Wraith *some of the same new toys that the new ship has. Tell the flight crew to report tomorrow for recertification at 0800.}*

{Copy that, sir. I'll pass your orders along. And... thanks.}

The next morning, curiosity got the better of Gabe, and he decided to head down to the hangar to catch a glimpse of the mysterious new ship. The vessel was a completely new type-class, a Nadir. It differed slightly from *Wraith,* the ship that normally carried the team when they deployed.

Unlike *Wraith,* this new vessel wasn't simply a modified version of a Helios fast attack craft; the Nadir took those modifications to an entirely new level. It was also bigger than *Wraith,* though it was a bit difficult to distinguish any features from this distance.

Oddly, the closer Gabe got to it, the more disoriented he became. It got to the point he was forced to focus on the people standing in front of it, instead of the ship itself.

"Start her systems up," he heard Snell call out as he drew to a stop.

He saw Hyer standing in the ship's open hatch, but she looked for all the worlds as if she were floating two meters above the deck, suspended in a sea of black nothingness. It looked almost as if she had opened up a door in spacetime, a portal to a ship that... wasn't there.

He saw her nod and duck back inside the ship.

Gabe looked over at Jonathan Case, the person nearest to him, and tilted his head in the direction of the vessel. "That's *Mirage*, I take it?"

At the pilot's nod, Gabe grunted, keeping his gaze fixed on the other man's face. "Not to put too fine a point on it, but I thought you could cycle those ships' skins so they looked normal and didn't play tricks on the eyes."

Jonathan glanced over at the ship and then back at Gabe, a look of amusement pulling at the corner of his mouth. "Yeah, sorry about that. We're cycling through *Mirage*'s outer hull settings, kind of a multi-point inspection. Hang on; let me have them put it on hold for a sec so we can calibrate your software uplink."

Gabe nodded his understanding and waited while Jonathan sauntered over to Snell and the two men briefly conferred.

"Okay, come on over," Jonathan called out, a laughing note in his voice as he added, "We can't have the team's second-in-command walking around the new ship like a drunken sailor—especially when she's about to be sent out on her first mission."

"Very funny, Case."

He followed the pilot gingerly, doing his best to look anywhere but directly at the ship.

"Just walk up and place your hand on *Mirage*'s hull," Jonathan encouraged. "I'll input your token into the ship so you can handshake with her systems."

Gabe's gaze wandered over to the figurative black hole where the ship sat, and he immediately tilted his head up to look at the hangar's overhead.

"Damn, that ship'll do a number on your vertigo," he muttered, and heard Jonathan smother a laugh.

"It's the ship's ultrablack surface. It's ten times blacker than *Wraith*'s coating."

"Shit, and I thought *Wraith* was impressive."

Both vessels evoked an eerie feeling of sensory deprivation when their skins were programmed to present a precisely aligned 'forest' of carbon nanotubes. The tubes were spaced in such a way that they absorbed all light that hit the surface across the visible, IR, and UV spectrums.

It was disorienting enough that military minds had programmed a virtual optical overlayer for the crews attached to the spacecraft. It allowed ship's personnel—and any passengers, like Gabe—to approach and interact with the vessel without being thrown by its lack of visual cues.

Gabe recalled someone explaining to him that the vertigo he experienced was because the surface suppressed all depth perception. This, in turn, made the human eye want to shy away from looking directly at it.

"Right, then. Keep going; you're almost there." Jonathan's voice held suppressed laughter, and Gabe shot him a murderous look.

"Smartass," he said under his breath, but sped up, ignoring the other man's mirth. "I'm not interested in getting a bloody nose over this."

"Okay, extend your arm. Contact should initiate an auto-update," Jonathan told him.

Gabe did as instructed, reaching out blindly until his palm landed on the curve of the ship. Suddenly, the craft's wireframe depiction snapped into sharp resolution on his overlay.

Gabe's low whistle pierced the air as the ship resolved on his overlay.

"Impressive," he whispered, sidling up to the craft and splaying his hand over its surface.

It was one thing to read that the spacecraft's profile had

been subtly altered. It was another to see it up close and personal. *Mirage* looked sleeker, somehow. Deadlier.

He skimmed the ship with his fingertips, feeling its slightly bumpy texture as he walked toward the ship's open hatch. At the same time, information began to pop up beside the wireframe.

Total hemispherical reflectance: 0.0003%.
Ablative strike plate: 230% to norm.
Composite interlayer: Phosphorene-Stanene Picofoam.

"What the hell's a phosphorene interlayer?" Gabe muttered.

"Oops, sorry about that," said Jonathan, and in the next instant, the data cut out. "That was a list of all the upgrades and improvements over the Helios."

Gabe crooked a smile and jerked his chin at the slumbering beast. "Have you or Micah taken her out yet?"

Jonathan grinned back at him, and planted his hands on hips. "Yeah, Micah took her out to the Badlands on that last mission. *Wraith* got the new plating too, while he was out dancing the asteroid tango with those smugglers."

Gabe followed Jonathan up the ramp and into the craft. He nodded a greeting to Will Morris, *Wraith*'s flight engineer, and smiled at Hyer, seated in the co-pilot's seat.

Jonathan slid into his cradle, and Gabe stepped up between him and Hyer to peer over his shoulder.

"So, what did all that stuff mean, anyway?" he tapped his temple to indicate the data feed that had appeared on his overlay.

"What, the list of features? You want the layman's version, or you want Specialist Morris here to spout fancy science shit no one understands, like 'twisted Weyl semimetals,' at you?"

Gabe held up his hands and sent an apologetic look the flight engineer's way. "No offense, Will, but let's keep it simple."

Will waved him off. "None taken, sir."

Jonathan continued the explanation. "Well, as you've

already seen, *Mirage* has a tunable strike plate, just like *Wraith*, but it's been completely redesigned from the ground up. When she's in active stealth mode, like she is right now, we can't be detected while we're at rest."

"But we're going to be moving," Gabe pointed out.

"Doesn't matter," Katie joined in. "*Mirage*'s energy cross-section is so low that even the Navy's sensors will write us off as a cloud of micrometeorite dust."

Jonathan jabbed a thumb back toward the ship's aft section. "Drives are twelve percent more efficient. Not only will that help mask our energy signature from other vessels, but the engineers also reduced the size of the tokamak plant. That lowers the mass, which makes for a more responsive ship."

Gabe gave another low whistle, impressed. "So, you're saying we're basically... a mirage."

Hyer shot him a wide grin. "Hey, good one, boss. I think there's hope for you yet."

"Now, why does that comment scare m—"

Gabe cut himself off and held up a hand as a ping came over his wire.

{SCIF. Fifteen minutes.}

Valenti's voice cut out as quickly as it had appeared.

Gabe motioned to Jonathan and Katie. "You heard the colonel."

"Don't have to tell me twice," Jonathan said under his breath as he swung the cradle around and stood.

Snell stuck his head inside the hatch, his eyes pinning first Jonathan, and then Katie. "I'll have the other crews hop onto this job with Will and Nina. We'll have her sorted and ready to fly by the time you receive your orders."

Gabe nodded his thanks, and the major slapped his hand against *Mirage*'s hide, and then stepped away.

"Ready?" Gabe asked as they jumped to the hangar deck.

"Stars, yes," Katie groaned. "This has been the longest week!"

Gabe inclined his head toward the lift. "Something tells me

things are about to start moving again—and quickly."

POOR CHOICES

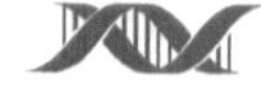

PRIME MINISTER'S OFFICE
PARLIAMENT HOUSE
ST. CLAIR TOWNSHIP, CERIBA

GARZA FOUND HIMSELF spending a lot of time inside his head, carrying on long conversations with his mirror self whenever one or the other wasn't in the middle of a sleep cycle or needing to focus.

They'd been tempted to stick with the use of '2.0,' something about the label appealing to the gallows humor his Marine unit had used back in his active-duty days. But after some debate, they'd decided on the same method Jonathan and Micah Case used.

Mentally, he now referred to himself by his—Raphael's—middle name, José.

He was glad the original Raphael, imprisoned at the maximum-security facility back in Akkadia, had the foresight to hide the mental connection they shared from their keepers. Had they known how effortlessly the two conversed, things might have gone down very differently.

Not only was it the lone edge he and his chiral twin had over their adversaries, but the familiar mental presence also kept him grounded and sane.

He'd been left alone this morning—a rarity these days. He sat at his desk, staring blindly down at the single-page daily brief that listed Parliament's most pressing issues.

The knowledge that he was a clone and not the original version of himself was an awareness that simmered at the back of his mind, ever-present.

Despite that, he realized his good fortune. He wasn't the *first* chiral clone. Though it was true that his position was what had caused him to be targeted, it also gave him access to classified information that others would not have.

He had been briefed on the Case mirror twins; he knew of their unique strengths and their greatest weaknesses. Knowledge was power, and forearmed with such information, he was able to beat back his encroaching panic to a manageable level and think with some clarity.

There was a lot to overcome, not the least of which was the need for chiral sustenance to keep him alive. If left to his own devices, he knew he would starve, for there was not a single thing growing on any planet in any of the settled worlds that would feed his mirror cells.

His keepers knew this, of course. It was one of two ways they kept him under their control.

"We can kill you fast, or we can kill you slow," Ed, his Akkadian keeper masquerading as his newest assistant, had told him the day he was inserted back into his—Raphael's—old life. "You'll be just as dead, either way."

The Akkadians had demonstrated as much to him and his other self back in the lab where he'd been brought to life. He and Raphael had been given a graphic demonstration of exactly how his quantum entanglement 'prison' worked.

José rubbed his hand over his chest at the memory. Getting shot hurt like hell. He'd experienced it a few times during his service as an active-duty Marine, and had thought those days were behind him—until that bastard Janus shot Raphael, point-blank, in the leg.

José hardly had time to process the scientist's unexpected actions before searing pain brought his attention to an identical hole in his own leg. He'd staggered back into the exam table, unable at first to comprehend what had happened.

Janus's action that day had driven home in a compelling way how narrow the thread was that held Garza's life. Should he forget, Ed reminded him of this fact each morning, when he doled out the supplements he needed to remain alive.

He reached down, fingering the time-release capsule he was to take with his food when his lunch was served.

Please don't let there be any more of those orange bars on the dessert menu.

He gagged a little, recalling the taste of pine tar that had clogged his throat when he'd bitten into one the other day.

I wonder what other 'tasty' surprises they have in store for me....

Raphael had tried not to laugh—and failed horribly—when José shared the incident with him. José had told him to stop being an asshole.

He was grateful he had someone to talk to, though. Ed and the other Akkadians who had infiltrated his protection detail were a stark reminder of the precariousness of his position. He knew that if he did not do exactly as he was told, the first casualties would be his family.

While he firmly believed in the vows he had taken to protect and defend the Alliance, he also recalled the solemn vow that he—or rather, Raphael—had made to his wife when they married. So he bided his time, agreeing to his keepers' demands, while continuing to seek ways to free himself and his family from the enemy's clutches.

He knew, as did Raphael, that at some point, he'd have to risk reaching out to someone for help. The problem was, who could they trust?

His thoughts had carried him through to the end of the briefing, and he looked up in mild surprise when a knock sounded outside his door, and his secretary, Ross, popped his head in.

"Assistant Director Sullivan to see you, sir."

José flicked a glance at the calendar on his overlay and noted the NSA briefing that had been put on his schedule earlier that morning.

"Thank you," he said. "Please show him in."

To his shock, his Akkadian keepers allowed Sullivan to enter alone.

José's heart raced. *Is this it? The opportunity we've been looking for?*

He stood to greet the assistant director while reaching out mentally to Raphael. The clouded, disjointed thoughts on the other end signaled the other man was sleeping.

"Sullivan, good morning."

José held up a hand to his aide, and Ross paused at the door.

"Coffee?" José asked.

The other man smiled, and the way he adjusted his suit cuffs briefly drew José's attention.

"That would be appreciated, Mister Prime Minister." Sullivan turned to the man at the door. "Cream, no sugar, please."

Ross shot José a questioning look, and he nodded a silent yes to the man's query. The door slid closed as the man retreated to get their drinks, and José gestured to the sitting area off to the side.

He braced for bad news.

"Okay, lay it on me," he said, and Sullivan's brow crinkled in confusion.

"Sir?"

José stared at the man, and some instinct told him not to mention the tell he'd picked up on.

He waved his comment away with a small smile. "Figure of speech. Or maybe you could call it a calculated guess. I've only been in office a little over a month, but if I've learned one thing already, it's that there's more bad news than good."

Sullivan's expression cleared. "Ah, no, actually, sir, there's nothing too pressing going on at the moment."

José's brows lifted at that. "Really?" He waved the daily brief at the man. "I see here Secretary Jamieson's recommending we cut the defensive screen in half, at the garrison guarding the Alpha Centauri gate."

"Maybe she thinks Asher Dent is less of a threat than the previous administration."

José sent the man a sardonic look. "And I'm sure you're about to tell me that would explain why Treasury's gone ahead and lifted all sanctions against Akkadia, as well?"

The other man's smile turned wry. "Maybe for once, the man in power there is someone we can reason with."

José felt the breakfast he'd eaten sour at Sullivan's words.

"Reason with?" He shook his head, an uncharacteristic bitterness tinging his voice. "The hell we can."

Sullivan's expression sharpened, but before he could respond, José stopped him with a meaningful look toward his office door. "Coffee should be here soon."

A look of understanding crossed Sullivan's face at José's unspoken warning to watch his words. The assistant director settled back into his seat, adopting a relaxed pose.

José clasped his hands and leaned forward, resting his forearms on his thighs. "Okay, besides what SECDEF and SECTREAS have been up to, is there anything else you have for me that wasn't included in the brief?"

He saw his secretary appear in the entrance, coffee service in hand. José waved him in as Sullivan began to detail the latest news from the Sol, Proxima, and Alpha Centauri systems.

He let the man drone on as Ross set down a tray with a steaming carafe and two china cups bearing the parliamentary crest, and then exited.

"The president of An-Yang has expressed an interest in attending this year's Founder's Cup."

Sullivan's statement caught José's attention, and he sent the AD a sharp look as, with a silent nod of thanks, he accepted his coffee from Ross.

"I didn't know he was a fan," said José as he took a sip.

Sullivan pushed a sheet of paper across the coffee table between them. "He would like an official invitation from your office, of course, before it is announced."

José picked up the brief and scanned it. "I don't see why not."

When his office door closed behind his assistant, José abruptly set the paper down and motioned to Sullivan's portfolio.

"Is there anything in there that might be worth an extra layer of security, by chance?"

He sent Sullivan what he hoped was a meaningful look, dipping his chin and silently urging the man to grasp the request he didn't dare state aloud.

The man blinked and then darted his eyes about the room, confused. "No, sir. Everything's standard today."

"Are you *certain*?" José's gaze drilled into the other man.

He let out a relieved breath when understanding dawned on the other man's face, and he reached into his pocket, removing a small device.

Sullivan set it on the table between them, and then shot him a quizzical look. With a small gesture, he said, "We're now being passively jammed, sir. None of your detail will be able to detect it. Was there something you needed to tell me?"

José let out a silent breath, once more reaching out to probe for his other self's mind. Raphael was still sleeping.

He's Duncan's right hand, and you'd trust Cutter with your life, he admonished himself. *So shit or get off the pot, Garza old man.*

"Yes. There is something you need to know. I need your help."

* * *

*You did **what**?*

José mentally replayed his conversation with Sullivan, wincing when he heard the alarm in Raphael's voice.

You know Cutter's tried to talk to me several times. I've seen him reserve time on my calendar, but Ed declines it every time.

Raphael made a sound of agreement. *Well, what's done is done. Wish you'd woken me.*

José grimaced. *Would it have made a difference?*

No, Raphael replied after a beat. *It was a smart move. He's Cutter's number two. He wouldn't have someone he didn't trust implicitly in a position that high in the NSA.*

José abruptly recalled Sullivan's seeming tension, the nervous habit he had of adjusting his cuffs, and stifled a sudden sense of foreboding.

You mentioned the Founder's Cup? Raphael's words brought José back to the conversation. *An-Yang is an ally. Think there'll be opportunity there?*

* * *

The next day, almost exactly to the hour, Jackie Garza arrived at a center for victims of the new psychotropic compound, Frenzy. This press junket was to raise awareness for the dangers of the drug; it was one of the platforms Jackie had chosen to take on as the wife of the new prime minister.

She smiled as she mounted the steps of the temporary stage that had been set up in front of the facility, and then waved to the holocameras.

"Thank you all for coming. I'm so proud of the rehabilitation work the Take Back Foundation has done in their first few months here." She let her smile drop and her expression fall into sober lines as she launched into her speech, which lasted the next few minutes.

"...and it's centers like the Take Back Foundation that are making real inroads to combat this dangerous drug," Jackie concluded. "But don't just take my word for it. Donating your time here will allow you to see for yourself the genuine difference this organization has made." One practiced smile later, and Jackie's duties were finished.

The agents assigned to her protection flanked her as she swept off the stage and toward the motorcade. From the corner of her eye, she saw two members of her detail slowly slip away.

She dismissed it, her mind on other matters. Smiling, she waved at the crowd of onlookers and reporters shouting questions, and then turned to duck into the waiting transport.

{Alert! Incoming! Aler—}

She looked around, confused at what the vehicle's security SI was saying and why it had cut off so abruptly. The agent beside her had an entirely different response. He cursed, his hand coming down on the top of her head, urging her inside the reinforced transport.

A loud, whistling sound pierced the air, and she saw an object smash into the front of the armored vehicle.

The vessel lurched, and she fought to stay on her feet as shouts of *"Missile!"* and *"Down!"* reached her ears. The agent behind her slammed into her and then slumped to the ground, his body dead weight.

She looked down and screamed when she saw half of his face had been blown off.

Another piercing whistle sounded, and then her world exploded in a ball of blinding light, fire, and searing pain.

* * *

José raced through the emergency room's entrance at St. Clair Medical Center, his eyes wild. "Where is she? Where's my wife?"

An orderly came up to him, hands held out to stop José from breaching the sterile room he'd just left. "Mister Prime Minister. Sir. You need to stop—"

"I *'need'* to see my wife. Where is she?"

He wasn't in the same fighting shape as he'd been when he'd been active duty, but he was still a Marine, and unlike Carlisle, he had not let himself go.

He used his bulk now, drawing himself up to his full height. Stepping menacingly toward the medic, he silently dared the man to try and stop him.

"Sir," one of his protection detail warned, and José whipped his head around, eyes glaring his hatred.

The man must have realized Garza was tightly wound, for he held up his hands. With a nod, he indicated the hallway where the orderly stood. "The doctor, sir."

José wheeled back around to face the woman.

The look on her face told him everything he needed to know.

"Fuck!" he roared. "*No!*"

His knees buckled, and he would have slammed to the floor if two of his detail hadn't stepped up to support him on either side. He stumbled forward, agony ripping through him.

The doctor lifted a placating hand. "She's not dead yet, sir, but she is in grave condition." She shook her head. "It's going to be touch and go, and the next few hours will be critical. But we're doing everything we can; you have my word."

Her voice had gentled as she spoke that last, and José gathered himself enough to give her a wordless nod of appreciation.

She spared his detail a sweeping glance, and then her eyes returned to his. "We'll keep you updated."

José shook off the hands that held him as the doctor retreated behind the doors of the operating theater.

"Get the *fuck* away from me." He glared at the agents surrounding him, hating that he didn't know who he could trust and who was traitor.

"If— If— you want to watch, sir, there's an observation room...."

Garza rounded on the orderly when the man began to speak.

The young man took a step back, eyes wide, and his voice faded on a hard swallow. Pointing to a stairwell, he then turned and bolted back the way he'd come.

"Bully for you, Mister Prime Minister. You just scared the shit out of one of the people trying to save your wife's life."

The voice came from his left, one of the men he knew was on Akkadia's payroll.

José closed the distance between them and slammed the heel of his hand, hard, against the operative's chest. "Do *not* mess with me right now," he growled.

He spun and took the steps three at a time, his chest tightening the closer he came to the viewing area.

Thank stars the place was empty.

Stepping up to the clearsteel wall, he looked down into the operating theater. Two teams of doctors hovered around a surgical suite, the blue glow that outlined the area telling José they were encased in an ES field.

Their movements were urgent, and he could hear low calls being made from the anesthetist as she relayed vitals to the chief surgeon—the man working urgently over the broken body of his wife.

Outwardly, José fought to remain calm. Inwardly, guilt ravaged and tore at him.

I did this to her.

His body thrummed with the need to take action, his mind racing as he turned over everything he'd done or said, scrutinizing it for where he went wrong. He kept coming back to the one data point he couldn't ignore. The lone outlier.

His meeting with Sullivan the morning before.

Damn it all to hell, how did they find out? Is Sullivan a traitor, or did they detect the jamming field?

Jackie's body looked so fragile from this far away, lying behind that sterile field. A sense of helplessness settled over him, the kind a man only felt when he'd failed those he loved. His presence here was less than useless, but he could not find it in himself to turn away while others fought for his wife's life.

This is all my fault.

The explosion that had nearly taken her life was being

investigated as an action taken by drug cartels, but the hard glint in Ed's eyes as he'd delivered the news earlier said otherwise.

A secured link had snapped into place between them, the words the man pushed into his head confirming what Ed's expression had telegraphed.

{We have eyes everywhere. There is nothing you can do that we will not see. Try to reach out for help again, and I promise you, she won't survive.}

José heard steps behind him and turned to see the object of his hate approaching.

"How is she doing?" Ed asked, a patently false sympathy painted on his face.

If the blistering rage that welled within José at that moment could have been transferred to pure energy, the man would have been incinerated on the spot.

He stared at Ed, hanging onto the thinnest thread of control.

The man knew it; he actually smiled.

{This is your one warning. It would be a shame for your children to grow up without a mother. It would be even worse if the prime minister should find himself both a widow and childless.}

José froze at the man's next words.

"I'll be leaving soon to pick up your daughters from preschool. Under the circumstances, I felt it best if I handled their safety... personally."

SCIF

Task Force Blue HQ
Humbolt Base

MICAH WAS ON an intercept with the SCIF just as Sam rounded the corner and headed his way.

"Hey, stranger," she smiled up at him as she came to a stop and the SI that controlled the entrance challenged their ID tokens.

"We have to stop meeting like this," he joked as the doors slid open. He reached out, tagging her gently on the elbow, just above where a medical gel pack encased her wrist. *{How are you feeling?}*

{Perfectly fine. I told you; these types of injuries respond very well to nanorepair.} She waved her hand at him.

{And that's why you've been avoiding me?}

Sam shot him a stern look. "I've been busy."

She tilted her head to indicate the open door, and then smiled mischievously. "At least your stomach's not growling like it was last time I saw you."

He groaned. "Hopefully this won't last *that* long...."

There were only two SCIFs on Humbolt Base. The Secured

Compartmentalized Information Facilities were fully sandboxed, able to block all external access.

Such extra measures were enacted only when extremely sensitive intelligence material needed to be shared—or in this case, special instructions given to the star nation's top special operations team.

Micah followed Sam inside, his eyes sweeping the room. There were eight people in attendance. Next to Jonathan sat Katie Hyer, and beyond her were Thad and Gabe. Cutter was flanked by Colonel Valenti and Harper Kinsley—the only NSA analyst fully read in on Task Force Blue and the chiral project.

If Micah had to gauge by the expression on her face, whatever Harper was here to share wasn't something they were going to be very happy to learn.

Other than Jonathan and Hyer, Micah was the only member of the flight crew in attendance. To his surprise, though, Ell was there as well. He hadn't realized she was still on Ceriba; he wondered about her inclusion.

Duncan Cutter looked up as they entered, smiling when his eyes landed on his niece.

"Hello, Sam," he greeted.

She murmured a hello in return as she slipped behind those already seated, angling for the two open chairs beside Micah's twin.

Once everyone was settled, Cutter cleared his throat and gave Valenti a nod.

"Takeko, activate SCIF," the colonel said, her words directed to the SI embedded inside her head.

The doors sealed, and Micah felt the familiar silence that came when his wire's connection to the base's network was severed.

{The SCIF has been secured,} announced the SI's voice, and Micah caught the look of unease that passed between Thad and Gabe. So did Jonathan.

Yeah, kind of creeps me out, too, his twin sent along their private connection.

Being different usually does that to people.

Micah felt annoyance behind the glare his doppelganger leveled at him.

*Don't compare the experimental tech in her head to what happened to you. It's **not** the same thing. No one's looking at you like that, so quit talking shit.*

Cutter's voice brought an end to their mental conversation. "Thank you all for coming." The director's gaze swept the table. "I don't have to tell you that what you hear goes no further than this room. I'll be adding to that number as the need arises, but for now, consider this information close-held. I believe you all know Harper Kinsley. She has something to show you." He sent Harper an expectant look.

The analyst turned to the holoscreen at the far end of the room, and it lit up. Micah was surprised when the recently appointed prime minister's face appeared.

Raphael Garza. He's only been in power, what? Three weeks? asked Jonathan.

Something like that, yes. Micah pulled his gaze from the image and turned back to Harper, his curiosity piqued.

"We intercepted a message, dropped from a deep cover agent on Eridu," she told them.

Thad leaned forward. "I take it this has something to do with the prime minister. Is his life in danger?"

Cutter and Harper exchanged glances.

"Yesterday afternoon, Garza's parliamentary press secretary announced his cabinet appointments," the director said.

Micah frowned at the apparent non sequitur. His gaze swung to Gabe when he saw the former NCIC agent straighten. "I saw that. Frankly, it surprised me. Garza's a Marine and a strong supporter of the military. I thought he'd be with us on this, but the people he selected...."

Cutter's expression took on a grim cast. "You weren't the only one. We thought so, too."

"It's been a few decades since he saw active duty," Thad

pointed out. "Maybe his position has changed."

Cutter shook his head slowly. "I...don't think so. Raphael Garza and I have spoken—recently, in fact. When it became clear that the governor-general was considering him for the position, I invited him to lunch and asked him point-blank where he stood."

The director's eyes cut to the prime minister's image on the holo. "Everything he told me indicated he supported a strong military. We discussed the potential threat Akkadia posed, even with its new leadership. Garza didn't trust easily, and wasn't convinced Dent was as altruistic as he made himself out to be."

"So what happened?" asked Gabe, leaning back in his seat and eyeing Cutter speculatively. "Because his choice for SECDEF is sure as hell not going to be good for the Navy."

Micah knew the secretary of defense cabinet position was one that could make life easier or much more miserable for the military and intelligence communities, depending on the individual's political leanings.

With growing concern, he looked between Gabe and Cutter. "Okay, this one's on me because I should have been paying attention. Who'd he appoint?"

Cutter nodded to the screen, and in the next instant, two other faces appeared, those of the newly named cabinet members.

"Jamieson."

At Cutter's mention of the woman's name, everything snapped into greater clarity.

Jamieson was an isolationist who believed the Alliance was far better off not sticking its nose into other star nations' business. She'd made her position clear on the Alliance's military presence at the heliopause of another nation's star system; in her eyes, it was onerously aggressive. When it was pointed out that the garrison was there to protect a Geminate-owned asset of strategic importance, she'd protested that the Alliance was nobler than this.

"We need to respect the integrity and honor of our esteemed neighbors," she'd been known to say on more than one occasion. *"Not everyone is out to get us, and to assume otherwise is both paranoid and delusional."*

It's not paranoid to protect our interests, Micah thought. *It's plain common sense.*

"This doesn't bode well for the Navy," Jonathan repeated quietly. "Or special forces."

Task Force Blue was the very definition of special forces. That meant they'd likely be impacted by this, as well.

Thad ran a hand over his close-cropped hair and let out a deep exhale. "Damn. Never knew a Marine not to have your back."

"I had every indication that he would," Cutter insisted. "That's what makes the message Harper is about to show you so troubling. It suggests Garza may have made those appointments under duress."

Thad straightened, eyes narrowing. "Duress... as in, an enemy agent got to him?" The Marine's voice was a low, threatening rumble.

"Possibly." Cutter's tone was noncommittal.

Sam shifted in her chair. "Have you approached him about this yet?"

Cutter shook his head. "The information we received yesterday may impact how and when we do so."

He turned to Harper, and Micah saw tension settle onto the analyst's shoulders as the director wordlessly ceded the floor to her.

She cleared her throat, and then indicated the holoscreen once more. Garza's image disappeared, to be replaced by text.

Prime Minister Garza being held in Akkadian maximum-security prison. AD Sullivan suspected of collusion. Proceed with caution.

Beside him, Micah saw Sam jolt upright, her spine snapping straight.

"Are you suggesting we have an imposter in Parliament? Or are you suggesting—"

Cutter studied his niece intently. "What are you thinking, Sam?"

Sam leaned around Micah to spear Katie Hyer with a questioning look. "Admiral Toland told me you were the first one to voice the thought that our victim the other night might be chiral."

At Katie's nod, she continued.

"Well, you were right. He was. The sample I took with my bracer wasn't enough to do much more, but it did confirm that. Harper used the visual file Micah sent Ell to identify his..." Sam stumbled over the next words. "... his donor."

Micah glanced over at Harper, lifting his brows in silent question.

"His name was Chris Williams," Harper supplied. "He worked at the NSA as an entry-level analyst. Just out of university last spring. We believe Chris was a 'test case' to see if they could control a pawn once they had him back in play." Harper's expression was bitter as she finger-quoted the words. "He'd just come back from a three-week vacation. He was supposed to have visited the casinos on Ganymede, but he never arrived."

Jonathan scrubbed at his face. "Hell of a vacation," he muttered under his breath.

Micah shot him a glance. "You think?"

Sympathy welled within him for a guy he'd never known. Williams hadn't asked for what had been done to him, any more than he had.

Dammit, he sought us out, asked for help—and we failed him.

He reached for the water pitcher in the center of the table. Sam silently pushed an empty glass his way, and he was proud of the fact his hand didn't shake as he filled it.

He looked over at Jonathan. *This shit's too close to home for my comfort, bro. We gotta shut those grav-suckers down.*

Yeah, his mirror twin agreed, and then said aloud, "How'd

they manage to kill him?"

Sam blew out a breath. "My guess is that their method of... bringing Chris's chiral twin to life is different than what Stinton did to you two in Luyten's Star. Their process must fully entangle the chiral pair, similar to what we've achieved in our research with the viruses."

She swallowed hard, and then added quietly, "That was the research they stole from us, when I was captured and held prisoner on that secret base in Proxima."

Harper took up the explanation. "If that's the case, then when the clone escaped, all the Akkadians had to do to stop him was shoot the original Williams, the man they still had imprisoned on Eridu. Both men died as a result."

The water Micah had downed sloshed uncomfortably in his stomach. He stared at the empty glass in his hands, thinking about what had been done to him and Jonathan.

This is shitty, bro.

His twin's thoughts flooded his mind in response. They were as emotionally charged as his own.

Those poor fuckers had it worse than even we did. They never had a chance.

Micah nodded in silent agreement.

Gabe lifted his chin to indicate the holo. "So, you think the same thing's happened to Garza? That the man your inside source saw imprisoned in Akkadia is the original, with the chiral Garza installed as our prime minister?"

Micah could feel the tension in the room as everyone waited to hear Cutter's response.

The director nodded. "Yes. It's a distinct possibility."

"Then we need to get confirmation that the man here on Ceriba is indeed chiral." Sam straightened and looked intently at her uncle. "That's easy enough to confirm. All we need is a tissue sample—"

Cutter cut her off with a shake of his head. "We can't go around asking one of the senior leaders of our star nation for a tissue sample. Not only would that tip our hand, it might also sign his death warrant, given what happened in Montpelier the other day."

Thad crossed his arms and sat back. "Okay, then. What do you propose?"

"If they're a chiral pair, we have to time this carefully, coordinate both rescues down to the minute."

Cutter looked first at Micah, and then at Jonathan. "I think we all know that the only way to guarantee instantaneous, untraceable communication between Akkadia and here is to use you two."

Micah had already come to the same conclusion. He exchanged a glance with his twin, who sent him a subtle nod.

Valenti took up the narrative, handing out orders in her usual clipped tone.

"We split you into two teams, Micah on one, Jonathan on the other. Your missions are the same. First, you recon. Confirm that Garza's indeed on Eridu and that the man here is his chiral clone and not a body double or imposter. Then we'll extract."

Cutter leaned forward. "Don't forget; it won't do Garza any good if we save only one of them. If they have the other, they'll still be able to eliminate them both."

"How do you plan to divvy this up?" Gabe asked Valenti.

The colonel's gaze landed on Micah. "We need a legitimate reason to get one or more of you close to the prime minister. Get that DNA sample. Give the man the opportunity to reach out for help if he's truly being coerced."

Micah carefully set down the empty glass he'd been rolling between his palms. "Why are you looking at me, Colonel?"

"You won't be flying the team to Akkadia. Jonathan will."

"If this has to do with chirality," Micah began, and Valenti lifted a hand.

"It does. If somehow the team is compromised and taken prisoner, I cannot let Akkadia get their hands on a chiral human."

"They have their own," Micah pointed out.

"And they don't know the differences between theirs and

ours. I'd like to keep it that way. Whatever edge we have, we use against them."

Micah nodded. "Understood. So where do I fit in?"

Cutter smiled. "Not sure if you've heard, Captain, but there is a sports event taking place within the next few weeks. The Founder's Cup."

"The starglider regatta?" Micah was surprised by the sudden topic change.

The director's smile widened. "I understand from Harper that you gentlemen have a bit of experience with the Founder's Cup."

Micah and Jonathan exchanged a look.

Jonathan shrugged. "I suppose you could say that."

Harper lifted a brow. "Founder's Cup champion two years in a row? I'd say it's a given."

"Would've been three," Jonathan grumbled, "except—"

"Except the spar cracked on the starglider the following year," Micah finished for him. "We—well, you—had to drop out."

Cutter motioned to the holoprojector. "Which provides us with a unique opportunity. Jiu Liam, the president of An-Yang, owes us a favor for cleaning out that nest of spies in the Badlands eighteen months ago. He'll be arriving from Shang to attend the regatta. We reached out to him very privately and asked if he'd consider challenging the prime minister to a friendly exhibition race."

Thad's brows rose. "Does the president of An-Yang know how to fly one of those things? For that matter, does Garza?"

Cutter chuckled. "Nope. Hasn't a clue." He motioned to Micah. "That's where you'll come in. You're going to be the prime minister's new personal trainer."

Micah blinked at that. "No offense, sir, but assigning me as Garza's trainer is a bad idea. The Akkadians will know instantly that we suspect something. It's not like I'm an unknown." He pointed to Sam. "Hell, they kidnapped her because of her connection to all this. There's no way they're going to believe this is a chance encounter."

Gabe nodded, a skeptical look on his face. "I agree. Plus, the Akkadians are going to have agents all over the man."

"You're right; they will." Cutter's gaze swung to where Micah and Sam sat. "Akkadia knows Williams sought you two out before they eliminated him. They can't be sure what he told you. If Garza's a clone, they'll expect us to make contact. So, that's what we do."

Katie's nose wrinkled. "But if they know, and we know, and they know that we know... then how can we get anything done? And how do we hide it from them?"

"Old magician's trick. We hide it in plain sight."

Katie's expression suggested that the director's comment hadn't cleared up anything for her.

Harper cut in. "While their eyes are on Micah and Sam, we'll be working with An-Yang to handle the swap from a different angle."

Thad's brow lifted. "Come again? And in words a Marine like me can understand."

"The swap will happen in midair, at the end of the exhibition race," said Valenti.

"What? How?" Micah asked.

"Shell game. Harper will fill you in on the details later," Cutter said. "But we'll need you to plant a tracker on Garza's starglider while you're training him."

Micah shook his head. "Won't be easy. They'll be watching me every second."

Valenti leaned in. "But they won't be watching Chief Hyer."

"Me?" Katie yelped, jerking in her seat as if she'd been zapped with an electrical current.

Cutter nodded. "You."

Thad sat back, scraping his palm against the stubble of his jaw as he stared thoughtfully back at the director. "So you're saying the whole training Garza thing is a big diversion."

Cutter shook his head. "Though it's true that the starglider he'll fly is equipped with an SI to autonomously fly the vessel, we still need to make sure he can land that thing if it fails."

He looked over at Micah. "Your mission is very real. You truly will need to give Garza a rudimentary understanding of how to pilot the craft—just in case."

"Understood," Micah murmured.

Cutter turned to his niece. "Sam, your mission is equally critical. There's still the possibility that Garza's a body double, or even a plant. We need that DNA sample before we break interstellar law by infiltrating a sovereign star nation to conduct an extraction. If we can seat you at Garza's table during the Founder's Dinner, can you retrieve that sample for us?"

Sam's brow furrowed. "I think so, yes."

Valenti's gaze bounced between Sam and Micah. "Neither of you will be going in alone. We'll have a Unit team there as backup."

Micah nodded but then sat back as an unhappy thought intruded.

Once the news leaked that a former two-time champion was tapped to train the prime minister, the fairgrounds would be crawling with reporters.

Sucks, bro.

Micah shot Jonathan a glare. *You think? You're off on a real assignment, while I'm playing decoy and having to sit my ass down in front of every journalist who wants a personal interest story about the Shadow Recon pilot who's the prime minister's personal trainer.*

Sometimes, you gotta suck it up.

Thad leaned over, purposely snaring Micah's gaze. The expression on his face told him that he knew full well he and Jonathan were having a private bitch session.

"Let the team do what they're trained to do," the Marine advised. "Boone and Asha can slip inside the fairgrounds undetected. The Akkadians'll never see them—and you'll never be without backup. Trust us to do our jobs, hoss."

Micah raised his hands in nonverbal capitulation and then

turned back to the colonel. "If I'm on Garza duty here, who's going in to retrieve the one on Eridu?"

"Thad. Jonathan. And Agent Cyr."

That got a reaction out of Thad. The Marine straightened, angling a questioning look Valenti's way.

In lieu of a response, the colonel gestured to Cutter.

The director turned to the petite woman seated beside Thad. "Since you were singled out by an Akkadian assassin eighteen months ago on Hawking, we plan to exploit that, if we can."

Ell's expression remained unchanged, but Micah sensed that she was about as excited at this turn of events as he'd been about training the prime minister.

"That wasn't—" began Ell, but Cutter held up a hand to cut her off.

"It might've been a chance encounter. You might have been the most convenient person for her to reach out to. Hell, you might've even been the only person she knew by name. Bottom line, it doesn't matter.

"Even if your... relationship with her is virtually nonexistent, it's more than anyone else can lay claim to. We're going to grab every advantage we can get in the situation. On the off-chance you can make contact with her while you're there, maybe convince her to help, then it's worth the risk."

Thad growled softly, and it was Valenti's turn to raise a warning hand.

Ell shot Thad a quick glance before returning her gaze to the director and nodding reluctantly. "Understood, sir."

"Jonathan will fly *Mirage*," Valenti continued. "By necessity, and because of his connection to Micah, he'll need to go with you to the prison in order to time the extraction perfectly."

"We're sending you through the Alpha Centauri gate with a garrison patrol doing an early rotation," explained Cutter. "It happens from time to time, so it shouldn't raise suspicions."

"Takeko, display file Eridu-One," Valenti instructed, and then turned to face the holo when a small sea of dots appeared, floating in a field of black. "*Invictus* is the flag for the cruiser squadron that will take you through gate transit. *Mirage* will travel inside her boat bay."

As she spoke, labels identifying additional Shadow Recon ships appeared above each icon representing one of the cruisers.

"We're sending *Wraith, Scimitar, Katana*, and *Eidolon*, too, along with eight direct-action Novastrikes. You'll all be hitching rides with the squadron. Once there, these ships will jump in closer to Eridu but remain on standby within the Sargon Straits. If you find you need an assist with a hot extraction, they'll be ready."

There were nods all around, and then Cutter cleared his throat.

"One more thing. For them to have snatched Garza out from under his protection detail tells me this was an inside job. At this point, we don't know which organizations have been compromised, so we assume the worst. No one outside this room is to know about this. This is highest-security, codeword access."

"Copy that," said Thad.

His words were echoed by those around the table.

"And here we thought Asher Dent might be a more reasonable leader for the Akkadian people," Gabe murmured.

"I don't think the words 'reasonable' and 'Akkadian' go together in any lexicon I've seen," Sam murmured.

"Ooh-rah," Thad agreed under his breath.

Valenti nodded to Alvarez. "You'll take the lead on the Ceriba op. I'll be going with Team Two to Akkadia. Admiral Toland will move over from the CID to take over in my absence."

Cutter stood. "You have your orders. I want *Mirage* ready to depart two hours after you've completed your briefings. Dismissed."

TEAM ERIDU BRIEFING

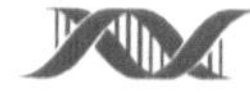

TASK FORCE BLUE HQ
HUMBOLT BASE

THE ALERT APPEARED on Ell's wire just as she was grabbing a sandwich to-go from the base commissary. With a regretful look, she tossed the prepackaged meal back into the chiller and headed back toward the special ops sector.

She cleared the security SI at the first checkpoint, murmuring her apologies to the line of soldiers as the specialist standing guard waved her to the front of the queue.

Her chrono told her she was still running behind, so she bypassed the lift, racing down the stairwell to where the team was meeting one level below. She came to a stop just outside the briefing room and looked inside. Spying Jonathan and Harper, she was relieved to see she wasn't the last to arrive.

The sound of footsteps had her peering over her shoulder to see Thad coming up behind her.

She lifted a brow and mimed looking at her wrist, as if checking one of those external chronos people used to wear.

Thad shot her a mock glare. "Don't go there with me, *cher*, especially when I can see you're winded from running here yourself."

Ell resisted the urge to smile at his growled warning. She settled for arching a brow in reply as she slipped past him into the room.

Thad sealed the door shut behind him, and Harper flipped the holoscreen on, launching immediately into the briefing. An image of the planet Eridu appeared, rotating slowly as she spoke.

"The facility you'll be breaching is located at the border of the Hohen Savannah and the Aksu Desert."

An icon appeared, pinpointing the spot.

"That's one of the most barren pieces of terrain on the Akkadian homeworld," she continued. "The land is subject to both monsoon rains and haboobs, depending on the season, and is not too far from Central Prefecture and their main space elevator."

The analyst spread her hands, and the projection's view exploded, a topographical map of Eridu zooming past as Harper zeroed in on a particular spot. Now the analyst appeared to be standing among a sea of dun-colored switchgrass, nearly a meter tall. She pointed to her right, and the image tracked in that direction.

Off in the distance, Ell could see a haze of green. She pointed to it. "What's that?"

"It's a rainforest that borders the savannah. Because of Eridu's botched terraforming, they have a real problem with acid rain, so it's not advised you spend any time there. Which reminds me...." She tossed a data chip to each of them.

Ell reflexively lifted her hand to catch it. As the chip hit her palm, she felt it handshake with her wire's data partition, and a file opened.

"You'll all be thrilled to know that you have appointments this afternoon in Medical for a few tweaks to your respiratory system. It'll allow you to blend in like natives—and breathe their toxic air without the headsets off-worlders need to use."

Jonathan grimaced. "Dammit, I hate it when they start

tinkering with our lattices. It's worse than a hundred-*g* burn, makes me wheeze for days afterward."

The lattice was a mesh weave of nanofilaments known as SmartCarbyne, tied to an onboard accelerometer, and connected to a person's wire. Ordinarily, it was deployed to protect the soft organs from crushing gravities only when the app detected dangerously high levels of acceleration.

Evidently, it could be modified to filter toxins, as well.

"Good news, hoss," Thad drawled, slapping his hand onto the pilot's shoulder. "Eridu's a long ways away. You'll have plenty of time to get used to it."

Harper coughed, drawing their attention back to the holo.

"Our assets on-planet say the best way to breach the facility is here." She moved her hands again, and the image shifted.

Ell saw the grasses thin into sparse clumps as the desert asserted itself.

Jonathan wrinkled his brow. "I don't see anything. Looks like just a bunch of dried grass and desert sand to me."

"That's because the prison is thirty meters below ground. There are entry shafts here, here, and here." As she spoke, areas on the screen lit up. "But they're monitored by both human and SI guards, and the surrounding area is heavily seeded with sensor arrays and listening platforms. Again, our local assets will have worked out a way to insert you into the prison, so for operational security purposes, we will defer to them. They'll give you the specifics once you're on site."

"What's this?" Jonathan pointed to a flat, rectangular space in the sand, several meters away from the shaft.

The indentation's straight lines confirmed that whatever was buried was of human origin.

"Those are hangar doors, very heavily guarded," Harper said. "The hangar bay serves as their main entrance. Supply shuttles run in and out of there once a week."

"Hangar doors, huh?" Jonathan leaned forward, expression focused.

"Yes. The doors retract to reveal an underground runway."

Jonathan nodded absently, fingers drumming a light cadence on the table's surface. His tone turned musing. "I could think of a few ways to get in there, maybe...."

"Take it up with the agents on site once you arrive," Harper cut in. "They've approached the prison to test defenses twice this past week. They'll know if something can or can't be done. Just know you'll need to approach with extreme care."

"Any idea of the layout inside?" Thad asked.

She nodded. "Our agent sent us a basic diagram with his last report, but it's a bit sketchy. They'll refine the data and have it ready for you when you get there. We do know the prime minister's being held on the fourth level, and the report indicates he's not alone. He has a cellmate."

Harper paused, and the expression on her face made Ell's gut tighten.

"Who?" she demanded of the analyst.

"Rin Zhou Enlai."

* * *

Thad saw Ell stiffen at Harper's mention of the name.

Enlai was the woman who'd been behind the viral attack against the Defense Summit on Hawking Habitat eighteen months earlier. That same woman was responsible for the kidnapping of Samantha Travis, and later, the death of thousands of citizens vacationing aboard a cruise ship when the virus slipped its leash.

Ell wasn't a bloodthirsty person. Years spent as a Unit sniper had trained her to be deliberate and methodical, so when she approached an assignment, it was with cool calculation.

But she'd been there, up close and personal, during the entire Hawking op; she'd helped apprehend the small terrorist cell Enlai had dispatched to carry out the deadly mission.

The expression that crossed her face now told Thad that the former sniper would have no trouble taking out the Akkadian woman—with extreme prejudice.

Come to think of it, neither will I.

"Orders?" he growled, turning to face Harper.

The sheet in the analyst's hands made a crinkling noise as she fiddled with it, causing Thad's eyes to narrow.

He had a bad feeling he knew what her nervous shuffling portended. If his guess was correct, he couldn't honestly say he blamed Cutter for wanting to keep Enlai alive, considering the vast wealth of information the former State Security Minister was likely to have.

"Your discretion," Harper said, confirming his suspicions. "If you can extract Minister Enlai without compromising the operation, then you're authorized to do so. If not, Garza remains your primary objective."

Thad's jaw worked as he turned Harper's words over in his mind. Slapping his hand down lightly on the table's surface, he nodded in reluctant acceptance.

"Copy that. So what's the plan for getting us to Eridu, and then sneaking us onto the planet?"

The image of the savannah disappeared entirely, to be replaced by a stellar landscape. A label appeared, identifying it as a region of space four AU from the Akkadian homeworld. A tiny dot grew in size until it resolved into a space platform.

"This is a first-stage customs clearance station, privately-held companies from every star nation have local office branches here. You'll be traveling with an Alliance freight company for the last leg of your transit. Their ships berth here," she said, dropping a pin on a section of the wheeled station, "and one of them in particular knows that a cloaked Navy vessel will rendezvous with them within the next few days."

Ell's startled inhale was echoed by Thad's immediate response.

"Whoa, hold on now, *cher.*"

He stood, marching over to the holoprojector. He sent Harper a silent questioning look, and she ceded control to him.

He zoomed out and then pointed to a spot half an AU beyond the station, toward the Alpha Centauri heliopause. His finger encircled the area, and the holoprojector obligingly highlighted it.

"That's an Akkadian defensive screen out there. We can't just appear practically on top of them and expect to remain unnoticed. They'll spot *Mirage*'s Casimir flare when we dump back into realspace."

His gaze swung to Jonathan. "Not disparaging your skills, there, hoss, but I'd like for us to have a fighting chance of getting this right."

The ghost of a grin creased Jonathan's face. "With the new drives, we won't be seen. The engineers at Siderius managed to find a way to dampen the flare of the Casimir bubble when it pops. Wouldn't've believed it myself if I hadn't reviewed the test footage Siderius sent along with the ship. *Mirage* appeared from out of nowhere while I was flying left seat on *Wraith*." He shook his head admiringly. "That ship appeared from out of nowhere just as pretty as you please, slicker than snot."

Thad shot the other man a jaundiced eye. " 'Than snot,' huh? Is that aviator talk?"

Jonathan winked. "That comes straight from a certain chief warrant who hails from the mining platforms."

Thad lifted his eyes to the ceiling and muttered, "Hyer's not even here, and yet she's here."

"Trust me," Jonathan's tone turned serious. "I don't want to be seen either. That far inside Akkadian space? They get a sniff of our signature, and we'll be blown out of the black. I wouldn't do this if I wasn't confident we would remain undetected."

"Fine. So we latch onto a merchie. How do we know that ship's captain can be trusted?" Thad's tone remained skeptical.

Harper gave him a wry smile. "She's naval reserve and Valenti vouches for her. That's all I know."

Jonathan leaned back, one arm draped along the back of an empty chair. Lifting a brow skeptically, the pilot voiced the question uppermost in Thad's mind.

"So we're going in as crew of a merchant ship? Won't we be scrutinized pretty heavily?"

Harper shook her head.

"You'll drop inside an Allied Worlds shipment—as cargo."

Jonathan shot up straight. "Hold up. As *cargo*?"

Harper nodded. "They're running contraband for one of the ministers. It won't be checked."

She indicated to the holoscreen projector, where the image changed from the Akkadian terrain to a man's face.

"That's Akkadia's minister of commerce, Vin Khavari. Vin has a real weakness for Cobalt Blue's Gold Label Reserve whiskey. In exchange for him looking the other way when the next shipment from Allied Worlds Freight arrives, the minister will receive a healthy-sized shipment of his favorite whiskey, duty-free and unreported."

"And exactly what does he think is being smuggled inside that shipping container?" Jonathan sounded doubtful.

"He believes one of the local cartels is smuggling drugs. No one will be allowed to scan the shipping container when it arrives." Her lips turned up in a wry smile. "We wouldn't want anyone to discover the minister's hidden case of gold label reserve. Another indication of how corrupt their system is, but since it can be manipulated in our favor, I'll take it."

Thad grunted.

Harper waited for follow-up questions; when none came, she continued the brief.

On the holo, a light haloed over one of the warehouses in the back of the trainyard.

"Two of our best assets will intercept the shipping container here. Their contact information is loaded onto your data chips, in case something should go wrong."

"Oh, *that* never happens," said Jonathan under his breath.

Ignoring him, Harper added, "If at all possible, we don't want these agents burned, so treat this information with care. Once you make contact, it's critical that you follow exactly what they tell you to do, even if it may seem to make little sense."

Her eyes drilled into each one of them individually, to drive her point home.

"They're deeply embedded with the Akkadians. They know the people, they speak the language fluently, they understand all the cultural ins and outs. They are your best hope for surviving this mission without harm."

Thad nodded. This was SOP with Unit teams. He glanced over at Jonathan; the man was chewing on his lower lip, expression contemplative. He'd doubtless heard this before, but both men knew this was the first time it would apply directly to him.

Harper reached for her notes once more, her expression carefully blank. Eyes cast downward, she concluded, "And... everything inside the shipping container is going to be placed in stasis—including you."

Thad jerked his head back and shot Harper a stern look. "No offense, *cher*, but I'm not too keen on the idea of trusting my life to someone on the other end who may or may not have my back, where a stasis unit is concerned."

Harper's eyes met his, and she nodded solemnly. "I understand your concern. All I can tell you is that our senior deep cover agent on site has assured us that he'll handle this himself. He'll personally receive the package from Allied Worlds Freight."

"And by 'package,' she means us," Jonathan interjected with a scowl.

Harper shot him a repressive look and continued. "With the minister's seal on it, the shipping container won't have to go through customs. The container should be offloaded and set inside the warehouse before anyone has a chance to get near it."

Thad worked his jaw back and forth as he thought about what she'd said.

Ell knew what was going through his mind; trust was earned in this business, and the higher the stakes, the more imperative it was that the people you partnered with could be trusted.

He shook his head. "Afraid I'm going to need more than that. *Names*, Harper. Tell me about this agent on the ground, the one calling the shots. Who is it?"

Without a word, Harper turned back to the projector and brought up a file.

Thad gave a low whistle when he saw the image of the man on the screen. "Okay, I'm in."

* * *

Surprise suffused Jonathan at Thad's sudden capitulation. "Just like that?"

Thad tilted his head toward the image of the man. "Morrison got me out of a jam a long, long time ago. Stuck out his neck and risked burning himself to do so, around a different star, in another deep cover situation. He's good people."

"One of the best cryptologists and human intelligence operatives the NSA has ever known," agreed Harper.

Her gaze swung to Jonathan. "So *now* will you agree to the plan?

After another long moment's consideration, he sighed, then muttered, "I still don't like the idea of traveling from here to Akkadia as a popsicle."

Harper cracked a smile. "You won't be frozen. Stasis isn't cryo. It simply places you in a state where all atomic function is suspended."

Jonathan regarded her silently for a beat before he nodded his agreement. "Popsicle it is. Sign me up."

"Good, because they're waiting for you in Medical. Best get going, flyboy. Oh, and Captain...."

Jonathan looked at her expectantly, but Harper wasn't looking at him; she was staring at the Marine captain.

She had also resumed fiddling with her sheet.

"There's just one more thing," she hedged.

Thad groaned aloud, and Ell looked from him to Harper, her

interest piqued.

"I'm not going to like this, am I?" the man asked, and Ell saw a reluctant smile tug at Harper's lips.

She shook her head. "Probably not, but it's been decided. We're adding one more member to your team." The analyst looked Thad straight in the eye. "You'll be taking one of the cats with you."

TEAM FOUNDER'S CUP

Task Force Blue HQ
Humbolt Base

THE MEETING WITH the home team progressed much more quickly. Gabe walked in right as Micah was describing Thad's response to the news that one of the cats would be joining their mission.

"Jonathan been ratting out the captain again?" Gabe asked Asha under the sound of Sam and Katie's laughter, as he pulled out a chair beside the medic.

On Asha's other side, Boone tipped his chair up onto its back legs. The move displaced him far enough that he could see around his teammate and make eye contact with Gabe. "Ratting him out and starting a betting pool on whether or not Thad'll find a way to squirrel out of it."

Gabe lifted a brow. "You in on this wager, soldier?"

Asha laughed. "He keeps his nose too clean for stuff like that. Or at least, that's what he'd like you to think."

She ducked as Boone took a halfhearted swipe at the back of her head. Gabe withheld comment, turning when the briefing room doors slid open once more to admit Harper.

Major Reid strode in just behind her. Whipcord lean, with dark eyes and hair, the major was Colonel Valenti's right hand, an officer who had worked her way up the ranks of the Special Reconnaissance Units after several exemplary tours. The woman had distinguished herself as a servant leader, earning the respect of the teams the hard way.

She was the kind of person equally willing to tackle the menial stuff and unafraid to listen to the wisdom of noncoms with years of experience under their belts. And yet, she was one of the most taciturn people Gabe had ever known. She never used two words when one would do, and even those she doled out sparingly.

"Major!" Asha called out when she spied the woman.

Both sniper and medic had served under Reid, Thad, too, for that matter. The major had led SRU Team Five for a full decade prior to Thad taking over as Unit commander, a role he'd held prior to the formation of Task Force Blue.

Boone straightened in his seat. "Good to see you again, ma'am."

The major nodded to them both, her expression virtually unreadable. Her gaze traveled past them and then landed on Micah. "So, you're the game piece they're putting in play on the local board?" she said as she came to a stop beside him.

Micah shrugged, looking a bit uncomfortable, though whether it was because of her scrutiny or because of the assignment, Gabe couldn't tell.

"Looks like it, ma'am. I can't say I'm looking forward to it, though."

The major jerked her chin to one side, as if dismissing Micah's words. "You forget; I've seen you work. You've flown us in and out of too many hotspots over the years for me to think this will be an issue. You'll do." She nodded decisively, as if by the strength of her words alone, she could wipe away his concerns.

Perhaps she can, Gabe thought, as he saw Micah's shoulders settle.

As the major turned to take a seat, Harper cleared her throat.

"Major, I don't believe you've met Doctor Travis or Chief Warrant Hyer yet. They're our other two, ah, 'game pieces' that'll be in play for this part of the mission."

Reid nodded curtly to the two women as Hyer raised a hand.

"About that…. What's my role, exactly?"

Harper tossed Katie the Douglass-Washburn ballcap she held in her hand. "You mean how will you go about planting that tracker on the starglider? You'll be joining the pit crew for the prime minister's exhibition race."

"Gotcha." Katie caught the cap, examined the logo on its bill, and then flipped it over her short blue curls. Tipping the bill of the cap back with one finger, she gave Harper a sloppy salute. "So I'm a grease monkey, then. Nothing I haven't done before."

Harper gave Katie a quick smile. "Keep an inside eye on Micah while you're at it. If anything looks suspicious, find a reason to step outside the tent and alert the team."

At Katie's nod, Harper gestured to the major.

"Major Reid has SRU Teams One and Four assigned to canvass the fairgrounds, where the stands and the starting line will be set up. Major?"

Reid's gaze swept the group. "Some of the team will be wearing drakeskin; the rest will be in plainclothes." She turned to Micah. "I've not been to a Founder's Cup. What are we looking at here, Captain? Top-level sketch on what to expect."

Micah pulled his lower lip, expression thoughtful. "The regatta's pretty much no different from any other major sporting event," he said after a moment. "Each team participating has a tent set up along the taxiway, where their stargliders are hangared during the event. There's also a large area set aside for vendors behind the stands. Fans can walk around and buy memorabilia from their favorite teams—you know, shirts, hats, posters, stuffed animals, things like that. Anything they can slap a logo on, they'll sell. And then there are food trucks scattered all around, where you can grab the kind of stuff your mom never let you eat when you were a kid."

Major Reid leaned forward. "Security?"

"I can answer that one." Harper waved a hand at the room's holoprojector, and it lit up with a diagram of the fairgrounds.

She pointed at a spot on the map. "Everyone enters through the registration tent, where security SIs will challenge each person's ID token. On the days the prime minister or the president of An-Yang is in attendance, agents from Protective Services will be on hand to vet attendees, as well."

The image altered.

"The tent housing the starglider that the prime minister will use will have around-the-clock protection, both from Parliament and the Navy. In addition, they've established a firewall inside the tent. No unauthorized signals in or out."

"They don't want to risk someone sneaking something in and setting it off remotely?" Micah guessed.

Boone was the one who answered. "SOP when top-level officials are in residence."

Reid nodded. "Okay, then. We'll double up the number of people in that location. You get in trouble, we should have someone there within thirty seconds." She glanced over at Micah and Hyer. "When you're inside that tent, though, you two will be on your own."

"We have a workaround," Gabe assured the major. He shot a questioning look at Harper.

A subtle shake of her head told him Reid hadn't been cleared to know about the unique chiral connection Micah shared with his twin—something no firewall could defeat.

"They'll have a way to reach us if they need our help," Gabe stated simply.

Harper blanked the screen. "I've sent each of you data files with the details. Bottom line: they're already expecting you out at the fairgrounds."

Micah made a startled sound and shot up in his seat. "We'd better get moving, then."

With a nod to Boone and Asha, Gabe stood. "So had we."

PART TWO: DEPLOYED

FAIRGROUNDS

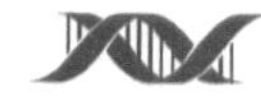

THE EVENT AREA reserved for the Founder's Cup was awash in color, just like Micah remembered from years past. Bright flags adorned the tents that housed the competitors, proclaiming each team's name and nationality.

Katie Hyer's face was glued to the row of clearsteel windows that lined the sides of the spaceport shuttle as it pulled to a stop at the entrance. When its doors opened, the passengers were met by a cacophony of sound, organized chaos that rose from the park-like expanse.

The place was swarming with people, the purpose-filled strides of team members and pit crews slicing through the sea of spectators like a mako through a school of slow-moving fish.

"Busier'n a cat coverin' crap on a marble floor."

Micah wasn't sure he was meant to hear Hyer's words, as they were muttered *sotto voce*, but they surprised a laugh out of him anyway.

"Interesting way to put it, but yeah. It's always like this right before the regatta begins." He inclined his head, indicating the registration tent. *{Go on ahead. We're not supposed to know each other, remember?}*

{Gotcha, Cap. No worries.}

She turned in that direction, her long legs and easy stride giving her a coltish look—Hyer dressed the part, too, straight down to her mechanics' coveralls.

Micah took another long moment to visually scan the area, picking out the icons of racing teams he recognized. He spied a team from An-Yang clustered between a flashy Ganymede tent and one from the cloud cities of Venus.

"They'll be the team to beat," he heard a voice say, and turned to see a woman with a newsnet holobadge around her neck, staring in the same direction.

"Nothing like a pilot who's grown up in the clouds to innately know how to handle an airframe," he agreed.

The woman thrust out her hand. "Janet Provo, SportsCentre. You're Micah Case, aren't you?"

He smiled as he took her hand. "In the flesh."

The reporter waved a hand around. "What's a two-time Founder's Cup champion think of our home teams' chances this year?"

Micah let his brow lift. "On or off the record?"

She grinned. "Oh, you'll know when I'm on the record, trust me. Wouldn't be very sporting of me to waylay you the second you arrived."

Micah let his gaze travel over the teams' banners once more. "They're up against some tough competition this year, but I think the Sirius Gems might have an edge over the Atlieka Hawks."

Provo shot him an assessing look. "Sounds like you've been keeping up on things." Her gaze returned to the fairgrounds. "Any truth in the rumor that you're here to help train Prime Minister Garza for that exhibition race An-Yang's president has challenged him to? And is this an official Navy assignment, or are you taking a personal vacation?"

Micah couldn't help the laugh that escaped him. "You people don't pull your punches, do you? I think you've missed your calling. You should contact the NSA, see if they have any analyst positions open—you'd be a sure bet."

The woman chuckled quietly. "Nah, where's the fun in that? Besides, my passion is sports, not political intrigue." She made a face at that last, but quickly pivoted back to the topic of Garza's race.

She motioned to the tents. "You realize you're walking into a feeding frenzy, don't you? Press'll be swarming all over you the minute you hit the fairgrounds."

Micah gave an easy shrug. "Not much I can do about it. When the Navy senses a photo op and cuts orders for you to be somewhere high-profile, you salute, say 'yessir,' and show up on time."

He let his eyes roam the tents once more as his tone turned nostalgic. "Not that I'm complaining. Been years since I've flown one of these babies. Can't wait to go up in one again."

Provo crossed her arms. "Is that really the wisest thing, then, to send in someone so rusty to train one of our star nation's top leaders?"

Micah popped off a cocky grin. "You forget what I do for a living, ma'am. I'm a Navy pilot, and I fly billion-credit machines every day." He nudged his shoulder in the direction of the tents. "You think a starglider's controls are a challenge? It's like riding a bike. Kinetic memory's ingrained," he tapped his forehead, "up here. And in here." He waggled his fingers at her.

She paused as if weighing his words, and then nodded. "Guess you might be right about that."

"Damn skippy I am. Now, if you'll excuse me, I hear registration closes at five. I'd better hustle or they won't let me in."

Provo smiled and fell into step beside him as he strode off. When he slid her a sidelong glance, her smile widened into a grin.

"Don't mind me. Just tagging along so I can see the dog and pony show." She pointed her finger at him. "You can thank me later for warming you up with softball questions. I like the La Cygne Lager they have on tap at the main food tent, by the way. In a frosty mug."

Micah tipped his head back, his laugh catching the attention of those nearby.

"I'll remember that, ma'am." He gave her a quick salute as he ducked inside the tent.

He moved to the back of a short queue just as Katie stepped up to a tired-looking woman at the registration desk and pulled out the papers she had tucked inside her mechanics' coveralls.

Micah grinned at the official's reaction when Katie handed over the old-fashioned document, then patted the pocket of his own flight suit, hearing the faint crinkle of his credentials.

"Ma'am?" he heard Katie prompt when the woman just sat blinking at the unfamiliar forms being held out to her.

Hyer began to reach for them, but then turned and frowned at the desktop SI when it beeped.

The unit had flagged the chief warrant's ID token, yet its indicator light flashed green.

{Uhh, Cap?} Katie's head began to turn, as if to seek him out.

{Don't turn around! We're not supposed to know each other. Let's just see how these weird NSA credentials play out.}

The registration lady glanced at one of the security guards standing against the back of the tent and motioned him over. The people waiting for admittance in front of him grumbled at the delay, but Micah's attention was fully on the interaction between the woman and the guard, as she asked the man to double-check Katie's info.

The guard glanced over at the holographic display, and his bored expression changed to one of interest. He cast a swift, probing look at Katie before scrolling carefully through the information her ID token had provided.

After a close look at the papers, he stepped back, waving Katie through.

Micah felt a smile pull at his lips when the chief exhaled a mental sigh of relief. He stepped forward as the line began to move once again, and Katie exited onto the fairgrounds.

When his time came, and the SI flagged his ID, the registration agent didn't look concerned; she merely waved the guard over.

Micah was subjected to the same intense scrutiny the man had given Katie, but moments later, he nodded and stepped back.

"Good to go. You can let him through."

* * *

It bothered Katie somewhat that she wasn't allowed to carry a weapon inside the fairgrounds. She'd become used to carrying a sidearm on her person at all times—something she'd not been expected to do as a pilot in the regular Navy, but with Task Force Blue, it was a requirement.

She catalogued her surroundings as she made her way to the tent housing the prime minister's starglider. Just as Micah had described in the briefing, the fairgrounds were teeming with people, merchandise, food carts, and street performers.

Her unease at not having a weapon on her returned, but then Gabe's voice rang inside her head, memories playing of the time they'd taken to the streets of St. Clair Township for a training session, and she'd wanted to know what weapon she'd be carrying.

He'd just looked at her, and then tapped the side of his head. *"This, right here, is your most important everyday carry."*

'Everyday carry'. She remembered thinking it had a cool, special forces ring to it.

The thought must've shown on her face, too, for the former NCIC agent had begun to laugh quietly.

"Don't get romanced by the lingo," he admonished. *"It's the weekend warriors who think they need to bring a lot to the party. For those in the field? That EDC list is very small."*

He'd gestured around him as they maneuvered their way through a busy lunchtime crowd. *"Tell me what you see. What strikes you as a possible weapon?"*

She'd looked blankly at him, but then dutifully glanced around.

There were street vendors, and an open-air café. A pair of stanchions were set up to handle the evening's queue at a theater for a show's opening night.

"I'm not—" she began, and he'd held up a hand.

"Loose brick." He pointed down at the edge of the sidewalk. *"Stanchions."*

She followed his hand as it traced an arc over to the open-air café. In a corner she hadn't noticed, a garden rake leaned against a wall.

"That rake handle would make a fine bo," he assessed, then pointed to a nearby chair. *"And that's light enough for you to swing, but hefty enough to make someone think twice about crossing you."*

"Yes, but—"

"All of these items are just tools that this weapon right here," he tapped Katie's forehead, *"can use to defeat any enemy."*

*I'm **not** unarmed,* she reminded herself now. *If the need arises, I'll just get creative....*

* * *

The familiar drone of aircraft reached Micah's ears as he exited the registration tent, the sound mingling with the bright peal of children's laughter and the call of street vendors. He'd half expected Provo to show up again, but he didn't spot her anywhere.

The Founder's Cup had a secured teamnet set up for participants, a localized, wireless network dedicated solely to those in the regatta. As Garza's trainer, Micah was included.

He accessed it now and found himself routed directly into the combat net that the Unit teams already in position had set up.

{*Welcome to the party,*} Gabe's familiar voice sounded inside his head.

Task Force Blue's second-in-command was leading this part of the operation.

{*Sitrep,*} the former NCIC agent ordered.

{*Hyer and I are in, though our ID tokens garnered a bit more scrutiny than most,*} he admitted.

{*That was expected. It's because you're cleared to be around the P-M.*}

Micah sent a mental nod as he pulled up a map of the fairgrounds. Comparing it to the map Cutter had given them, he frowned.

{*Interesting,*} he murmured. {*They kept the tent with Garza's ship off the list.*}

{*Smart move, if you ask me,*} he heard Boone reply.

{*World's worst-kept secret, if you ask me,*} a new voice countered, and Micah's overlay identified its owner as Shawna, the demolitions expert from Team Two. {*If the starglider's number one manufacturer isn't already at the top of everyone's list, then the sheer number of security agents would be a dead giveaway.*}

{*Shit, Shade, why'n't you jinx us while you're at it?*} another voice intervened.

{*Shut up, Moog.*}

Lips twitching in amusement, Micah let the team's banter wash over him as he went back to the event map Cutter had provided. Locating the Douglass-Washburn Corporation's aeronautics division's tent, he angled his steps in that direction.

Shawna was right; the company was the premier maker of stargliders and had been chosen as the host of the exhibition race. It was in that tent the starglider Prime Minister Garza would be flying could be found.

With the newsnet reporter's warning of the 'feeding frenzy' echoing in his ear, Micah kept a wary eye on his surroundings as he moved. He half expected to be ambushed by a horde of journalists waiting to jump out at him from behind every vendor's booth.

Sucks to be you, bro.

Not even Jonathan's teasing voice could cut through his dread at the thought of facing the people he knew were awaiting him.

Should get hazard pay for this, you know, he grumbled back, as his path dumped him into the row of tents where Douglass-Washburn had set up shop.

It was easy to see what Shawna had meant; though there were plenty of onlookers in the vicinity, the sheer number of reporters and news media outlets that were represented was significantly greater than outside any other tent. Interspersed with them and forming a tight ring around the tent itself were men and women who were clearly not mere spectators.

How's the setup look? his twin asked.

Micah tried to get a better feel for the number of agents surrounding the tent without putting his head on a swivel.

They're canvassing the area pretty heavily. Several layers of on-duty personnel, all of them carrying and all of them in uniform.

Uniform? Jonathan's voice sounded surprised.

Micah sent him a mental laugh. *You know what I mean. Black suits. No identifiable markings. Expressionless faces. Eyes hidden behind visors. Yeah, uniform.*

How many do you think are undercover, either as reporters, or wearing drakeskins?

Micah sent him a mental shrug. *Good question. The drakeskins only have enough juice for a set number of hours before they have to be powered down and the heat buildup dissipated,* he reminded Jonathan. *So they're probably swapping out every four hours or so.*

What about the prime minister? You spot him yet?

The soon-to-be trainer pushed his way past a small knot of cameramen and reporters. *Don't think he's here. The opening ceremonies don't begin for another few hours, but I'm sure he's at the main stadium. He's involved in the pre-event ceremony, isn't he?*

He had nearly made it to the first line of security forces when a sharp exclamation sounded from behind him.

In the next instant, he was surrounded by the news media, microdrone holorecorders hovering around his face as reporters began pelting him with questions.

Micah growled under his breath, causing Katie to cackle in genuine amusement from where she stood at the tent's entrance.

{Watch it, Chief.}

{Sorry, sir. I'm just part of the pit crew.} She grinned and then slipped inside, abandoning him to the ministrations of the paparazzi.

Forcing a smile, he turned to face them.

"Are you the same Micah Case who won the Founder's Cup two years in a row?"

"Is it true the prime minister has been challenged to a race with the president of An-Yang?"

"Are you still active-duty Navy? What does the Navy think about you taking time off to train the prime minister?"

The security detail standing guard in front of the D-W tent to ensure the prime minister's safety was reinforced by a small contingent of Navy soldiers. Both were there for one purpose, and one purpose only: to prevent anyone with ill intentions from tinkering with the starglider Garza would eventually pilot.

Micah had come dressed in his Navy flight suit, so it would be evident to those standing guard that he was in the same service branch as they were. However, he received no help warding off the horde of hungry journalists from those quarters.

He glared back at the nearest guard who dared to smirk in amusement at his predicament.

Micah was certain the man's sentiment was shared by the

rest, but he was the only Navy soldier whose eyes weren't covered by shades or a half-helmet, so Micah couldn't be certain.

Bastard, he muttered silently, only half kidding.

His comment elicited a mental laugh from Jonathan.

Can't fault the guy for doing his job.

I can if it means not aiding a fellow soldier.

"Mister Case!" The nearest reporter shoved a holorecording microdrone into his face. "How long has it been since you've flown stargliders? You've been retired from racing for at least ten years, isn't that correct? What makes you think you can help the prime minister?"

Ignoring the man's second question, Micah chose to address the first.

"Wow, has it really been ten years?" He looked off into the distance, affecting a thoughtful frown. Plastering an *aw-shucks* grin on his face, he shrugged. "Well, since I fly for the Navy, I suppose you could say I've still got it. Oh, and by the way, it's *Captain* Case, not Mister."

He gave one of the female reporters nearby a wink, and she took that as an opening.

"So, Captain, is it true that you're going to be the prime minister's personal trainer?"

"Well...." Micah let his voice fade as he attempted to look humble while still sounding credible. "All I can say is I'm honored the Navy chose me out of all its pilots to be the one to help the prime minister learn the ins and outs of the stargliders."

"Ah, come on now, Captain, no need to be modest here. You would've won three Founder's Cups if that spar on your ship hadn't broken back in '36, am I right?"

Micah played to the opening the reporter gave him. "I'm surprised you remember that. Yeah, that kind of burned, but life's made up of moments like that... times that change your destiny. That's when I decided to fly for the Navy. Besides, winning isn't everything. Safety always comes first—especially when you're talking about one of the leaders of this great star nation."

"So it's true, then? The president of An-Yang challenged the prime minister to a friendly race?"

Micah nodded. "He has, and the loser has committed to donate a generous amount of money to the Wounded Warriors Project. So not only is it a friendly race, but in the end, everyone wins."

By the time he managed to extricate himself from the press twenty minutes later, his cheeks ached from smiling, and the tension running down his spine was no joke.

He quickly ducked inside the tent—and came to an abrupt halt when he found himself on the receiving end of a deadly firearm.

DEPARTURE

SHADOW RECON HANGAR
HUMBOLT BASE
CERIBAN ORBIT

BACK AT THE BASE, Humbolt's main hangar bay was hopping. Jonathan pulled up short as he stepped from the lift, nearly plowing into Daz as she rushed past.

The pilot, who'd flown the drone-scouting mission prior to Sam's rescue from the Akkadian lab, called out a quick "Sorry!" as she raced for *Wraith*'s cockpit.

Ordinarily, the woman flew second seat on *Wraith*'s sister ship, *Katana*, but with *Mirage* now in service, the ship Jonathan had flown for years had been reassigned.

"This place is busy," observed Thad as Jonathan and Ell stepped up beside him.

"Yup."

They'd only had time to get four of the Shadow Recon Helios and a dozen of the specially outfitted Novastrikes upgraded with the new Scharnhorst drives. Colonel Valenti had pulled them all for this mission.

Jonathan could see two more flight crews loading up from

where he stood; Johnson was at *Scimitar*'s controls, with Ryan piloting *Eidolon*. In addition, four fireteams from SRU Three and Five were spread evenly between the Nadir and the Helios ships.

The small fleet would leave within the hour for Leavitt Station. They'd travel at three times the speed of light, the Scharnhorst drives' maximum accel. However, even at those speeds, transit time would still be nearly five hours.

On the other end of the hangar, a light cruiser and three destroyers were busy rearranging their boat bays to make room for the stealthed Unit vessels that would shortly arrive. Once secured, the small battlegroup would transit the gate to Alpha Centauri, ostensibly to relieve the garrison on the other side.

"Guess we'd better move if we don't want to be left behind," Jonathan chuckled, breaking into a jog and arrowing for the corner that held *Mirage*.

Nina looked down at them as they approached. "Perfect timing," she called out, using a handhold above the aft hatch to pike herself off the top of the Nadir and drop into the cargo hold. "We just finished our walkaround. Yuki's in there, pre-flighting her."

She turned to Thad after flashing Ell a quick smile of greeting. "Colonel's inside, said to tell you to come find her when you arrived."

Thad slapped Jonathan on the shoulder as he passed. "Duty calls."

"For you and me both," he nodded, turning on his heels and following the Marine inside.

* * *

The trip to Leavitt was a bit of a letdown after the rush of preparations leading up to departure. Comms didn't work in Scharnhorst space, so the crew and passengers were left with several hours of downtime as the ship, enveloped in its Casimir bubble, crossed the Procyon System to its heliopause.

Thad glanced at the woman seated beside him before reaching over and laying his hand on her knee—the bioidentical replacement for the one she'd lost in the Straits of Sargon so many years ago.

When Ell met his eyes, he gave her leg a squeeze and then dropped his hand. The contact had allowed him to initiate a private, peer-to-peer connection with her.

{You doing okay, cher?*}*

Her inscrutable eyes met his unblinkingly.

{Ell-o-dieeee,} he coaxed, drawing her name out as he had so many times in the past.

She stayed silent for a beat, and then gave him a small nod. *{I'll be fine. I won't let you down.}*

Thad let out a low growl. *{That's not what I asked, and you know it. I have every faith in you. I don't think you know the meaning of the word quit.}* He tapped his temple. *{What about up here? Need your head in the game, Ell.}*

He saw her flare of anger, and immediately felt like an ass for bringing it up.

The flicker of emotion was a mere echo of what he'd seen from her that fateful day her leg had been left a mangled ruin. But he'd held her together then, and he would do so now, if she needed.

He knew she wouldn't; Ell was a woman supremely in control. He'd only seen her break down once, when she'd learned she was one of the few humans whose body rejected the bioidentical nerve implants used to attach cloned limbs.

The utter devastation on her face had wrecked him.

It was then that he'd reached out to Gabe.

He hadn't seen Alvarez since Basic. Their paths had diverged after that; he'd gone into the Marines, while Alvarez had entered the NCIC. Reaching out to the man so many years after had been an act of desperation on Thad's part, not knowing where else to turn.

Alvarez had given Ell a lifeline when he'd talked her into

changing career paths and joining the Criminal Investigation Command, and she'd grabbed onto it with both hands.

Gabe would never know how deep Thad's gratitude ran for his part in bringing purpose back into her life... even though it had meant she would exit his.

When Valenti asked Thad to pull together a team and handed him Task Force Blue to build from the ground up, Gabe had been an easy choice as his second. It hadn't hurt that the man somehow managed to become involved, all on his own, in the events that went down in Luyten's Star.

And Ell? Just as Thad had resigned himself to life without her, she'd ended up in the center of it once more. Only, she was back under his command for this op, and once again off-limits.

Dammit.

Lock it down, Severance.

The anger he'd provoked in Ell faded from her eyes, and he wondered what she saw in his that caused them to change.

She placed her hand on top of his and squeezed. *{I think you know where my head's at.}*

"It's been nine years, Thad," she added aloud. "I'm fine, I've learned to live with the pain. I might not be able to run the Unit course and qualify any longer, but I can do this. Trust me, I won't let you down."

Their conversation was interrupted by an alert from the ship's SI.

{Transition to realspace will commence in five... four....}

They broke apart, both turning to look at *Mirage*'s forward screens. A slight tremor ran through the ship, and then Thad saw an alert pop up on his wire's overlay, informing him that the network for Leavitt Station was now available.

The view in front of them was... unexpected.

Thad let out a low whistle. "Talk about precision flying...."

"I know they said these new drives didn't need to observe the fifty-kilometer rule, but...." Ell's words drifted off, and she shook her head in wonder.

Invictus, the light cruiser that would be transporting *Mirage,* completely filled the ship's forward field of view. Over the landscape of silvery-grey hull were emblazoned enormous letters—a 'T,' a 'U,' and part of the 'S' from the ship's name.

Jonathan manipulated the image, tapping into a feed from the space station's constellation of satellite drones. They could now see that *Mirage* was snugged up against the light cruiser's boat bay entrance.

In a low tone, Ell murmured, "I can't believe how close we are to that ship."

Thad nodded. "I know what you mean. I feel like I can reach out and touch the surface of the damn thing."

* * *

Jonathan smiled at their exchange. He didn't blame them; he felt pretty much the same, and he'd flown them here.

"You should try it from the driver's seat," he called back to them. "It's hella impressive up here, too."

He sank back into his connection with the SyntheticVision system as the maw of the ship before them began to open. He nudged *Mirage* a bit to center her, and then eased her over the cruiser's threshold, careful to match vector and speed with the enormous vessel.

The coordinated dance of thrusters came to an abrupt halt as the ship settled onto *Invictus*'s deck. Jonathan felt his pilot's seat right itself as *Mirage* 'gimbaled' the cockpit into proper orientation, but he knew the induced gravity from the cruiser would have their passengers feeling as if they were now sitting sideways.

{Hang on, reconfiguring cabin,} Will called out.

Like all Alliance Navy ships, *Mirage*'s interior was made from ActiveFiber. Coating surfaces with the self-assembling nanomaterial was a system the Navy had worked out ages ago. With a simple command, Will reordered *Mirage*'s modular walls, seating, and even the ship's plumbing to reflect the new orientation.

As a cruiser, *Invictus*'s boat bay was roomy enough to accommodate *Mirage* without losing any of its normal complement of Novastrike fighters, shuttles, and the lone pinnace ordinarily found within its bulkheads. It was a bit of a squeeze, though.

Jonathan tried not to hold his breath as the cruiser's boatswain's mate in yellow coveralls directed the flight deck's blue-shirted tractor driver to slot *Mirage* into an impossibly tight space.

"Captain's compliments, Colonel," Will's voice cut in, drawing Jonathan's attention away from the accident just begging to happen.

He saw the flight engineer turn to face Valenti.

"He's extended an invitation to join him on a tour of the ship, and has offered temporary billets for the teams and flight crews."

The courtesy was appreciated. The plan was to maintain a steady two *g*s, a believable rate of acceleration within the Navy's 'hurry up and wait' mentality. That put *Invictus*—currently fifteen million kilometers from the gate—at a little over fifteen hours away. It also meant they'd be on board *Invictus* overnight.

Though everyone on *Mirage* had endured worse than being stuck in the Nadir's cramped quarters for that amount of time, they'd all be much more comfortable bunking with the cruiser's crew.

Jonathan glanced over his shoulder in time to catch Valenti's quick nod.

"Tell him we'll be there as soon as *Mirage* is parked."

"They'd just better not scratch the new paint job," Jonathan muttered under his breath, just loud enough for the flight crew to hear.

It pulled a smothered laugh from Yuki, but it was Will who responded.

"No paint to mess up, Cap."

"Fine. Carbon nanotube woo-woo shit, then," he tossed

back.

A boot slammed into his cradle, rocking him forward.

"What was that for?" He spun his seat around and glared at Nina.

"We have guests, sir. Behave."

Jonathan coughed. "Hello pot, meet kettle."

They were interrupted by the squeal of a sharp object against metal, sounding from aft of the cabin. More precisely, it was the scrape of claws against metal, applied to the door of a crate. The noise was accompanied by an annoyed mental voice.

{Are we there yet? Need out.}

Thad groaned and shot Jonathan a look.

Jonathan gestured to his pilot's console. "Don't look at me. I'm working."

Thad turned his glower on Nina.

The gunner kicked back in her seat, stretching her legs out in front of her. She cocked her head at Thad and gave him a wicked grin as she interlaced her hands behind her head. "Don't tell me the big bad Marine's afraid of the widdle kitty."

"*Kitty*? That's a damn extortionist—"

{Not my fault you owe Pascal steaks. Now let me out.}

"Joule's right," Jonathan pointed out. "She's not the extortionist. You have a clean slate where she's concerned."

Thad groaned once more, rising to his feet and stomping down the aisle toward the crate that held the hunting cat. "I'm sure *that* won't last long."

Nina snickered quietly as she and Yuki exchanged knowing glances.

"What's the betting pool up to now?" Ell asked.

Jonathan looked from Ell to Nina. "Wait. There's a pool? And you didn't let me in on it?"

Nina frowned. "You're disqualified. So is she." The gunner waved a hand in Ell's direction. "Since you're both on the mission, you'd be able to influence the outcome."

"But the pool?" Jonathan repeated.

"Oh, that. I think they're laying odds that he'll owe Joule

more steaks than he currently owes Pascal by the time you guys get back."

Chuckling, Jonathan turned back to monitoring the forward screen just as the tractor shut down and *Mirage* stopped moving.

Letting out a relieved breath, he unwebbed. "Ladies and gentlemen, we have arrived."

The scrabbling of claws sounded alongside booted feet as Thad returned from the aft compartment, Joule in tow. At his appearance, Valenti, who had remained quiet during the crew's ribbing, stood.

She pointed to Jonathan and Thad. "You two, with me. Ship's XO is waiting for us in the boat bay."

Thad nodded and then paused to look at Ell. "You want to come along, *cher*? Despite what the captain's message said about officers, your NCIC credentials will open any doors you like."

The former sniper shook her head, her hand sinking deep into Joule's scruff. "I'll stay here with the ship."

Her quiet voice just barely reached Jonathan as he came to a stop in front of the Marine.

Thad reached over and squeezed Ell's shoulder. "Do me a favor and keep her out of trouble, will you?"

"Captain." Valenti's voice had both men turning to face her. She looked pointedly down at Joule, and then back up at Thad. "That's a trained working cat. She gets into trouble, it's the handler's fault, not the cat's."

Jonathan heard the other man stifle a sigh as he followed the Marine toward the hatch where the colonel waited.

"Ma'am, yes, ma'am."

Thad's muttered *"Damn cat"* had Jonathan biting off a laugh as they descended the ramp to the boat bay, but it was quickly forgotten as he took in their surroundings.

This was his first opportunity to see inside the new, Hauptman-class light cruisers. His first impression was that it was big; the bay alone was as spacious as their hangar back on

Humbolt.

He saw the ship's placard as they approached the doors that led from the bay into the ship's lower passageway, and made a mental note to get a better look at it on the way back. If he recalled correctly, *Invictus*'s keel had been laid at the Sirius shipyards above his homeworld more than a decade ago, but the titanium crest adhered to the bulkhead just inside the bay's entrance would confirm it for him.

After a quick greeting, Hinckley, the ship's XO, launched into a brief explanation of how *Invictus* was laid out.

"I know you special forces types don't spend a whole lot of time with the regular Navy, so forgive me if I'm stating the obvious," the man said, pointing to a color-coded strip that ran along the port side wall.

Over *Mirage*'s shipnet, Nina quipped, *{Remedial Navy 101 for the Marine, coming right up.}*

Thad responded with an inaudible subsonic growl.

Valenti shot them a repressive look before returning her attention to the XO, who, thankfully, remained oblivious as he continued his spiel.

Jonathan let the man's words wash over him as he looked around.

Alliance Navy ships were laid out in a uniform manner fleet-wide. Passageways running tip to stern were numbered, while cross corridors were given an alpha designation. Colors were used to designate different levels.

For example, the coordinates of Delta-Seventeen-Yellow would tell any naval personnel, as well as the small squadron of Marines assigned to the ship, exactly where an individual was on *Invictus* at any given moment in time.

They were currently amidships at India-Two-Blue.

"*Invictus* doesn't go all the way through on all levels, so if you need to make your way from here to the bridge," Hinkley was saying, "you need to make note of which color you're on. Green goes all the way through. Red is restricted to Engineering. Seven is the central passageway that runs the length of the ship on every level except Red, where the driveshaft for the weapons bays and the tokamak are accessed."

They stopped at a lift, and the XO's security token ID allowed them entrance. Jonathan saw a quick *'Denied'* flash over his own overlay when the lift challenged his ident and the SI operating ship security didn't recognize him as part of the crew.

The XO eyed him knowingly. "Caught that, did you?"

He nodded.

"Access to this level and this particular lift is only for ship's personnel. You'll have access to the boat bay, the D-FAC, and your temporary quarters," he told them, using Navy shorthand for the dining facility.

They murmured acknowledgment as they boarded the lift, which delivered them in short order to the ship's CIC.

The Combat Information Center on board *Invictus* was small but serviceable, with a large battlespace holotank taking up much of the room's center.

As he entered, Jonathan saw that the captain, Hemry, had their destination pulled up on the display: a customs staging platform in a section of space nearly four AU from the planet Eridu. Merchant ships from every star system converged there to begin their journey through Akkadia's extensive security checks.

After introductions were made between those in the CIC, Valenti turned to the holotank, and then shot Hemry a questioning look.

"I thought it might be worth discussing your plans, in case you find you need backup from the garrison," the captain explained. "Our anti-drone and anti-platform capabilities—"

He stopped when the colonel raised a hand.

"This job requires stealth and precision strikes. That's why we brought the direct-action ships with us. We're not authorized to start a war—which we could easily provoke, if a ship of this class were to show up unannounced and uninvited.

If *Mirage* is detected, we'll send the Helios and Novastrikes in first."

"Very well, then. In that case, I'm sure you've reviewed this information, but a new report just came in I thought you might like to see."

Hemry manipulated the image, widening the field of view until a diamond-shaped pattern emerged, surrounding the space platform at the ten-million-kilometer mark.

Jonathan moved closer to study the placement of the stealthed sensor drones, then gave the captain an appreciative look. "I'm not sure how you managed to get specs on those listening stations, but thanks. This takes all the guesswork out of it for us."

Hemry smiled. "Griffins, Captain Case. The garrison in Alpha Centauri received permission to send a pair of them through on a fast fly-by." He indicated the image. "Data's about an hour old."

Jonathan nodded his understanding.

Griffins were stealth reconnaissance drones with small but mighty fusion reactors hidden behind layers of high-performance electromagnetic shielding. Their cross-sectional return was so small, even Alliance ship scans would dismiss them as a blip from a system's heliospheric current sheet.

He opened his mouth to ask how close the drones had managed to approach, when the XO held up a hand to forestall him.

The man's gaze grew distant, indicating he was receiving an incoming ping, and conversation halted as he listened to the message.

Seconds later, he turned to Hemry after flashing the group a smile.

"Good news. Leavitt STC has us priority routed. As soon as we arrive, we pop to the head of the queue."

Hemry chuckled. "Bet that pissed off some of the merchies. They've been waiting in line for hours, and we just jumped to the front of the list, and we haven't even arrived yet."

"Do you have an ETA for transit?" Jonathan asked.

The XO nodded. "I've forwarded it to your flight crew."

"Well, then." Valenti straightened. "Thank you for the tour, Captain. We'll get out of your hair and let you be about your business."

Taking the colonel's unspoken cue, the XO led the way out of the CIC to show them to their assigned quarters.

Thad looked over at Jonathan as they strode down the corridor. *{Smooth sailing, hoss. Wonder how your counterpart's faring.}*

SIMULATOR RIDE

Douglass-Washburn Tent
Founder's Cup Fairgrounds
Bezier Foothills, Ceriba

MICAH STOOD VERY still at the tent entrance as two very lethal weapons were shoved against his skull. The security agents holding the weapons looked like they meant business.

"Name's Micah Case," he told them calmly. "I was ordered to report here—"

"We know who you are. Don't talk. Don't move."

Micah remained frozen in place while the agents confirmed his identity. His wire pinged as their security tokens challenged his own.

He'd lost the area network connection to Ceriba's planetary net the moment he stepped foot inside—Cutter had warned them to expect this. It was why Jonathan was on standby. His mirror twin was the only person Micah would be able to contact if things went sideways.

As if conjured by his thoughts, Jonathan's voice filtered through his head.

How's Hyer settling in?

Kinda busy here. Two agents holding me at gunpoint, and I'm cut off from the network.

He sent Jonathan a mental image, and then belatedly added, *Hyer bailed on me the minute the vultures descended.*

Can't imagine why. His twin paused. *Are they going to give you network access?*

Whatever connectivity Micah was allowed would be provided behind a secured, monitored, and fully encrypted firewall.

I'm about to find out.

Seconds passed, and then one of the agents nodded and stepped back, his weapon snapping into the high ready position.

"He's clear."

Before moving further into the tent, Micah turned to the first weapon-wielding agent.

"I've been instructed to let you know that I need to report in periodically to my superiors. I understand I need to go through the firewall to do that?"

The agent looked at her partner, and wordless communication passed between the two. The woman nodded, and stepped back, holstering her weapon.

"We'll submit your ID to the list," she told him.

In the next instant, a secured network token appeared over his wire.

"Everything you say, send, or share will be recorded and scrutinized," she warned.

Micah nodded. "Understood."

He had his wire handshake with the encrypted channel, and saw the message, *'Limited Connectivity,'* flash on his overhead.

He lifted a brow at that.

One side of the agent's mouth curled up into a non-smile. "The minute your security token has been cleared, you'll have full connectivity."

He nodded and moved past them, stepping more fully into the tent.

Tell Gabe I'm in.

Will do, Jonathan responded, then paused for a beat. *Done. They expect to hear from you as soon as you're free to contact them. You see the chief?*

Micah's steps brought him more fully inside the tent and closer to the ship at its center. His eyes traced the ship's lines as he walked toward it.

He nodded silently to the two mechanics standing beside a workbench, his eyes shifting to take in Katie Hyer's presence as well. She was kneeling beside what looked to be replacement spars. He didn't let his gaze linger, continuing his inspection of the tent that was their temporary hangar for the regatta.

Yeah, she seems to have integrated with the pit crew no problem.

He stopped in front of the starglider, hands on hips as he looked up at its fuselage.

I have eyes on the ship Garza'll be flying. It's a newer model than the one we flew, but the airframe's the same.

So, you think you can teach a jarhead how to fly?

Jack was one, Micah reminded Jonathan. *Marines do have pilots in their ranks, you know.*

Yeah, but Garza wasn't one of them.

Micah sent a mental shrug. *The operating system on his starglider will have an autopilot. I'll also be tied into the system and can take over at any time.*

Unless they manage to hack the system and boot you out.

Dude. Stop it with the cheerful thoughts.

Micah began a slow, cursory walk-around, at a distance calculated to ensure none of the agents got antsy.

He'd requested and received permission to fly a test run of the exhibition match's course ahead of any real hands-on training he might give the prime minister—but not with this ship. Douglass-Washburn agreed to provide an identical unit for him to use.

The fairgrounds were set between Montpelier and St. Clair Township, on a flat plain just at the base of the Bezier

Mountain range. All of the ships would take off from a dirt strip marked off through the center of the fairgrounds.

The Founder's Cup was a three-heat race that blended triathlon with regatta, and was set to run for three consecutive days.

The stargliders that competed were unique vessels. The air-breathing, magneto-plasma propulsion system gave them both atmospheric and non-atmospheric capabilities, while a secondary, ducted, multiple impeller drive allowed them to dip below the surface of Ceriba's oceans.

In addition, the ships each had a variable-geometry surface that could be reprogrammed to work optimally with the fluid dynamics of each of the three legs of the race.

{Which course will they fly for the exhibition?} asked his mirror twin. *{I'm guessing it's the first leg.}*

The first leg was atmospheric and was held on day one. Its course wound through some of the most beautiful terrain the planet had to offer. Stretching ten kilometers along the Bezier Foothills, the terrain funneled into a long, chute-like gulch. The gorge walls that rose on either side were a mere kilometer apart.

Micah shook his head. *{Nah, too many twists and turns. With another ship alongside, jockeying for position within that same one-kilometer-wide, narrow chute? Too risky.}*.

Surprise coursed through their connection. *{Well, it can't be day two.}*

The ships taking off from the fairgrounds for the second heat would arrow straight for the coastline, dipping into the Marianas Ocean, the course running straight through the Carcassonne Trench.

Micah sent Jonathan a second mental head-shake. *{Nah, they're not going to send novices through a protected sea life preserve. One miscalculation, and they'd be scraping their hulls against coral walls. And before you ask, it's not the third leg, either. Well, not exactly....}*

The final day of the race, the ships would shoot skyward,

guided between holographic flags projected by microdrones hovering in the air, creating a corridor that led past the planet's stratosphere. From there, a series of pylons had been set in nearspace, a course each starglider must maneuver through before returning to the planet's surface.

{So...?}

Micah laughed quietly at his other self's impatience. *{It's a variant of day three, only atmospheric. Simple oval racetrack, pylon drones. Very straightforward.}*

Jonathan made a disappointed noise. *{Boring.}*

{You sound like Pascal when you say that.}

Still, Micah understood his twin's sentiment. He envied those flying the regatta; it was much more fun than the racetrack he'd be setting up for Garza.

He hadn't flown something as small and maneuverable as the starglider in ages. It was criminal to use such a fine flying machine for such an easy course, but given the pilots involved, simple meant safe.

He stopped at the nose of the craft and looked over once again at the two mechanics. Hooking a thumb in the direction of the starglider's cockpit, he asked, "Mind if I take a look inside?"

The engineer standing beside Katie reluctantly set aside the part he was working on, grabbed a rag, and began to wipe his hands as he ambled over.

Micah saw the moment recognition flared in the other man's eyes. His footsteps increased, and he closed the distance more rapidly, all reluctance shed.

"Hey, aren't you that —?"

"Yeah," Micah nodded. "I'm that guy."

A chuckle rumbled in the man's chest as he tipped his chin toward the vessel. "They wrangle you into this party, too, then?"

Micah barked a short laugh. "Yep. Falls under 'and other duties, as assigned.' That's the Navy way. We go where they tell us to."

The mechanic cocked his head. "Not a bad posting for a few days' work, though," he observed.

Micah turned back to the starglider and let his eyes roam its surface controls. "Can't argue that. Sure beats deployment out on the front, or at one of the gates." He tilted his head to indicate the cockpit. "Mind if I take a look?"

The other man stuffed his rag in the back pocket of his coveralls and turned toward the hatch. "Not at all. Come give her a once over." He shot a look over his shoulder. "Just keep your hands off the controls, mind you." His eyes flicked over to where the prime minister's protection detail stood. "Don't want to give those folks any more reason to feel antsy, know what I mean?"

Micah gave him an understanding nod. "That's a good copy. Hands off."

The mechanic hoisted himself up inside the glider, and Micah followed, his optical augments automatically adjusting for the dimmer interior.

He took in the clearsteel nose shield and the holographic control panels and gave a low whistle.

"I see you guys have made a few improvements since I've flown."

The mechanic squinted at Micah. "My guess is the model you used likely didn't have any kind of autopilot SI installed either, did it?'

Micah grinned over at him. "Not hardly. Unless the rules have changed, no Founder's Cup participant would be allowed to use one anyway."

"That's true," the man allowed, "but this isn't for the regatta. This is an exhibition race between two major political figures, and the bosses made it clear there were to be no accidents under my watch. So, SI it is."

Micah tipped his head in the general direction of the pit, outside the ship. "How many people are on the team's pit crew, anyway? I was lucky to have one, and that was only because regulations required it."

The mechanic shot him a sardonic look. "Three from Douglass, on-site at all times, and then your Navy has sent some young upstart to check over our work, make sure we don't do anything stupid."

Micah grinned at the man's peeved tone and jerked his chin in the direction of the pit. "That girl out there? Looks awfully young."

She'd kick your ass if she heard you calling her a girl.

Micah sent Jonathan an annoyed mental grunt. *Shut up. I'm playing to the audience here.*

Unaware of the mental exchange going on around him, the mechanic scrubbed at his stubble, considering Micah's words. "Those were my first thoughts, but she's already elbow-deep in grease. Girl knows what's what, too. Have to admit, she's the first Navy mechanic I've ever seen who's that capable at that age."

Micah hid a smile.

Don't tell the chief warrant, Jonathan warned. *It'll go to her head.*

Nah, Alvarez'll keep her ego knocked down to proper size.

Jonathan laughed. *He brought her into the program, she's his responsibility. Isn't that what Thad said? Like a foundling under Gabe's care.*

Dare you to tell her that to her face.

Jonathan sent him a look of mock terror. *Not sure about you, brother, but I value my life.*

Then it's a good thing we're not this new breed of chiral man. You bite it, I might feel your pain, but I won't end up joining you.

Asshole.

Back at you.

His attention was brought back by the mechanic's description of the display as he wrapped up his tour of the cockpit.

Micah reached for the yoke, but the mechanic knocked it away.

"Don't touch," the man reiterated. "Not anything. Those are

the rules, and I intend to abide by them."

Micah lifted his hands in wordless acknowledgment and then backed out of the ship.

He glanced around as he jumped down from the hatch, nodding in satisfaction. "Looks like the prime minister's in good hands. You have a sim set up somewhere that I can use for initial training?"

The man pointed toward the back of the tent, where two consoles were set up, side by side. "Standard setup. One's slaved to the other so you can monitor Garza's input. You'll be able to make small corrections, or provide instructions so he can do it on his own."

Micah spared him a brief glance. "Mind if I go check it out?" His voice turned dry. "I assume you won't have any problem if I place my hands on those."

The mechanic lifted a brow. "I forgot for a hot minute what wiseasses all you pilots are." Grabbing the rag out of his back pocket he waved it vaguely toward the consoles. "Be my guest. I gotta get back to work."

With that, the man pivoted and marched back toward the piece of equipment he'd abandoned in the mechanics' pit.

Micah's eyes flickered briefly over to Katie. She looked up as the mechanic approached, her gaze shifting to meet his before settling on the man once more.

Micah was relieved to see her treat him just like any other Navy pilot, with a courteous nod and nothing more.

He spent the next two hours running a simulation of the course that Garza would race in the exhibition, and then cycled over to run each of the three legs of the Founder's Cup regatta. It served to both dust the cobwebs off his skills, and offer a brief window of fun during this assignment.

Besides, he was curious about what changes had been made to the course since he'd run it back in '36.

Not much, Jonathan murmured.

No, he agreed.

Micah looked up when he heard footsteps approaching.

Katie held a bottled water in each hand.

"Excuse me, sir." She awkwardly juggled the water bottles as she attempted a salute. "Captain, sir. Sorry."

Micah returned the salute, an amused gleam in his eyes as he replied, "At ease."

He had to hand it to Katie; her acting abilities were on par.

He accepted the water she offered, and then nodded to the console. "Ever flown one of these?"

Katie tilted her head, eyeing the console critically. "No, sir, haven't had that pleasure."

Micah sat back with an expansive wave of his hand. "Well, Chief, I'm supposed to be teaching the prime minister how to fly one of these things. You think the Navy—or your bosses over there in the pit crew—would mind if I borrowed you for a brief run to test my teaching abilities?"

Understanding dawned in Katie's eyes, and then it was gone as she affected a concerned look. "Don't know, sir, but I'll go ask. Be right back."

Smart move, observed Jonathan. *You still feel you got the short end of the stick with this assignment?*

You saw the onslaught when I got here, Micah retorted. *What do you think? I'll face the same thing when I leave, and then a repeat performance every day until the end of the regatta. Not to mention the fact that Cutter basically painted a big ol' target on my back that says, 'Hey, Akkadians, come get me.'*

Jonathan sent him a mental eyeroll. *That's a heck of a lot more excitement than I've got going on. I'm just the bus driver. And now that we're at Leavitt Station, I'm not even that. I'm cargo.*

Yeah, but at the other end? You'll actually get to shoot at things.

Not if things go as planned, countered Jonathan.

When have things ever gone as planned?

Okay, fine. We call it a draw, then.

Micah sat up when he saw Katie approach. *Looks like those Douglass mechanics have approved her as my guinea pig.*

Ought to be fun. Katie's going to take to that like a duck to water.

She will, agreed Micah.

He signed off with Jonathan as Katie came to a stop in front of him.

"Well?" he asked.

"All yours, sir, at least until shift's end."

"Great." He patted the seat beside him. "Web in, and let's get going."

He held the webbing out so that Katie would be forced to take it from his hand. When she did, a direct peer-to-peer connection snapped into place between them. It allowed them to bypass the firewalled network, hiding their conversation from the protection detail.

Micah kept up a stream of general information, which Katie interspersed with nods and *uh-huhs* as they went along. The chatter was simplistic enough to allow them both to focus on the real exchange happening over their wires.

{Got anything to report?} she asked.

{Not much.}

Katie made a mental face, turning her head to look at the starglider. *{We're going to have to sneak in after the mechanics have left, if I'm to plant a tracker on that ship. They won't let me near the thing.}*

Micah grimaced slightly as he reached into the console and activated it. *{Yeah, I didn't dare try anything while your boss gave me the tour.}*

{Did you see them sweep the ship after you exited?} she asked.

{No, but that just proves my point. You can't fault them for doing their jobs.}

Katie blew out an annoyed breath. *{Except that **some** of them are playing for the other team. Wish we knew who.}*

Once she was webbed in, Micah reached for the helmet and a pair of gauntlets that sat in the space between the two consoles.

Katie eyed them with some suspicion. "Wraparound visor? Why not just use our HUDs?"

He shook his head. "Doesn't work that way."

She took the helmet from him, flipping it upside down and peering inside. "You're kidding, right? This tech looks like it's at least a hundred years old, maybe more."

Micah lifted a brow. "Well, the starglider's a piece of anachronistic tech, made to behave as if it came from pre-Diaspora times." He extended the gauntlets to her. "These have haptic responses built into them, so you'll be able to experience the feel of the starglider's controls, even in the sim."

Katie huffed as she took them. "They look like relics from the first mech suit ever invented."

Micah said nothing; he merely donned his own helmet.

Slipping his hands into his set of gauntlets, he took a position behind her, arms crossed.

Katie eyed him doubtfully. "You know, you look a bit... intimidating, standing there behind me like that."

Micah inclined his helmeted head, but remained silent otherwise.

Katie's eyes widened slightly as she hastily amended, "Sir."

Micah gestured with one gauntleted hand. "Put it on."

His voice sounded muffled and a bit hollow even to his own ears; he could imagine what he sounded like to the chief.

Katie made a face at the equipment in her hands, but then gave a little shrug and placed it on her head.

Micah could tell the moment her helmet activated by her swiftly indrawn breath.

"Oh, this is funky."

She jerked her head from side to side, craning her head back and around in an attempt to get used to the odd sensation.

"I feel like I'm inside a tin can," she complained.

Her actions pulled an involuntary chuckle from Micah.

"You remind me of a cat who stuck his head inside a bag of spiced nuts, only to find he can't get out of it."

Katie sputtered a laugh. "I *feel* like a cat stuck inside a bag of spiced nuts. Or a ferret."

Her helmet stilled suddenly.

{Hold that thought.} Her words resonated through his head as she turned to face him. *{What if... What if we get Snotface or Sneaky Pete to plant the tracking device on the ship? No one would suspect an animal, would they?}*

One of her gauntleted hands gestured vaguely as she continued. *{I mean, the fairgrounds are pretty much butted up right against the Bezier Foothills. There are bound to be field animals out here, and I can't imagine the protection detail is that well-versed on the various critters native to this part of the world.}*

Micah tilted his head. *{Huh. That... actually isn't a bad idea. We'll talk it over with Gabe once we're out of here for the day. For now....}* He motioned for her to turn around.

She obediently placed her hands on the console.

{We really should see if I can teach you to fly one of these things.}

{I'm a Navy pilot, Micah. I think I can handle it,} she replied tartly.

{Well, pretend not to be. I've never officially taught anyone how to fly before, so it wouldn't be a bad idea for me to get a bit of practice in before Garza shows up.}

*{**Now** you tell me....}*

FERRETS

BEZIER FOOTHILLS
OUTSIDE FOUNDER'S CUP FAIRGROUNDS
CERIBA

AFTER COMPLETING THREE rounds of the simulated race with Katie, Micah released the chief warrant back to the mechanics' pit and exited the tent. The gauntlet of journalists was slightly smaller than the one that had pounced on him when he'd first arrived, and he let out a relieved breath when he made it to the edge of the fairgrounds without incident.

Gabriel Alvarez was leaning against a low fence, a basket of waffle fries in one hand. He popped one into his mouth and straightened when he caught sight of Micah. Snagging a napkin from the pile underneath the boat-shaped, paper container, he handed the snack over to Micah, who accepted with a smile of thanks.

"You done for the day?" Gabe asked.

"Looks like," Micah said. He glanced over his shoulder at the sea of tents he'd just left. "You get a chance to wander through and see the sights, or were you stationed outside the perimeter?"

Alvarez chuckled and nodded at the fries in Micah's hand. "Where do you think those came from?"

"Point." Micah saluted him with one of the aforementioned pieces of fried potato before popping it into his mouth.

He fell into step beside Gabe as the other man began an easy stroll along the fence line that marked the event's outer perimeter.

"See anything worth mentioning today?"

Gabe shook his head. "Nope. Not a thing." He shaded one hand against the stadium lighting that had turned on now that the sun had set, and pointed at a graceful, curved spindle nestled against a stand of trees. "Boone's on overwatch up there."

Micah followed his line of sight. The fairgrounds' tallest permanent structure rose twenty meters into the air. It would serve as the regatta's traffic control tower.

Gabe then swung his head back toward the tents. "Asha's been strolling around as well."

He reached over and helped himself to another fry, and then rested his forearms on the railing as one of the stargliders flew past, ending its evening test run. His eyes didn't leave the ship as it taxied to a stop and then turned toward its team's tent.

{Sam has the DNA sampling software ready to go,} he continued, brushing salt from his hands. *{You or Hyer able to get the tracker planted?}*

Micah settled against the railing beside the other man. *{Not a chance. That ship's locked down so tight, they're eating coal and crapping diamonds.}*

Gabe slid him a sidelong glance. *{I see you've been spending too much time with a certain chief warrant.}*

Micah barked a laugh. "You might be right."

{Diamonds or not, we still need to plant a tracking device on that ship.}

Micah nodded, popping another fry into his mouth. Chewing thoughtfully, he watched Gabe's face. *{Hyer had an idea about that, actually. It's a bit unorthodox, but I think it has merit.}*

He shared Katie's idea about using the ferrets to plant the tracker. He wasn't sure what he expected out of Alvarez, but the other man's eyes narrowed as he nodded.

{That worked for us on Hawking, at the Merki Institute. Don't see why it wouldn't work here. Should be easier, in fact. I'd imagine it's a bit more believable to see an animal at a fairground like this, than it was in the middle of downtown Midland.}

Micah cracked a smile at the memory that conjured. The security detail at the Institute had begun as skeptics, but turned into believers the moment Snotface found the first viral bomb tucked into the ceiling of one of the institute's lifts.

{Yeah, getting one of them to the tent won't be a problem. It's inside that we might hit a snag,} he admitted. *{I wouldn't be surprised if security didn't have a stealthed surveillance swarm surrounding the ship. They had all sorts of shit active inside that tent.}*

He licked the salt off of his fingers, folded the paper basket, and shoved it and the remaining napkins into a nearby recycling bin.

{I can tell you that there was some active jamming going on the minute I entered,} he continued as he returned to the fence. *{Even my wire's optics ended up being slaved to Protective Services' firewall. I'm certain it's because they didn't want anyone to see what was really going on in there.}*

Gabe turned to face the parking area. *{Okay, why don't we set one of the ferrets loose at the edge of the fairgrounds, and direct them to the Douglass-Washburn tent?}*

Micah nodded and straightened, shoving his hands into his pockets. *{That'll work. Once he's inside, it's best if he wanders randomly through the tent a bit, too. Sniff around, climb all over shit, plant the tracker while doing it. That way, his actions will look natural.}*

{We'll have to run it by Cutter, but I think we have ourselves a plan.}

*{I had an idea about the DNA, too. I might be able to get it

while training Garza, and then we won't have to risk Sam at the dinner.}

Micah felt Gabe's eyes land on him.

{How so? You just said they have surveillance everywhere.}

Micah's mouth kicked up in a smile. *{The way the training simulators are set up, both teacher and student are required to wear a helmet and a pair of gauntleted gloves. Get me that DNA sampler inside a Faraday sheath, and I'll coat the gloves with it. When we're done with our first session, I'll extract it from the gloves after he's worn them.}*

{If you're caught smuggling that DNA tech, you're going to have some explaining to do,} warned the other man.

Gabe pushed away from the fence and clapped him on the shoulder. "Come on. Let's head back." *{We'll set up Operation Ferret as soon as we get to the base. Let's plan to head down, with ferrets, at oh-three-hundred.}*

* * *

The Bezier Foothills were shrouded in the nocturnal silence of the wilderness. It made arrival by shuttlecraft problematic; sound carried far in the crisp night air over the plains.

The vessel Micah flew had the same EM-suppression package that *Wraith* and *Mirage* boasted, but it had also been outfitted with a stealth cloud. The swarm of microdrones that enveloped the ship in a spherical screen veiled its presence by dampening the sound waves made by the shuttle's emissions.

They also functioned as a series of baffles, dissipating the air currents it stirred while cutting through the air. This made the craft slightly more detectable than the ships Shadow Recon flew—but not by much.

As he came in on approach, Micah could see that the fairgrounds' lights had been reduced from event levels to the soft glow by which the area's SI and human guards monitored the empty space.

He'd been told that Teams One and Four had rotated

fireteams and that, even now, drakeskin-clad operatives remained deployed within the fairgrounds. They formed a corridor of sorts, spread out from the shuttle's targeted landing zone to their objective, the tent housing Garza's starglider.

Also on duty tonight were Harper and Sam. The women had their hands busy, keeping the ferrets out of trouble. And stretched out in the shuttle's aisle was Joule's chiral counterpart, Pascal. Black as the night itself, the large, panther-sized feline would be on standby to offer a distraction within the fairgrounds if the selected ferret, Snotface, encountered any problems after insertion.

The plan was to use Snotface's mirror twin, Sneaky Pete, to communicate with the other ferret once he inserted into the fairgrounds. Like Micah and Jonathan, the animals shared a mental quantum connection with their chiral counterpart. This was how they'd direct Snotface into position once he breached the tent.

Micah could only hope this would work; If Snotface were caught with the tracker, he didn't think they'd get a second shot at the ship.

The fallback was to rely on the starglider's own transponder, but if they could track the ship in such a public way, then so could the Akkadians within Garza's detail. With a tracker installed, they could use the override Douglass-Washburn had built into the craft and shut down the transponder, effectively 'disappearing' it—and the prime minister.

While Micah flew, Harper held Snotface, letting Sam work on the cloaking device they would attach to his collar. It could be remotely activated, shrouding the ferret from view if he needed a quick escape.

Micah glanced over at the cabin's internal feed as the Bezier range neared. He saw Snotface's chiral twin, Sneaky Pete, on the seat beside Harper, inquisitive nose twitching as he avidly watched Sam work.

Sam held up the small disk, showing it to Snotface. "This,"

she spoke slowly, in a deliberate manner, "will make you invisible. Do you understand what that means?"

{No one see me? Like on mission to catch bad guys!}

Micah saw Sam's lips twitch as her hands fiddled with the unit.

"Mm-hmm," she said, "just like when the teams go out on a mission."

What she didn't bother to explain was the disk used refraction to bend incident light waves. It tied directly into the simple evanescent device implanted into the ferret's brain.

Snotface's communications chip was different from human wire implants. Identical to the ones inside the big cats' heads, it had no data partition or memory cache, no lattice of SmartCarbyne nanofloss threaded throughout the body for it to control.

The comm implant did, however, include a small cluster of short fibers that led to specific spots in the ferret's brain. These fibers monitored neural data, translating thought into rudimentary speech. That data also happened to register certain other neural activity—neurons that controlled the ferret's motor functions.

When these neurons fired, sending messages to Snotface's limbs, the implant's feed allowed the device in Sam's hand to predict which way the small mammal was going to move and where he would place his limbs. It would then direct a magnetically controlled cloud of light-bending chaff to cloak the animal's movements.

It wasn't perfect. In strong light, a wave-like ripple would outline Snotface's form whenever he moved, giving away his location. But in the fairgrounds' shadows and the minimal lighting of the tents, Snotface would blend in with ease.

Sam sat back. "There. That should do it."

Micah returned his attention to the shuttle's flight controls, their destination looming large in the forward holo. Disengaging the vessel's SI, he took full manual control, setting the shuttle down at the mission's landing zone. Sheltered as it was in the lee of a hill, and with its own passive stealth activated, the ship should remain undetected.

{We're here,} he sent over the ship's net to Major Reid and the team, seated aft of Sam and Harper.

His words were met by a chorus of mental voices as he placed the vessel in standby mode.

Unwebbing from his pilot's cradle, he rotated to face the cabin. He nodded to Major Reid as she made her way to the front, and then met Sam's eyes. "You ready?"

She nodded.

"Is he?"

She nodded again.

He looked down at the small animal. "Snotface?"

The ferret jerked around at the sound of his name, the motion accompanied by an inquisitive noise. He squirmed in Sam's arms and, when she released him, pattered over to where Micah sat, swarming up into his lap.

Despite the fact that they'd been enhanced by the same crazed scientist who had brought him to life, Micah knew the ferrets still didn't have a comprehension level—or attention span—greater than that of a young child.

He also knew this bothered Major Reid. It concerned him, too, truth be told. But he'd seen Snotface's performance in the Hawking Habitat, up close and personal. He knew the ferret could do it, if they could just impart the seriousness of the situation to the animal.

Micah lifted Snotface up and stared into his eyes as Reid stopped beside the first row of seats. "You got this, little guy? You understand what you need to do?"

Snotface's whiskers twitched, and he reached one paw up to swipe at his muzzle in a washing motion. After a moment's contemplation, he replied.

{Put little shiny piece on big shiny ship.}

Micah resisted the urge to sigh as he settled the ferret in his lap.

He looked over at Harper and made a motion with his hand.

She dropped the tracker into his open palm.

"That's right. Put little shiny piece onto big shiny ship."

He held the small tracker between thumb and forefinger.

"This thing is your small shiny. All you have to do is place it on the ship, just like we practiced, remember?"

He mimed placing the tracker against the shuttle's bulkhead.

"You get it up there, and we'll do the rest. Place little shiny on big shiny."

{Then I get to keep?}

"No… no." He exhaled a short, frustrated breath, his fist closing on the tracker. "Little shiny has to *stay* where you put it."

Snotface's nose crinkled, and he reached a small paw toward the device.

Reid's voice cut in. "This isn't going to work."

"Yes, it will," Harper protested, pushing to her feet.

"Wait." Micah shot his hand out in front of him as an idea struck him.

He reached into the pocket of his flight suit and pulled out the challenge coin he'd been given when he'd first achieved his captaincy within Shadow Recon.

Focusing once more on the ferret, he held up the coin in one hand, and the tracker in the other. "You put the tracker on the ship like we discussed, and when you get back, I'll give you *this* shiny instead. Deal?"

The ferret reached for the challenge coin with both tiny paws. *{Gimme, gimme, want to see.}*

"Nope." Micah palmed the coin, wagging his finger at the inquisitive ferret. "You don't get the new shiny until you put the little shiny on the big shiny."

Reid groaned.

{Is this giving anyone else a headache?} one of the operatives on Team Two said over the net.

Micah ignored the voice, his attention fully on the creature in his lap.

The ferret's eyes turned calculating, and Micah could practically see the thoughts whirling inside his little brain.

{Okay. Deal.}

Micah's eyes slid shut and he released another soundless breath as he set the small animal down onto the deck. "He's all yours," he told Harper, feeling as if he'd just won a hard-fought battle.

He ignored the laughing look the analyst shot his way as she pulled Snotface into her arms.

She reached up to activate the cloak that would hide the ferret from the view of the guards monitoring the fairgrounds, and in a blink, Snotface disappeared.

Harper stood, nodding to Reid. "We're ready, Major."

Reid's lips compressed, but she refrained from further comment. Pivoting on her heel, she led the way aft to the open hatch, then flicked her finger at the hunting cat.

Pascal chuffed quietly and rose from his haunches, padding behind her.

As he passed one of the operatives from Team One, the man bent down to activate the cloaking disk attached to the cat's working vest. The material was made from the same camouflage material used to create the teams' drakeskin suits, which would afford the animal protection against stray gunshots.

Like Snotface, Pascal's disk was tied to the team's combat net, so when the cat disappeared from view right before Micah's eyes, the feline's location popped up on his HUD, the blip generated by IFF code embedded inside identifying him as a 'friendly.'

A slight ripple gave away his movement under the shuttle's harsh interior lighting as Pascal slipped into the darkness.

Harper handed Snotface over to one of the team members who was suited up and ready to depart. "You'll take him all the way to the outside of the tent?"

The man nodded briefly in response.

Harper stepped back with her own nod, and then melted

into the background while Major Reid gave the team their final instructions.

Micah saw each member of the fireteam doing last-minute weapons checks, then heard them sound off over the combat net before activating their own drakeskin suits and disappearing from view.

{*ETA, ten minutes,*} one reported.

Micah exchanged a glance with Sam, turning back to the shuttle's cockpit. He pulled up the various feeds coming from the drakeskin suits of the team advancing toward the tent, and tossed them up onto the ship's forward screen.

As he cycled through them, he paused on the feed of the operative carrying the ferret as the man stopped at the edge of the tent. He saw the figure crouch, setting Snotface on the ground. Then the man pulled out a knife and went to work digging at the hard-packed dirt beside the tent, careful not to touch its canvas sides.

Sensors woven into the material would alert those guarding the tent if it was disturbed. By gaining entrance this way, it would look like the ferret had burrowed his way in, which would explain to anyone who might catch sight of the creature how he could have evaded detection.

{*In you go, little one,*} they heard the operative say as he stepped back.

The device cloaking the ferret disappeared in a blip when Snotface crossed through into the heavily firewalled area.

Over the combat net, Micah heard, {*Asset is in.*}

Reid turned and looked at him. "Okay, Case. You're up."

Micah swiveled his chair to face Sneaky Pete, held in Harper's arms. Forearms braced on knees, the captain clasped his hands loosely and leaned toward the little animal.

"Okay, buddy, tell me what's going on. Talk to Snotface. Tell us what he's seeing."

The ferret stared up at him with bright eyes. {*Smells like Chief Katie,*} he sent after a moment.

Micah chuckled. "That's right, Katie was there. Smells like

grease, doesn't it?"

{And lots of shinies. Oooooh, round shiny, I keep?}

"No," said Micah hastily. Pulling his challenge coin from his pocket, he knelt on the shuttle's deck in front of Sneaky Pete. Holding the coin up, he said, "Remind Snotface we have an agreement."

Sneaky Pete stared at him, whiskers arching, and then he tilted his head to one side, as if listening. *{Snotface at ship. Put little shiny up inside?}*

"Tell him to hurry. We want him out of there as fast as possible," said Harper.

{Hokay. Little shiny on big shiny. Snotface bring me round ball with Katie smell on them.}

"No!" Micah instinctively lurched forward, but then caught himself. "Tell him he needs to leave before the bad guys find him."

{Uh-oh, too late.}

An alert sounded, and Micah swung his attention to the shuttle's forward screens. There, he saw several figures converging on the tent.

Reid stiffened. "Something must have tipped them off."

Micah's lips thinned as he looked up at the major with a brief nod. "We knew that was a possibility, the way they have that tent locked down. If they find him, the worst that can happen is—"

"The worst that can happen is they *kill* him!" Harper interrupted. Her hands tightened around Sneaky Pete. "Tell him to run, Pete!"

At her sharp words, the ferret in her arms began to shiver, eyes wide and ears flattening. *{They hurt Snotface?}*

Micah grasped Harper's arm and gave her a warning headshake.

Leaning forward, he brushed a hand over Sneaky Pete's head. "We won't let that happen," he reassured him. "But to protect him, we need to get him out of that tent. Do you understand?"

The tension from the humans was bleeding over to the creature, who was now vibrating with fear.

"Come on, buddy," Micah urged. "You can do this. Tell Snotface to get back to the tunnel they dug—"

Pete chittered nervously. *{Bad men chase! Bad men in tent! Snotface scared! Hurt—}*

Harper gasped. "They're firing at him?"

{Pascal!} Micah interrupted. *{I need that diversion!}*

The ripping snarl of a Ceriban hunting cat in full tracking mode ripped through the open plains.

A jumble of voices sounded over the combat net, the sound eliciting startled exclamations from the teams' operatives, despite being forewarned.

A quick glance up at the shuttle's forward screen told Micah it had done the same to the opposition. Icons moved erratically, agents jolted into action by the hunting cat's savage cry.

{Pascal,} Micah barked. *{Again!}*

Another feral roar sliced through the night, the sound chilling in the dark. Micah could almost taste the confusion and terror the panther-like animal evoked as the icons on the feed began to scatter.

He turned back to the ferret. "Sneaky Pete?"

The ferret reached up and patted Micah on the chin. *{Snotface back outside now.}*

Micah exhaled and glanced back up at the major. Her eyes were defocused; he could tell she was speaking privately on Team One's combat channel.

After a moment, she looked down at him, jerking her chin in a brief nod. "Asset has been contained, cloaking device reinitialized. The team is en route to the LZ."

Reid shifted and crossed her arms, a look of grudging admiration playing across her face. The expression was subtle, easily missed. "I have to admit, I didn't think that would work."

"It almost didn't." Micah rocked back on his heels and pushed to his feet. "It's not a success if they find it. We have to hope that they don't do another sweep before the race. If they do…" He sighed and gestured vaguely about. "I'm out of ideas."

GATE TRANSIT

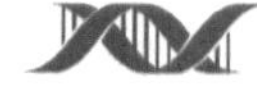

JONATHAN'S MORNING BEGAN with Micah's recount of the night's escapades.

*Dude. That's **two** ferret ops you've completed. You're now the designated Ferret Handler,* he declared.

Micah mentally flipped him off, and then groaned, exhaustion clear in his mental tone.

I gotta grab a few hours' sleep before I meet Garza. Go bug someone else.

His words caused Jonathan to chuckle aloud. He rose from his temporary billet on the cruiser, after a quick glance at his chrono. He had just enough time to grab a shower and some grub before reporting back to *Mirage.*

Twenty minutes later, he strode into the ship's dining facility, where a table of Shadow Recon pilots waved him over. He grabbed a pile of food and some coffee, and joined them, sliding into an empty chair between Yuki and Daz.

He was midway through his meal when Valenti's voice

sounded over the task force's mission combat net.

{You have one hour to report to your respective ships. We arrive at the gate in two hours.}

He checked his chrono again. It had just rolled over to 0800.

Beside him, Daz chased the last bite of egg on her plate with the piece of toast in her hand. Popping it into her mouth, she mumbled, "Gotta run."

Jonathan buried his grin behind his mug as he took a sip of coffee, but a jab in his side from Yuki's elbow told him she'd caught it anyway.

"Stop it. You were the same way when you captained your first ship. Cut her some slack. She's doing great."

"She is," he agreed, "and she deserves *Wraith*. She's an outstanding pilot."

He felt a tug of loss over the ship he'd spent the past few tours captaining, but shrugged it off; they had *Mirage* now, and she was a damn fine vessel.

Yuki pushed away from the table. "Just enough time for me to get in a quick run down at the gym."

She scooped up her tray and ambled over to the corner recycler.

Jonathan crooked a brow at Will, seated across from him. "You're not joining her?"

The man who was both *Mirage*'s flight engineer and its crew chief looked mildly surprised. "She didn't tell you? The gym's in Marine country."

Jonathan groaned. "She challenged one of them, didn't she?"

Will ran a hand over the top of his blond crew cut, tilting his head back as he studied the D-FAC's ceiling. "Maybe."

Jonathan resisted the urge to grind his teeth. "Do I need to go bail her out?"

The normally mild-mannered man grinned suddenly. "Nope. I pinged Thad. He's on his way to intercept her."

Jonathan shook his head. "She's going to kick your ass when she finds out you snitched."

Will just shrugged. "I figure she'll be too busy flying to do that. If all else fails, I'll tell her you sent Thad after her, not me."

Jonathan wadded up his napkin and fired it across the table. "Bastard."

* * *

Within half an hour, everyone was back on board their assigned Shadow Recon vessel. Joule was in her crate, and the flight crews were at their stations and webbed into their seats.

Will patched the feed from *Invictus*'s sensors onto *Mirage*'s forward screens. From his seat beside Ell in *Mirage*'s cabin, Thad had a front-row view.

He found himself unable to look away from the Calabi-Yau gate's otherworldly glow as the cruiser approached the front of the queue. A flash heralded a fresh cycle as another ship readied itself to transit.

Thad sat mesmerized as the vessel crept forward until it was seized by the wildly coruscating extra-dimensional light given off by the compactified branes in the center of its maw. It disappeared in a blink, collapsing into blackness, as the next ship advanced slowly into position.

"Third in the queue," announced Will.

Yuki, seated to his left, seemed deeply immersed in her connection with the ship and did not respond.

Thad saw Jonathan give the specialist a thumbs-up in silent reply just as a secondary display showed *Invictus* side-slipping into position—and then they were number two.

A wave from Jonathan's hand shifted the secondary feed from space traffic control onto the main screens. Thad saw icons marching forward toward the gate, each separated by a fifty-kilometer distance, STC's indicators highlighting the ones in the queue as red. The vessel transiting was limned in green, and the one next up had a yellow tag.

A grouping of six tiny triangles on the screen represented their small task group. Three ships floated in the black ahead of *Mirage*, two were on their six.

"Awfully tight there, hoss."

Thad could hear the smile in Jonathan's voice as he replied, "Once we get to the other side, they'll spread out a bit."

As the countdown clock neared zero, the formation moved into position. When it was time, the destroyers in front of *Mirage* eased forward... and disappeared. Between one instant and the next, *Mirage* left the Procyon star system and entered Alpha Centauri.

After the extra-dimensional lights faded from the ship's main holoscreens, Thad could see the vessels ahead of them engaging thrusters to move away from the gate, clearing the way for the ships behind them to transit. They maintained their loose formation and, once they cleared the area, lit up their fusion drives.

Jonathan tossed a glance over his shoulder.

"That's it, folks. We'll jump the minute we hit the fifteen-million-klick mark, about another two hours or so."

"And then?" asked Valenti.

Jonathan made a humming sound as he made some sort of mental calculation Thad likely couldn't follow. "The customs clearance station's a good thirty-three AU from here. That puts us at about an hour twenty in Scharnhorst space before we arrive."

"Thank you, Captain." The colonel turned to Will. "All-call to the task force. Tell them to stand down. Take a nap, grab some grub. And be ready to go again at..." she paused to check her chrono, "thirteen hundred, ship time."

The flight engineer nodded and turned to his console.

Jonathan swung around once more, his gaze bouncing between Thad and the colonel. "If it's all the same to you, I'd like to take one more look at any fresh data *Invictus* might have managed to capture, before they dump us out into the black."

Valenti shot him an inquiring look. "Any particular reason why?"

Thad saw a look of unease cross the pilot's face, but then he shrugged it away.

"I'd like to take a look at the task force's disbursement once *Mirage* departs. I know we'll have Micah as a communications conduit to them, but just in case something goes wrong and I can't reach him, I want to know for myself exactly where they're going to be hiding within the Straits, in case we need to call for an evac."

Thad hoped like hell nothing happened to Micah, but he could see the other man's point.

Valenti nodded her understanding. "I'll ping the captain and set something up."

REGATTA

DOUGLASS-WASHBURN TENT
FOUNDER'S CUP FAIRGROUNDS
BEZIER FOOTHILLS, CERIBA

MICAH LURCHED AWAKE to a piercing sound that hammered through his mind like a bad hangover. He gripped his head in his hands, croaking out, "Alarm off!"

With a groan, he rolled tiredly to his feet. Operation Ferret had put a significant dent in his sleep schedule. By the time the Unit team had returned with Snotface, it had been well past rack time and he was feeling it today.

Cracking one eye open, he looked blearily around his quarters, his optics automatically cycling to night vision. Other than the boots he'd left by the door, and yesterday's discarded flight suit, the room was Navy-neat.

"Good," he muttered. "Least I won't break my neck on the way to the lav."

The chrono on his optical overlay informed him he'd better hustle if he intended to make it down to the fairgrounds before the prime minister arrived.

With a sigh, he ordered the lights in the room to full

strength, wincing under their bright glare.

A message from Major Reid was sitting in his inbox, flashing silently at him. He scrolled through its contents while he showered, skimming through last night's after-action report.

According to the assets that had stayed behind to monitor those guarding the fairgrounds, the rest of the overnight had been unremarkable. Nothing to suggest they might have discovered a tracker planted on the starglider.

"Let's just hope things stay that way," he murmured.

Half an hour later, Micah found himself in the queue for the space elevator, waiting for the next car to arrive that would whisk him down to the surface. He checked in with Jonathan while he waited, but quickly discovered his counterpart was in the middle of a planning session.

Deciding to leave his twin to his work, Micah boarded the elevator car when it pulled into the terminal, and then sat back to wait while they dropped to the planet's surface.

The shuttle ride to the fairgrounds was equally uneventful, and Micah soon found himself flashing his ID token at the security SI staffing the event's entrance.

Only a smattering of reporters greeted him, calling out quick questions as he passed. He guessed the rest were covering the regatta's progress, given that today was the first official day of the race. Micah scrubbed through the newsnets to see how the Alliance teams he'd picked were faring.

He paused when he came to a live feed hosted by the reporter who'd first waylaid him outside registration. Popping it up onto his overlay, he listened to Provo's play-by-play description of the ships' progress as he turned down the row of tents that led to his destination.

The rich aroma of freshly brewed coffee arrested his motion, and he detoured by a vendor's cart to get his morning fix.

Well, morning for me, at least.

Today, the number of Navy personnel and security agents far outnumbered the journalists outside the Douglass-

Washburn tent. It made sense; Garza was scheduled to arrive for his first training session in a few hours.

Ducking inside, Micah found himself once more subjected to intense scrutiny. Like the day before, he stood perfectly still, though now with a hot cup of java in hand, while waiting for the protective detail to scan him before allowing him entrance.

A quick glance over at the mechanics' pit showed Katie was already there. Since she hadn't been involved in last night's escapade, it was likely the chief warrant had been here for hours. She was currently buried elbow-deep inside a piece of equipment.

Make that head-deep, he thought with some amusement, as Katie's voice echoed eerily from inside a carbon composite tail section.

"Try it now," he heard her say, and the chief mechanic obligingly moved the control surface she was studying up and down.

The head mechanic looked up as Micah passed, giving a quick two-fingered wave. Micah lifted his coffee in silent response to the man, and then turned toward the simulators.

He spared his wrist a quick glance, the Faraday cuff encircling it hidden under his flight suit's sleeve. Inside was the DNA sampling nano it was his job to deploy before Garza arrived.

He took a casual sip, his eyes taking in the starglider as he walked by, before straying past it to the various agents lining the inside of the tent. He turned toward the simulators, the back of his neck itching under the eyes of those watching him.

He set his coffee down and booted up both units, cycling them through a full diagnostics check while he visually inspected the helmet and pair of gauntlets both he and Garza would wear. He deliberately ignored his surroundings, giving the impression he was fully absorbed in his task.

He slipped a hand inside Garza's gauntlet, ostensibly to test its haptic feedback. After running it through its paces, he reached over to pull it off, right hand casually triggering the

Faraday cuff and setting the DNA-sampling nano free.

The small machines were programmed to handshake with his own wire's data partition once activated. He saw a green indicator light flash briefly on his overlay as they settled, coating the inside of the glove. Satisfied they were in position, he removed his hand, and the light winked out.

He maintained his pretense, testing the other gloves in the same way, settling first one and then the other helmet on his head to confirm their interface. He'd just removed the second helmet when a sound at the tent's entrance caught his attention.

A pair of agents entered, taking up positions on either side of the opening, their watchful eyes scanning the interior. Moments later, Garza stepped inside.

The prime minister nodded pleasantly to the agents stationed inside the tent before his eyes roamed toward the mechanics' pit, and then on to where Micah stood.

Taking that as his cue, Micah set down the helmet in his hands and walked over to greet the man, extending a hand. "Mister Prime Minister, it's nice to meet you. I'm—"

Micah stopped abruptly, dropping his outstretched limb, when the two agents flanking Garza shifted subtly in front of him, barring his way.

Message received. Don't touch the merchandise.

Garza pushed the two men gently apart. "You must be Captain Case," he said with a slight smile.

Micah clasped his hands behind his back and nodded respectfully. "Yessir."

The prime minister lifted a slightly amused brow and jerked his chin in the direction of the starglider. "Think you can train an old jarhead how to fly that thing? And in time to beat the president of An-Yang?"

Micah grinned. "No contest, sir. It'll be a walk in the park."

He gestured Garza toward the back of the tent, explaining his helmet and gloves on the way.

The prime minister accepted the information with a silent

nod of thanks, then asked, "So, what's on the agenda for today?"

Micah looked thoughtfully at the man, his gaze cutting toward the starglider in the center of the tent. "I think the first order of business is to familiarize you with the ship's controls. What would you say to flying the course for today's regatta?"

Garza's eyebrows rose into his hairline. "That's a bit ambitious, isn't it?"

"You'll just be shadowing me," he assured the man.

Micah gestured to the simulation units sitting passively against the tent's back wall. "Your hands will be on the stick, don't get me wrong. But there's no danger. It'll give you a good feel for how the ship maneuvers. Plus—" he shot a conspiratorial grin Garza's way, "it'll be fun."

Garza regarded him for a beat, and then nodded. "You're the boss. What do I do with this?" He gestured to the helmet in his hands.

"Put it on." Micah pointed to the display. "It's already booted up and ready to go."

He donned his own helmet, its hardware depositing him into the system's wraparound holographic environment.

Garza made a fascinated noise, his voice sounding over the communication system built into the sim's helmet. "For old tech, this is pretty impressive," the man murmured.

"Wait until the simulation begins," Micah said, glancing around at the frozen tableau. "It gets better."

"This is the first leg of the race, you say?" Garza asked as he took a seat and Micah flipped through snapshots of the course the racing teams were currently running.

"It is."

"Something tells me there are a few significant differences between what I'll be doing and what they're facing on today's course," said the prime minister.

Micah chuckled, changing the visual over to the one for the exhibition course. "True. As you can see, your race will be on a traditional oval track. Just turns and straightaways. Pretty straightforward, no pun intended."

"In other words, I'll be going around in circles. That pretty much sums up the average day in the life of a politician. I should be an expert in that by now," he deadpanned.

Micah couldn't constrain the laugh that escaped; he hadn't expected the man to have such a dry sense of humor.

"That's pretty much it, yes." He cleared his throat, changing the sim's landscape once more, and calling Garza's attention back to it. "Here. I'll take you through the first leg of the race. Keep your hands on the controls so you can feel what I'm doing."

He began the simulation, taking it nice and easy. After a few minutes, Garza made a pensive noise.

"It's been a while since I've been through this part of the country. I forgot how beautiful it is."

"One of the most scenic places on the planet," Micah agreed.

As instructed, Garza's hands stayed on the yoke, riding the controls along with him. When they entered into the gorge, Micah centered the simulated starglider in the middle of the one-kilometer-wide stretch and then handed the controls over to Garza completely.

"You have the ship."

The prime minister didn't respond verbally, as an experienced pilot would. He just grabbed the yoke, wiggling it experimentally back and forth a bit.

The simulated craft obliged, dipping its nose and then yawing left and right.

"It's... very responsive," he heard the man say.

The surprise in his voice caused Micah to grin inside his helmet. "That's one of the best things about a starglider."

Micah took the controls back after a few kilometers and headed back to the fairgrounds. From there, he took Garza through basic takeoffs and landings before showing the man what he could expect in certain situations, such as a power outage, or if he accidentally put the small craft into a stall or a spin.

Not that the man would be required to recover from such unusual attitudes; that's what the Synthetic Intelligence aboard the craft was there to prevent. Still, the aviator in Micah wouldn't allow him to set Garza loose—even with training wheels—until he'd been given a taste of what to expect should something go wrong.

In the short time he'd spent with Garza, he'd sensed the prime minister was a man whose first instinct was to gather what information he could about a situation, and let that guide his response. As such, knowing what was happening would go a long way toward putting his mind at ease, should his starglider end up in an odd configuration. In such a situation, the SI would take over, wrenching the craft back into normal flight mode, but at least Garza would know what was going on.

The simulation came to an end when the virtual starglider touched down once more at the fairground's landing strip. Micah took off his helmet and saw Garza sit back with a sigh.

"That was exhilarating."

Micah bit back a grin. "I'd agree with that, but it's what I do for a living, so I might be a bit prejudiced. You ready to have a go at that racetrack?"

Garza straightened once more. "Let's do it."

The racetrack the prime minister would be flying on the day of the exhibition race was four kilometers long by one and a half wide. It would inscribe a long, narrow oval in the air a safe distance away, above the Bezier Foothills. It would be easily seen from the fairgrounds' stadium seating.

The oval was defined by a pair of autonomous drones hovering two kilometers in the air at each end of the course. These projected holographic pylons through which the contestants must thread their ships.

Micah took Garza through several laps before allowing the prime minister to take full control of the sim. After he was confident the man could handle it on his own, he introduced him to techniques that would aid him in banking and turning without losing speed or altitude.

After an hour of practice, he called for Garza to return to the simulated landing strip, and brought the rehearsal to a close.

"So? How'd that feel?" he asked, pulling off his helmet.

Garza set his helmet on his lap and reached up to run a hand through his sweaty hair, only to knock himself in the forehead with the thick gauntlets. He shot Micah a rueful smile, and then stripped himself of the clunky gloves.

Micah reached out a hand to take them from him, but was forestalled by a security agent, who intercepted them before he could.

Damn.

In the excitement of the flight, he'd forgotten they were even here.

One of them stepped forward and relieved the prime minister of his helmet, and Micah ground his teeth quietly while plastering a smile on his face and forcing himself to pay attention to Garza's response.

"I think maybe, just maybe, I won't embarrass the Alliance after all," he was saying as he stood. The man gave Micah a grudging half smile. "Doesn't hurt that I have a former Founder's Cup winner and one of our top Navy assets to train me, either. "

Micah dipped his head. "It's my pleasure, sir."

Another agent approached; the woman who had screened Micah when he'd first entered. She stopped in front of Garza, and the prime minister's expression blanked.

"Excuse me, sir." The woman's voice was cold. "You have a call scheduled with the governor-general in half an hour. We should really be going."

"Looks like duty calls," Garza told Micah, shooting an inscrutable look toward the men who flanked him.

The change that had come over the man caused Micah's attention to sharpen. He'd lay good credits on these three being Akkadians, if Garza's response was any gauge.

Without acknowledging the woman who'd spoken— something that struck Micah as uncharacteristic of the PM— Garza turned, extending his hand for Micah to shake.

The gesture caused the two men on either side of him to

shift uncomfortably.

As he returned the man's handshake, Micah silently cursed the fact that he had none of the DNA sampling nano left. All of it had been dumped inside the gauntlet now in the agent's hands.

"I understand you'll be joining us for dinner tonight?" Garza looked at him expectantly.

Micah blinked. He'd forgotten that the Founder's Dinner was this evening, and that Cutter had arranged for him and Sam to be seated at the prime minister's table for the event.

"Yes, thank you for the invitation."

"Least I could do to thank you for teaching an old Marine how to fly. I'll see you this evening, then." Garza straightened his jacket with a short tug, gave Micah a brief nod, and then turned to follow the female agent to the tent's entrance.

Micah saw that the agent had set Garza's equipment beside the simulator. He decided it was worth one more attempt, and after racking his own helmet and gloves, reached for the ones the agent had set aside.

The man stepped forward to intercept him.

Pretending ignorance didn't work; when Micah shifted to move around him, the agent countered the move, making it clear that Micah would not be allowed near Garza's equipment.

Micah threw him a pointed, annoyed look as he crossed his arms. "Look, you're preventing me from doing my job."

"No one comes into contact with any of the prime minister's equipment," countered the agent.

Micah hid his consternation behind a look of derision, and gestured to the sim units. "There is literally nothing there that can harm him. These are all passive-response sims. Hell, the tech's more than a century out of date. I fail to see the problem here."

The guard remained implacable.

Micah threw his hands in the air. "Okay, fine. Then *you* put everything back the way it was."

He stalked off toward the mechanics' pit.

The crew chief who had given him the tour of the starglider

the day before shot him a sympathetic look as he came to a stop in front of them.

"Don't take it too hard," he said in a low tone with a look back toward the agent. "Rumor has it they found something in the tent overnight. They've been a bit jumpy ever since."

Does he mean Snotface, or something more? Micah adopted a sardonic tone to hide his trepidation. "Not my fault they didn't do their jobs. Don't see why he had to take it out on me."

The mechanic grabbed a flathead screwdriver, and began picking grease from beneath his fingernails. Tilting his head thoughtfully, he mused, "I might not be Alliance Navy, but I've been around plenty of bosses in my time." He chuckled darkly. "Someone screws up by the numbers? After they get done being chewed out, they always find someone else to take it out on. Know what I mean?"

The truth of the man's statement startled a rueful laugh from Micah.

"Yeah," he admitted. "Been there."

The mechanic motioned toward the back of the tent. "Leastwise, sounds like your protest about getting things cleaned up got through to them. They're checking the systems out like good little soldiers."

That last prompted Micah to glance at the sim units. He forced a chuckle at the mechanic's words while inwardly cursing.

He suspected that they were doing a bit more than just putting the equipment back where it belonged. He had a feeling he'd better get out of here before they found something he'd really rather they not—like DNA sampling nano.

"Well," he gave the mechanic a casual wave, "guess my work here for the day is done. Be seeing you."

He angled for the entrance to the tent, breathing a little easier after exiting into the bright sunlight. The minute the combat net snapped back into place, he contacted Gabe to update him on the situation.

Dammit. Not only did he fail to retrieve the DNA, but he was certain he'd been made. Where did that leave their next move?

KATIE'S WAR

BEZIER FOOTHILLS
OUTSIDE FOUNDER'S CUP FAIRGROUNDS
CERIBA

WHILE MICAH EXCHANGED heated words with the agents at the back of the tent, Katie Hyer sidled closer she could hear.

She kept her head down, pulling at the bill of her cap until it rode low on her forehead, hiding her eyes. She bent over the instrument in her hands, faking an intense interest in it.

When she caught onto the pissing contest the security agents were waging with Micah, she shook her head and muttered, "Asswipes."

Behind her, she heard a choked laugh, and pivoted to see the chief mechanic standing with a grin on his face.

He hocked and spat, wiping his grizzled chin with the dirty rag in his hands. From behind his hand, he murmured, "Girl, you've got that right."

Her lips twitched.

He motioned her to follow him back to the pit, jutting his chin toward Micah and Garza's goons. "The way they're posturing reeks of make-work to me. I mean, look around you."

The mechanic twisted, gesturing around the Douglass-Washburn tent. "There's just not a whole lot inside here that would threaten the likes of Garza, so I figure they gotta make shit up. Makes them look like they're doing their jobs."

Katie just nodded.

Under normal circumstances, she'd agree, but she knew it was likely there were enemy agents in the tent with them, right now.

Of course, I can't exactly come out and tell the guy that....

The mechanic beside her snorted, and teased, "You ain't got that thing cleared yet?"

She looked up in confusion, and then down at the object in her hands. The pitot-static tube was a simple flow-measurement device that read atmospheric speed and pressure changes. It had been built into the starglider's fuselage as a mechanical backup to more sophisticated systems.

Seeing as the thing was probably the simplest piece of equipment on the entire starglider, it certainly hadn't warranted the amount of attention Katie was giving it, and the man knew it. The amusement in his tone informed her that he was well aware of the fact that she'd been eavesdropping, but wasn't going to give her away.

She smiled a silent thanks that morphed into a mischievous half grin. "You never know," she drawled. "Some bird might've decided to take a crap in it."

The man hooted a laugh, slapping the table with his grease-stained rag. "While it was in your hands? Bold bird. Microscopic one, too."

Still chuckling, the man turned to walk away just as Micah passed the pit.

Katie made fleeting eye contact with the captain as he stopped to chat with the chief mechanic for a bit. She caught his slight headshake, confirming her concerns.

He'd been unable to retrieve the DNA sample from Garza's gloves.

I'll have to risk it myself.

She chanced another look at the back of the tent, where the agents had finished setting the equipment down and were in the process of shutting off the simulators. One of the men had a glove in his hand, and turned to shoot a suspicious look Micah's way.

Uh-oh. Maybe there won't be anything for me to retrieve, after all.

Had Katie's eyes not been on that agent at that exact moment, she would have missed the signal the man passed to his counterparts at the front of the tent.

Ducking her head once more, she peered up from underneath the bill of her cap to see a pair of agents duck out of the tent and turn to follow Micah's departing figure.

Dammit. Now what do I do?

The encrypted network set up inside the tent meant that she didn't dare try to contact anyone.

On impulse, she grabbed an empty bucket and turned to the grizzled man beside her. "You know, I just realized we're getting low on cleaner. You have extra stored in the crates stashed against the back of the tent, right?"

The mechanic nodded absently, his gaze once more on the spar he'd been working on.

Katie wiped her hands on her coveralls and stepped away from the table. "Cool. Be right back." She pivoted and jogged toward the tent's entrance.

Deciding that the best way to hide was in plain sight, she turned halfway to the opening. Voice raised, she asked the mechanic, "Want anything else while I'm gone? A beer, or maybe one of those roasted turkey leg things they sell at the vendor carts?"

The mechanic pulled off his hat, wiped his brow, and cast his eyes overhead in thought. Settling his hat back in place, he called out, "Funnel cake."

"Oh yeah." Katie gave him a thumbs-up. "Now you're talking."

Exiting the tent, she turned the opposite direction Micah had left to get to the back of the tent where the spare parts were stored. She'd planned on ditching the bucket there, too, but as she moved to set it down, an open bin filled with small, metallic parts and ball bearings caught her eye.

Dipping her hand into the container, her hands connected with the small, round spheres, and impulse had her scooping them into her bucket, along with a few small bits of unfinished metal with jagged edges.

Better to be armed with something unconventional than not to be armed at all.

At the front of the tent once more, Katie spied Micah up ahead. She was relieved to see that the man and woman following him seemed content to do just that. Still, she set out after them, keeping a generous space between herself and the agents.

Then a man stepped out from between two tents, his eyes on Micah.

Something about the intensity of his stare got Katie's hackles up. From this distance, she couldn't tell who the man was, just that he was in uniform.

He reached out a hand, tagging Micah on the elbow, and they exchanged a few words, the man gesturing off to one side.

By the way his attention kept wandering to the two agents following him, Katie suspected the reason he'd intercepted Micah was to maneuver the pilot away from the crowd.

She scanned their surroundings. The tents were lined up back to back, in long rows broken by narrow alleys every third or fourth tent, where vendors stored their overstock. She spied one of those alleys just ahead.

Gripping her bucket more firmly in her hands, she darted down it, skip-jogging her way around a stack of boxes labeled with the event's logo. Exiting into the next row over, she raced ahead, weaving her way through evening event-goers as she looked for an alleyway that would put her past the spot where the stranger had waylaid Micah.

As she went, she pushed a mental alert to Gabe.

{Boss!} she hollered. *{They're going after Micah!}*

Annoyed shouts followed in her wake as Katie wove her way recklessly through the crowd. She ignored them, her focus split between her connection with Gabe, and that elusive alleyway between the tents she needed to find in order to get on the other side of Micah's stalkers.

{Where?} Gabe demanded, and Katie dropped a pin on her best estimation of where Micah now was.

{Don't let him out of your sight,} Gabe ordered. *{ETA two minutes.}*

{Copy that.}

Katie exhaled when she spied the alley, leaping over a tent peg as she careened around the corner and into the darkened passage between the tents. She poked her head out the other side, and saw she'd guessed right.

The agents were converging, but slowly, as if unwilling to draw undue attention. The stranger in the uniform was still trying to engage Micah in conversation.

*Dammit. I'm not sure he **has** two minutes....*

Katie looked around for additional makeshift weapons. Since she was supposed to be a pit crew mechanic, she was unarmed, except for her bucket of scrap and ball bearings. That didn't deter her.

Gabriel Alvarez's lesson on improvising once more flashed through her head as she glanced around, seeing the fairgrounds through the lens the former NCIC agent had taught her to use.

A guy-wire anchoring a tent nearby looked promising. She grabbed one of the sharp metal bits and sawed at the end of the thin cable until it came free. Sending up a silent apology to the tent's owner, she coiled the wire that had once helped anchor the structure, she laid it across the alley's opening, covering it with a bit of dirt. The remainder, she tucked behind a portable recycle bin.

As an afterthought, she jiggled the tent peg and then pulled, surprised to find the thing was nearly a meter in length when it came free of the ground. She hefted the solid bar in her hand, and then tucked it under one arm.

A quick dash to a nearby tent garnered Katie a *'Temporarily Closed'* signboard from a vendor who had briefly stepped away. Setting it across the buried wire blocked the alley, keeping casual sightseers from wandering into what she feared might soon become a war zone.

Her gaze next caught on a crate labeled *'lanyards'* and the thick band holding the crate closed that looked like it was made of a rubber-like material.

She pulled it off and tested it, anchoring each end of the band to the metal tent peg.

That'll make a decent slingshot.

Battlefield laid, Katie tucked the bit of metal she'd used to slice the cable inside her coveralls pocket. Dipping her hand once more into the bucket, she ran her fingers through the ball bearings, smiling in smug satisfaction at the memory of the last time she'd used the spheres.

Setting the bucket where she could easily grab it, she crept back down the alleyway to peer around the corner—just in time to see one of the agents slap something against the back of Micah's neck.

She pinged Gabe in alarm.

{They just ziptied him!}

SOS

GNS *INVICTUS*
GEMINATE ALLIANCE

AT THE EXACT moment the Akkadian mole inside Protective Services got the drop on Micah with the suppression nanopackage, his mirror twin, Jonathan was standing beside Colonel Valenti in the CIC just off *Invictus*'s bridge.

A shaft of alarm zinged through Jonathan like an arrow, the emotion not his own. He stiffened, then whipped his head blindly around.

Valenti stopped midsentence, sensing something was amiss. "Captain?"

"It's our... *agent* embedded with the Founder's Cup team." Jonathan picked his words carefully, as if treading through a minefield, conscious of the presence of personnel not read into the situation. "He's been compromised."

Immediately, Valenti pushed away from the CIC's holotank. Turning to the captain, she said, "Apologies, but this is a matter of some urgency."

The captain's lips firmed, but he nodded his understanding.

"Case, you're with me." With those words, Valenti turned

and stalked from the CIC.

Jonathan fell into step beside her, and an encrypted combat net snapped into place.

{Report,} the colonel snapped.

{They just got him with an Akkadian ziptie.} Jonathan's words were terse. *{All I got before he lost consciousness was that he was out in the fairgrounds somewhere. Someone in uniform waylaid him, and then two agents hit him from behind.}*

Valenti widened the net with a thought, bringing Thad and Ell in on the conversation.

{Contact Toland. Tell her Micah's been compromised. He's under Akkadian control.}

* * *

A specialist from the team's headquarters element met Sam at Humbolt's security checkpoint, approving her entry into Task Force Blue territory.

"Admiral Toland's in the bullpen, waiting for you, Doc," the woman said with a smile.

Sam matched it with one of her own, though hers was a bit forced. NCIC had just completed their investigation into the attack on the CID transport, and the admiral had asked her here to review their findings.

She followed the specialist through the warren of corridors and lifts until the woman drew to a stop outside the bullpen. "Wait here; I'll get her."

Sam nodded, but when the door slid open, she heard a voice call out, "Admiral! Urgent message from *Mirage.*"

She pushed her way through, ignoring the specialist's protests.

Tala Valenti's face resolved on the main holotank, the colonel standing inside *Mirage*'s cockpit. Beside her, Sam could see Jonathan, seated in his pilot's cradle. His forehead was pinched together, his eyes dark with concern.

Valenti recapped the situation in crisp, staccato-like

sentences, and then turned the comm over to Jonathan, who gave them Micah's last known location before his consciousness faded.

Sam clenched her hands, silently cursing the fact they were out of real-time range. Her mind raced to find a way—*any* way—to trace Micah before it was too late.

An idea occurred to her, and she pivoted. "Admiral," she said urgently, causing the other woman to pause Jonathan's message mid-word. "I know Jonathan doesn't think he can reach Micah, now that he's unconscious, but I think he can... though it might get a bit tricky."

"In what way?" asked Toland.

"Micah's not truly unconscious," she explained. "A ziptie—I guess Akkadians call their version a 'shackle'— doesn't just interfere with motor control. It also hijacks executive function."

"Executive function?" The admiral's brows drew together in a frown.

"It's what allows you to control and coordinate cognitive abilities. Attention, memory, the ability to form words. Discipline and willpower. It's a finite thing, and can be depleted. That's what's happened to Micah."

She paused, grasping for a way to explain how a ziptie affected the prefrontal cortex.

"Being subjected to an Akkadian shackle is like... like he has the security token to fly *Mirage*, but the ship's fusion reactor's offline, and its hydrogen tanks have been emptied. Until he's able to get fuel to them, he's not going anywhere."

"I'm not following, Doctor. It sounds like you're saying there's no way Jonathan can reach him while he's under the influence."

Sam held up a finger. "Under normal circumstances, you'd be right. They can't connect if one of them is unconscious, but they *can* still sense one another."

Her hand dropped, and her voice sped up, excitement coloring it. "What's more, in the past, when they both merged with that 3-D sim run by the ship's SI...." Her voice faded as she sought the name.

"It's actually the nav system's situational awareness app," Harper supplied, stepping forward. "It's called SyntheticVision."

Sam pointed at Harper. "Yes! That." She turned back to the admiral. "When they merged with *Wraith*'s SyntheticVision system, this strange synergy happened."

She began to pace as she ticked off the traits she'd seen the two men exhibit.

"Their synapses fired faster, their response times were off the charts, higher than any augmented human—both physical reaction time and mental processing speed. It's possible that if he tries to connect with Micah while merged with the ship, he could trigger that gestalt."

"You're suggesting he try this *now*?" The admiral sounded skeptical. "They're inside *Invictus*'s boat bay. They can't fire up the Nadir's drives right now."

"They won't have to," Harper assured her, her voice confident. "Just engaging the SI should do it, don't you think, Doc?"

Sam nodded her agreement, turning back to Toland. "With the SI added to the merge, Jonathan just might be able to punch through the rate-limiting aspect of the shackles—lend Micah some of his own resources, if you will. Or at least get him to share his location."

Toland nodded. "It's worth a try. We can't allow Micah to fall into the hands of the Akkadians."

She turned to the communications agent, who'd been standing off to one side, waiting for instructions.

"Recap that for Jonathan."

The man nodded. "On it, ma'am."

* * *

Jonathan kept pace with Colonel Valenti as they raced down *Invictus*'s long corridor.

"Can you feel him?" The colonel slid him a quick glance.

"Yes, but it...." His words faded as he struggled to find the right ones. "It's foggy. I can tell he's there, I can feel his presence, but that's about it."

They'd just made it to the lift when Will pinged them.

{Got a response from the admiral, ma'am.} The flight engineer followed his words with the recorded file.

Valenti shared it with Jonathan as they stepped inside the lift and it whisked them down to the boat bay's level. Admiral Toland's voice came over the wire first.

{All assets have been contacted and are converging on his last known location, but we'd like Captain Case to help us pinpoint it.}

Her voice was replaced by Sam's.

{Jonathan, I understand you can't communicate with Micah while he's unconscious, but I think you can still locate him.}

Jonathan shook his head. "That's the one thing we've found that weakens with distance, ma'am. The closer we are, the more precise—"

Sam's recorded voice overrode his protests.

{Hear me out on this. Try to initiate a gestalt. I know it's a long shot, but you have to try. Spool up Mirage's *SyntheticVision system, and then reach out to Micah* **while** *you're merged with the ship. Even though he's not conscious, the thread's still there. Lean into the connection a bit, see if you can magnify it.}*

Valenti looked over at Jonathan, raising her brows in question.

He nodded. "That... could work."

They hit the boat bay at a run, arrowing toward the Nadir's extended ramp.

"Bring up *Mirage*'s SI," Jonathan called out as he hit the top of the ramp.

Yuki pivoted in the copilot's cradle, dipping her hand into the cockpit's holographic console.

"Better warn *Invictus*," Nina counseled. "Last thing we need is for someone on the bridge to think we're trying to spin up our drives while this cruiser's in flight and the boat bay's doors are closed."

"On it," Will said, turning to his own console, his hands dancing across its controls.

Jonathan slid into his cradle, plunging into his connection with *Mirage* faster than he'd ever done before.

The connection was meant to allow a pilot's consciousness to enter into a form of merge with the ship's Synthetic Intelligence. It was an odd feeling, doing such a thing from inside a larger ship. He'd certainly never tried it when a ship like *Invictus* was in motion.

The merge faithfully recreated *Mirage*'s immediate surroundings, so instead of the inky blackness of space that he was used to seeing, he got a good view of the cruiser's hangar.

He pushed outward, sensors piercing through *Invictus*'s hull until he was once more surrounded by the comforting familiarity of the void beyond.

He reached for Micah, using the SyntheticVision system to enhance his connection to his twin. He was still unable to rouse him, but his other self's presence did seem to crystallize inside his head.

He turned, seeking Micah's whereabouts in a way not too dissimilar from how a ship's sensors would tune to a beacon. He felt a familiar tug in the direction of his chiral self, and followed the invisible line forward.

The thread that connected him to *Mirage* grew thinner the farther along the line he traveled, but he didn't have time to worry about that. He needed Micah's coordinates, and he needed them *now*.

A sort of a map appeared inside his head—not so much a set of coordinates as it was a ghostly representation of what Micah had seen and experienced that day—the fairgrounds, the tent, Katie's mechanics' pit. Until finally, Jonathan saw the vendor tent his twin had been passing just as the shackling app was slapped against his neck.

He placed the spark that was Micah's consciousness as a

mental overlay on top of the ghostly projection, and his heart rate sped up when he saw it moving.

He'd found him.

He tried to push the information to Valenti, but his connection to his physical surroundings seemed tinny and distant. He heard the colonel shout at him, but had a difficult time making out her words.

He felt her do something on her end, and suddenly the connection between himself and *Mirage* boosted, doubling and then tripling in thickness.

He again tried pushing the projection to her, willing her to see the blip that represented Micah, just as he did.

He felt confusion from her end; he had the impression that she was jumbling the images around, not quite certain what to do with them.

He dropped a pin on top of the spark that was Micah, ordering his mind to force a correlation, and willing his wire to attach coordinates to that spark.

His implant initially refused, unable to resolve their unique, chiral connection with a solid data point that its system was familiar with, but Jonathan kept at it until he found something that would stick.

He felt more than heard comprehension from Valenti, and then her presence receded.

Jonathan once more turned his attention to his twin, his focus extending even more fully, until *Mirage* was once more the thinnest of threads.

His action provoked an angry response from the colonel. Again, he couldn't hear her words, but her intent was clear. She was ordering him to retreat.

Everything in him rebelled, but then he felt a shock, an electric discharge, and heard clearly her angry words.

*{That is an **order**, Captain!}*

With great reluctance, Jonathan pulled away from Micah, until the gestalt between *Mirage*, himself, and his twin faded.

* * *

Sam closed her eyes in relief as the telemetry came through.

She understood better than most the risks Jonathan was taking on behalf of his twin, yet she couldn't bring herself to regret the man's actions.

She stood by, hands clenching and unclenching in a sort of tense anticipation, as Toland relayed the information to Major Reid, and the Unit teams sprang into action.

Toland flipped through several feeds streamed from the drakeskin-clad operators, projecting them into the bullpen's holotank.

Sam inhaled sharply when she saw Micah's form walking with an unnatural stiffness that suggested the unconscious man's carbyne lattice was engaged and he was being led by his captors through the fairgrounds to an undisclosed location.

Teams One and Four closed on the agents, but were still too far away to engage. Then, from out of nowhere, Katie Hyer appeared.

GESTALT

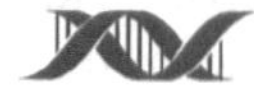

BEZIER FOOTHILLS
OUTSIDE FOUNDER'S CUP FAIRGROUNDS
CERIBA

KATIE WATCHED MICAH'S eyes roll up in his head the moment the agent slapped the suppression nanopackage on the back of his neck. As his knees gave out, the two agents came up alongside him in a practiced move that told Katie this wasn't the first time they'd done this maneuver.

{*Thirty seconds out,*} Gabe's voice came across.

{*Too long. I'm engaging.*}

{*Hyer, no! Stand down, Chief, that's an—*}

Katie blocked out Gabe's words as she stepped out of the alley and pulled out her makeshift slingshot. Notching the jagged bit of metal at the center of the band, she drew it taut against her cheekbone.

Zeroing in on the officer's forehead, she let the small piece of metal fly. It went rocketing through the air, hitting the man in the center of his left eye socket with a satisfying *thwack*.

The man bellowed in pain, hand rising belatedly to protect his face as he staggered a step backward. He whipped his head around to where Katie stood. "Get her!"

The agents dropped Micah and went racing forward.

Flinging the lanyard away, Katie turned and bolted back down the alley. Bending mid-stride, she scooped up the bucket of ball bearings with one hand as she flew past. Hefting it over her shoulder, she let its contents fall behind her, scattering small, metal spheres in her wake.

A shout was followed by the whine of a weapon discharging. Katie had jinked at the sound of the woman's raised voice. It was the only thing that kept her from the full brunt of the direct-energy beam that struck to her left, the beam's edge just clipping her left leg.

The muscles in her thigh jerked, nerve endings jangling at the near-miss.

She careened around the corner and slid to a stop behind the recycling bin, her hand scrabbling for the tripwire. Cries and thuds reached her ears as the two agents slipped on the pebbled offering she'd left for them.

Scuffling noises and more curses told Katie the two were having trouble finding their feet. She used the precious few extra seconds to change her appearance, flinging off the cap and then ripping the Founder's Cup shirt over her head.

Thundering footsteps told her they had cleared the ball bearing minefield and were seconds away from reaching the end of the alley. Taking up the tripwire cable, she timed their approach carefully, and with a savage pull, jerked the wire taut just as they came flush with the opening.

From the narrow slit between tent and recycle bin, she watched as the signboard went flying, cracking the man under the chin. In the next instant, he went sprawling face first into pedestrian traffic, the woman tripping over him as she, too, fell.

Katie's HUD alerted her to the presence of two shadowed figures racing around the corner. Wheeling around, she intended to beat it to the back of the tent, but a ping stopped her in her tracks.

{'S okay, Chief. Cavalry's here. Good job taking these two down.}

* * *

Micah felt Jonathan's presence prodding at him, and he fought to throw off the effects of the nano-suppression packet that had dragged him into the twilight of unconsciousness. He was dimly aware of a fight happening around him, and yet was utterly helpless to assist.

Suddenly, he felt a figure kneel beside him, and an invisible hand smacked a rectification code onto the back of his neck. The code neutralized the subjugation nanopackage, and his consciousness came roaring back.

With it came a connection unlike anything Micah or Jonathan had ever before experienced.

It thundered into existence, a thing of incredible power. The Micah side of the merge immediately recognized the danger lurking in its depths, and instinctively tried to pull back, but the Jonathan part of the merge latched on with fierce intensity.

The Micah half shuddered under the tsunami of thought and emotion that overlaid his own. He staggered under the sensation, oblivious to the fact that his physical body was being bolstered by invisible, drakeskin-clad suits—team operators who had been sent to guard him.

He pushed against the gestalt, fighting to tear free. {{*Pull back!*}} he yelled into the mental maelstrom. {{*Retreat!*}}

Slowly, the howling diminished to the point where the Micah part could sense that they were two individual identities once more, inexorably intertwined yet separate.

It suddenly came to him that the gestalt had a distinctly mechanical edge to it. Horror struck as he realized the Jonathan part had nearly subsumed himself within the SyntheticVision system in his effort to reach his unconscious twin.

He felt more than heard the immense effort his mirror twin brought to bear as he wrenched himself away, struggling to put mental distance between their two selves.

The merge surged once more as movement distracted

Jonathan/Micah from their efforts. They saw Katie Hyer rush forward, saw the ghostly outline of a form they shouldn't be able to see raise a weapon, targeting the chief warrant.

Micah crouched, and with a bellow, launched himself at the invisible enemy. Unable to see the Akkadian gunning for her, Katie faltered at the sight of Micah rushing her.

{{Look out!}} the merge cried out, and Hyer pivoted, eyes skittered around, looking for a foe she could not see.

The cloaked enemy turned at Micah's shout, weapon swinging around to draw a bead on him.

With a guttural yell, Micah pushed off into a flying tackle, his shoulder impacting with the man's solar plexus. The two went down, and Micah heard the chief warrant yell out for Gabe.

Moments later, he felt the burning sting of a directed energy weapon as the blast glanced off his shoulder, hitting his opponent in the head. The figure beneath him went slack, and Micah rolled up to a sitting position, slapping at his shoulder with his free hand to try to work the sting out of it.

In the back of the merged mind, the Jonathan part recognized that this enhanced vision, the seeming ability to see a stealthed opponent, was something entirely new.

Katie stooped, hooking a hand beneath Micah's arm, and hauled him to his feet. *{You okay?}* Her voice came across the team's combat net.

{{Yes.}}

But the merge's attention wasn't on Katie; it was on the battle raging around them.

Micah's head snapped up, and he called out, *{{Boone! To your right, three o'clock. Alvarez, two coming up on your six.}}*

He knew the merge made it difficult for those on the combat net to distinguish between his and Jonathan's voices.

Katie shook her head convulsively and muttered, "Damn, but that shit's weird."

Training had her placing her back to Micah's as they faced off against what, to the chief, were invisible opponents.

Micah glanced at the weapon in her hand. She was

brandishing what looked like some sort of short metal pole she'd found somewhere.

{{*A tent stake?*}} the Jonathan-Micah merge thought.

{{*Possibly,*}} they agreed.

The only weapon he had at the moment was the weird, enhanced vision that the gestalt provided. Still, the merge wielded it to their advantage, calling out enemy locations as he assumed an overwatch position over the combat net.

The battle itself, though violent, was over in a matter of minutes. When all was settled, Micah bent, ripping the hood from the unconscious man who had gone after Katie.

He looked up when Gabe knelt beside him. {{*Never seen them before.*}}

He shook his head slightly at the mental echo.

{{*This is getting weird, brother. Think it might be time for you to pull out.*}}

The Jonathan part of the merge sent mental acquiescence, and Micah felt his twin's mind fade from its altered state back to the normal presence inside his head.

Micah sagged slightly, fighting a sudden onslaught of fatigue. Gabe and Boone caught him, guiding him to the ground as Asha came running toward them, donning a field bracer.

"That was some talent you showed just now," murmured Gabe as Asha knelt beside him and began a quick exam. "Are you really able to see them, despite the stealth they're wearing?"

Micah sent his eyes roaming around the immediate area, scanning the figures where they lay. Some were partially uncloaked, their hoods removed. Others....

He blinked, and suddenly they disappeared.

{*Gone, now.*} He shook his head and cleared his throat before adding aloud, "That's a new one for the books." His voice sounded rusty, like it always did after a gestalt.

"I'd say." Gabe eyed him thoughtfully. "The colonel's going to want to hear about this. The director, too, for that matter."

Micah nodded. "Not sure it's worth the danger Jonathan put

himself in to try it again, though. He stretched himself pretty thin."

He paused, Jonathan sending the impression of Valenti chewing him out. Jonathan tried to hide Micah's awareness of her words, but the verbal punch they bestowed upon his twin echoed in his thoughts.

"Colonel's pretty chapped about it, too."

Gabe's brow lifted in silent query.

"He went catatonic on them," Micah explained. "They couldn't rouse him. Thought they were about to lose him." He blinked, his gaze refocusing on his surroundings. "Not an advantage I'd want to press."

"Not with that price tag, no," agreed Gabe, helping Micah to his feet. "Sounds like the colonel's already aware, then, and doesn't approve. Glad to hear it."

Gabe took a few steps toward the nearest prisoner. With a booted foot, he gently nudged the woman's unconscious form. As she rolled onto her back, Micah recognized her as one of the agents that had been guarding the entrance of the Douglass-Washburn tent.

"Well, it looks like we've identified at least one of our moles," he murmured.

"That was one of the two people I saw Garza's agent motion to," Katie said as she stepped up beside them. She lifted her chin, pointing to another downed figure a few meters away. "That's the other one."

"What about the officer you said you saw, the one who stopped Micah in the first place?" Gabe asked.

"He was dressed in a general's uniform," Micah supplied. "Guy seemed familiar, too."

Gabe looked at him sharply. "You get an ID on the man?"

Micah chuckled. "No, but it won't be very hard to find him." He glanced over at Katie. "Just look for the guy trying to hold his left eyeball in. Somebody popped him in the head."

Katie grinned, tossing a small chunk of steel in the air with her right her hand. "Got 'im right good, too. Last I saw, the asshole was bleeding like a stuck pig and whining like a baby."

Gabe nodded, and Micah could tell the man was working hard not to smile at Katie's attitude. "Head wounds will do that." He looked around. "Anyone see the man the chief warrant nailed?"

There were headshakes and murmured noes. Then a call came in from over the combat net.

{Just checked with the fairgrounds, sir. Interestingly enough, the security feed from the sector you're in encountered a glitch and is currently nonfunctional.}

"Great, so we have no record of the incident. Bit suspicious, isn't it?" asked Micah.

"More than a little." Gabe shook his head. "This is really starting to piss me off."

Micah lifted a brow but said nothing as the other man turned to address the operatives doing the bagging and tagging.

"Haul them back to base as soon as you're done securing them," Gabe ordered.

He motioned Boone and Asha over, and then turned to face Micah once more. "They'll escort you and Katie back to the base. Try to stay out of trouble between now and dinnertime. I hear you have an event tonight. You feel up for it?"

Micah frowned. "Yeah, I almost forgot. Founder's Cup Dinner. That gives us one last chance at the prime minister before the race... that is, if they'll let me within two meters of him, after today."

He gave Gabe a wry look. "Too bad we can't get the event planners to tweak tonight's menu. If they served something with an orange glaze, we wouldn't need a DNA test to confirm Garza's a clone. His reaction would tell us all we need to know." Remembered distaste had him grimacing. "Damn stuff tastes like turpentine mixed with pine, at least to chiral taste buds."

Gabe's brows lifted at the description. "You're right. I'm sure that'd be a hard pass for him."

He glanced around, body telegraphing a restless energy at

odds with his usual buttoned-down demeanor. Nodding to himself as if coming to an inner decision, his gaze swung back to Micah.

"Go. I have a man in a general's uniform to hunt... and hopefully at least a few eyewitnesses to find and interview."

THE DAGGER

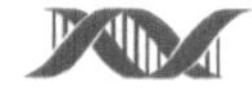

SHAR-KALI CORRECTIONAL FACILITY
AND REEDUCATION CENTER
AKSU DESERT

IT HAD TAKEN the Dagger a full week of careful probing before she traced Clint Janus to a secret research laboratory that Asher Dent had privately funded for the man. The lab had been buried underground, hidden inside the Shar-Kali Correctional Facility.

It struck her that there was a certain irony to its location. In her opinion, this was precisely where Janus belonged—only, as a prisoner. Instead, he freely roamed the halls, treating the place as if it were his own personal playground.

She'd contacted a soldier who'd been in her graduating class at the Junxun Academy; through the grapevine, she'd learned the man had served a tour as the head of the facility's prison guard. For a price, he'd shown her how to circumvent its security. Out of fear and respect for a member of the Assassin's Guild, he would tell no one of their transaction.

Earlier that day, Dacina had dressed as one of the cleaning crew and melded silently into the background, unnoticed by prison personnel. She'd openly walked the facility's halls, memorizing points of ingress, the structure's strengths and weaknesses.

That completed, she'd slipped away to change into the stealth Yinshen armor that was her traditional garb. When she returned, she tracked Janus down once more, following silently behind as he stalked irritably down the prison's halls.

Something had annoyed him while she'd been gone. Dacina hadn't yet discovered its source.

She paused two meters behind the man as he swiped impatiently at the pad that secured his laboratory entrance and cursed at the delay.

She smiled inwardly, knowing the app she'd applied to the doors earlier was likely the cause of it. The packet was opportunistic... it piggybacked off Janus's ID token, insinuating her own into the lab's security protocol, thus allowing Dacina entrance whenever she desired.

She had a feeling it would come in handy in the near future.

Dacina slid quietly in behind the biochemist as he entered the room, seeking the shadows as she always did. Oblivious to the lethal killer who stood a mere handsbreadth away, Janus tossed the package he'd gone to retrieve onto a countertop filled with equipment the Dagger knew nothing about.

"All the fucking way up to the fucking shipping department," he grumbled. "They couldn't have spared one of their trained monkeys to deliver it to me?"

The doctor's complaint washed over Dacina like so much white noise, his whine all too familiar from the months she'd spent as his keeper on deGrasse. She crept silently along the lab's wall, her movements too gradual to even stir the air.

The scientist ignored the package, turning instead to a console—above which floated a holoprojection of a timetable with a list of names.

While his back was turned, the Dagger positioned herself so she could gain a better look at the package's contents, whenever Janus deigned to open it. He wouldn't wait too long.

Dacina knew from her own carefully curated network of informants that the package carried the seal of the State Assembly House, and had been sent directly from the premier himself. Whatever was inside would get her one step closer to learning what had passed between Janus and Dent in the premier's closed-door meeting the previous week.

After a long moment spent glowering at the holoprojection, Janus wheeled, rounding on the offending package. He swiped at the seal with his personal ID token, and it opened, revealing a small stasis chamber, which then uncovered three cylindrical tubes filled with an unidentified substance, the holostickers on their sides reading *'Biohazard.'*

Janus made an annoyed sound. "I *told* him I'd need an assistant if he persists in moving up the timeline!"

Despite his ire, the biochemist lifted each tube with great care, transferring them to a chiller against the lab's far wall, where they joined other such specimens.

Dacina made note of where he placed the tubes, and when he turned away to activate a console, she stepped forward.

Peering through the cooler's transparent, clearsteel door, she read the ident tags off each one.

> Kuytu, Shen. Minister of Information.
> Obati, Mei-Win. Minister of the People's Court.
> Nawane, Ong. Minister of the Standing Committee.

Had her Yinshen suit's stealth properties not been activated, she knew her expression would have betrayed the confusion she felt.

Why is the premier sending Clint Janus biological samples of these three ministers?

A shrill alert sounded, and she pivoted in time to see a reminder pop up in the holoscreen of the console where Janus worked. He was due in interrogation to monitor Garza during another round of questioning. The session was scheduled to commence in ten minutes, in the prison sector.

Janus made another annoyed sound. Reaching for a medical bracer, he rose and stomped from the lab, leaving the console he'd been working on active.

The Dagger drifted over to it. The alert was still projected, along with Garza's file. She paged through it, committing the information to memory, noting the identity of the person with whom he shared a cell.

Rin Zhou Enlai.

Dacina had been around long enough to know how the system worked. This was an anomaly, a departure from prison procedure.

This was an Akkadian power play.

The assassin had no doubt that somehow, Rin Zhou had orchestrated this. How she'd managed to pull this off, and right under Dent's nose, Dacina had no clue.

Her loyalists must be better placed and more organized than I realized.

Pulling her thoughts from speculation on the strength of Enlai's hidden cadre of followers, Dacina returned her attention to her objective: discovering what, exactly, Asher Dent wanted Janus to do—the task he kept hidden from Che Josza, his own minister of state security.

Carefully reaching into the holographic controls, Dacina inserted a worm that would perform a more detailed search, funneling all suspicious data to her. As it disappeared into the background, she began a more cursory search, flipping through Janus's calendar.

She began with the day she'd seen the biochemist slipping out of Dent's office alone, and with a Cheshire grin on his face. A notation labeled 'Project Obelus' caught her attention, and she did a quick search. A file of the same name caught her eye; its contents had her inhaling a harsh breath.

A quick look at the file's tamper protocol revealed that any attempt to copy it or send it to an unauthorized user would result in it being flagged.

She stifled her annoyance. It wouldn't stop her from

recording what she saw on the lab's holo, nor would it keep her from drawing upon her Assassin's Guild training to commit its contents to memory. It did, however, keep it from being used as concrete evidence.

Recordings could be fabricated; a secured file's metadata could not.

Leaving the worm to its search, she backed out of the system with cool efficiency, looking around the lab one final time. Task complete, she slipped from the room and prepared to exit the prison.

She was halfway back to Central Prefecture when a ping over her wire announced the arrival of a secured transmission. It had been delivered to the evanescent version of a dead drop she'd set up for an informant she'd cultivated inside the Geminate Alliance.

Opening it, she felt the first stirrings of a plan begin to form.

The message warned of Alliance special forces operatives landing soon on Eridu. Their mission: to confirm the rumor that the empire held Raphael Garza prisoner.

Attached to the dispatch were the dossiers of the three agents. One face in particular stood out.

Dacina allowed a small smile to tease at her lips.

If Asher Dent was about to embark upon what she thought, then the Dagger would embrace an ages-old war philosophy.

The enemy of my enemy is my friend.

Elodie Cyr didn't know it yet, but she was about to acquire a secret partner.

MERCHANT SHIP

AWF *Swallow*
ALLIED WORLDS FREIGHT HAULER
CUSTOMS PORT ENTRANCE
ERIDU ORBIT

JONATHAN KNEW HE'D been unusually withdrawn since he'd ended the gestalt with Micah hours earlier. Thankfully, everyone had been too busy with the transition from *Invictus*'s boat bay and the subsequent jump to Scharnhorst space for anyone to corner him and ask about it.

Now, though, he could practically feel Yuki's eyes drilling into him as he secured the ship.

Mirage was safely ensconced inside its Casimir bubble, the ship ghosting deeper into Akkadian territory at three times the speed of light, their rendezvous with the Allied Worlds merchant ship now less than an hour away.

Before Yuki could voice the questions he saw burning in her eyes, Jonathan quickly excused himself and headed aft for the head. Ducking past the row where Thad and Ell were seated, he shifted his gaze away from them, giving Valenti a terse nod, still recovering from her earlier tongue-lashing.

He made quick use of the facilities, and then, loath to head back to the cockpit, and craving a few precious minutes of solitude, he slipped quietly into the Nadir's small galley.

Jonathan grabbed a pod of water from the chiller and took a seat on one of the benches, out of sight of those aboard. Tipping his head back until it rested against the coolness of the bulkhead, he closed his eyes, shutting out his surroundings.

Gingerly, he reached out with his mind to touch Micah's essence; not wanting to risk reestablishing the gestalt, but needing to reassure himself of his mirror twin's safety. Not sensing anything amiss, he pulled back, rolling his shoulders forward and giving his neck a quick crack to relieve some of the tension.

The silence he found himself in now was both comforting and disturbing. He knew he needed to confess to someone how compelling, how almost *addicting*, that last gestalt had felt. He hadn't wanted to return to himself, and had only done so when Micah's alarm had spiked.

He also knew that if he hadn't returned when he did... he would have been lost forever.

With a sigh, he cupped the water between his hands and stared down into the clear bioplastic container. A small pocket of air moved about as he squeezed, idly rotating the pod around in his hands.

A scuff of boots alerted him that he was no longer alone. He looked up and saw Thad leaning against the doorframe.

"Mind if I join you?"

Wordlessly, Jonathan gestured to the bench seat across from him.

Ignoring this, the Marine walked over to where Jonathan sat, and parked himself beside him. "You've been talking to Micah?" he asked in a low voice.

Startled by the implication behind the question, Jonathan slid a sideways glance at the big man. "You were there on *Invictus* when it happened," he replied. "You saw. Thank stars Katie reacted the way she did—and that the rest of the team was able to get to him before those grav-suckers could take him."

Thad stared back at him. "That's not what I'm talking about, *ami*. I think you know that." The Marine leaned forward and interlaced his fingers, bracing his forearms on his knees, and turned dark eyes on him, pinning him with a knowing look. "You two can communicate in Scharnhorst space, can't you?"

His words formed a question, but his tone told Jonathan that he already knew the answer.

Jonathan considered denying it, but he was just too damn exhausted. He gave a small shrug. "Yeah," he said simply. "We can."

"You've been keeping it from... who? Everyone? The director? The colonel?"

Jonathan sat back and tossed his pod of water onto the table in front of them. "We haven't told anyone. Well, Sam knows, but she's the only one."

Thad said nothing, only continued to look at him.

After a moment, Jonathan tried to explain. "The three of us agreed that maybe it'd be too tempting for the powers that be to know that we had such an ability."

He gestured vaguely around. "Just look at the hard-on the higher-ups got when they learned that the two of us can communicate mentally in a way that's totally untraceable, unhackable, unjammable."

Jonathan laughed, the sound bitter to his own ears. "Let's see. Distance and light lag don't impact it, either. It was enough to make some in the Alliance lobby for a chiral cloning program of their own."

He didn't bother to hide the rancor that laced his words, and saw understanding dawn in Thad's eyes.

"Can you imagine what they would do if they knew that not even Scharnhorst space could stop us?" Jonathan asked quietly.

Thad worked his jaw as he turned the pilot's words over in his head. He looked down, contemplating his interlaced hands.

Finally sucking in a breath, he nodded. "I get it, hoss. I do.

And off the record? I think you're right. Thanks for coming clean with me, though. It's a good ace for us to have up our sleeves. And on this op, we just might need it."

Jonathan felt tension leach from his shoulders when the Marine abruptly stood, rapped his knuckles on the table, and then exited.

He stared after the other man for a beat. Then, popping the lid off the water, he tipped his head back and downed it.

Tossing the now-empty container into the recycler, he stood and returned to the cockpit.

* * *

An hour later, silently and with virtually no detectable emissions signature, the Nadir spacecraft slipped from Scharnhorst space back into realspace. Thad noted that the location Jonathan had chosen for the transition was just outside the lane assigned to ships that came and went from the Alpha Centauri gate.

From where he sat in *Mirage's* front row of passenger seats, the Marine could see that the pilot had timed their exit to coincide with the crossing of a large commercial vessel.

The ship shuddered slightly as it settled into realspace. The effect was noticeably smoother than when ships like *Wraith* shed their bubbles, and Thad marveled at the Nadir's capabilities.

Despite its advanced stealth and the much-diminished Casmir flare, the energy from a translation out of Scharnhorst space had to go somewhere, but what little remained to be detected was effectively shielded by the ship that floated between their location and the outer customs yard.

Valenti was already unwebbed and up. She gripped the beam separating the cockpit from the main cabin to steady herself as she pointed to an icon on the ship's forward screens. "There."

A ship whose transponder ID token sported the Allied

Worlds Freight logo lit up.

"That's our ship. The *Swallow*. They're expecting us."

Jonathan obligingly turned *Mirage*'s nose toward the massive freighter, moored at the Akkadian customs clearance station. Minutes later, he'd snugged the fully cloaked ship up against a hatch on the vessel's topside.

Valenti herself was standing in the airlock, handling the coupling. *{Remember to blank the screens,}* she called out to Jonathan just before she cycled the airlock. *{Captain Knorr is naval reserve, but* Mirage *is classified.}*

{Yes, ma'am,} he replied, and Thad saw him do something to his pilot's boards.

In the next instant, every indicator went dark.

Shaking off the slightly creepy feeling that came in the wake of such absence, Thad stood and motioned the pilot from the cockpit. "Come on, Case. Time to go."

Jonathan nodded and then murmured a few words to Yuki as he transferred control of the ship over to the lieutenant.

The Unit team member that would be subbing as copilot nodded as he sidled past Thad, and the three entered into a prearranged dance. Jonathan unwebbed and stood, Yuki slid into the pilot's cradle he'd just vacated, and then the Marine backfilled Yuki's position.

Ell rose as Jonathan came to a stop beside her and Thad, and the Marine captain wordlessly waved them both aft.

A screen above the weapons locker flared to life as they approached. It showed a feed from the airlock. Thad watched the colonel cycle the hatch, saw a woman dressed in a standard civilian ship's suit on the other side.

The colonel—or rather, Takeko, the SI embedded inside Valenti's head—had given them a brief sitrep on the merchanter before they docked. The woman was a retired naval ship's commander who had captained the flagship for the Alliance's Strike Force Ready Group One [SFRG-1]. That flagship was the one the Special Recon Units had staged from, during the border skirmishes that had plagued the Atliekas two decades ago.

She knew spec ops. She and Valenti had a history. She'd also been Valenti's personal pick for this leg of the mission.

The woman saluted, and then the two shook hands. Valenti motioned her into the airlock, cycling it shut behind her.

Thad returned his attention to the kit bag he'd packed before they departed *Invictus*. Ell was already performing a gear check, and Jonathan had gone to fetch Joule's crate from *Mirage*'s cargo bay.

Thad had just resealed his duffel and slung it over his shoulder when Valenti called his name.

She launched into introductions with her usual peremptory manner. Pointing to each in turn, she identified them. "This is Naval Reserve Captain Bev Knorr. SRU Captain Thad Severance. NCIC Agent Elodie Cyr. Shadow Recon Captain Jonathan Case, and," she gestured to the crate, "their working cat, Joule."

The reserve captain nodded. "I understand you're my cargo for this next Eridu run."

Thad nodded. "Yes, ma'am. That we are."

Valenti motioned to the airlock, and Thad led the way, pausing beside Joule's crate to switch it on.

The unit rose on one side, causing the big cat to scramble for footing.

"Sorry," the Marine muttered, swinging the back of the crate around until it lined up better with one of the maglev coil stripes indicated on *Mirage*'s deck. "Still getting used to the new ship."

{Don't see why I can't just walk. Got four perfectly good paws.}

Jonathan coughed quietly into his hand, earning him a stern look from the colonel.

"Gotta keep you hidden on the other end until we reach the savannah. That's why."

The only response to Thad's explanation was a loud, feline chuff.

Why do I get the feeling I owe her a steak for that?

At the airlock, Valenti held up a hand. Giving Jonathan a look rife with meaning, she said, "Your special contact will be waiting to hear from you. He'll let us know you've arrived safely."

Thad and Jonathan exchanged a glance at her oblique reference to Micah.

The pilot gave the colonel a brief nod. "Understood, ma'am."

Valenti stepped back. "We'll be on standby. If you need us, send word, and we'll jump in."

This time, it was Thad who nodded. "Copy."

Valenti cycled the hatch, and they filed onto the merchant ship, the team following Captain Knorr as she led the way aft through an almost eerily silent ship, stopping only when they arrived at its cargo bay.

Ell voiced Thad's thoughts. "Quiet around here."

The Navy captain nodded. "That's by design. We're in third watch, and the bridge crew has been informed that I have Navy business to attend to. Beyond that, the only other person involved is my supply officer."

Thad ground to a halt at her words, but Knorr shook her head, smiling, apparently having anticipated his reaction.

"Also naval reserve, also vetted by Valenti."

Thad resumed walking.

After another few minutes had passed, Knorr slid him a glance. "I see the colonel hasn't changed in the years since I served under her. Still as no-nonsense as ever."

Thad felt his lips twitch.

Too bad I can't tell you about Takeko. She and that damn SI really are a perfect match.

Aloud, he merely nodded. "You called it, ma'am."

A soft laugh rippled from Knorr at that, and she motioned them down a side passage.

They drew to a stop in front of a large, boxcar-like shipping container. She coded in a command, and the container's doors swung open.

Placing her hand on the open frame, Knorr stared inside the dark recess.

"Stasis shipping container. Once switched on, all molecular activity inside this box stops." She made a slashing motion with her hand to emphasize her point.

"The entire unit is essentially one enormous tau-neu chamber, only without the niceties of a stasis pod. You sure you want to do this?" She shot them a doubtful look.

Thad leaned closer to peer inside. The container was filled with pallets of boxes, stacked from floor to ceiling. Crates were everywhere, some bearing tamper-lock seals, others with holographic stickers marked *fragile, handle with care.'* One sported the logo of a Cobalt distillery.

The place had very few spots where a trio of humans might maglock themselves to the container's walls and settle in for a long stasis trip between the stars.

Thad hooked a hand around the back of his neck and squeezed. "Not particularly, no," he admitted. "But I know the agent on the other end, and I trust him."

The woman eyed him knowingly. "Yes, but it's the between-here-and-there part that's a little goosey for you, isn't it?"

Thad kicked his head over in a quick tic, silently acknowledging the truth of the woman's words. "Didn't sign up for easy, though."

Brows lifted, the former Navy fleet officer refrained from commenting. Instead, she motioned her ship's supply officer forward. The man had been waiting quietly beside the unit, a weapons-filled maglev cart beside him.

"Everything the colonel asked for, plus a few other things we thought might be of service along the way," the man informed them by way of greeting.

Ell stepped forward, peering down curiously at the assortment. She cocked an eyebrow. "You do know that we'll be in stasis the entire way? From our point of view, between one blink and the next, we'll be there."

Knorr pursed her lips. "I know, but we'll be transferring you over to an Akkadian merchant ship—a civvy ship in foreign territory. What if someone gets curious and decides to see for himself what's inside this tin can?"

She rapped the side of the container. "You folks are used to this spy shit. I was only the bus driver, ferrying Unit teams in and out, and that was long before your time. So humor me, please."

Understanding creased Ell's face, and she sent the woman and her supply officer a small smile. "Please extend our thanks to your company, if it's appropriate, for their cooperation."

Knorr stepped back with a small grin. "Comes with the territory. They hired me knowing I was in the reserves and could be called back at any time. That explained the detour. The rest, well...." She patted the container and turned to her companion. "I never saw anything else. Did you?"

The supply officer met her gaze, a bland expression on his face. "No idea what you're talking about, skipper."

Thad suppressed a smile, opting to reach out a hand instead. "Thanks."

The woman clasped his in her own and gave it a perfunctory shake.

Slapping her palms against her ship coveralls, she stepped back. "Welp, I guess this is it. The orders we have are to go ahead and initiate stasis. You want to get settled, and then we'll close the door and seal you in?"

Thad saw that Jonathan had already wedged himself into a corner in the back, between a stack of crates and pallet that declared it was full of something perishable called raspberry oranges. Behind him was Joule's crate.

The pilot had wisely chosen the rear of the container, leaving the more combat experienced to cover the door.

Thad gave him a silent nod, and then moved to find his own hidden position. He chose a cubby closer to the front and settled onto the floor, his back pressed against the metal wall. Ordering his suit to maglock him to the container's surface, he curled one hand around the CUSP directed-energy pistol holstered at his ankle.

Ell took the space across from him.

When they were settled, Thad called out to the captain, "Ready."

"Good hunting," the woman replied.

The door swung shut, enveloping them in blackness. He heard a low hum… and then there was nothing.

* * *

Thad came to abruptly, blinking away disorientation as light speared the darkness. As the sliver widened, he realized someone had cracked open the container's seal, releasing them from stasis.

He tensed, his hand tightening around the weapon strapped to his ankle.

Did we make it to Eridu, or was the captain right, and we're dealing with a nosy customs inspector… or worse?

Thad gripped the direct energy pistol in his hand as he heard cautious footsteps approach.

THE DINNER

Driscoll Opera Haus
St. Clair Township
Ceriba

THE FOUNDER'S CUP dinner was set up in the Driscoll Opera Haus's ballroom, an ancient and opulent structure that dated back to early colonization days. Many a state function had been staged here, but this was the first opportunity Micah had ever had to see it from the inside.

He was dressed in his Navy black, the blue of the special forces a thin stripe edging the side of the suit and running down each leg. Rather than holopips, this suit had kept with ancient tradition, with physical, magnetized pins that displayed his ribbons and service medals. They were clipped to the flap of his suit pocket and affixed to his suit's black pauldron. His rank insignia stripes were displayed on the shoulder opposite the pauldron, as well as at the cuffs of each sleeve.

He shifted uncomfortably, the awards he was allowed to show still comprising a healthy-sized salad of glitter that many outside the military seemed often over-impressed by.

It brought to mind the times he and his fellow shadow recon

flight teams had been on leave during the first two tours. The commander of his flight crew at the time, Rafe Zander, had introduced him to—and warned him about—the 'Navy bunnies' that frequented the bars at Port Humbolt.

"They see you in that ship suit, and you're going to be propositioned more than once tonight," his commander had predicted.

Zander'd been right, and though Micah might have initially enjoyed the ego boost, it had grown old quickly. He preferred someone who wasn't an easy conquest. Someone... like Sam.

He looked over at the woman whose hand rested on his arm. Her gown swept the floor in a graceful cascade, and she'd done something with her hair so it sparkled under the chandeliers.

Feeling his eyes on her, she turned, green eyes alight with interest in everything she saw. It was a stark contrast to the expression those eyes had held when he'd first met her.

Of course, back then, I was pissed as hell at the thought of having to play babysitter to some scientist on some sort of secret mission for her uncle.

Sam pursed her lips. "Penny for your thoughts."

Micah's mouth creased in a grin. "I was just thinking about first impressions."

One blonde brow arched elegantly. "Are you referring to the one you made on me? Or are you thinking about the one we're making here?"

He laughed. "I didn't exactly win you over that first day, did I?"

Her tone was colored with wry amusement. "You were a cocky naval aviator who saw me as some sort of punishment assignment. I believe your first words to me were, 'I don't babysit.'"

His grin widened. "Hate to say it, but you're wrong. Those words were directed toward your uncle, not you."

"Same difference, but okay, we'll go with it."

She squinted as she studied him, head cocked slightly to one side. "If that's the case, then it's hard to know exactly what your first words might have been. You froze me out for some time, Captain." He felt a fingernail dig gently into his side as she poked him in the ribs. "You were a tough nut to crack."

He caught her hand, rescuing his ribs from further abuse by interlacing his fingers through hers.

"How does that saying go? 'The tougher they are, the harder they fall'?"

Sam laughed. "Not exactly, but it'll do."

She inclined her head toward the entrance that armed naval soldiers stood guarding, and several black-suit-clad, expressionless security agents milled about. *{You think there are any ringers inside that detail?}*

*{I can pretty much guarantee it. We also have no idea how many visitors on the list are Akkadian. Aside from our own people and your uncle, trust **no one**.}*

At his own words, concern flooded him, and he squeezed her hand, willing her to look him in the eye. *{I'm not kidding, Sam. They'd kill to get their hands on you again. I'm not about to let that happen.}*

She returned the squeeze. *{That goes for you, too, you know.}*

Something caught her attention, and she lifted a hand with a wave.

"There's my uncle."

* * *

Duncan Cutter looked up as his niece and Micah Case stopped in front of him. Favoring Sam with a smile, he nodded a greeting to the man at her side. "You two ready?"

Sam reached out a hand to clasp his, turning it slightly so they could both see the lacing of gold filigree that etched her palm. It gleamed under the opera house's chandelier lighting, tracing its way past her wrist and disappearing under her sleeve.

It was unlike any bracer Micah had ever seen; the ones he

was used to her wearing were thick with hardware.

He lifted a brow as he met her eyes.

"All set," she murmured. "Just the essentials this time."

She dropped her hand as chimes sounded, announcing that dinner was served. They followed the crowd as the dining room doors opened, and the guests migrated into the ballroom.

They had purposely skipped the cocktail hour, not wanting to give the Akkadians another opportunity to make a grab for Sam—or him.

Micah remained watchful as they followed Duncan to one of the front tables. Two people were already present: the prime minister's newest assistant, Ed, and one of his security agents.

Cutter nodded pleasantly to the man and woman, and pulled out a seat for Sam beside the one earmarked for Garza.

"I'm sorry," the woman interposed smoothly. "That seat is taken."

Micah saw Sam glance questioningly over at her uncle, and the man nodded, signifying silently she was to cooperate.

He pulled out the next available chair, and Sam sank into it. Cutter motioned for Micah to take the seat beside Sam, grabbing the next one over for himself.

Once seated, Sam leaned in and pointed to the decanter of red wine resting at the center of the table. "Would either of you like a glass?" She casually touched the back of Micah's hand, sending him a reassuring, *{Don't worry. I've got this.}*

The trio enjoyed their drinks and idle chat as the chairs around them became occupied.

When the ballroom was filled and everyone seated, a stir at a side entrance caught Micah's attention, and he saw a phalanx of guards appear, all dressed in black, their watchful eyes scanning the crowd. Behind them, he could see Jiu Liam, the dynastic president of An-Yang, standing beside Prime Minister Garza.

At a nod from one of the security agents, the two men stepped into the ballroom, their detail spreading out to surround them.

The leaders parted when Jiu Liam stopped at the An-Yang table, where Alliance trade representatives chatted with their An-Yang counterparts. Garza continued on, smiling a greeting as he approached.

Micah and the director stood, but Garza waved them back down.

Micah could swear he saw relief and maybe a flare of hope flash across the prime minister's face when he and Cutter exchanged hellos. With a full two meters of round table separating Garza from the NSA director, Micah didn't see how the man could ask for help, if he was indeed hoping for the opportunity.

Garza sat, leaning over to hear something his assistant said to him. Micah didn't miss the subtle flare of anger, quickly banked.

Micah's gaze shot to Cutter to see if the man had caught it, and he received a subtle nod in return.

As the meal progressed, Sam made a few valiant attempts to reach Garza, but they were all summarily blocked by the female agent seated between them.

"How's your wife?" he heard Cutter ask, and Garza's fork froze momentarily on its way down to his plate.

"She's doing well, all things considered."

To Micah's ear, it sounded as if the prime minister had chosen his words with care. His attention sharpened when the man's assistant chimed in.

"She's very lucky to be alive, though I understand she's not out of the woods just yet."

The patently false expression of sympathy plastered on the man's face hit Micah with the same impact waving a red flag at a bull would have.

He fisted his hand around his steak knife, wanting nothing more than to shove it through the aide's eye socket, but a kick under the table from Cutter had him relaxing back in his seat.

He couldn't miss the slight stiffening of Garza's pose, nor the way the man's knuckles whitened around his water glass as he lifted it to take a sip.

Sam was refilling her own water glass from the carafe at the center of the table. Before she set it down, she looked over at Garza, and with a smile, offered, "May I top you off, Mister Prime Minister?"

He smiled and extended his glass. "Thank you, that would be appreciated."

The agent between him and Sam went to intercept the carafe, but Sam fumbled it, spilling its contents onto the table, the pool of water rushing straight toward Garza's lap.

"I'm so sorry!" Sam gasped, reaching her napkin across, and in the process, tipping over the agent's red wine.

It crested over the cuff of Garza's right hand just before the man scooted away from the dripping tablecloth.

Apologizing profusely, Sam reached across once more to try to dab at Garza's wet sleeve, but the agent's hand snapped out and grabbed Sam's arm in a bruising grip.

Micah was immediately on the agent, his hand over hers. "Let her go," he said pleasantly, but the look he shot the woman was anything but. "She was just trying to help."

The agent knocked his hand away as she let go of Sam. She looked like she was one breath away from going for a weapon, when one of the nearby catering staff intervened.

The woman removed the towel that had been slung over her shoulder and bent over Garza, murmuring an apology.

The agent's head whipped around, her attention now firmly on the ballroom waitress. "Hand me that towel," she demanded.

She scrutinized the fabric closely—an action Micah assumed meant she was probing it for foreign substances—then handed it back to the woman and, with a wordless gesture, ordered her to proceed.

The waitress bent to her task, applying the towel to Garza's jacket and pants leg, its absorbent ActiveFiber material efficiently wicking the moisture away from the prime minister's clothing.

"Excuse me, sir," Micah heard her murmur as she grasped his wrist with her left hand, her attention on the red wine staining the cuff of his white shirt.

As she dabbed, Micah noticed she wore no jewelry except for a plain gold band that adorned her ring finger.

A few seconds later, she straightened, and stepped away. "There you go, sir. I apologize for the inconvenience, and I'll be right back with a fresh glass of water for you."

Micah sat back, frustrated, as the waitress told the agent that she would also bring out a refill for her red wine.

Dammit.

He knew Sam wasn't normally that clumsy; no doubt, that had been her attempt to make contact with Garza and, in the process, take a sample with the bracer disguised as jewelry around her arm.

His mood grew more foul when he chanced to catch the contemptuous glance of Garza's assistant. The man wasn't exactly *smiling*—he wouldn't be that overt about it—but there was a knowing glint in his eye that told Micah that he, too, knew Sam wasn't the clumsy type.

As dessert was served, the emcee for the evening invited Garza to come to the stage, along with the president of An-Yang, to talk about the foundation that would benefit from the exhibition race, thanks to the generous donation of the one who lost the race.

Garza stood, and Micah's jaw clenched in anger when he saw both his assistant and the agent stand.

He knew... he *knew* that they were planning to spirit the man away after this. That meant their window of opportunity had now officially closed.

Micah forced himself to smile at the appropriate times as the two leaders engaged in a jovial bit of ribbing, but inside, he was steaming mad.

The whole evening had been a bust.

* * *

Micah tossed his napkin down in the center of his plate as Garza was escorted off stage and out a side door, disgusted by how the entire evening had turned out. "What a colossal waste of time," he muttered softly.

He braced his hands against the table, but before he could shove his chair back, Cutter's hand came down on his forearm.

{No scenes.}

The words came over a private channel the director forced into his head.

Cutter's hand squeezed, and he gave Micah a warning look. *{This is a high-profile event, and you're here as Garza's trainer. Newsnet reporters are present, so plaster a smile on your face, Captain, and look like you're enjoying yourself. And in case it wasn't perfectly clear—that's an order.}*

On a sharp inhale, Micah nodded, reaching for his wineglass.

Cutter flashed a brief smile of approval before turning to Samantha to ask a question.

The people across the table seemed not to have noticed, their attention on the stage as the next speaker approached the lectern. Micah glanced surreptitiously around, relaxing when it appeared his aborted action had gone unnoticed.

It was another hour before the ceremony was over, and they could exit into the cool evening. Coming to a stop, Duncan turned to look at Capitol Hill, the star nation's government center glowing softly under its nighttime illumination. Micah followed his gaze.

"Come on," Cutter said abruptly as a transport pulled up to the curb. "You're both with me."

Micah peered inside, unsurprised to see Gabriel Alvarez at its controls.

They piled inside, the silence broken only by occasional idle chatter as Gabe expertly piloted them to the headquarters of the National Security Agency. By unspoken agreement, the silence held as they passed through security and into the warren of underground tunnels that linked the NSA to

Parliament House.

The destination Cutter led them to was directly beneath the government seat, in a SCIF buried dozens of floors below the Great Hall.

As they were ushered through its doors, Micah was surprised to see both Admiral Toland and Major Reid already inside. Between the two sat a young woman whose face looked vaguely familiar.

Micah began to turn toward Gabe, but then his head swung sharply back around when the pieces came together in his mind.

The woman was dressed exactly like the waitress at the Driscoll.

He slanted Cutter a questioning glance, and caught a mix of anticipation and barely contained elation on the man's face. No one said a word until the doors sealed and the connection to the planetary network cut off.

"I told you you'd make a kickass spy."

It was the last thing Micah expected to hear, especially from Sam. His head jerked around in surprise, only to see her attention directed toward the stranger in the room.

"What the hell?" He looked around in confusion.

Gabe appeared equally bewildered, but Reid, Toland, and Cutter all seemed as pleased as Sam sounded.

The director clapped a hand on his shoulder. "Afraid you were the victim of a bit of subterfuge, tonight, Captain. Sorry we didn't have the time to let you in on it."

Cutter grinned. "By the way, your barely concealed frustration toward the end was a nice touch. Really ramped up the believability factor."

Micah scowled. "Believability factor? Believability about *what?*"

Sam shot him an apologetic look. "It was a last-minute idea we came up with. I didn't have a chance to introduce you to Linnet before we put the plan into play."

"Linnet?" Micah turned to stare at the woman seated

between Toland and Reid.

"Linnet Thompson. We were college roommates," Sam said, as if that explained everything. "Linnet, this is Captain Micah Case."

The brunette smiled. "I've heard a lot about you, Captain."

A mischievous twinkle in her eyes told Micah it'd be best not to pursue those details just yet.

"Linnet was Admiral Toland's first choice for the position Clint Janus filled on deGrasse Torus," Sam added. "It nearly got her killed."

"Come again?" Confusion colored Micah's voice.

"I was employed at the Merki Institute on Hawking," Linnet explained. "At the time, I had a year left on my contract, so I couldn't accept." She shrugged. "Turns out Akkadia had already dispatched an assassin to eliminate me, but they called her off when I turned down the admiral's offer."

Micah glanced at the Admiral Toland. "She's aware of what happened on deGrasse?"

"Only peripherally, and only because she recently left Merki to join Project Rufus at the CID. I just got into town this morning."

As Rufus was the code name for the classified chiral project under Toland's leadership, Micah supposed she knew a bit more than just the 'peripheral' things.

"In any case, she was our backup plan in case Doctor Travis's attempts to obtain a sample of Garza's DNA were blocked." Admiral Toland glanced at Cutter. "From what I hear, that's exactly what happened."

"It worked, too." Sam's voice was smug. "No one paid any attention to the waitstaff who came to Garza's rescue, they were too busy preventing me from touching him."

Micah looked over at the woman by his side. "You could have said something ahead of time."

"No time," Reid interjected. "It came together fast. There was someone on the waitstaff with similar physical features, and we were able to substitute Linnet in her place at the last-minute."

"So you're saying you got the sample from Garza after all?" Micah pressed.

Linnet nodded.

He turned to Cutter. "So... I was just window dressing."

"You were the distraction we needed in order for them to forget Linnet was there. Waitstaff often disappear into the woodwork, and we needed to ensure that that was the case today."

"And Sam's attempt?"

Cutter smiled. "Was a legitimate one. But it was also a bit more predictable. It also provided further cover to hide Linnet's attempt."

Micah considered the man's words, nodding reluctantly. He turned to Linnet. "How'd you do it?"

Linnet lifted her left hand.

Micah saw the simple golden band he'd noticed around her ring finger earlier. When she rotated her palm outward, he recognized the same intricate web of circuitry that laced Sam's, descending down her wrist and wrapping around her forearm.

"You're wearing a bracer."

She nodded.

"And you got the sample?"

"I did."

"And?"

Linnet's gaze shifted to the director, her expression suddenly sad. "I'm afraid you were right, Director Cutter. The man who was there tonight is chiral."

MORRISON

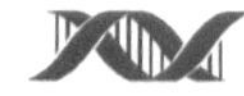

Location: Unknown

THAD FOUGHT A wave of vertigo, the disorientation something he'd been warned about. While perfectly safe, stasis used for shipping wasn't built for comfort. It was an instantaneous thing, not the gradual return to consciousness that stasis pods built for humans employed.

He blinked hard, fingers tightening around the CUSP energy pistol in his grip. Across the aisle, Ell stirred. Mentally triggering his suit to release its magnetic grip on the container's walls and floor, he held up a warning hand as he strained to focus on the footsteps drawing closer.

An alert came across his wire, indicating an incoming communication request from an unknown source. Ignoring it for the moment, Thad slipped a hand inside the pocket of his tactical vest, where he retrieved a pair of surveillance microdrones that he released into the air.

The feed from the small machines told him there were two figures standing at the entrance. Both wore concealing garments that shrouded their faces, obscuring their identities. They were armed, with one focused inward, while the other kept watch outside the shipping container.

In the next instant, the drones sent a warning ping to his overlay, letting him know they'd detected another set of drones in the air. Telemetry from the feed indicated they were of Alliance origin.

Thad relaxed slightly at that.

He accepted the ping, and heard the correct challenge phrase uttered from a voice he recognized.

{Morrison?}

{Severance. Long time, buddy.}

{Who's your friend?}

{Aviva. She's good people. Been with the NSA since '37.}

{Copy that. Coming out.}

Thad motioned Ell to cover him, and Jonathan to sit tight. He kept to the shadows as he made his way forward, stopping just inside the lip of the container, where Morrison stood.

What limited view he had of the outside reminded him of old 2-D photos of pre-diaspora trainyards back on Earth. Empty maglev tracks stretched as far as the eye could see. Old, worn-out boxcars were lined up in long rows, just visible between shabby, rusted warehouse buildings.

"Sitrep?" he asked in a low voice as he turned to face the Agency man.

Morrison inclined his head outside. "You're in the warehouse district at the back of the shipyards adjacent to the main spaceport. Base of the elevator, just outside Central Prefecture. We requested that Allied Worlds drop you in this spot because this sector has the weakest security."

The agent shot Thad a warning look and then added, "That doesn't translate to *no* security, though. We need to get moving. Got any equipment you plan to bring along?"

Thad shook his head. "Let me get a lay of the land, first."

The lower part of Morrison's swarthy face—what little he could see of it, hidden as it was under a cowl—creased into a grin, white teeth flashing as he motioned Thad forward. "That's a good copy, amigo."

The man shifted to one side, widening Thad's field of view, but before the Marine could move, Morrison put out a hand to stop him.

"Look, but don't step out. Not dressed like that."

Thad cocked a brow at the man and glanced down at the plain tan shirt and pants he'd been given to wear over his drakeskin suit. Then his eyes landed on the agent.

Morrison was shrouded from head to toe in some sort of local robe, made of a coarse, off-white material.

Morrison's eyes met his knowingly as he hefted a bundle of cloth in his hands, tossing them to Thad. "They got the inside dress right, but you'll still need a robe if you want to blend in. Put that on before you stick your head out and take a look around."

"Robe, huh?"

Catching the bundle midair, Thad dropped it on top of a nearby crate and untied the package. Several articles of clothing were inside, the fabric of each similar to what Morrison wore.

"Loose weave lets air in," Morrison explained, "and the light color reflects that damned star's heat. Least miserable way to get around, considering most of these folks don't have the credits for the kind of temperature-modulating clothing we're used to."

Thad nodded his understanding.

He held up the top piece; the cloak fell to mid-calf, hitting the tops of his boots. He shrugged into it, flipping the cloak's hood over his head. When he turned back to the entrance, Morrison gave him a silent thumbs-up.

Edging his way out into the sunlight, Thad started to call his microdrones forward, but Morrison shook his head.

"Trust me, we don't want those outside the container. They'll set off alarms for sure."

The woman whose gaze was tracking back and forth from one side of the building to the other shot the two men a look at that comment.

Morrison took that as an invitation to introduce the two operatives to each other.

"Aviva, this is Captain Severance. Thad Severance, Agent Aviva Hebbart."

Hebbart jerked a quick nod, her eyes returning immediately to the surrounding area.

As satisfied as he could be with the situation, Thad turned back to Morrison. "I have two more inside."

The other man's brows lifted. "I was told you'd only have one with you."

He shifted another bundle of cloth he'd tucked under his arm, and held it out to Thad as Jonathan and Ell edged closer to the container's opening. Morrison eyed the three of them doubtfully.

"We only brought the two bundles of clothing. You'll have to make do. Sort through it and figure out how you can split it three ways."

Ell was already sifting through what was left of the first parcel, so Thad tossed the bundle in his hands to Jonathan.

The man's pilot reflexes snatched it nimbly out of the air.

With an impatient sound, the woman standing guard reached up and unwound the scarf she wore around her neck. "Here." She tossed the material to Morrison, motioning to Ell. "Hand that to her."

"Thanks," said Ell, taking the scarf from the man. She studied the material, sliding it through her hands before murmuring, "I can work with this."

With a quick flip of her wrist and a few deft twists, she had the material wound into a believable cowl. Thad shook his head, completely unable to fathom how she'd done that.

A bemused look crossed Jonathan's face. "Watched her the entire time, and I still couldn't tell you how she managed that."

The look of disdain on Ell's face was priceless. "Really? I can accurately place a shot five thousand meters away, and you're impressed by the way I tossed a scarf over my head?"

Thad stifled his flare of amusement, totally inappropriate to the situation, but damn. He could tell the normally stoic sniper was one step away from cuffing the pilot on the back of the head. Since the woman rarely showed emotion, it was funny as hell.

Instead, she opted for a scathing, "Shouldn't we be going?" and lifted an eyebrow to emphasize her point.

As if on cue, Aviva called out in a low voice, "Time to move. We have another five minutes until the guards come this direction. We can only keep the SIs offline for another two."

Thad nodded to Jonathan. "Grab the equipment—and the cat."

Morrison's eyebrows rose at that last, but he handed over two woven, rucksack-like bags. "Prioritize what you need to fit inside these. Hustle, amigo."

Thad passed them to Ell, who, with a quick nod, disappeared into the back. A few seconds later, she and Jonathan returned, rucksacks bulging.

All three hopped to the ground, Jonathan directing Joule's crate over the lip of the container. Morrison swung the doors closed, and then motioned Ell to his side.

"It's best if we split up," he explained when Thad lifted a questioning brow. "You two go with Aviva. We'll rendezvous at the safehouse."

Before they headed out, Morrison instructed them all to pull their hoods forward.

"To shield our faces from the locals?" asked Thad.

Morrison shook his head. "The locals learn early in life that it's not healthy to pay too much attention to their neighbors— or to anyone else on the street, for that matter." He pointed to a pair of tall posts Thad could just make out in the distance. "The Empire has a 'social monitoring system' in place. Cameras embedded at every street corner, outside nearly every business, too."

"Geez, controlling much?" Jonathan muttered.

"Welcome to Akkadia," Aviva said in a dry voice.

Thad clapped a berobed Jonathan on the shoulder and

steered him toward Aviva. "See you in twenty."

* * *

As Morrison had predicted, not many spared them a second glance as they wound their way through narrow streets and down a steep hill. The echoing din of an indoor city market grew louder as they neared its base.

Peering inside as they passed, Thad caught brief glimpses of produce stalls, booths had been worn away in some places, revealing a scarred and pitted surface.

From what Thad could see, the dun-colored undercoating matched the description of the formation material used by the original settlers. That meant this building had to be going on three centuries now.

Footsteps heralded the arrival of Ell and Morrison.

As he came to a stop beside them, Morrison lifted a cupped hand, and a pair of microdrones exited the man's palm. They flew to a stairwell that descended beneath the building's ground floor, hovering before a shadowed doorway.

"I set up an ActiveFiber early warning system," Morrison explained. "It's crude, but effective. Anyone trying to breach the safehouse would have disturbed the threads sealing the door."

After a moment, he gave a crisp nod and stepped forward. "We're good to go."

The spare apartment was surprisingly large, taking up half the basement. A swift look around suggested to Thad that the two agents spent more time on their spycraft than they did on creature comforts.

Aviva motioned to the back of the building. "Bedrooms and a lav back there, if you need to refresh yourselves or change."

Nodding her thanks, Ell stepped into the narrow hallway.

Thad was certain it was more about the NCIC agent's desire to secure the area for herself than her need to use the head.

He stayed in the main room with Jonathan, who bent to release Joule from her confines. The big cat slunk from the crate, eyes wary and head on a swivel as she surveyed her surroundings.

Morrison took in her vest. "Working cat?"

Thad nodded. "Part of the team."

The agent frowned. "That seems excessive, hauling an animal all the way out here."

Aviva made a sound of dissent. "Considering where they're infiltrating, it makes sense. Depending on how well-trained it is, the cat should be able to get away with a lot more than a human could."

Joule turned glittering green eyes on the woman. *{Not an **it**.}*

A look of startlement crossed Aviva's face.

"Did that thing just talk?" Morrison asked.

Joule's head whipped around to face the man, eyes narrowing. *{Not a **thing**, either.}*

"Holy shit," he breathed. "He did."

If a cat could roll its eyes, Joule would be doing so.

*{Am a **she**.}*

"Careful," Jonathan cautioned. "Piss off one of the cats, and you'll end up using half your credits bailing yourself out." Crooking a thumb Thad's way, he added, "He owes her brother at least fifty steaks by now."

"Thirty," Thad corrected.

The pilot scoffed. "That's what you think." He returned his attention to the agents before him. "Joule's a result of a classified experiment. First animal to be implanted with a device that allows rudimentary communication." He carefully avoided any mention of the cat's chirally-paired twin.

"Huh," Morrison's brows rose, but he wisely refrained from commenting any further.

A noise from behind Thad told him Ell had returned. She stepped up next to him, but her gaze was fixed on a pair of transom windows set above the apartment's door. They were the basement's only source of natural illumination, bleeding a small shaft of dirty sunlight across the carpeted floor.

"What's bothering you, *cher*?"

Her eyes remained focused on the door. "We're certain that there are no listening devices planted anywhere outside this building that could be directed our way?"

Morrison tried and failed not to look affronted at her questioning of his skills, but it was Aviva who responded to Ell's query.

"The ActiveFiber that Agent Morrison has deployed around the perimeter of this apartment is seeded with small, noise-canceling devices programmed to emit occasional bursts of conversation. The kind of thing you'd expect to hear from any apartment in this area. If anyone is listening in, they're hearing about how bad the local brew tastes, or Morrison complaining about his wages being garnished."

Aviva's words seemed to convince Ell. She looked thoughtfully at the door before turning to Aviva with a nod. "What's the plan, then?"

Aviva held a holoprojector in her palm. At Ell's inquiry, she thumbed it on. "We have an update on the prison. I was able to get my hands on the latest diagram, plus access codes to control the security SIs that monitor those shafts you'll be using to infiltrate."

Thad whistled. "How'd you manage that?"

Morrison chuckled. "She has her ways."

They were interrupted by a flash, followed by a loud clap of thunder, the rumble receding in the distance.

"Heat lightning?" Thad asked.

"No. It's monsoon season." She flicked the projector off, tucking it away in her robes. "I'd thought the rains wouldn't come for another few hours; this moves the timetable up. Get ready, we leave as soon as the rains hit."

Joule's ears flattened, followed by Jonathan's yelped, "What? I thought Eridu had acid rain. Isn't that going to be dangerous?"

The agent shook her head. "Don't get me wrong; over time, they'll eat through even the hardest surface. But a little bit of exposure won't hurt you. It's not like the acid rain that, say, a pre-terraformed Venus once had."

Jonathan's expression turned contemplative, and he turned away to try to calm the big cat, who was making it clear she did not like this turn of events.

"Why move while it rains?"

Ell's quiet question earned her a shrug from Aviva.

"Rain in Central Prefecture is rare enough that it'll serve as a nice distraction. People will be more focused on that than they are anything else."

Ell hummed thoughtfully and Aviva cocked her head as another rumble hit. Nodding to herself, the agent reached for a kit bag and began to load it up.

"Gather your things. We move out in an hour."

CARROT AND STICK

Shar-Kali Correctional Facility
and Reeducation Center
Aksu Desert

"It is time."

At Rin Zhou's words, Raphael turned to face his cellmate. The woman stood with her hand out, the jamming device blinking in her open palm.

"Time?"

"I have told you of my proposition. You have not given me an answer. Now, your time has run out."

Raphael's eyes narrowed. "That sounds suspiciously like a threat."

"I merely state fact. Your people have come for you. Mine are tracking them, monitoring their progress."

Raphael stiffened. "So then I was right; you *are* threatening me."

"My people are waiting for instructions. I could tell them to sound the alarm, or...." Rin Zhou tilted her head, her eyes as keen as a raptor's. "You can support our uprising, and help us unseat a truly evil man."

Raphael stared at her, and then gestured around expansively. "Not sure you've noticed, but I'm not in any position to help anyone right now."

Rin Zhou gave him a look that would have made Raphael's Marine drill instructor proud. "Your people are on this planet now, and are in contact with special forces troops lurking in the Sargon Straits. Combined with my loyalists, their numbers will suffice."

"And if I were to turn down your offer?"

The former minister cocked her head, the action reinforcing his impression of a bird of prey.

"Then I will have no choice but to reveal their presence to the Akkadian fleet."

MONSOON

Central Prefecture
Eridu, Akkadia

ELL STOOD IN the shadows outside the safehouse's basement entrance, quietly studying the street traffic, while Morrison reset his ActiveFiber warning system.

She was surprised at the press of bodies that crowded the narrow path, even during a downpour such as this. Central Prefecture was a congested place, and she reminded herself that this was another reason why its citizens paid those around them little mind.

The only concession the residents seemed to make for the downpour was the exchange of the traditional cloak for a sturdy oilskin covering. Everywhere she looked, people bustled around her, their heads down, rain dripping from wide-brimmed hats to plop on the pitted pavement.

Ell followed Thad up the stairs to street-level, where they merged with the pedestrian traffic. By unspoken agreement, they closed ranks around Joule, invisible behind a cloak laced with light-bending nano.

Her gaze wandered to the man who strode just ahead of her,

eyes catching on the long, dark-hued fingers that secured the duffel he shouldered. She thought, not for the first time, that his hands could belong to an artist.

The hulking Marine would likely snort at the idea before breaking into that rich, deep laugh of his—the kind that came from the core of a person.

The man in front of her made an annoyed sound, dancing around a pedestrian who had stopped abruptly in the middle of the street.

{Heads up, cher.}

The warning sounded just as she, too, was forced to jink sideways to avoid the man. She glanced down at Joule to make sure the detour hadn't impacted the cat.

As if she'd sensed Ell's regard, the cat's mental voice sounded in her head.

{Wet,} Joule complained. *{Hate the wet.}*

On her overlay, Ell could see the big feline's shadowed form high-stepping her way around puddles, head hunched beneath the drakeskin hood.

{Our destination's just up ahead,} Aviva announced, and Ell wondered if Joule had sent the complaint to the agent, as well.

They drew to a stop at a transport platform lined with vehicles and filled with people waiting to board. Aviva motioned them to a queue, just as the first bus pulled away with a wheeze and a groan.

Jonathan made a choked sound. *{**That's** our ride?}*

The kindest word Ell could think of to describe the caravan they joined was 'rustic'.

Each one had seen better days, that much was obvious. She would have been worried about radiation leakage from the small fission drives if she hadn't seen for herself that the reactors used were the modular, sealed type often seen in backwater areas such as this. They required no maintenance, were virtually tamper-proof, and had a guaranteed energy output well into the next century.

The units traded performance for safety, however, and only

provided enough juice for a conveyance such as this to crawl along. Given the rough terrain, she supposed that made sense.

The track they were following was pitted with deep grooves, carved into the rutted landscape. Vibrations from the drive shaft combined with the vehicle's lack of suspension to deliver a jarring experience.

{Hardscrabble existence,} Ell murmured.

{Keep your head down,} advised Aviva as she handed over a few strips of pastirma, a local, spiced jerky, to chew on. *{But yes, it is. Most are families who fell out of favor with the last premier, or who disagree with the current one's policies. Some have lived this meager existence for generations.}*

Ell sank her teeth into the tough, cured meat and averted her gaze, staring down at the coarse threads of the cloak she wore as she chewed. It looked homespun—an oddity throughout the settled worlds, where highly automated manufactured goods were the norm.

She glanced at Aviva when the woman resumed her narrative.

{It's not always bleak. Earn their trust, get inside their homes, and you'll often find the same kind of family dynamics we had as kids growing up. Except for the fact that they're living under the threat of death every single day.}

{Oh, is that all.} Jonathan's sardonic words had Ell twisting around to give him a warning look.

{Be careful how you judge.} Aviva's voice held censure. *{Don't think that normal, everyday life is exclusive to Coalition and Alliance worlds. People here fall in love, marry, raise families, and die, too.}*

The agent gestured outward, through windows that had lost their panes many seasons ago. *{If I were you, I'd be spending my time on this trip familiarizing myself a bit better with my surroundings instead of criticizing it. Study the savannah, get a feel for what you're going to be traveling through to get to the prison.}*

Ell saw a look of shame cross Jonathan's face before he

ducked his head and turned to look out the open window.

{You'll have to excuse Aviva,} Morrison said, his tone light. *{She's the best Human Intelligence operative I've ever seen, but part of what makes her that way is her ability to connect with the natives. It's difficult not to sympathize with the people oppressed by this regime.}*

Ell nodded her understanding, and did as Aviva suggested.

Grasslands extended as far as the eye could see, except for a faint green blush in the distance where the rainforest began. The rain had stopped half an hour ago, leaving the brownish-green terrain covered in glistening drops of dew.

She saw slow-moving shapes on the horizon. Thad must have spotted them, too.

{What kind of animal life are we going to encounter out here?} she heard him ask.

{Mostly grazing animals,} Morrison replied. *{But a few predators. One of the things those terraforming Eridu did correctly was strive to maintain a balance between predator and prey.}*

{Otherwise, the herd animals would overrun the ecosystem?} Ell guessed.

He sent a mental nod.

She shot the man a glance. *{What's the size of the predators?}*

He smiled, his eyes sliding down to where Joule's invisible form crouched at Jonathan's feet.

{Smaller cats, mainly. They're cunning—much like your Joule, I'd imagine.}

Joule chuffed at that but refrained from commenting.

{They shouldn't be too much of a problem,} he went on, *{especially with your companion along to keep them at bay. They usually avoid humans.}*

Jonathan grunted at that, and she caught the faintest whisper, sent privately to herself and Thad.

{Should have brought Pascal with us, too.}

Ell hid a grin behind a bite of jerky, anticipating Thad's response to Jonathan's mention of Joule's chiral twin.

*{Hoss, the Navy doesn't **pay** me enough to bring that beast along.}*

She knew his complaints were empty, and that, if forced, he'd admit he enjoyed his verbal sparring with the feline.

Her gaze landed thoughtfully on Thad.

This situation had brought the big Marine back into her life. She'd thought her career with the teams was behind her, and their paths unlikely to cross. Yet they'd been thrown together repeatedly over the past three years, her new career with the NCIC intersecting with Task Force Blue again and again.

Back when she'd first been with the teams, Ell had refused to admit the attraction she felt for the tall, dark-skinned man sitting in front of her. What else could she do? Fraternization was frowned upon, especially between enlisted and commissioned officers. He'd been a lieutenant, she a sergeant.

Maybe, though, after all this is over….

She turned back to the view out the windows, letting her thoughts drift away.

* * *

Two hours later, the bus rattled to a stop at a platform that was little more than a glorified shack, with a weathered sign creaking in the light breeze. Her wire's translation chip conveniently interpreted the Aka'a script for her:

Drangiana Zh'abad (town). Administrative Unit, Level Three.

Cheerful, Ell thought. *And not terribly inventive.*

"This is where we get off," Aviva said, rising to her feet and shouldering her duffel.

She moved out into the aisle, Thad following immediately after.

"Looks little more than a shantytown," Ell murmured to Thad under her breath as she stepped up behind him. "Or shanty-zh'abad, I suppose."

He nodded wordless agreement.

They stepped off onto the hard-baked dirt in front of the ramshackle building, their legs doing that funny thing that happened when the body, used to hours of constant movement, ended up on solid ground once more.

Ell ignored the lingering sensation of pitch and vibration that her nervous system insisted she still experienced, knowing it'd catch up soon enough. Instead, she turned to look in the direction Morrison pointed.

"We have a skimmer stored in a garage two blocks off the next street. It'll get us to the spot where we'll stage from. Not the best place to hole up, but it'll do."

The villagers who had followed them off the transport faded from view as they dispersed into their respective homes. Morrison motioned for them to split up once more into separate groups, like they had in Central Prefecture.

Ell joined him when he waved her forward, Jonathan falling into step on her other side. Behind them, Thad did much the same, accompanying Aviva. Joule trailed behind.

"We'll turn left at the next intersection," Morrison subvocalized. "Aviva's widening the space between our group and the two of them, just in case. Even though it's clear to the locals that we're not from around here, large groups of people tend to make them uneasy."

His words had Ell's sniper training reasserting itself—or perhaps it was a little bit of the NCIC agent in her by now, too. After so many years, it was bound to have an impact.

She kept a careful eye on their surroundings, her gaze taking in the meager dwellings, the shuttered windows, a furtive hand twitching a curtain corner aside to peer out at them. All these things combined to inform her that their passage was not going unremarked.

The smells of hot, greasy food and the sour, biting odor of whatever local brew was being served assaulted her nose as they passed by the open door of the next building—obviously the town's tavern. She kept her head firmly pointed forward, but she flicked her eyes to the establishment's dingy windows, taking quick mental snapshots of its occupants in brief, one-second glances.

She could see a handful of large forms hunched over a bar, nursing their drinks. Closer to the entrance, three more figures sat at a table, deep in conversation.

Heads turned at their passage, and Ell stiffened, her hand automatically seeking the carbyne-tipped blade she wore in a sheath strapped to the inside of her wrist.

{Don't worry,} Morrison sent. *{They think we're with a Coalition mining concern, extracting the metals found in Eridu's outer crust.}*

Jonathan jerked his head in surprise. *{I thought this planet was terraformed.}*

{It is. Or was. I won't talk about all the ways they failed, but I will say this—the planet was here before the colonists got to it, and it already had its own core, and a minimal amount of basic building blocks, cyanobacteria and the like, already in place.}

Morrison's gaze swept the dusty road ahead, and Ell saw the man squint as he looked up at the swiftly clearing sky overhead.

{What screwed the process up was actually how they misjudged the effects that tampering would have on this world's tectonic plates and the materials in the upper magma, just beneath its crust. The release of sulfuric acid was several orders of magnitude greater than they had anticipated, and not even seeding the atmosphere could counteract it.}

The agent shot her a sardonic look and added with mordant humor, *{That doesn't mean that what's bad for the colonists can't be good for business, though.}*

Ell held his glance. *{So there really is material worth mining beneath the planet's surface?}*

{Oh yes,} Morrison assured her. *{And the Akkadian Empire's only too happy to trade with privately held mining companies— for an exorbitant fee.}*

He made a small gesture with his hand, encompassing the

shantytown. *{Where do you think all these people work, and who do you think they work for? The empire entices Coalition companies here with cheap Akkadian labor, and then pockets the vast majority of the profits for itself.}*

Ell shook her head but relaxed marginally at his words.

It made sense. More, his reasoning provided a believable explanation for their presence here, and at the moment, that was all she cared about.

Morrison drew to a stop in front of the garage, and its doors slid open. He motioned them inside.

The skimmer was a sturdy one, and completely within character for the type of cover they had created.

"Where are we headed?" she asked as Jonathan opened the door for Joule to jump inside.

For answer, Morrison pushed a map over their connection.

"There's an abandoned hunter's hide five klicks away from the prison." He highlighted the spot. "It's as close as we can get without risking detection."

The scrape of footsteps had Ell whipping her head around, her hand instinctively going for the knife she had strapped to the inside of her wrist.

"It's just me," Thad's voice called softly, as if he knew she'd have a bead on him.

A second later, his shadow cleared the doorway.

Morrison brought the big Marine to speed as Aviva stepped toward the skimmer and began running an efficient check for fuel readiness and any possible tampering that might have occurred while the vessel was in storage.

Thad flung the rucksack from his shoulder, setting it down gently onto the packed dirt floor. Turning to Morrison, he looked around. "What else needs to be done here?"

The agent shook his head. "Nothing. They expect us to grab the skimmer and leave. That's the routine we've established over the past several months, so to do so today won't raise any eyebrows."

"Except for the fact that there are three strangers tagging

along with you today."

Jonathan's skeptical comment earned him another sharp look from Aviva.

"We've staged a few prospecting runs over the last week," she said in a brusque tone, motioning for them to load their gear in the back. "We brought locals with us from the city, different people each time. The people in this village are used to strange faces. Morrison and I are the only constant."

"Sounds like you've thought of everything, then." Thad wedged his duffel into a corner before taking Ell's pack from her hands.

"That's what the NSA pays us to do," Aviva pointed out, placing her hands on her hips. "And right now, they're paying us to get you to that prison. So, do you want to stand here jawing about it, or can we go?"

PART THREE: DECEIVED

INTELLIGENCE BRIEFING

AKKADIAN HOME FLEET FLAGSHIP
PORT AKKADIA
IN ORBIT ABOVE ERIDU

AS THE FIVE Geminate operatives traversed Eridu's savannah, Che Josza was busy high above the planet, attending to matters that his position demanded he oversee. Today, that meant the monthly briefing aboard a *Hendijan*-class battleship, the flagship for the Akkadian home fleet.

Hands clasped behind him, he resisted the urge to rock back on his heels as the ship's captain droned on in excruciating detail about the home fleet's readiness. An image projected onto the holoscreens displayed a panoramic image of Port Akkadia.

It was an impressive view, with more than seventy-five ships moored there. Unfortunately, the captain seemed intent upon enumerating the status of every last stars-cursed one of them.

"In addition to our carriers, destroyers, battleships, and light attack cruisers, we have almost one hundred and fifty small support vessels assigned to this complement of ships."

Che suppressed a groan. *Ancestors, please, no. If he starts in on every last attack craft....*

His expression remained fixed, while inwardly, he wondered how quickly he could break in to graciously extricate himself. Granting the citizen captain an audience with the minister of state security was a courtesy expected during Che's visit. He didn't want the man to lose face by cutting him off, but Che wasn't sure how much longer he could hold out.

"These smaller vessels range in size from large cargo transports to small pinnaces, to the Hydra Mark III and Hydra Mark IV classes, our nimble and deadliest fighters."

Che stifled a sigh and glanced over at the man standing to his left. As the leader of Home Fleet, Citizen Admiral Li's duties often conflicted with Che's visits, and so it was rare that their paths crossed.

Che caught a rare show of humor on the man's face, his lips twitching in amusement. It was an unguarded moment the man seldom showed.

Li quickly hid his half-smile behind a carefully blank face when he saw Che watching him, but then took pity on him and stepped forward. "Citizen Captain, I'm afraid the citizen minister is needed in the wardroom. Thank you for your update; I'm sure he appreciates all your hard work on behalf of the premier."

"Indeed," Che murmured as the citizen captain bowed. Che returned it with a nod.

The admiral waved a hand toward the bridge's exit. "Shall we, Citizen Minister?"

Che nodded gratefully and followed the admiral out.

From the corner of his eye, he saw a shadow disengage from the bulkhead, falling into step beside him. His Dagger's hand curled around the blade at her waist, brown eyes watchful in an expressionless face.

As if feeling the weight of his regard, her gaze skimmed his before drifting to the corridor beyond. The turning of her head set the beads woven into the braids that framed her face shifting under the ship's harsh lights.

To most, she would appear inscrutable, but Che was not most people. Years in her proximity had gifted him the ability to read her microexpressions and the subtle cues of her body. At the moment, she was relaxed. Guarded, but relaxed.

They entered the wardroom, where Citizen Agent Ahura waited to brief him. These meetings were routine, monthly in-person reports as befitted the sensitive nature of the information the intelligence officer curated.

At Che's entrance, the man looked up, moving from a command console to stand beside the room's central holotank.

"Citizen Minister Josza, sir." The man nodded respectfully.

Che thanked the citizen admiral, who bowed his way out. Dacina sealed the door, a minute dip of her head signaling that the room was now secure.

"What do you bring me today?" Che asked.

The man pressed his hand against the surface of the tank, and the star system sprang into ghostly relief between them.

"A detailed snapshot of movements around the Calabi-Yau gate at our heliopause," Ahura said. He pointed, and a small grouping of icons shuffled, like playing pieces being recalled as fresh ones were handed out.

"The garrison changed over?" Che asked, and Ahura nodded. "Any indication why?"

The man shrugged. "Scuttlebutt has it the Geminate Navy bumped up a refit. There's no unusual movement, no indication this is anything other than that."

Che hummed thoughtfully, but then nodded, motioning for the man to continue.

Unlike the citizen captain, Ahura knew the meaning of a high-level briefing. His update was concise, his words economical.

"That's it. Except... there is one more rather odd thing." The citizen intelligence officer pursed his lips in a pensive scowl. "Each flagship commander has been ordered back to Eridu for a medical exam. That's..." Ahura paused as if to check his notes, "fifteen citizen captains in all."

Che's brows lifted. "Really? When each of their ships has a fully staffed medical department?"

"I managed to obtain a copy of the orders. They clearly specify where they're to go, and who they're to see."

The intelligence officer dipped his chin, and a ping sounded over Che's wire, notifying him of an incoming file.

Bringing it up on his overlay, Che quickly scanned through its contents. The more he read, the higher his brows tried to climb.

"They've been specifically ordered to see Clint Janus?" He didn't bother tempering the incredulousness in his voice.

His words elicited an almost imperceptible sound from his Dagger.

Che's gaze shot to where she stood against the bulkhead, her body still and posture held ramrod straight. Dacina never made her presence known; when she did, it was done purposely.

She returned his gaze, expression bland, but he sensed an awareness in her stare that had not been there before.

She knows something.

Turning back to Ahura, Che drummed his fingers thoughtfully on the surface of the holographic tank and adopted a casual tone, as if this news hadn't just set off all sorts of alarms.

"Tell me. What do you think of this recall?" He used his 'teaching voice,' the tone he'd used to such great effect when he'd led the Junxun years ago.

Considering that the man before him had once been a promising student, the tactic was effective. As Che had intended, it engendered the desired response. Almost reflexively, the officer fell back into the familiar byplay of teacher and student.

The intelligence officer squinted off into the distance. After a moment, he said, "It's been a standard year and a half since we were shut out of the Proxima Badlands. I'd say that we managed to salvage enough research from the installation An-Yang shut down to revive that program."

Che made an encouraging noise, rolling his hand in a silent order for the man to continue.

Ahura, fortified by Che's response, began to warm to the idea. "Best guess? We now have a viable bioweapon, and the citizen captains are being recalled so they can be inoculated against it."

As guesses went, it was a good one. An educated one. It showed that Che had chosen well when placing Ahura as chief intelligence officer over the fleet. It was even possible the man was correct.

But Che's gut was telling him otherwise.

Regardless, it was neither Ahura's burden nor his responsibility to figure out what was really going on between Janus and Dent.

"It's possible," Che said, pitching the tone of his voice to suggest that exact thing, while officially refusing to acknowledge it.

Not wanting to encourage Ahura to get himself into trouble by pursuing this any further, Che decided the best course was to abandon the topic.

"What other news do you have for me?"

Ahura straightened, dragging his attention back to the briefing. "That's about it, sir. Things have been quiet since the premier's inauguration. The Coalition and the Alliance both seem to have backed off."

"What of the standing orders to the fleet?"

The officer frowned. "Premier Dent has been, somewhat... less aggressive than his predecessor. Fleet-wide, we've been ordered to play nice with the garrison at the gate. Same with the border we share with Khufu. To be honest, there are a lot of citizen captains who have grown weary of their patrols."

"Is it becoming a morale problem?"

The man shook his head. "Not yet, though they wouldn't say no to a little action."

Che cracked a smile at that. "Understandable. I'll see what I can do, talk to Citizen Minister Hatami about ways to liven things up a bit."

Warren Hatami was Akkadia's minister of defense, a solid man, if a little lacking in creativity.

Che pushed away from the holotank. "Excellent work, as usual. I'm due planetside for a briefing soon. If there's nothing else, I'll leave you to it."

Ahura nodded. "I'll see you next month, sir."

Che responded with a nod of his own.

I hope you do, Ahura. I hope you do. Who knows what will transpire before then.

* * *

As they exited the wardroom and headed for the shuttle bay, Dacina remained quiet, but Che could see tension radiating from her shoulders. Something was wrong, and he needed to find out what it was.

It wasn't until they were ensconced in their ship, with the pinnace's SI engaged to return them to the planet's surface, that he felt comfortable broaching the topic.

Che enacted full security protocols before turning to face his Dagger.

"I saw your reaction back there, when he mentioned the recall."

He waited. Finally, she stirred.

"You know I have been working to discover what was discussed between Janus and the premier."

Che's brows drew down. "You think this is part of that."

"I do. I have my suspicions as to why, but I need time to gain proof before presenting it to you."

He considered her words, and then nodded. "Very well."

He reached for the ship's controls, but halted when her hand fell on his arm.

"The Garza clone. He has been in play for a week now, yes?"

Che nodded, surprised at her change of topic.

"His actions—the directors he was forced to appoint, under Premier Dent's orders... they are clearly out of character for him," she hedged.

Once more, Che nodded.

"Clint Janus killed the chiral agent in front of Doctor Travis and Captain Case, but not before he spoke to them. We must assume the Alliance now knows we have the technology to chirally clone humans. They will seek confirmation of this soon."

Her words puzzled him.

"None of this is news."

"Correct. Yet sometimes patterns can only be seen when looking back at where they began to form."

Che felt a brief stirring of annoyance. "What are you trying to say, Dacina?"

The Dagger's eyes burned with a dark intensity. "I made a promise to you, my General, eighteen months ago."

Che knew she was referring to the incident on Hawking, where she'd taken matters into her own hands. She'd given up the location of the assault team to the Geminate—a team he'd been tasked to lead. And then, she'd covered for him, claiming he'd ordered her actions.

Her words were all that had saved him from death—or worse—at Asher Dent's hands.

"I do not regret the actions I took then, and I would do the same again," she assured him stoically. "It saved your life, and there was no time to warn you. But I gave you my word that I would not act again without your consent."

She bowed, and though seated, it was clear by the accompanying gesture that it was the bow of subservience. "I require that consent now."

A chill coursed down Che's spine.

"Exactly what action do you feel you need to take?"

"The Alliance's intelligence network is convinced we have their prime minister. They are coming for him."

Che sat back, rubbing his chin thoughtfully. This had always been a possibility, something he and Dent had discussed. It was why the roster guarding the Shar-Kali Facility had been doubled.

Dacina wasn't done.

"The warden running Shar-Kali has made a tactical error."

Her words mystified him somewhat; they were almost non-sequitur. Almost... but not quite. "And what would that be?"

"The former minister of state security is also a resident there. The two are cellmates."

Che blinked, shocked that someone at Shar-Kali had been so slack.

"Are you telling me that the warden of that prison has placed Rin Zhou Enlai in the same cell as Raphael Garza? And he didn't think that placing two high-value prisoners together might be cause for concern?"

A fluid movement suggested a shrug. "I cannot comment on that. It is as much a possibility that the guards were bribed to arrange such a thing by loyalists as it is laziness on the part of the warden."

Her words were vague, and they began to annoy him.

"Loyalists? To Rin Zhou?" Che heard the sharpness in his own voice.

Dacina nodded. "She has offered to help Garza escape. For a price."

Che had a feeling he wasn't going to like what she said next. "What would that be?"

"He is to assist her in a coup."

Dacina held up a hand, forestalling his nascent protest.

"My informants tell me that Enlai's loyalists are strong, but would most likely fail in this attempt without assistance. Even if she secures Garza's support, it will do her no good. He's a prisoner himself. His hands are tied."

Che shook his head. "Not necessarily. If Rin Zhou's network is as robust as you say, she could arrange to have the Alliance's infiltration team meet with Garza."

Dacina's expression remained inscrutable. "The Geminate do not involve themselves with the politics of other star nations. They will not aid the overthrow of a sitting government."

Che smiled thinly and shook his head. "Are you willing to bet the empire on that?"

RECON

Hohen Savannah
Eridu, Akkadia

THE SKIMMER AVIVA piloted stopped under the shade of a grove of massive umbrella trees, their intertwined canopies spreading wide above gnarled, bent trunks.

"This is it," Morrison announced from the front passenger seat, pointing to a pile of metal tucked up against the trunk of the largest tree.

Calling it a hide seemed a bit generous, in Jonathan's opinion. The structure was little more than four corrugated metal walls listing drunkenly to one side, held together by an equally weathered corrugated metal roof.

Jonathan opened the skimmer's passenger door, and Joule leapt outside, the black panther-like animal's ears flicking in annoyance as leftover droplets of rain fell sporadically from the canopy of leaves overhead.

The humans followed her out, each grabbing a load from the back. When Jonathan stepped into the hide, he dropped his pack at the base of the nearest wall.

It wasn't much to look at, and its interior wasn't any better, boasting only two pieces of furniture: a cot, and a low table that ran the length of one corrugated wall.

Joule padded over to the corner where an animal had left a smelly pile of refuse. After one disdainful sniff, the big cat began to prowl along the perimeter, head lifted and mouth slightly open as she scented the air.

{No human smell, other than theirs.} The cat's head swung around to indicate Morrison and Aviva.

"Any other animals we need to worry about?" Jonathan asked.

Joule gave a sneeze. *{Scaly-crawlers. Naked rats. Taste bad. Too stringy. Dogs with bad breath.}*

"Bad—" Thad turned to regard the midnight-furred animal and then pinned Jonathan with a look. "Wanna translate that for me, hoss?"

It was Aviva who replied. "I'm guessing she's referring to lizards, mole rats, and... hyenas?" Amusement laced her voice. "By the sound of it, she's not impressed."

"How far are we from the prison?" Jonathan asked.

Morrison waved a hand. "Five klicks that way." He squinted up into the sky. "Shouldn't have to worry about any more rain, which ought to make your furry friend happy."

Jonathan nodded.

"What about the skimmer?" Thad asked.

"We can't hide its heat signature, so we don't bother to try. That's why he's not wearing stealth." Aviva motioned to her partner. "I'll stay behind in the hide as your contact, while—"

"While *I'm* your alibi," Morrison cut in. He pointed. "The mine shaft's about three klicks west of us. Prison security monitoring the area might be a bit surprised to see only one heat signature leaving the hide, but we've varied the number of people in our party enough over the last several weeks to hopefully avert suspicion."

"Let's get started." Aviva began rummaging through the box she'd placed on the table when she came in.

"Okay then." Thad searched through the team's supplies and

rose with a camper's shovel in his hand. Clapping Jonathan on the shoulder, he held it out to him and motioned to the smelly pile. "New guy on an op gets latrine duty. Have at it, *ami*."

Jonathan shot Thad a glare he hoped promised retribution if he ever had the Marine at his mercy in a small aircraft.

Snatching the shovel out of the other man's hand, he stalked toward the offending clump of manure. With a heavy sigh that turned into a cough when he caught a good whiff of the stuff he was to remove, he set himself to the onerous task.

When he stepped back inside, Jonathan heard Aviva instructing Thad and Ell on the placement of security devices around the hide's perimeter.

"With the active sweeps the prison conducts, all we can afford are passive recon sensors around the perimeter," the agent explained, handing them each a stack of the tech. "Anything else will set off an alarm."

Thad and Ell nodded and disappeared to set out the sensors.

Turning to the two agents, Jonathan spread out his hands. "Anything else I can do to help?"

From where he was seated on the cot, Morrison shook his head. "We keep things pretty simple out of necessity. The less complex it is, the less there is to go wrong.

"Speaking of which, it's about time I headed out to check the mine. I'll be sure to move about plenty, keep their eyes off you as best I can." He stood just as Thad and Ell reentered, and sent the Marine a questioning look. "Will two hours be long enough?"

Thad glanced at Ell and then Jonathan before nodding at Morrison. "We'll make it work." The Marine captain turned in a circle, and then shot Jonathan a questioning look. "Where's Joule?"

He hooked a thumb outside. "She's familiarizing herself with the area."

"Call her back. It's time to send her to the shaft."

Jonathan nodded, and a few minutes later, the cat came loping toward them.

He stepped forward and dropped to one knee as she came to a stop. Taking her head between his palms, Jonathan stared into the cat's big green eyes. "Be careful out there. Don't take any chances. If you spot any humans, behave exactly as one of your wild siblings would, and get the heck out of Dodge."

Joule reared her head, eyes narrowing in irritation. *{Don't know Dodge. Humans show up, I leave. Not Pascal. Not stupid, either.}*

"Not saying you are, just making a point."

The cat brought her paw up and rested it on Jonathan's knee. *{You want point?}*

He felt her claws flex, the tips piercing his pant leg ever so slightly.

"Okay, okay! I get it," he said hastily. "Retract the claws already. I apologize for ever questioning you."

The cat made a noise Jonathan swore sounded satisfied, chuffing lightly as she sat back on her haunches.

{I wear that?} She nosed at Jonathan's hands.

He looked down at the black collar he held. "Yes," he said, then reached around and fastened it behind her scruff. It blended in seamlessly with her black fur.

Evenly spaced around the accessory's length were several holorecorders that had been harvested from a set of surveillance drones. These would transmit back to the hide, allowing the team to see what Joule saw.

"Collar in place." Jonathan stepped back, looking questioningly at Thad, who gave him a thumbs-up.

"Signal's five by five."

"Alright then. Looks like you're good to go," he told the animal, ruffling the fur behind her ear. "Just... stay away from humans, and don't pick any fights. It's their territory, you're just a guest here."

If the cat were capable of rolling its eyes, he was pretty sure Joule would be doing it about now.

{Not Pascal,} she reminded him once again. *{Pascal is punk.}*

Thad chuckled. "Pascal the punk. I like it."

{I tell him you said that.}

A look of alarm crossed Thad's face, and he rapidly shook his head. "No need to do that. We'll just keep that between ourselves, okay, *cher*?"

*{Not share. Nothing **to** share.}* Joule's head swung to stare pointedly at Thad, her eyes narrowing into slits. *{Pascal not share any of his steaks.}*

Thad groaned. "I knew it. I *knew* I wasn't getting out of this without being blackmailed. Damn cats."

Joule's jaw dropped, fangs flashing as the big animal gave the feline version of a grin. *{Human not think fast as cat.}*

Jonathan decided now would be a good time to get things back on track. He turned to Joule. "Are you ready to go?"

The big cat lifted her head and sneezed once. *{Been ready. Back soon.}*

With that, she slipped off into the savannah.

* * *

They followed the cat's progress visually as she slid between clumps of switchgrass, bluestem, and thatch. With its angle so low to the ground, the feed from the cameras gave the impression of great speed as the panther-like animal raced through the grasses.

The view became dizzying at times, with the cat leaping over bushes, skidding around rocky promontories, and dodging trees. Thad had to close his eyes more than once.

"Damn cat," he muttered, but there was no heat in his voice.

"Look at how fast she's going. Won't that be a red flag?" Ell asked.

The data coming from the cameras around her neck showed Joule's pace topping out at thirty kilometers per hour.

Aviva shook her head. "I've seen leopards chasing down prey. They easily reach fifty kilometers an hour."

Thad cocked a brow at the agent. "Think she's on their radar already?"

"Oh, you can be sure of it. But they're used to the wildlife around here, so they'll dismiss her as soon as they identify what she is." She sent a sideways look Jonathan's way. "Good training, by the way. Her behavior's very natural; it won't raise suspicion."

Jonathan nodded but refrained from any further comment.

{Okay, am here.} Joule's mental voice cut into the video feed as the cat slowed to a walk.

Ahead, they could see a round patch of switchgrass, rising a little more than a meter tall. The cat paused to sniff around the base of the nearest clump.

"Too uniform to be natural," Ell murmured, and Aviva nodded.

"They planted that grass to cover the shaft."

The recorders gave them a good view of the smooth metal column, rising almost to the tops of the stalks. Joule lifted her head and scented the air before pacing carefully around its circumference.

{Humans here hours ago.}

"They patrol the area physically twice a day, weather permitting," Aviva explained. "In the morning, and just before sunset."

"What about SIs?" Thad asked as Joule reared up onto her hind legs and hooked her front paws around its rim.

The agent bent down, reaching into one of the bags. Thad heard the slight clink of metal, and when she held out a hand, he saw she had several Bravo Charlies resting in her palm.

He took a pair from her, and Ell did the same.

"Breaching canisters, updated with the prison's latest security routines."

Thad pocketed the BCs in his tac vest with a nod of thanks. "And the SIs?" he repeated.

Aviva smiled mysteriously. "They'll already be offline when you infiltrate."

The sound of nails scraping against metal brought his attention back to the video feed.

"Careful," Jonathan warned, both audibly and directly to the cat via their connection. "Don't give them a reason to think you're too interested in that."

The cat made a sound halfway between a chuff and a grunt. *{Metal stuck. Won't come loose.}*

Her words confused Thad until she leaned further in, and he could see a grate covering the top.

"That grate's not your problem, kitty," he told her. "Just give us a quick look down in there, and then back away."

Joule obligingly stretched to her full height and then peered down. They could hear sniffing sounds as the feline made her own scent study of the human-made artifact.

The recorders in her collar had plenty of time to capture the view inside, and Aviva cycled them through the full EM spectrum before nodding in satisfaction.

"Okay, we got what we need. Get out of there," Jonathan instructed the hunting cat.

Joule gave another chuff and pushed herself off the grill, landing lightly on the ground.

They heard the sound of claws scratching against dirt, and then the sound of liquid hitting metal.

Ell turned to Jonathan, one brow lifting. "Did she just *pee* on it?"

Joule's tone managed to sound offended. *{You **said** act natural.}*

"That's fine, just fine," Jonathan said hastily, laughter in his voice. "Move on. Keep scouting around, see what else you can find, and then make your way back here."

Another chuff was their only response.

Aviva unfolded a flat, 2-D display and spread it out on the cot. The simple low-tech device had minimal energy requirements, rendering it untraceable. Triggering it on, she accessed the recording Joule had captured.

"Here's what she saw."

The view shifted, zooming past the grate as the big cat leaned forward and peered down inside.

"Enhancing," Aviva said.

Details appeared over the top of the image. It measured a little more than a meter in diameter, and Thad could see handrails welded to one side. Between them, slight indentations in the metal formed rungs, the toeholds roughened for traction.

"Look," Ell pointed to the center, where something rotated in the distance. "Ventilation fan," she guessed.

Aviva nodded her agreement. "You'll have to use a breaching canister on its motor, too."

"Agreed," Thad murmured. "Any idea what's beyond it?"

Aviva flipped the image over to a diagram she'd acquired of the prison. "According to this, that shaft leads directly into environmental."

Thad scrubbed at the stubble of his jaw with the flat of his hand, eyeing the 2-D image thoughtfully. He nodded. "We can work with that." Turning to Ell, he asked, "Ready to go spring a prisoner, *cher*?"

DAGGER'S DOZEN

Junxun Training Center
Central Prefecture
Eridu, Akkadia

THE JUNXUN CADET school was a long-standing fixture within Central Prefecture. The Dagger had lived within its walls years ago, as a raw recruit. Now, she studied its austere lines as she approached its rear entrance.

These were the killing fields. The sparring arena had earned its moniker in the usual way—via the spilled blood of students not fast enough to dodge the deadly blade.

A set of sturdy metal stairs affixed to the back of the building led up to the observation platform, where instructors stood weighing the merits of each pupil's prowess. As Dacina mounted them, she stepped firmly, deliberately, her boots heralding her arrival. Their tread's open weave lent her footsteps a hollow, bell-like ring, an audible warning to those above that someone approached.

Another individual had preceded her up these steps. The woman she'd come to meet stood at the forward end of the observation deck, resting her hands on the railing as she looked out on the field. Below her, the current crop of Junxun candidates sparred.

The institute's headmistress was someone Dacina knew well. Citizen General Serae Etesav had progressed through the cadre two classes behind her own. The woman excelled in both spycraft and close-quarters combat.

Rather than following Dacina into the ranks of the Tèzhǒng, it had been decided that Serae's skills were best used elsewhere. She'd been ordered to pursue the path of an officer, regardless of what her personal preferences were.

Serae knew how to play the game, though, and the woman swiftly rose within the echelon. It had been a few years since the two women had crossed paths, and yet the Dagger knew Serae's skills remained honed to a fine edge.

She also knew, thanks to her contacts within the loyalist group, that Serae held no love for Asher Dent.

The other woman pressed a button set into the railing as Dacina came to a stop beside her, and an isolation screen sprang into place.

It wasn't unusual to invoke such screens at the academy; they enabled drill instructors to discuss the progress of their students below. Over the years, they had also been used to mask conversations between ambitious officers, seeking to elevate themselves.

Today, it could be argued that this one cloaked talk of treason.

{How many warriors do you need?} asked Serae.

{A squadron, no more.} Dacina turned, allowing her gaze to follow the progress of the cadet who had just been defeated as he was assisted off the field, clutching a bloodied arm.

The casual head turn also allowed her to make brief eye contact with Serae. *{They must hold your highest confidence, and unwavering loyalty.}*

{Understood.}

The Dagger caught the slightest headshake from the other woman, and the flavor of her tone turned bitter with her next words.

{Political infighting, assassination, uprisings. None of this is particularly new to the Akkadian people. But never would I have thought I would be at the forefront of such an endeavor.}

*{You know **nothing**.}* Dacina's voice cut her off sharply. *{It is safer that way. The less you know, the less you can give up should we fail.}*

Serae sent Dacina a world-wise look. *{Let me help. There are packets that will need to be delivered. Proof you'll need to present. I can take care of that for you.}*

After a moment's hesitation, Dacina acknowledged this with a silent nod.

A moment later, an alert flashed on her overlay, signifying that a file awaited. She granted permission for it to download onto the data partition of the implant embedded inside her head.

She stared at its icon a moment, knowing that this was the first of many steps of trust she must take. Opening the file could trigger a cascade that would lead to brain death, if she had made an error in judgment and Serae was not the Loyalist she believed her to be.

On a silent inhale, she opened the file. The relieved breath that she exhaled was featherlight, but no less intense despite the fact it was hidden.

On her overlay were displayed twelve names.

{The Dagger's Dozen,} Serae's voice sounded inside her head with a dark chuckle.

Dacina lifted a brow. *{You make that sound as if it holds a special meaning.}*

{Only that your reputation precedes you. They will be honored to hold that title.}

Abruptly, Serae pushed away from the railing. *{The necessary forms have been drawn up, and we'll doctor the records after the fact. Officially, they will show these men and women were transferred over to serve a tour with the prison guard. Unofficially, they report only to you.}*

Dacina inclined her head in thanks. *{You gave them the code to contact me once they arrive at Shar-Kali?}*

The slightest lift of her head was the headmistress' response. *{They will be ready when you arrive.}*

Dacina straightened. She had a rendezvous with Rin Zhou to keep; a meeting she dare not miss. She turned to go, but stopped when Serae faced her.

{May these twelve warriors be the weapon you wield to free us from the abomination.}

The words, spoken so formally, struck a chord deep within Dacina.

She turned to fully face Serae. Folding her hands at her midriff, one atop the other, she bowed formally over them. *{The People are in your debt.}*

With that, she left.

PROPOSAL

Minister's Office
Ministry of State Security
Eridu, Akkadia

"You did *what?!?*" Che's pacing abruptly halted as he turned to stare incredulously at the assassin standing silently against the dark wood paneling of his office.

As had become custom, they'd instituted an informal version of a SCIF each time they conversed. The first level cut them off from all communication; the second fed innocuous yet believable conversation to any listening devices that might be pointed in the direction of his office.

Che was very glad for those precautions today; what his Dagger had done was nothing short of treason. Certainly, he could see no pathway through that would lead to anything less than his own death.

He dragged a hand roughly through his hair. "You actually *spoke* to Rin Zhou about this?"

She stared at him, eyes drilling into his, willing him to make connections that his mind balked at.

"Are you..." He shook his head. "Are you *really* suggesting that I support a revolution? Have you forgotten so quickly that I am the sole reason Rin Zhou Enlai is in prison in the first place?"

Dacina shifted. For her, the subtle movement was the equivalent of an impatient shout. "I explained to her that you hold no love for the man, and that you are committed to his downfall."

Che made a rude sound. "There is no reality I can conceive of where Rin Zhou would allow me to live."

"There is," Dacina corrected him. "I have been working the channels. If we can deliver Geminate support to Enlai in our bid to install her as premier, unseating Asher Dent, then your position will remain unchanged."

The Dagger leaned forward as Che began to shake his head. Her eyes held a rare pleading. "Hear me out. I believe this will sway you." Expression grave, she reached out a hand.

Bemused, Che stretched out his own to meet hers, but when she uncurled her fingers, there was nothing in her palm for him to retrieve.

He began to withdraw, but Dacina's strong fingers latched around his, initiating a secured peer-to-peer connection.

{This information is too sensitive to transfer over a wireless connection,} she insisted in his mind. *{Too sensitive to speak aloud.}*

A file transferred over their connection.

{I found this on the system Clint Janus had installed inside his lab.}

Che shot her a sharp glance.

He scanned the file once, quickly, and felt his face pale.

Swallowing hard, he scanned the document a second time, reading more thoroughly.

He speared her with a hard look. *{And you're **certain** of this? There can be no mistake.}*

The Dagger shook her head. *{No mistake. I overheard his conversation with the premier myself. I saw the files. I saw the **vials.**}*

Alarm shot through Che at her admission. If she'd been caught, not only would her life be forfeit, but his as well. Everyone high-up within the government knew her to be his shadow.

"You were careful?" he pressed.

His words came out sharper than he'd intended. When her expression shifted subtly, he realized he had just offended the assassin.

Of course she'd been careful. She always was.

{Dent is ordering clones of all these military men?} he summated. *{Chiral clones? To what purpose?}*

Now her expression held a hint of sardonic amusement. It was as close as she would ever come to saying, *"Exactly what you think it means."*

{Obelus is far more ambitious than Dent ever let on,} she hinted.

{He plans to control the entire corps?} Che guessed. *{All our military might?}*

The thought was staggering.

The Dagger stared unblinkingly back. *{There is more.}*

Her words snapped his attention from the file displayed on his overlay and back to her.

{What?} he demanded.

A second file appeared beside the first.

With some apprehension, Che toggled it open. The names listed in the document leapt out at him—his own among them. The plan was so daring, so devious, he could hardly wrap his brain around it.

He heard Dacina's next words as if from a distance.

{Obelus is far more insidious than controlling our adversaries' governments. He will accept nothing less than complete control over his own people. If he succeeds, he will become unstoppable.}

{And Rin Zhou knows all this?}

Dacina dipped her head. *{She does. She has a core group of loyal followers ready to act on her behalf.}*

"This is suicide…" Che muttered aloud. "You realize that,

don't you?"
    "It is suicide if we don't."

COMMITMENT

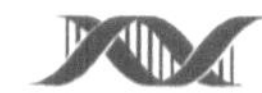

SHAR-KALI CORRECTIONAL FACILITY
AND REEDUCATION CENTER
AKSU DESERT

"PRIME MINISTER GARZA, I invoke the Responsibility to Protect Doctrine."

Rin Zhou's words had Raphael jerking his head around.

After her threat to expose the special forces teams, they'd fallen into a stiff silence. Apparently, that had now come to an end.

He figured she'd try again to manipulate him. But this?

Raphael stared at the woman as if she'd lost her mind. "You want to invoke the *Responsibility to Protect Doctrine*?"

"Yes." The woman stood, unruffled. "It is a moral obligation held by every civilization within the broader interstellar community. Should a star nation—"

"I know what the damn doctrine states," the prime minister snapped, but the woman continued, talking over him.

"Should a star nation fail in its responsibility to protect its own people, either through inability or lack of willingness to do so, then the greater interstellar community is duty-bound to step in," Rin Zhou finished.

"That doctrine has never once been invoked."

"I beg to differ."

The former minister leaned forward, her expression predatory. "Pre-diaspora, in the late twentieth century, in Kosovo. In the twenty-first century, in the Ivory Coast and Libya. In the late twenty-second century, it was invoked at the Europa colony, and in the early twenty-third—"

"Enough! I don't need a history lesson." Raphael shook his head, laughing humorlessly as he began to pace. "Oh, this is rich, coming from you. Especially after the bioterror weapon you tried to unleash at the Defense Summit."

Rin Zhou wisely kept silent.

Raphael continued to pace.

Do it.

José's voice sounded inside his head, causing him to break his stride.

*She's invoking that damn doctrine as a way to get us to support her coup. We don't **fund** coups. It goes against Alliance policy.* Raphael took a seat on his cot and buried his head in his hands.

His doppelganger sighed. *Well, we aren't exactly funding it. We'll be fighting it.*

Same difference, Raphael snarled.

It's either that, or... His mirror twin hesitated. *Or deny them control over **our** nation.*

You're talking suicide.

Forcing them to eliminate us, corrected José.

Same difference.

Raphael's gut clenched. He wasn't the type of man to shy away from the ultimate sacrifice, but he hated that such a decision might also doom three innocents. His wife. His twin daughters, who had yet to truly experience all life had to offer.

José's voice cut in again. *You saw how I tried to reach out to Cutter at the Founder's Cup dinner. It was impossible. They have me sewn up so tight, we'll never be free. Unless....*

Raphael's jaw clenched. *Unless we give her what she's asking for,* he finished.

His twin sent a mental nod. *She's right, you know. We can't allow Dent to get away with this, to enslave others like he did to us.*

Hell, you and I know she's the lesser evil, but that doesn't give us the right to commit the Alliance to this course, Raphael pointed out.

Between the doctrine she invoked and what Dent has done to us, I think we could make a case that the man presents a clear and present danger to the settled worlds. I seriously doubt you'll get push-back from Cutter.

José was making a compelling argument, but Raphael forced himself to step back and play devil's advocate.

What about the governor-general? She has a responsibility to the people. This could have long-reaching repercussions. It could impact our relationship with the Coalition of Worlds for years to come.

There was a pause from the other end. When José returned, his mental tone held a deep weariness.

Do you really think any one of those governments wouldn't support this, once they learn the truth? For that matter, do you think Asher Dent will be satisfied with just one star nation, once he's turned the Alliance into his puppet regime?

Raphael closed his eyes. *Dear god, we're really doing this, aren't we?* He opened them and shifted his gaze back to Rin Zhou, giving a slight nod. "All right. You have a deal."

SURPRISE INSPECTION

SHAR-KALI CORRECTIONAL FACILITY
AND REEDUCATION CENTER
AKSU DESERT

AFTER THE DAGGER'S shocking revelation, Che knew time was their worst enemy. If this plan had any chance for success, they had to act fast. Which was why, less than an hour later, he found himself staring out a skimmer's windscreen at clumps of switchgrass as they sped toward the prison.

On an inhale, he turned to look over at the Dagger, who was piloting the transport with a practiced hand.

"Everything is in place? You're certain this will work?"

Dacina's dark eyes shifted briefly to him. "It is, and I am. Do not worry, my General. All will go as planned."

"How do you know the Alliance has sent in a special forces team, when no whisper of this has reached my ears?" Che persisted.

"Channels," was all she said.

"This is bothersome," Che muttered. "I'm the minister of state security. If the leader of the intelligence branch for the entire Akkadian Empire doesn't know about this, then what else is being kept from me?"

"I told you; I intercepted it before it could go through regular agencies in order to prevent the premier's faithful from learning about it."

She spared him another glance. "At the moment, we stand as counter-faction to the premier's faction. It would be a mistake to allow sensitive information to pass through standard means, despite their level of encryption. If the special forces team we plan to partner with ends up at the mercy of Asher Dent, we fail… and Akkadia falls."

Her logic, as always, was impeccable.

"He would just as soon see them cloned and put back into play, the same as Garza," Che murmured, acknowledging her truth. "I should have thought of that myself."

Suddenly, he felt weary, even a bit inept.

"You've been busy keeping them occupied so that no one suspects," she reminded him.

It was true. In order to bolster the appearance of his loyalty to Dent, Che had ordered Tèzhǒng operatives to attempt to obtain Micah Case and Samantha Travis.

In addition, he'd proposed similar acquisitions inside various other planetary governments, starting with the Commonwealth of Ganymede, and moving on to the Democratic Free States of Mars. As Class-A worlds, both were on the priority list that Dent had approved.

He'd also suggested to the premier the possibility of forays into Class-B space, but Dent had demurred, wanting to see progress from the bigger fish before they went any farther afield. So Che had backed off.

It was a fine line he danced between convincing the premier of his complete loyalty, and raising the man's suspicions. Asher Dent had a very finely honed BS meter. Che had no intention of underestimating the man.

His thoughts returned to the present, and he pushed his concerns behind him as the Dagger slowed the shuttle, transmitting the security signal that would allow them access to the Shar-Kali Correctional Facility. The massive hangar doors began to slide open, tilting up slightly so as to shed the sand that had been deposited by the winds.

"As our esteemed opponents in the Geminate star system would say," Che murmured, " 'it's showtime.' "

* * *

The lab that had been built to accommodate Clint Janus was oddly familiar to Che, and he realized abruptly why that was; Janus had recreated the laboratory where he'd served undercover as the assistant to the Geminate Navy's chief scientist.

Che glanced over at Dacina and caught her faint nod, confirming his guess.

She would know; he'd dispatched her to that same facility three years earlier, to keep watch over Janus as the man obtained samples and stole Alliance research. She had then sent him footage of the facility in her reports.

The Dagger had destroyed the lab when she'd blown up deGrasse Torus—yet here it stood, once again.

Che circled the lab slowly, examining every instrument as he awaited Clint Janus's arrival. He paused when he came to an alcove at the back of the laboratory, where an immense piece of equipment stood.

The machine in question had an arm that hung ponderously out from its isocenter, the gantry that held it in place able to rotate freely on all three axes. The indentation perfectly positioned beneath it appeared to be fully retracted.

Beneath the unit, which held the very scientific title of 'Polarized DBC 3-D Prototype B,' was a well of bioink, suspended in a tank of hydrogel.

At its core, the machine housed a digital-to-biological converter capable of printing complex biological material from diagrams of detailed molecular structures. However, before the program could begin, the bioink reservoir would first be infused with stem cells, harvested from a preselected host. Then the two-stage process would commence.

First, a single molecule was printed using a method that produced high-fidelity structures, rapidly and continuously. The molecule was then sent through an adaptive optical centrifuge that used short pulses of linearly polarized lasers to induce a highly excited, specific rotational state. Only then did the machine send the molecule to the second stage, the more complex printing of organic structures like organs and tissue.

The result was a perfect, chiral reproduction of the original.

"So... this is where he prints his chiral clones."

Dacina nodded. "It is."

They both turned at the sound of footsteps approaching. The doors slid open, admitting the man Che had come to see.

He felt an irrational urge to laugh at the look of utter surprise that crossed Janus's face when he realized who was standing inside his laboratory.

"Cit– Citizen Minister," the scientist stuttered, stumbling to a halt. Janus's eyes flickered to the left, and his face turned noticeably whiter when he took in the identity of the woman by Che's side. The man swallowed hard, his Adam's Apple bobbing up and down.

Janus jerked his eyes back over to Che. "What can I do for you, Citizen Minister?" His words were faint.

The man's visceral reaction to the Dagger was too much; Che allowed his amusement to show.

With a smile, he gestured expansively to the room. "You can give me a tour, Citizen Doctor."

"I was unaware one had been scheduled," Janus said after a beat, his gaze shifting from uncomfortable to crafty.

That caught Che's attention.

{Observe the look in his eyes,} he told Dacina.

She made a noise that sounded a bit like a mental hum. *{He believes he knows something you don't.}*

Che clasped his hands at the small of his back and began to

pace slowly, his gaze casting about casually as if perusing various items in the room.

"Well, it wouldn't be a surprise inspection if I let you know about it ahead of time, now would it?"

The Dagger shifted, as planned, drawing a flinch from Janus.

Che glanced over at her as if only just now recalling her presence. "*Ahh.*" He breathed the word, turning back to Janus with a bland smile. "I seem to have forgotten the unpleasantness you experienced at the hands of my tool here. Allow me to put you at ease."

He turned to Dacina and nodded. "You are dismissed."

The Dagger drew herself up and gave a bow of deep respect. "Citizen Minister, I live to serve."

With military precision, she pivoted and marched out the door.

Phase one complete, Che thought. *The rest is up to her. Now all I have to do is keep this arrogant, self-important prick occupied.*

INSERTION

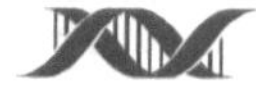

SHAR-KALI CORRECTIONAL FACILITY
AND REEDUCATION CENTER
AKSU DESERT

IT TOOK THAD, Jonathan, and Ell about half an hour to trace Joule's steps to the shaft. They'd stopped once, hunkering down in the tall grasses, when a skimmer went speeding by. It disappeared in the direction of the prison, causing Thad to risk pinging Aviva.

{*Any idea who that might be?*}

{ *We tracked them to the prison hangar. Sometimes they get special deliveries. No indication you were spotted.*}

Thad motioned for the trio to continue. When they arrived, Jonathan spotted the big cat hidden beneath the sweep of a sand-raisin bush.

She stared unblinkingly out at them from deep within its dense foliage, her pelt blending in with the shadows that had grown deeper as dusk neared.

Jonathan knelt beside the bush, reaching in to retrieve the cameras strung about her neck, while Thad and Ell continued on to the shaft.

Thad could see the grille that rested at its lip, patterned in long, parallel lines that looked just wide enough for him to insert his fingers between.

He dipped into his tactical vest, withdrew one of the Bravo Charlies that Aviva had given them, and slapped the nano package onto the grate.

He and Ell both tensed, waiting for some indication that an alarm had been tripped.

Silence greeted them. After a few seconds had passed, Thad felt comfortable enough to drop a surveillance microdrone inside.

The fact that its signal did not immediately cut off once it disappeared from sight suggested the BC was functioning as Aviva had promised.

{Looks like her contact inside the ministry came through. I think it's safe to proceed. Removing the grate.}

Thad pulled on the cover and cursed softly as he realized he'd sorely misjudged its mass. With a silent "*oof,*" he wrenched up on the metal plate, putting his back into it.

As the rounded metal plate began to swing upward, Ell stepped in, lending her strength to the task.

{That's going to be fun to lift from inside.} Her mental voice was strained as they muscled the hinged lid to its upright position.

{Let's just hope we're not in a hurry on our way back up. You ready?}

For answer, she levered herself over the side, hooking her toes into the shallow indentations that served as rungs. He could see her silhouetted form send him a quick glance before she grabbed the railings and began to ease her way down.

Thad looked over to where Jonathan stood, one hand placed on Joule's head.

{We'll stay close by,} the pilot assured him.

The Marine nodded and then pressed a ball of ActiveFiber against the metal rim. When he pulled his hand away, a small amount of the material remained adhered to the frame, while the rest stuck to the palm of his glove. A thin fiber communications line extruded between the two, spooling out behind him as he turned to follow Ell.

He spared Jonathan one last look. *{I'll check back in at the top of the hour. Stay hidden until it's time to connect to the fiber.}*

{Copy.}

Thad saw Jonathan lift a hand right before he moved out of sight.

{I'm at the fan,} Ell called from below.

Thad cycled his optics to night vision, craning his neck until he could see the slow turn of blades beneath him. It spanned the full diameter of the metal cylinder, windmilling at a stately pace.

He kept his eyes on Ell as he descended. His climb was mainly done by feel, toes scraping the sides until they found purchase at the next indentation. As he lowered himself rung by rung, Ell's shadowed figure leaned forward to place a second Bravo Charlie onto the center of the motor.

The breaching canister's blinking light flashed from red to green just as he came to a stop immediately above her. He heard a low thrumming cut off, and watched as the blades feathered to a stop.

Ell's silhouette turned to look up at him, and he gave her a nod.

{After you, cher.*}*

It was a much tighter fit for his broad shoulders to squeeze through than for the former sniper's lithe frame, but Thad managed—until he found himself dangling from one of the blades when his foot slipped off the indentations in the wall.

He looked down and realized the conduit ended a mere two meters below him, and decided he'd drop the rest of the way. Still, habit had him releasing a cloud of colloid audio chaff in order to muffle the sound of his landing before he let go.

Ell looked over at him as he took a knee beside her.

He pointed to their exit, a vent that fed fresh air into the prison's environmental control center, and said, *{You take one end, I'll take the other.}*

Once they had the enclosure loose enough to hinge outward into the room, Thad directed the surveillance drone inside, ordering it to sweep for monitoring devices.

{Looks clear,} he told Ell.

He unholstered his CUSP, bringing the weapon up and pointing it out at the room.

He nodded. *{Go.}*

She slipped through, and he dropped lightly beside her.

Ell glanced his way. *{This is too easy....}*

CONFIRMATION

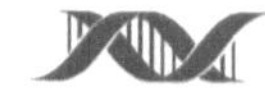

SHAR-KALI CORRECTIONAL FACILITY
AND REEDUCATION CENTER
AKSU DESERT

THE TRACKER THE Dagger's inside source had managed to plant onto the two Alliance operatives flashed to active status the moment they breached the facility.

Knowing the other woman was quite capable in her own right, Dacina didn't worry about Ell or her partner getting caught. Instead, she focused her energies on gathering her small cadre of twelve warriors and ordering them to their prearranged spots.

If things went as planned, not only would she shortly be coming face-to-face with the former sniper, but she would yet again be partnering with the woman.

A voice broke in suddenly over the private, encrypted channel she'd established for the Dagger's Dozen.

{Team one in place.}

On its heels came a second voice.

{Team two is spread out among the guard. All report readiness.}

{Good,} Dacina replied. *{Remember the plan. Drive the Alliance agents toward the ravine at all costs. And remind the prison guards who accompany you that these people are to be taken alive and unharmed, or they will pay the price.}*

{As you say, Fermanedh.*}*

Dacina was not their *fermanedh*, their commander, but she remained silent and let it ride.

Her players in position, the Dagger settled in to watch and wait.

* * *

Thad wasn't necessarily a superstitious man, but Ell's words about their insertion being too easy caused a ripple of apprehension to curl around his spine.

{Let's not borrow trouble, cher.*}*

His internal chronometer told him they had forty-five minutes, give or take, before their first contact window with Jonathan lapsed.

Maybe it would be a good idea to snoop around their network systems before proceeding any further.

He nodded to the door and the keypad beside it. *{Think you can hack their system through that?}*

Ell stepped forward, dipping a hand inside her tac vest. *{Worth a try. I have one more of Aviva's Bravo Charlies left. Let's see how robust their network security really is.}*

A few minutes later, she made a pleased sound. *{We're in.}* She forwarded him the connection.

When he accepted it, his overlay flooded with information, and they settled in to review the data.

Something caught his eye, and he highlighted it, pushing it to Ell. *{Is this what I think it is?}*

She studied it silently for several minutes.

{If you're thinking it's a lab and there's some sort of experiment going on here, then I have to say I agree with your assessment.}

She held up a hand. *{Wait. There's more information here.}*

She brought up a secured data file that linked the lab's access with approved ID tokens.

Thad let out a low, mental whistle. *{Well, well, well. Would you look at that. I guess we found our traitor.}*

Before him floated a familiar name: Clint Janus, the biochemist who had gone missing shortly after the foiled attempt to attack the Defense Summit.

{What are you up to, Doctor?} he murmured.

There was a pause, and then another name floated to the foreground.

Ell highlighted it. *{Look who just arrived for an unscheduled tour of the prison today.}*

Thad studied the name Ell had found: Che Josza. *{Guess we know who was in that transport. Isn't he their minister of state security now?}*

{Yes.} The tension in Ell's mental tone suggested that she also recalled the woman who was Che's right hand; the assassin who would very likely be with him.

{You might end up bumping into your buddy after all,} he observed. *{Stay frosty, cher.}*

{Oh, I will, believe me.}

{She is not to be underestimated.}

*{I **know**.}*

Her voice held an edge that warned Thad he was entering dangerous territory, so he backed off.

{Looks like Aviva's contact gave her accurate intel,} he said, switching topics back to their objective. *{Prisoners are being held four levels below that lab you just spotted. Got a roster for me?}*

In response, up popped a list of names with corresponding head shots.

Thad began to scroll through them, pausing here and there to note names and dates. His jaw clenched as he noted several with Geminate nationality.

He had to forcibly stop his teeth from grinding when he saw how many of those were deceased.

{Wait, stop. That one right there.} He zoomed in on the man's image.

Ell pursed her lips. *{That's the guy who stopped Micah and Sam outside the restaurant, isn't it?}*

He nodded, and she began to manipulate the feed.

{Hang on, I think I found him listed as one of the—}

Her voice stuttered to a stop, and she wordlessly displayed the notation that had been added to the man's prison record.

> Chris Williams: Junior analyst-in-training.
> National Security Agency, Geminate Alliance.
> Obtained March 24 while vacationing Ganymede.
> First session in cloning lab: April 3.
> Viable subject created: April 5.
> Subject terminated.

{Any others that they've done this to?} Thad asked quietly.

{Other than Garza?} Ell shook her head. *{No. There's a listing of several who were briefly 'held as guests,' but then let go.}*

{What the—? 'Held as guests'? Is that what they call torture and brainwashing now?} Thad felt anger surge. *{Show me.}*

Another list popped up, and the name at the top snagged his eye.

General Harris Carlisle, Vice Chief of Joint Operations.

"That bastard? The Akkadians know how to pick them, don't they." The Marine's voice was soft—very, very soft—but it reeked of disapproval. "Shit, I'll bet he holds the land speed record for fastest enemy asset turned into an Akkadian spy."

Though a general, Carlisle garnered little respect. It was a known fact the man had never seen combat; it was also well-known that he liked to let civilians think that he had. Rumor had it that his office was littered with articles of war that had never seen a minute's use: a sniper rifle, a carbyne-tipped combat blade.

On the general's walls, holopictures were proudly displayed of him standing beside special recon teams—people whose lives were endangered by the public display of such images, and yet the general didn't seem to care.

For him, it was nothing but an ego trip. Stolen valor.

It didn't surprise Thad in the least to learn the man had been turned.

{Package that up, and let's send it up to Jonathan over that fiber line before we go any further. He can begin transmitting it to Micah while we infiltrate. It will be my great pleasure to take that fils-putain *down.}*

{Copy that.} Ell's response was terse, but those two words held a wealth of emotion.

She crossed the room on light feet, reaching up to where the fiber clung to the side of the vent.

{Done,} she said after a moment.

{Okay then,} Thad straightened. *{Let's do this.}*

TRAITORS NAMED

TASK FORCE BLUE HQ
HUMBOLT BASE

BACK AT TASK Force Blue headquarters, Micah walked the room restlessly, maintaining a light touch with Jonathan as Ell and Thad breached the facility.

Gabe gave Micah a questioning look as he passed. He shook his head; no news.

Off to one side, Katie had her feet propped up on a console, and was rotating a pair of Chinese medicine balls in one palm. The spheres made a light clacking sound Micah could hear above the murmur of voices that came from the headquarters element staffing the communications array.

You there?

Micah came to an abrupt halt, his head jerking around to seek Toland's gaze.

The admiral held up a hand, bringing the casual conversation in the room to a stop. "Captain?"

Micah focused on his connection with Jonathan. *That was fast. Recon over?*

Jonathan gave a mental shake of his head. *No, but they*

managed to break into the prison's network and found a shit-ton of intel that they thought you should have. They sent it up to me so I could update you while they obtain visual confirmation that Garza is here.

*You have **non**-visual confirmation?*

Yes.

Micah motioned to Toland as he grabbed a seat at the table. *I'm going to repeat everything you say aloud, and they're going to record it. If I say something wrong, stop me.*

They went through all the information Ell had discovered on the prisoners. When they got to the list of victims' names, Micah had to swallow and clear his throat before continuing.

That all you have for us?

No.

Micah felt a swell of anger emanating from Jonathan.

This next list isn't victims. It's agents. Moles. Traitors.

They began anew, Micah repeating back what Jonathan shared. When his twin reported on Clint Janus and his lab, Micah felt his anger build. So when Jonathan sent the intel on Harris Carlisle....

Micah shot to his feet. "That fucking bastard!"

Gabe, who'd taken a seat beside him, stood and placed a hand on his shoulder. "Report, Captain."

The man's calm, steady tone pierced the haze of red that had clouded Micah's vision.

He turned blindly to face Gabe, and then pushed an image onto the bullpen's holotank. "Recognize this asshole?"

An exclamation from Katie Hyer confirmed it.

"Hey! That's the creep I nailed in the eye!"

"That is General Harris Carlisle." Toland's voice was devoid of emotion—the way it got when she was very angry. "He's the vice chair of the joint operating committee."

Micah met her eyes. "He's also a traitor. No wonder I've always hated that guy."

TRIGGERED

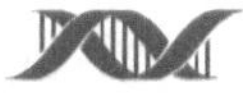

ELL SLID THE environmental room's door open a crack, far enough to release a reconnaissance microdrone.

{Hallway's clear,} she reported a second later.

She palmed the door fully open and slipped through, Thad following at her six. A map settled onto his overlay, their destination highlighted and waypoints identified.

They'd agreed earlier that they'd stick to maintenance shafts when they could.

Wordlessly, Ell pointed up ahead, and Thad saw the microdrone dip inside the stairwell located beside a bank of lifts. They caught up to it just in time to see the tiny machine plummet four stories to the detention floor.

{Clear.} Ell wrapped her hands and feet around the ladder's side rails, and dropped.

He followed after.

{Hang on.} Thad caught her just as she was about to step out into the hall.

If what he suspected was true, this area's security would be far more difficult to get past than the level they had just left.

He released his own microdrone, and almost immediately, a warning ping sounded.

He ordered the drone to retreat as he studied its sensor feed, then shared the warning that flashed on his HUD with Ell.

{Well, shit. Colloid mist,} she muttered. *{Sorry. Should have seen that one coming.}*

Her disgusted comment brought a grin to Thad's face, which he didn't bother to hide, since his suit's hood shrouded it from her view.

{No worries. Remember back when Jack rigged those paintball guns for that op at Cobalt Mining?}

Her head cranked around in his direction. *{You mean those paintballs he injected with the tagging program? Yes, I remember.}*

He jerked his chin in the direction of the hallway. *{That mist'll do the same thing to us.}*

She tilted her head, and then pointed. *{Okay then, how about we use that little guy for recon?}*

Thad followed her shadowed hand and spied a cleaning bot parked in its charging station across the corridor. *{Good idea. That'll do nicely.}*

He directed one of the microdrones toward the resting bot. It floated across the hallway, coming to rest in the crevice between the automaton's forward sensors. He then ordered the drone to inject a filament of nanomaterial into the sensors, using the connection to deliver the breaching code.

After a moment, he nodded. *{Okay. Control's ours. Now let's see what this thing's programmed to do.}*

Thad threw the cleaning bot's routine up onto his HUD, sharing the connection with Ell.

{Looks like its standard setting sweeps the corridors,} he said. *{If we have it run its regular loop, it'll give us a good feel for how many prison guards we're up against.}*

{Works for me.} Ell highlighted a subroutine in the program.

{They send the bots in to clean the cells, too.}

Almost instinctively, Thad leaned forward as he scrolled down, seeking the number of Garza's cell. *{Bingo.}*

Ell made a satisfied noise. *{Okay, then. Bot's in play.}*

They sent it off to make its rounds, and Thad's gut tightened at the tally of guards they were up against on this level. Between them and the colloid mist, their chances of getting Garza out safely weren't good.

{They sure as hell aren't taking any chances, are they?} he murmured.

He tensed as the bot came to a stop in front of the cell that held the prime minister, but the guards seemed oblivious to the little machine.

It docked with a small service hatch and then cycled through to the other side.

He heard Ell suck in a breath as the hatch opened, and they got a clear visual of the cell's inhabitant.

They now had a positive ID.

Their connection to the microdrone abruptly cut out, and Thad jerked.

{What the fuck?}

Ell pointed, highlighting the message error:

Connection Lost.

{My guess? Faraday cage.}

Thad scowled at the readout. *{Makes sense. Doesn't mean I have to like it, though.}*

He saw Ell's outline move in a graceful shrug. *{The drone has its commands. It will ping Garza with the challenge codes whether we're there to watch or not.}*

Thad grunted his agreement, and then stood. *{Stay here and keep watch. It's about time to update Jonathan. I'll retrace our steps, report in, and be back here before the bot's completed its cleaning routine.}*

* * *

Dacina paced the halls of the prison, her focus intent on the tracking app on her overlay that showed the location of Elodie Cyr and her companion. She'd waited as they made it down to the level that held Garza, and now they appeared to be hunkered down just out of range of the enhanced security.

She wasn't concerned the operatives would try to free him just yet. She'd studied the Special Reconnaissance Unit; the Alliance Navy's special forces were consummate professionals. They knew to recon first and act second. This was their recon stage. They would observe and assess, and then come back later to act.

They had no way to know this, but when they did come back, it would be under completely different circumstances—circumstances Dacina would dictate.

She patiently observed, waiting for the right moment to spring her trap.

It was almost time....

The two blips on her overlay separated. One began to retrace his steps, presumably to report in, while the other remained behind to monitor the prison cells.

The Dagger determined they'd had enough time to confirm Garza's presence.

She triggered the alarm.

TELOMERES

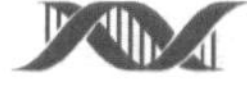

TASK FORCE BLUE HQ
HUMBOLT BASE

SAM HADN'T SEEN Micah in two days. He'd been tied up in Task Force Blue's bullpen, reporting everything Jonathan shared, while she'd been holed up in the CID, studying the chiral samples Linnet had obtained from Garza.

She'd been right to assume they'd used her viral research as the launching point for this leap to living organisms. The entanglement markers were much stronger in Garza's sample than they were in the samples she had from Jonathan and Micah... or even the ferrets and cats, for that matter.

It's all in the spin—

A tone sounded behind Sam, interrupting her thoughts. The most recent round of tests was done.

She set up another series, and then turned to pull up the analysis that had just completed.

Her eyes widened in shock.

Wondering how in the hell they'd missed this in their initial evaluation, Sam reached for the secured channel that would connect her directly to Admiral Toland.

* * *

Duncan Cutter had been home a grand total of five minutes. He'd kicked off his shoes, tossed a portfolio full of briefs onto the table beside his favorite chair, and grabbed a bottle of New Willet. He'd just settled in, bourbon in one hand, reports in the other, when a priority ping came across his wire from Admiral Toland.

Although the secured channel she used to contact him used the latest encryption algorithm, it was monitored by the National Security Agency, and therefore subject to hacking by any well-placed mole they had yet to find.

Toland's message reflected this. He could hear her pick her words carefully.

{At your earliest convenience, could you swing by, sir? We'd like to share our latest findings on the current health challenges we discussed at our last meeting.}

Over the recording, the admiral's voice paused.

{Pardon the late hour, I was catching up on old correspondence. I await your response.}

Duncan didn't have to be a telepath to read between those lines. For Toland to reach out to him via these channels at such a late hour meant that it was likely they'd discovered something in Garza's sample. Something he needed to know.

With a regretful look at the drink he'd just poured, he sealed his portfolio and pushed away from his desk. As he headed for the door, he pinged his security detail for an escort.

The agent on duty was one he'd known for many years, and he smiled when he saw her familiar face.

"Awfully late to be going somewhere, sir," she commented.

He gave a tired smile. "Unfortunately, it can't be helped. No rest for the wicked, Sara."

She nodded, her eyes everywhere except on him, alert for any danger. She shifted as a transport rounded the corner.

"Where to, sir? she asked, holding the door open for him.

"The CID, Montpelier."

***

A trio of solemn faces greeted him as he entered the secret wing of the CID dedicated to chiral research.

"What's going on?" His gaze swept from Toland, to Linnet, and then over to his niece.

Sam's brows were furrowed, eyes dark.

From worry?

"Sam?"

She looked to Toland for permission, and the admiral nodded.

"It's about the Prime Minister."

"He's not chiral after all?"

"Oh no, he is," she assured him. "It's just that…well, there's more."

"Have they turned him into some sort of a ticking time bomb?"

Linnet laughed, but it was a harsh sound, and there was no humor in it.

He looked over at the woman he had known since Sam's college days, when she'd come to live with him after her parents died. He knew the biochemist well enough to know that something had spooked her.

He turned back to Sam. "Spit it out. What kind of time bomb are we dealing with here?"

"The kind that will only kill Raphael Garza. But it *will* kill him."

Sam gestured, and the conference room's holodisplay lit up. On it appeared a medical diagram.

He could identify the double helix of DNA, but beyond that, it was gibberish. Lifting a brow, he turned his attention back to Sam, silently waiting for her to explain.

"Are you familiar with telomeres?" she asked.

He shrugged. "Only that they shorten as we age. Aren't they

what hold DNA together, kind of keep it from unraveling?"

Sam nodded. "In this instance, the telomeres of chiral Garza are severely foreshortened." Her expression grew grave. "Duncan…. He doesn't have long to live."

Cutter's gaze shot to the admiral and then back to his niece. "How much time?"

Sam hesitated. "Less than we'd like. We need to get chiral Garza into stasis as soon as possible."

CAPTURED

SHAR-KALI CORRECTIONAL FACILITY
AND REEDUCATION CENTER
AKSU DESERT

THAD WAS HALFWAY back to the shaft when an alarm began shrieking through the prison.

Unrelated? Dammit, can't take the chance.

Pivoting, he hauled ass back to Ell, nearly running her over when she appeared suddenly in front of him.

{Time for us to leave.} he said hurriedly.

She fell into step beside him. *{Have we been made?}*

{No clue. Not sticking around to find out.}

She pointed toward an intersection they were fast approaching. *{There's a maintenance tunnel at that juncture.}*

Thad altered direction toward it.

The sound of pounding footsteps approaching wrung a burst of speed from him, but Ell dropped behind.

A glance back showed her silhouette fumbling for something in her tactical vest.

{Hang on; I can create a diversion.}

{Whatever you're doing, do it while moving, Sergeant.} He

dropped back as he snapped the order, tagging her elbow and urging her along.

She sped up, gloved hand still working something inside her vest. She made a sound of satisfaction, and he caught the glint of a reconnaissance drone in her hand.

{We both know who's coming.} He barely kept the impatience from his voice, driven by the need to get them out of the line of fire.

She shook her head and he saw the thing float away from her palm and go jetting off back the way they'd come.

*{I altered its stealth profile and programmed it to send small updates at irregular intervals. That last is meaningless, really, because you're right; we **do** know who's coming for us.}*

Thad's head snapped up when he heard a shout followed by the pounding of feet as prison guards turned in the direction the drone had flown.

He lifted a brow, though he knew she couldn't see it. *{Tweaked its stealth...?}*

{Just enough so that it's now leaking a signal. Reads like a ghost signature. That, coupled with the brief EM bursts each time it sends out a 'recon update,' will hopefully buy us some time.}

He grinned. *{You made a human-sized Dazzler.}*

Dazzlers were the Navy pilot's purview. The stealth drones that employed ECM—electronic countermeasures—had the ability to mimic the footprint of a much larger ship, or make it appear in different or even multiple locations to confuse targeting systems.

He'd been on more than a few missions where the Shadow Recon flight crew had used them to lure an enemy away.

He slipped inside the maintenance passage and picked up the pace. When they came to the exit that would spill them into the corridor across from enviro, he slowed, manually sliding the door open a crack.

The corridor was empty.

{Come on.}

They hurried through the room, and back up into the shaft.

Thad secured the vent behind them, while Ell began to climb.

{*That ECM drone's about to come to the end of its useful life,*} she warned.

{*Where'd you send it, anyway?*}

{*To one of the other shafts. As soon as they find out there aren't any humans attached to that signal, they'll be coming for us.*}

Thad spared a glance at the Bravo Charlie on the fan as he squeezed his way between its blades, happy to see the breaching app still blinking a reassuring green.

They climbed as quickly as the footholds gouged into the side of the shaft would allow, until Ell paused at the top, her hands pushing against the grille.

Jonathan must have been watching for the movement; in an instant, he was there, helping Ell push the heavy metal out of the way. She then tumbled over the side, and Thad followed.

The moment they were back on the grass, Jonathan dropped the grate, which fell with a muted clang.

{*Joule says there are people coming.*}

{*She's right.*}

They took off, Thad setting the pace.

{*Try not to disturb the switchgrass if you can avoid it,*} he called out as he wove a path through the starlit terrain. {*Aim for rock if you can, dirt patches second.*}

The instructions were for Jonathan's benefit; a seasoned soldier, Ell needed no such reminder.

As they traversed the rock-strewn plateau, Thad tossed the map of the area onto the small combat net the three shared.

{*Fallback point Alpha,*} he called out, dropping a pin onto a nearby ravine that had been carved into the earth over countless monsoon seasons. It was the most logical rally point.

The Akkadians would know this, as well.

That was shortly proved when a shout went up and the chatter of unsuppressed gunfire erupted from behind them.

Thad saw Joule arrow off at an angle, the animal's sleek, black form running full-out, body stretched low to the ground.

Another shout told him their enemy was closing in.

Thad cursed and increased his speed. His legs pumped, gaze sweeping the terrain, evaluating the stand of trees they were fast approaching. They had no choice; the ravine provided the best defilade, and that was all that mattered at the moment.

As the scrub-covered land began to slope, chips of stone went flying as bullets carved chunks out of the rock formation on his left.

{Low profile!} he roared as he began maneuvering through the terrain, keeping as many obstacles as possible between himself and their pursuers.

He swung his rifle up, thumbing its reticle to auto-detect, and turned, firing over his shoulder as he went.

The high-pitched whine of his weapon had suppressor chaff to attenuate it, but any well-trained soldier would be able to zero in on its location.

He dodged just in time, the dirt in front of him kicking up as bullets stitched their way through the grass.

The team careened through the brush, closing in on the umbrella trees lining the ravine's edge.

{Go for the far right,} Ell said, veering in that direction. *{It has the thickest coverage.}*

The tops of the trees seemed to come alive, the canopy dancing overhead as gunfire ripped into it. Shredded leaves rained down on them as they passed beneath.

{They're shooting over our heads,} panted Jonathan.

{That's because they've been ordered to take us alive,} Ell replied.

She ducked beneath the canopy of the first tree, Jonathan hot on her heels. Thad skittered around a sandpaper raisin bush, the plant's berries dancing as he passed.

His heels dug hard into the packed earth as he pushed off a piece of exposed rock, then he was in the cover of the trees, branches slapping against his face as he raced past.

The undergrowth was denser than he'd anticipated, and he found himself jinking right, then left, in order to avoid the smaller saplings that were somehow managing to shove their way up through the hardened earth.

He swung around the gnarled trunk of the last tree and then burst out into the switchgrass that spanned the distance between the trees and the ravine.

Another round ripped through the grass on their right, causing Thad to swerve sharply in the other direction.

{Double-time, Sergeant,} he barked.

Ell responded by increasing her speed, though it was apparent her cloned leg was giving her issues. His suit's predictive systems indicated her silhouette had a pronounced limp.

More rock exploded on his right, bullets turning small bits of limestone into tiny missiles. The projectiles peppered them like shrapnel, digging into their suits, but the tough drakeskins' liquid armor held, diffusing their impact.

He rejoined the others just in time to see Jonathan leap into a shallow depression three steps ahead of Ell; the latter dropped into a skid, sliding over the crevice's lip and landing beside the pilot.

Jonathan turned to help the former sniper to her feet just as Thad touched down beside them.

{Go, go!} Thad hooked a hand beneath Ell's arm, urging her forward, Jonathan on her other side.

Between the two men, she half-hopped, half-skipped, doing her best to assist as they pulled her along.

Ahead, the ravine widened into one of many trenches that peppered the landscape, created by acid rains that fell season after season, wearing away at the savannah's surface. This one carved a natural corridor that angled gently to the west.

{Where's Joule?} Thad asked, abruptly remembering the animal.

{I sent her on ahead when the bullets started flying. Didn't want her to get hit by a stray round. She's looping around, approaching the hide from an alternate angle.}

{Good thinking,} Thad replied. *{Now if we can just shake*

these fools, we can—}

Aw, fuck, he cursed mentally as they rounded a corner and abruptly came face to face with a trio of armed Akkadian soldiers.

* * *

Dacina raced to join the team poised to spring her trap, keeping one eye on her two targets as she went, to ensure they didn't surprise her. She was pleased to see their movements matched her predictions.

The prison feed she'd hacked showed its guards spilling out from Shar-Kali's three primary access points. Gunfire began snapping, the sound carrying far in the still night of the desert. As they closed on their quarry, the high-pitched whine of bullets increased in volume, whistling through the air as they passed over her head.

{Nonlethal.} She barked the reminder to the six Junxun she'd planted within the prison guard's ranks. *{They must make it to the ravine. Place your shots carefully; herd them to me.}*

Answering clicks came her way just as she made it to the site of the ambush. Crouching in a clump of switchgrass, Dacina waited beside three of Serae's Junxun soldiers. Two of them held a Ghillie camouflage net, stretched out on the ground between them.

Off to her left by several meters, her demolitions team was doing a final check on their part of the fabrication. They looked her way, giving the hand sign for 'all set' before backing away from the spot where a shaped charge was buried, and taking cover behind a group of rocks, weapons up and ready to fire.

Everything was as ready as Dacina could make it. The rest lay in the hands of the Geminate warriors heading her way.

A loud *crash* came through the brush, drawing her attention back to the ravine. In the darkness, her optics' enhanced night vision showed the shrouded forms of three people slipping down into the ravine, disappearing from sight.

"Very good," she murmured aloud, and then connected with the team dispersed among the guards. *{They have made the ravine. Delay the guards as long as you can.}*

The sound of the three stealthed humans heading rapidly her way grew louder, though it was oddly muted. She realized they must be using some sort of audio-dampening field to further hide their progress from the guards.

It was a noble attempt, but the crushed grasses from their feet, and the branches disturbed by their passage marked their positions as surely as if they weren't clad in drakeskin.

{Hold steady,} she warned.

She snapped her eyes over to the two men who held the Ghillie net, and both nodded crisply, ready to use it.

And then three Geminate figures came racing around the bend.

* * *

Ell quickly took in the Akkadians before her. They weren't dressed as prison guards; these were Junxun, she could tell that much despite the fact they were clad in stealth suits.

The cloud of dust the soldiers' feet had kicked up slowly settled around them as a fourth person joined the three, unmasking her hood to expose her face.

{Well, damn,} Ell said quietly.

They were face to face with a very familiar figure—the Akkadian assassin from the Hawking Habitat.

"Down! Get down—quickly! There is little time," the Dagger hissed harshly as she gestured with the rifle in her hand.

Two of the three soldiers flanking the woman bent to pick up a length of camouflage netting. They dragged it forward, their intent clear.

For some reason Ell couldn't determine, the assassin wished to hide them from those who were in pursuit.

Though she didn't trust the Dagger's motives, she wasn't about to look a gift horse in the mouth. They needed the assist, so they'd just have to deal with the consequences later.

She looked over at Thad with a subtle nod.

The Marine took a knee and gave a quick hand motion, signaling for her and Jonathan to follow. They dropped beside him, and the two soldiers tossed the ghillie net over their forms.

"For this to work, you must remain still and be completely silent," the Dagger whispered. "And keep your heads down if you do not wish to be injured in the fallout."

With those cryptic words, she pivoted and ran swiftly to join her soldiers, calling out, "Blow it!"

The camouflage netting had a loose enough weave that Ell could see through it. She observed as the shaped charge the assassin had set detonated several meters away, rock shards and debris spewing outward, the energy directed away from the depression where they lay.

Even as the rubble settled, the assassin was out from under cover, her rifle in her hands and pointed at the impact crater.

The soldiers with her hurried to join the Dagger, positioning themselves in a semi-circle, their weapons poised, muzzles pointing down at what Ell knew to be an imaginary foe.

It was stagecraft, pure and simple.

But to what end?

* * *

The Dagger stood with her cadre of cadets, waiting for the prison guards to burst through the ravine. She could hear them race around the corner, and then skid to an abrupt halt behind her.

"Where are they?" the lead guard demanded.

Dacina snapped her rifle up into its ready position and turned to face them, her cold gaze landing on the man who had spoken.

"Dead," she said flatly, pointing to the crater made by the shaped charge.

The leader of the guards who had been pursuing the Geminate agents kicked a nearby rock and said with some disgust, "Doctor Janus isn't going to like this. He pinged and explicitly told us they were to be taken alive."

Dacina lifted one brow. "That will not be happening. I should not need to remind you that the doctor does not have the authority to order someone detained rather than eliminated."

The man who had spoken shot her a smug look that suggested he knew something she did not. "He wanted them for the premier's program."

Dacina's eyes hardened. She removed the band that constrained her hair and stepped into the light mounted on the guard's rifle. She heard the satisfying sound of a sharp inhale when the light caught the beads woven into her braids—one bead, one kill.

The man took an involuntary step back when he realized to whom he had spoken.

"*Assassin.*" The sibilant whisper traveled fast among those who stood behind him.

Dacina spared a glance over her shoulder, her voice cold and hard as she addressed one of the Dozen who stood beside the small crater.

"Have a cleanup crew gather what DNA they can from the site, and present it to the doctor. Perhaps he will find some use for the remains."

One of the Junxun bowed his head. "It will be as you say, Dagger."

She turned back to the insolent prison guard, whose face was now as pale as one of her victims.

"The doctor will have to make do with what we can find."

He swallowed hard. Wisely, he refrained from speaking.

She turned to look at the contingent of guards who had accompanied the leader; they stood as if not quite knowing what to do next.

This was easily remedied. Her voice cracked through the

silence. "Why do you loiter about? There is a prison to guard. It is a wonder the prisoners aren't running the facility."

Her words struck home. Even her Junxun plants within the guard jumped. With alacrity, they turned and began to jog back toward the prison.

Dacina waited, watching her hacked feed until she was certain they were well on their way back to the facility, before slinging the rifle over her shoulder and kneeling to lift the ghillie net from her prize.

"Elodie Cyr."

A soft *snick* sounded, and in the next moment, the woman she had once named *zhídé de duìshǒu*, a 'worthy opponent,' peeled her hood from her face.

Ell nodded warily. "Dacina Zian."

"Well met," the Dagger responded.

She stepped forward, hand weaving in the complex Junxun sign for 'esteemed warrior'—though she didn't necessarily expect the other woman to know its meaning.

"I have a proposition for you. Your people and mine share a common problem. I need your help to stop it."

PRISON INSPECTION

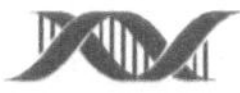

Shar-Kali Correctional Facility
and Reeducation Center
Aksu Desert

JONATHAN TOOK HIS cues from Thad and Ell, and when the other two rose to their feet, he followed.

While trapped under the ghillie net, watching the staged drama play out before them, he'd reached out to Morrison to check on Joule, and was relieved to hear the big cat had returned to the hide unscathed.

"Need *our* help?" he heard Thad ask sharply. "What for?"

The assassin stepped closer, her cold eyes causing a chill to chase down Jonathan's spine. Her words, spoken in a low tone, were innocuous enough, and yet her stance, the bite in her voice, everything about the woman promised death.

"I know what our premier has done to your prime minister. I can help you free him."

Thad stepped forward to meet her toe to toe, his action causing the Dagger's soldiers to shift in warning. Jonathan had to give the Marine props; it took balls of steel to go up against a killer like that.

"What?" asked Thad, gesturing to himself, Ell, and Jonathan. "You want to pass us off as part of your elite soldier unit, doing some sort of prison inspection or something?"

The woman stared back unblinkingly. "Exactly so."

Ell stepped up, placing a hand on Thad's arm. "You said we share a common problem. What is that?"

The assassin turned to her after a hard look at the big Marine. "He plans to do to every other star nation what he has done to yours. He must be stopped."

Shock reeled through Jonathan at her words.

Ell's new pal had just made a compelling case for pooling resources, and yet something didn't quite ring true about her words. He couldn't understand why such aggression would bother this Akkadian.

Why does she care?

His thoughts derailed as the woman motioned to one of her soldiers, and the man stepped forward, thrusting a stealth suit into Jonathan's hands.

"Put it on," the Dagger ordered.

He frowned. "What's wrong with mine?"

"This one has Akkadian IFF. Your stealth will not be questioned."

This had to be the strangest exfil Jonathan had ever been part of—not that he'd been on this side of an exfil before.

He fingered the Yinshen suit, shooting Thad a questioning look. "Your call," he told the Marine.

Thad turned to the assassin, hooking a thumb toward Jonathan. "Why him and not either of us?"

The faintest look of annoyance crossed her face. "You infiltrated the prison's network, so you cannot possibly have missed it. Clint Janus has a lab here." She gestured to the pilot. "You know as well as I do that his is a face the doctor will recognize."

Thad's expression hardened at mention of the man, but it was nothing compared to the anger Jonathan felt.

He immediately began to don the Akkadian suit. "If this plan includes taking Janus down, I'm in."

Ell's gaze swung from him to their new pal, and she picked up where Thad left off. "So, you help us recover Garza and eliminate Janus and his lab, and in return, we help you, what? Spring Rin Zhou?"

"Yes. The minister of state security will explain when we arrive."

"Hold up." Jonathan looked up from his attempt to figure out how to get the suit on correctly. "Isn't Rin Zhou the person your current boss replaced?"

Seeing him struggle, the assassin waved one of her men over to help him.

"He is, but there are... extenuating circumstances. In this, they are unified."

Jonathan doubted that but he let it ride, his attention back on the suit he'd just stepped into.

He wasn't certain if it was because it was Akkadian design, or if it was just the subconscious knowledge that he was using enemy tech, but the thing felt uncomfortable and ill-fitting.

The soldier tweaked the Yinshen's collar, adjusted the chest plate, and then slapped him on the shoulder in the universal 'good to go' signal all special forces warriors seemed to use.

Jonathan nodded his thanks, palms smoothing over the material's foreign pattern. From what he could tell, it was made of a liquid armor similar to that of their own drakeskin.

He felt a sinuous brush along his left leg as Joule announced her arrival. He looked down, but saw nothing.

{Joule?}

{You know any other cats out here?}

He suppressed a grin.

{Reinforcements just arrived,} he informed Thad. *{Joule's here.}*

The Marine's expression didn't change. *{You had Morrison send her back out?}*

{After suiting her up, yeah. Light-bending nano for the win.}

{Good thinking. She'll be our ace in the hole, just in case Ell's

BFF turns on us.}

Jonathan hid a grin at the dark look Ell shot Thad at that last remark. *{That's a good copy.}*

{Won't the colloid mist catch her?}

Ell's words had Thad turning to the Akkadian.

Tilting his head to indicate Jonathan, he explained, "They run a mist down on that level that'll tag him, even in a stealth suit. You really want him incognito, we're going to have to turn that off."

"I already did," said the Dagger. "It is no longer a problem."

Thad crossed his arms. "Well, then it looks like you have yourself three—" he angled his head toward Jonathan and corrected himself, "*two* new soldiers, and one Yinshen-suited spook."

The assassin didn't respond; instead, she motioned for another soldier to hand Thad and Ell their own change of clothes.

"How should we address you?" Ell asked as they donned the uniforms.

"You can call me Dagger, or..." she hesitated, "*Fermanedh.*"

Jonathan's wire helpfully provided a translation of the Aka'a word: 'Commander.'

Interesting that she seems uncomfortable with the title....

The woman indicated they should move out. "Citizen Minister Josza is currently conducting a tour of the facility," she told them as they headed that direction. "Later this evening, he will personally interview the prisoners Garza and Enlai."

{Interrogate, you mean,} Jonathan muttered over their team's connection.

"It is customary for someone at his level of importance within the government to have an advance team sweep the facility to ensure his safety," the assassin continued, unaware of his side remark. "It will not be unreasonable for us to enter their cells to perform a preliminary inspection."

It was the most they'd ever heard the assassin say at one time.

"I see," Ell said, voice thoughtful.

Her limp was barely noticeable now, but the uniform she wore looked odd on her.

Equally strange was seeing Thaddeus Severance in a Tèzhŏng ostovar's battle dress.

"And then?" Thad asked.

"And then the former citizen minister and the present citizen minister will explain to you exactly why we must join forces."

"To do what?" Ell prodded, but the assassin refused to say anything further as they arrived at Shar-Kali.

At a signal none could hear, the hangar doors retracted, sand spilling off as they hinged upward. They didn't open fully—just enough for humans to pass through.

They moved single-file through the opening, Jonathan lingering until all of the soldiers had passed inside the hangar.

Joule pressed against his leg, and he silently motioned her forward before stepping inside himself.

{Stay close to me,} he murmured to the cat.

He received a mental growl in response.

* * *

It felt surreal to Thad, standing in the midst of Akkadia's most secure prison, wearing the uniform of one of their elite soldiers. Despite the fact he carried a loaded weapon—a fact that astonished him—he still felt naked and exposed, this deep inside enemy territory.

{Easy does it,} Ell's amused voice penetrated his thoughts. *{Shoulders look a bit tense there, Captain. You belong here, don't forget.}*

{Not about to forget I'm wearing an enemy's uniform, cher.}

They marched through the compound, conducting what appeared to be a standard drill, inspecting each level for security, and then moving on.

When they reached level four, where the most secured cells

were located, Thad smiled inwardly as he caught a glimpse of the cleaning bot docked in the corridor.

The microdrone it had delivered to Garza's cell was a bit of intel the assassin knew nothing about—and he intended to keep it that way.

As they approached the cell that housed the former minister of state security, a prison guard stepped forward. The moment he spied her signature braids, his bluster fled like a balloon deflating.

"We require entry," the assassin stated. "The citizen minister will not be allowed inside these walls until I have seen for myself that his safety is assured."

The battle of wills… was no battle at all. The man fairly tripped over himself in his haste to open the door.

Thad was surprised when the guard found the courage to try and join them. He hid a smile at the man's poorly-concealed flinch when the Dagger held up her hand.

"It would not do for you to abandon your post."

"But protocol—"

"We are of the Tèzhǒng," the assassin said in a deceptively mild tone. "You doubt our ability to defend ourselves against an old woman and a Geminate political prisoner?"

The guard shook his head rapidly and stepped away.

On his overlay, Thad saw the shadowed figures of Jonathan and Joule slip inside just as the assassin closed the door. When he turned, he saw that both Rin Zhou and Garza were standing, looking warily at the newcomers.

They remained silent until the assassin spoke.

"Minister." She bowed her head.

Enlai's eyes narrowed. "Greetings, Dagger. I half expected our earlier encounter to be our last."

The assassin did not respond; she merely stared steadily back at the woman.

Thad used that opportunity to access the data the microdrone had begun feeding him the moment they entered the room. He relaxed minutely when he saw that not only had

Garza accurately answered the challenge questions, but he'd volunteered every scrap of intel he had about the facility.

He saw the Dagger motion to Jonathan, and then his suit deactivated. By the look on the pilot's face, he hadn't been the one to do it.

Garza startled when Jonathan appeared, his eyes widening.

Rin Zhou's gaze held no such surprise. "Are you the original," she asked, "or are you the clone?"

* * *

The former minister of state security was staring at him with the same sort of fascination someone would give a scientific exhibit in a museum. It reminded Jonathan of a display he'd seen as a kid—a collection of dead insects, their wings pinned open to show their varied patterns and colors.

He started forward, angry at the clinical detachment he heard in her tone.

Thad's arm snapped up, the back of his hand smacking him in the chest, effectively stopping him.

It couldn't stop his words.

"Micah's not a thing, he's a person! An individual. A living, thinking, breathing individual. And *your* people did that to him."

Rin Zhou dipped her chin and looked at him from under lowered brows. "Come now, Captain. It was your own chief scientist who did that to you, not any of my people."

"But it was one of your people who enabled him."

"Be that as it may, sometimes scientific advances require sacrifice."

Jonathan surged forward, shoving against Thad's fisted hand.

"Careful," the big Marine growled, but then turned to Rin Zhou. "Watch your words. Minister of state security or not, I'll let him come at you."

"What they did to him, and to Micah, was unconscionable."

Ell stepped forward, her quiet voice cutting through the tension.

"On that, we agree." Rin Zhou swiveled her head to look the sniper in the eye. "And that is precisely why you will help me."

Ell shifted, hands tightening on the rifle slung across her chest. "You seem awfully confident of that."

Rin Zhou seemed unruffled by the threat Ell posed. She merely nodded and then turned to face Thad. "I assume you're here to break this gentleman out?" A fluid hand gesture indicated the man standing silently beside her.

At their silence, Enlai continued.

"Your prime minister and I have spoken at length about a proposition I offered. He has accepted."

"Proposition?" Thad asked in a dangerous voice.

Rin Zhou's gaze turned to the assassin, favoring the warrior with a puzzled look. "You didn't tell them?"

* * *

Thad felt himself tense as the assassin stepped between him and Rin Zhou. Reflex prodded him to reach for the pistol holstered at his side; he curled his hand in a fist, consciously fighting the urge.

Her gaze drilled into his. "Listen to her," was all she said.

Thad broke eye contact with the Dagger long enough to shoot Garza a questioning look.

The prime minister dipped his head slightly in a faint nod.

"All right, then." Thad braced, feet apart. "Let us have it."

"You're all well aware that we can now chirally clone humans." Rin Zhou indicated the prime minister beside her. "What I suspect our Dagger has told you is that Asher Dent's plans extend far beyond the Geminate Alliance. Raphael Garza is just the first step in Project Obelus."

"Obelus?" Ell asked. "Isn't that...." She wrinkled her forehead in concentration.

The word seemed familiar to him too, yet elusive.

Something he might've heard in school, years ago.

That was confirmed by Garza's next words.

"Obelus is a mathematical term. The name for the symbol representing division."

"An apt word, wouldn't you say?" Rin Zhou turned a knowing look on Garza.

He nodded. "Obelus is the code name for Dent's plans to control every leader in every government in the settled worlds."

"And that's why you support this." Thad stared at the prime minister.

"She invoked the Responsibility to Protect Doctrine. We have an obligation to assist."

Thad could hear the gravity in Garza's voice, the weight of duty falling heavy on the man.

"What's Dent's end game?" he asked, though he suspected he already knew.

Enlai scoffed. "Nothing short of total space supremacy, across all the settled worlds."

Silence descended after Rin Zhou's statement.

Thad looked at Garza; the proof was right in front of them, and yet, how could they trust the woman who had nearly loosed a viral weapon that would have killed millions?

"And you support this?" Thad asked Garza one last time.

He saw the reservation in the man's eyes, and yet he nodded.

"She's not done," the prime minister told them. "There's more."

Thad turned to Rin Zhou.

"It is this 'more' that will convince you of our sincerity," she assured him. "Not only has he targeted the known worlds, but he has also targeted his own. Everyone in a position of power within the Akkadian Empire is scheduled to be chirally cloned and enslaved. The only person in on this plan is the same man he's tasked to carry out his orders."

Thad exchanged a look with Jonathan and Ell. He had a

funny feeling he knew the answer to this next question, too, and yet he had to ask.

"And that person would be?"

"Clint Janus."

DECISION TIME

Task Force Blue HQ
Humbolt Base

IT TOOK THE Navy and NSA half an hour to establish a secured channel between Humbolt base and Akkadia that they felt wouldn't be traceable. That gave Duncan's people time to set up a series of cutout nodes on their end, too, ensuring the enemy would have no way to pinpoint or trace the communication.

But then, finally, Thad's face appeared in the tank .He was flanked by Ell and Jonathan.

"Sir." Thad nodded, and then panned the holorecorder so that Duncan could see Raphael Garza.

Beside him stood Rin Zhou. Beside her, Che Josza.

In the shadows, Cutter could just make out a figure that looked vaguely familiar. When she turned her head, and he caught sight of the beads in her hair, he knew.

The assassin.

"Director Cutter," Rin Zhou began in her flat, accented voice. "As I've already told your prime minister, I am invoking the Responsibility to Protect Doctrine. I officially request your intervention."

As she laid out Dent's plans, Duncan could see why Garza felt the Alliance should agree to it.

"This is a weighty decision, sir," he told the prime minister. "I don't have the authority to commit to it on my own. Give me two hours."

Che Josza spoke up for the first time. "That is about all we can afford you, Director Cutter. I have arranged for Minister Enlai and your prime minister to be released from their cells under the pretext of an interrogation. Two hours from now, we need to have seized control of this prison."

Duncan nodded. "Understood."

The holotank fell dark.

"I think it's clear to everyone here that Dent is up to no good." Duncan glanced around the table. "Do we believe Rin Zhou that Dent's plans extend even to enslaving his own people? Harper, you've studied that woman. What do you think?"

Her brows drew together. After a moment, she stated, "The former minister's actions are consistent with the strong nationalistic loyalty she exhibited during her tenure as minister of state security."

"Then you believe her," Gabe stated.

Harper nodded. "I do. I think she's just as disgusted by Dent as we are."

"Yes, but can we *trust* her?" Cutter pressed.

The analyst grimaced. "Now, that is a more difficult question to answer. What she's proposing is ambitious. No Akkadian has ever asked for an outside source to assist them."

She chewed on her lower lip, expression pensive. "Here's the thing... historically, coups have been internal. You could say they've been used as proof that the person who succeeds is strong enough to both defend the position and lead the people. Strength is a very important quality to Akkadian culture, its significance is deeply ingrained in the people."

It was a long lecture from the analyst, but it was her job to put things into perspective for Duncan, to help him make informed decisions.

What Harper had just done was remind him that he couldn't judge the Akkadians by the Alliance's own meter stick.

"She's playing the old 'the enemy of my enemy is my friend,' card," said Major Reid, her voice dry.

"She is." Cutter nodded. "But if we're going to exchange trite phrases, we might consider, 'Hold your friends close but hold your enemies closer.'"

He pushed away from the table, his eye on the chrono displayed on his overlay. "Looks like I'm about to crash the governor-general's lunch."

* * *

Governor-General Laura Castro had insisted that there be one place in her home where she could retreat without agents hovering protectively over her. That place was in a small breakfast nook just off the mansion's expansive kitchens.

It was here that Duncan was now led.

Even though Castro had won the battle and there were no live agents within the room, two security SIs still watched over her. These, Duncan could deal with.

He nodded politely to the security agents posted before the door, then turned to his escort, another pair of agents who had met him at the mansion's entrance, and held out a hand.

"Thank you, James." He shook, and then extended his hand again. "Rick, good seeing you again."

The two men nodded and retreated back to their posts when the lead of the governor-general's detail stepped forward.

The woman gave him an apologetic smile. "Sorry, Director Cutter, but you know the rules. In order to be allowed in, especially with the An-Yang president in residence right now, we have to give you a Level One scan."

Duncan returned her smile with a wry one of his own.

"Understood. Not my first; won't be my last. I'm not going to promise to enjoy it, though."

The man beside her chuckled. "Can't think of a single person who would."

The thorough background check was invasive. Such scrutiny was unpleasant, but necessary to ensure he'd not secreted a harmful app or damaging subroutine somewhere on his person or within his wire's data partition. He'd only had to suffer through it once before, when he'd been recruited from college to join the NSA as its newest junior analyst.

It was every bit as uncomfortable now as he recalled it being many years ago.

That done, the agents opened the door, allowing him access to the room. He thanked them as he crossed the threshold.

The governor-general had risen at the sound of the door opening and stood, smiling a welcome.

Duncan returned it with a smile and small nod of his own before turning and bowing formally to the other person in the room. "President Jiu. Madame Governor-General. Thank you both for letting me join you today."

Jiu Liam, the Imperial President of the Shang Dynasty of the star nation of An-Yang, took Duncan's proffered hand with a smile. "Please, call me Liam," the president offered.

"Thank you, sir," Duncan murmured, and then turned to shake Laura Castro's hand.

Through the physical contact, he initiated a private connection, pushing an NSA-sealed file to her.

She stared at him for a beat, one brow lifted, before accepting it. *{And here I thought you had come for the tea.}*

Her droll mental tone rolled over him, and his smile widened.

{Really, Director. If you're going to make a practice of this, I'd advise making a few dry runs to throw people off so they don't become suspicious.}

He tilted his head, acknowledging her point. *{I'll do that. And I do like your teas.}* Aloud, he said, "Thank you for letting me crash your meal. I'd heard Chef Tio was making her famous Midnight Blossom Povitica for dessert." He clapped his hands and looked around hopefully.

Jiu Liam chuckled. "I take it that's the sweet, flaky loaf with the little seeds on the top?" He gestured to the platter at the center of the table.

"It is, indeed." Duncan turned to engage Jiu in a lengthy conversation, comparing Shang and Geminate cuisines, giving Laura Castro a chance to review the file.

He prayed she'd come to the same conclusion he and those leading the special forces had, and support his recommendation.

"Holmes, Watson."

Duncan paused as the governor-general's voice cut into their conversation. He turned to see Laura addressing the sensor pickups the SIs used to monitor the room.

"Suspend recording. Sable-Copper-Keyhole," she spoke the codeword sequence without concern for the two men present.

Protective Services will be inventing another new set of words about now.

The SIs spoke in tandem. *{Security token authorization required.}*

He and Jiu Liam waited while Castro submitted her token. Once the SIs had confirmed that recording had been suspended, the governor-general turned and pinned him with a stern look.

"This had better be from an unimpeachable source, Duncan."

His lips thinned. "It is. I've seen it myself."

She sighed. "Liam, it appears we're about to go to war. Care to join us?"

PART FOUR: DEPOSED

EXHIBITION RACE

DOUGLASS-WASHBURN TESTING FACILITY
BEZIÉR PROVING GROUNDS

DUNCAN CUTTER WASN'T used to reading another star nation into an operation, especially not at the expense of his own, but in some ways, that was exactly what was going on here today.

Once the governor-general had shared the information the team on Eridu supplied, and the doctrine that Rin Zhou had invoked, Jiu Liam had needed little persuasion; An-Yang was now fully invested in support of their plan.

Those involved had converged at a secret military testing facility known as the Bezier Proving Grounds. The doors to the hangar they stood inside were open, the runway mere meters away. Attached to the hangar's backside was a four-story building owned by Douglass-Washburn, the company's on-site testing facility.

Though the location was the nearest secured site to the fairgrounds, that wasn't its biggest selling point. That belonged to the Douglass-Washburn mission control room, and the console where Micah Case was seated—the one tied directly into Garza's starglider.

When the time came, it was from here Micah would commandeer Garza's ship, and divert it to the Proving Grounds, where a team stood by, ready to hustle the prime minister to safety.

The woman seated beside Micah had been introduced to Duncan as Douglass-Washburn's chief test pilot. Isobel would be the one to pilot the decoy plane in the aerial shell game that was about to transpire.

Duncan turned to his left, where Sam stood beside Admiral Toland. His niece's hand rested lightly on a stasis pod that floated between the two women, ready to receive the chiral man, and she and the admiral were flanked by a pair of drakeskin-clad operators. Their lone duty was to protect Sam and her charge, and the only person they reported to was Cutter himself.

Aside from Sam, Micah, and a small complement of highly trained mission specialists supplied by Douglass, the only other people involved in the rescue of Garza's twin were Major Reid's Unit teams, and the security team from An-Yang.

Duncan looked over at the An-Yang delegation—and Jiu Liam. Few realized it, but the man flying in today's exhibition race wouldn't be the star nation's president; it would be Liam's body double. A capable pilot, the An-Yang officer had spent the past few hours in close discussion with Micah, ironing out the details of the operation from the air.

A flicker from one of the holoscreens caught Duncan's attention, and he saw two stargliders taxiing toward the fairgrounds' runway.

{Ships are rolling,} he heard over his wire.

With nothing else to do but wait for the race to begin, he sidled over to Sam and the admiral. "Tell me again that this will work," he said in a low voice.

Sam stared back at him, resolute. "It will," she said in an equally low tone.

After a pause, she added, "The one time Micah coded was when Jonathan crashed in the portable surgi-suite on board

Wraith. I had to put Jonathan into stasis to save him, and from the timeline we managed to piece together, that's when Micah revived."

"And you've tested this between them since?" Duncan pressed.

Sam nodded. "Of course. When one of them is in stasis, the connection to the other is completely cut off. A tau-neu pod engenders total molecular cessation. It's like... a signal put on pause. The receiving unit will continue to operate and function, given its last set of instructions, until the signal is reinstated."

"And if something goes wrong, and we're unable to rescue them both?"

He saw concern crease Sam's brow.

"That is a little more difficult for us to judge," she admitted. "But we should be able to stabilize him if we take him out of stasis and he starts to crash. We can keep him there indefinitely until we figure out how to solve the problem."

She exchanged a guarded look with the admiral, and Toland decided to shoulder the explanation.

Turning to Cutter, she carefully stated, "One theory, sir, is that if one of them is killed and it doesn't appear the other will survive without his paired partner, then we might be able to force a quantum entanglement connection by replicating the chiral cloning."

Cutter's gaze cut from Toland to Sam and back. "You mean... a third Garza?" he said incredulously.

Toland lifted a cautionary hand. "It's just a working theory. We may be able to figure out a way around it without having to resort to something so drastic. We certainly aren't going to attempt such a thing without thoroughly researching it first— and without trying to get his permission to do it, if it comes to that."

Duncan stared back at her doubtfully. "You think you'll be able to get *permission* under those conditions?"

"I think we've all learned our lessons in that regard," she said.

Cutter stared back at the admiral as he considered her words.

Before he could respond, his attention was drawn to the main screens when he heard a voice call out, "They're taking off!"

"Showtime," he heard the test pilot say under her breath as she gripped the yoke.

The president of An-Yang stepped up beside Duncan with a polite nod. "Best wishes on your success," he murmured.

Duncan returned the nod with an equally grave one of his own. "Thank you for your help with this."

The other man inclined his head. "We have a common enemy. You helped us excise the nest in our backyard. It's only fair we do the same."

On a third screen, Cutter saw a starglider identical to the one Garza's clone was seated in idling at the end of the tarmac just outside the building in which they stood.

Once the three laps of the exhibition race were completed, the two competitors would participate in a victory roll that would lead them behind the crown of the Bezier Foothills. For a short while, both ships would be obscured; it was then that Garza's ship would be swapped out for the one idling on the runway just outside the Douglass-Washburn hangar.

At that point, the transponder codes would be switched, with Garza's ship being piloted by Micah. He would guide the ship here and land, while the test pilot, Isobel, joined the president's body double in a flashy landing back at the fairgrounds.

The timing was critical, but if all went as planned, Garza would be down on the Proving Grounds' runway and hustled inside the stasis unit before the Akkadian moles back at the fairgrounds discovered the shell game that had transpired.

DROPSHIP

Akkadian home fleet flagship
Port Akkadia
in orbit above Eridu

In nearspace above Eridu, Citizen Intelligence Officer Ahura found himself in the uncomfortable position of having to order a fleet admiral around.

The security packet from Che Josza that had provoked such rash behavior had arrived just minutes ago, delivered by a forbidding-looking man whose beaded braids signified an assassin of high rank within the Tèzhŏng. He stood beside Ahura in silent support as the intelligence officer faced off against Admiral Li.

To Ahura's great surprise, the man was surprisingly easy to convince.

Li turned to stare thoughtfully out at the starscape displayed on his office holoscreen. "This operation," he began. "Does it have anything to do with the recall of the fleet commanders?"

Ahura hesitated. "It... might. But not in the way you think."

"Good."

Li turned decisively and speared Ahura with a knowing look. "Something is going on. What, I don't know." He held up a hand. "And I don't *want* to know. I'm a simple man, Citizen Agent. Give me a clear enemy to fight, and I'm all in. But this recall for 'testing' that the premier's office ordered the other day...."

Li's voice turned sour. "It reeks of politics and intrigue. You say I need to loan you a dropship, but you can't tell me about the mission. And the people operating the dropship will never be able to speak about it. Yet I find it interesting this dropship is to deliver... someone... to the very spot my commanders have been ordered to report for testing."

Ahura knew the quality that often defined a good intelligence officer was the ability to know when to bluff and went to remain silent. In this instance, his instincts told him to do both.

He stoically stared back at Li, refusing to confirm or deny a thing—though inside, his heart was racing.

After a few moments, Li slapped the palm of his hand against his pants leg. "I've had a bad feeling about that recall from the start. You want a dropship?" He jerked a nod. "It's yours to command."

As Ahura boarded a shuttle, wondering how the hell an intelligence spook had just ended up in command of a ship, the people he was destined to meet were receiving their own marching orders.

* * *

A little more than two AU away, four Shadow Recon ships floated silently among a sea of stones, deep inside the Akkadian asteroid belt known as the Straits of Sargon.

While their co-pilots commanded fleets of stealthed drones forming protective spheres around the invisible ships, their comm officers were busy trying to unravel a puzzle.

Colonel Tala Valenti, the small battlegroup's commander,

presided over it all with quiet intensity. Of concern to her at the moment was something *Mirage*'s flight engineer had brought to her attention. Over the past day, no less than fifteen shuttles had flushed from capital ships, inbound to the Akkadian homeworld.

"Correct me if I'm wrong, ma'am," Will said, "but aren't every one of these ships coming from an Akkadian flagship?"

Will had configured the ship's ActiveFiber to form a jumpseat for Tala, so she could review the sensor feed with him. She bent forward to peer at the ident codes as Will backtraced each shuttle's flight path.

"They are," she confirmed, sitting back in the seat, eyes narrowing as she considered the display.

"Now, why would they be sending a representative in person, when they have access to Ford-Svaiter nodes?" Yuki murmured, putting voice to the same thought that had formed in Tala's mind.

"Good question, Lieutenant."

"Never known a military to spend a credit when they can do it on the cheap another way," said Taylor, the Marine co-pilot who sat on Yuki's left.

The Ford-Svaiter tech housed inside the Starshot buoys provided the settled worlds with instantaneous communication. The network of autonomous satellites was spread throughout each star system, a constellation that covered the bulk of occupied space within the heliosphere.

Though communication via Starshot was instantaneous, the buoys themselves were each spaced an AU apart, and latency between them was dependent on the speed of light. It took light a bit longer than eight minutes to travel that distance. That meant the very worst light lag one would experience in any populated area was half that—a fact every military ship knew intimately.

This, in turn, suggested that the people traveling in those shuttles were going to Eridu for more than just a little chat.

"See if you can't tap into some intraship chatter," Tala

instructed. "That activity's unusual enough for people to gossip—"

Takeko's voice interrupted the conversation.

{Incoming from Task Force Blue headquarters.}

Tala rose, holding her hand up to indicate she was listening to a message, and stepped away from the cockpit.

Head down, she paced *Mirage*'s cabin as Micah Case's voice came across her wire.

{Colonel, we have a situation.}

Quickly, he recapped the events that had most recently transpired on the Akkadian homeworld.

{Admiral Toland has okayed the fireteams to assist.}

He paused, and when he returned, his voice held an odd tenor.

{As strange as it may sound, you are ordered to rendezvous with an Akkadian dropship above Eridu's south pole. Apparently, my twin has managed to find himself an Akkadian co-conspirator.}

There was another pause. Then Micah's voice was back to its normal, brisk delivery.

{The admiral also said to remind you that the ship drives' new capabilities need to remain a secret. It is up to your discretion on how to handle that. Standing by, waiting for your response.}

The recording ended, and Tala instructed Takeko to push it to Will.

She picked up her pace as she crossed aft to the cargo bay, where the fireteam aboard *Mirage* had holed up. Alert eyes landed on her when she appeared at the bay doors.

"We've been greenlit for a mission," she told the soldiers. "Gear up."

Tala wheeled, retracing her steps to the cockpit and replaying the message for herself as she went.

She considered the mechanics of the situation they faced. They were hiding inside a densely populated asteroid field, deep inside enemy territory. Despite the fact they'd bolstered the existing constellation of comm buoys by seeding the area with their own stealth military ones, there was still fifteen seconds of lag—too long to comfortably hold live conversation.

My discretion, indeed.

Stopping behind Will's station, she silently instructed her SI to send Micah's message to the man's console. Aloud, she added, "Takeko, what is the least-time intercept to Eridu?"

Her words elicited a startled sound from Yuki, who twisted around to stare at her.

"Something going on, Colonel?"

Tala nodded to Will. "Specialist Morris?"

In response, the flight engineer pushed Micah's recording to the cockpit's speakers. "Colonel just received a message from Humbolt," he explained.

The recording played. Once it came to an end, Tala looked around at the flight crew. "Okay, you heard Captain Case. How are we going to hide these new drives?"

Nina made a troubled sound. "That's not going to be easy, Colonel. These drives don't have the same Casimir flare the old ones do. We appear from out of nowhere, whoever's looking will notice something's different."

"*Mirage*'s strike plate has been upgraded, too," Yuki reminded them. "If we retune to visible, they'll know exactly how good our stealth is. They'll pick it all up on scan, which means they'll study it and try to reverse engineer it."

"What if...." Will's voice faded, his expression one of concentration. "What if we take the jump uncloaked?"

Nina turned, frowning. "Did you hit your head or something? How does that help us?"

"Hang on, hear me out. What if we tell Micah to have Jonathan suggest that we've been hanging out around Eridu this whole time?"

"Not following," the Marine co-pilot frowned.

Tala held up a hand, and said slowly, "I think I am." She turned to Will. "Are you suggesting that we purposely misdirect them?"

He nodded. "Everyone knows that when a ship leaves

Scharnhorst space, the Casimir bubble lets off a pretty decent flare. But like Yuki pointed out, there's no visible flash with these new drives. If we imply we're already above Eridu, then when we shed the bubble, it'll mistakenly be attributed to the energy we use when coming out of stealth."

"So... they'll naturally associate their readings with our stealth technology, and not our drives," Tala clarified, and Will nodded.

"That's the idea. Seed a bit of confusion and misdirection within the intelligence community."

Yuki's face creased into a grin. "Dang, Will, you're devious. I like it."

Tala nodded. "I'll contact Micah, get him started on your disinformation campaign. You work on bringing the other ships up to speed on the plan."

"Hey, Colonel? What happens once we arrive?"

"We'll be rendezvousing with an Akkadian dropship. The fireteams from *Mirage*, *Wraith*, *Katana*, and *Eidolon* will transfer over, and from there, they'll be transported down to hook up with the team already in place."

Will frowned. "How are they going to hide this from their own military?"

"Under the pretense of a drill, conducted jointly by the Junxun Cadet Academy and the Akkadian home fleet."

The Marine copilot shook his head. "Not sure I want to know how they managed to pull that one off."

Ignoring his comment, Tala turned back to face Yuki. "ETA?"

"From here to Eridu's south pole? Eighteen minutes and some change."

"Very well. Since this was your idea," Tala waggled a finger between Yuki and Will, "record a detailed explanation of your plan, and have it ready to go in two minutes. I'll append it to my reply."

They nodded, and Tala retreated to her cabin, leaving them to their work as she crafted her own response to Task Force Blue.

Half an hour later, using coordinates Micah had assured them were exact, four Shadow Recon ships jumped into Scharnhorst space. Eighteen minutes after that, they reappeared… a scant fifty meters from an Akkadian dropship's starboard docking collar.

It took three minutes for the fireteams, poised inside the ships' airlocks, to launch themselves across the void into the open maw of the enemy ship.

Another three minutes after that, the four ships jumped back into Scharnhorst space, their collective crew numbers now decreased by sixteen warriors.

PAPERWORK

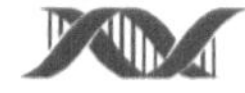

DEFENSE MINISTRY
CENTRAL PREFECTURE, ERIDU

SERAE ETESAV WAS more than just Dacina Zian's sister in combat. Like the 'Fierce Dagger,' Serae, too, had been abandoned to the Junxun as a young, nameless girl. Also like Dacina, it hadn't taken long for Serae to earn her own name.

Serae Etesav, 'Strikes Swiftly,' had done more than follow in Dacina's footsteps; she had become a champion of the killing fields in her own right.

Serae tried to follow Dacina into the Tèzhŏng, but the Ministry of State Security had refused her petition. Deep inside her heart of hearts, Strikes Swiftly knew why; Serae lacked that indefinable something, a quality that bled from Dacina's eyes. It was the soul of a stone-cold killer.

It hadn't kept Serae from covertly following her battle-sister's career, though. She became the Dagger's most staunch, yet silent, supporter.

When Dacina had asked for the Dozen, Serae gave without question. But when the Dagger had explained why, Serae demanded, by the right of vengeance, that she play a part.

Her request had led her to the Defense Ministry today.

Behind her blank façade, a fierce satisfaction burned. Today's strike would be swift and brilliant—and utterly unexpected.

She nodded curtly to the ostovars at the entrance, the two soldiers snapping to crisp attention at the sight of the general first-class, who neared.

Her face allowed her entrance into the building; her security token allowed her passage into the antechamber of the offices of Warren Hatami, Akkadia's minister of defense.

She checked her chrono; the dropship would be making its high-speed burn right about now, which meant....

Hatami's secretary burst out of his cramped cubicle, a frantic expression on his face.

"Your pardon, Citizen General. I need to see the Citizen Minister *immediately.*"

* * *

Warren Hatami had been trying to clear his desk of mounds of data cubes for the past two days. He'd had no idea when he accepted the position years earlier that the job came with so much paperwork.

*And why, by the ancestors, is it called **paper**work, when there's no paper involved?*

He knew his peers had their underlings manage most of the work, but Warren believed in keeping his fingers involved in the everyday aspects of the posting, and endeavored—as much as one could, with the constraints of the empire—to support his citizen generals, admirals, and commanders to the best of his ability.

More than once, his work ethic had been remarked upon, the citizen minister of the interior once even accusing him of trying to run the military as a meritocracy.

He had just signed off on the last file in the data cube inserted into his console when his doors flew open to reveal his wide-eyed secretary.

Or maybe that should be wild-eyed, he thought, his gaze shifting to the woman who stood coolly behind him.

The contrast was so marked, he almost smiled, but then he recalled himself and opted for disapproving instead.

"I explicitly said I was not to be disturbed," he said in a stern voice.

The man flinched, but forged ahead. "The premier's office pinged. They demand to know why a dropship is landing in the Aksu Desert without advance warning!"

"A dropship?" Startlement had Warren rising halfway from his chair.

"Are you speaking of the joint Junxun-fleet exercise the citizen minister approved last week?" Serae's voice sounded amused and slightly bored.

The secretary spun around. "You *know* of this?"

Citizen General Serae lifted a brow. "Of course I do. I was the one who requested it, along with Admiral Li."

Warren blinked in confusion, his mind drawing a blank. "I approved this?" He glanced around at the data cubes, scattered haphazardly about his desk.

The citizen general inclined her head. "Indeed. You signed the approval just yesterday, Citizen Minister. I dropped by to express my thanks. The latest cadet class has been a bit... unruly of late, and when I happened to mention it to the citizen admiral, he suggested we combine forces to keep our respective branches on their toes with a surprise drill."

Warren relaxed back into his seat. With a casual hand-wave in Serae's direction, he told his secretary, "See? That's all it is. Please reassure the premier's office this is routine, nothing more."

He returned his attention to his *paperwork*, his mind already puzzling out the next round of requests, heedless of the private smile that played about Serae's mouth as the Junxun leader pivoted and exited his domain.

SHAR-KALI INITIATIVE

Shar-Kali Correctional Facility
and Reeducation Center
Aksu Desert

CHE HAD STASHED Garza and Rin Zhou in a nearby conference room, leaving Ell, Jonathan, and Joule to protect them. Thad, Morrison, and Aviva—the woman his Dagger had flipped to their side—accompanied Che to visit the prison's warden.

He'd asked the facility's overseer to show them to the prison's security center so that they might watch the 'joint exercise' firsthand. Control of this room was critical to their mission's success; it was the heart of the entire complex, and it was located mere steps from the warden's office.

A side glance told Che the man still hadn't recovered from the shock of his arrival.

Still, the same explanation he'd used on the doctor, that of a surprise inspection, had worked on the warden, mainly because it held the ring of truth to it.

He ignored the man, trusting Dacina's watchful eyes, and turned his focus to the next phase.

The guards working the control center handed it over with

little fanfare. Before the warden even had a chance to open his mouth, Che's Dagger informed the men that they were relieved of duty.

They stood, swapping positions with a mix of Junxun and Geminate off-worlders.

Of course, the warden had no way of knowing this.

Che studied the wall dedicated to the prison's stream of holographic feeds, the images changing rapidly under the hands of the woman seated at the controls.

Under the pretext of realigning external sensors to better view the exercise about to commence, the Alliance agent the Dagger had recruited was busy severing communications with the outside.

It was their good fortune that Aviva had turned out to be what the Alliance called a 'signals intelligence specialist.' Her expertise guaranteed that no whisper of today's actions escaped.

The man who had been her partner stood glowering beside the giant Marine, both sporting poorly masked expressions of outrage.

Aviva turned to Che and gave a small nod, studiously ignoring the compatriots she had betrayed.

"The middle feed should give you the best view of the exercise, Citizen Minister," she said. "The dropship is scheduled to arrive within the next five minutes."

The warden sucked in a breath, awe painted on his face at the sight of the ship that came in on a hard burn.

It flipped, hovering in the air as it popped its hatches. Invisible bodies dropped from them, equally invisible thrusters halting their HALO descent.

Once clear, the ship climbed in a flare of light from its drives' energy plume, disappearing into the stratosphere.

"Assets down," Aviva said.

"Impressive," the warden murmured.

"This is just the beginning," responded Che, sending the Dagger the signal.

In a swift move, Dacina stepped up behind the man and, with a sharp blow to the back of his skull, rendered him unconscious. A shackling patch ensured he would remain that way.

One of her Junxun lifted him from the room, returning the warden to his office, until the operation was complete.

The feed projected on the wall showed the Unit soldiers had rendezvoused with their Junxun counterparts and were, even now, infiltrating via the three shafts. Their objective was twofold: secure the hangar and subdue the guards.

That left Clint Janus to the people inside this room.

Che looked over at Thad Severance. "Are you ready?"

* * *

At Che's question, Thad glanced at Morrison, who gave him a brief chin lift.

Thad ignored Aviva. It'd be a cold day in hell before he trusted her on an op. If he were a betting man, he'd guess the assassin knew this, too, which was why Aviva would remain stationed in this room.

Turning his back on the woman, Thad nodded to Che. "Let's do this."

He let the assassin lead. Swinging past the conference room so that Ell, Jonathan, and Joule could join them, they traversed the corridors at a steady clip, weapons holstered so as not to draw attention.

When they reached the intersection that led to the lab, the Dagger increased her pace, closing on the pair of guards that stood beside the security-coded entrance.

Words were exchanged. Thad watched as two of Dacina's soldiers moved forward at her hand signal, ostensibly to take the guards' place, but with sudden swiftness, they turned on the two men. A few vicious, well-placed strikes later, the guards were no longer a factor.

"Access is coming—"

The Dagger's words cut off as the security-coded doors' telltales turned green, and they slid open.

The hallway beyond the portal was short, with doors leading to rooms the prison's map had labeled as 'testing'. Thad didn't want to know what Janus had done to his subjects behind those doors. Fortunately, that wasn't the focus of this mission. Their objective, the lab, lay at the end of the passage.

He drew his weapon, and the rest did the same, the group spreading out as they approached. Dacina launched a drone that sniffed the door for all evidence of recent use—and for traps.

"Clear," she reported.

Stepping up to the door's palmpad, the assassin laid her hand on it.

The doors slid open, unleashing a barrage of weapons fire from inside.

* * *

Dacina dove for cover, the lance of directed-energy beams searing a path through the air mere centimeters from her head.

"That's not Janus!" she heard Ell call out, the sniper's back pressed to the wall on the other side of the door. "The angle's too high."

Dacina crouched, studying the firing pattern with a critical eye. "It's also automated," she noted after a second.

She heard Ell's Marine curse.

"Damned fool's set off the room's defense systems."

"But why?" a stealthed Garza asked.

"He must have tried to communicate with someone on the outside and realized he was blocked," Rin Zhou speculated.

"That alone shouldn't have done it," countered Ell. "Surely, networks go down on occasion—especially in the desert."

"Then he tried to reach the warden, and when the man didn't respond...."

Dacina reached out to the asset she'd turned. {Can you

deactivate the defensive grid in Janus's lab?}

{Working on it....} There was a pause. *{Is what you're after time-sensitive?}*

{Only Janus.}

{I'm reading no life signs on scan. He's not in there.}

Dacina hit the palmpad, and the doors slid shut, sealing the defensive screen inside. "He must be headed for the hangar. He'll try to escape, get word out."

"Janus is smart enough to suspect we have eyes on that hangar," protested Thad. "You know the layout here. Where else could he hole up?"

Dacina considered the options, and then nodded to her left. "The laundry facility and waste reclamation plants are adjacent to the hangar bay, on this side." Indicating with her chin, she added, "The kitchen and prison dining facility are in that direction, on the other side."

"So we split up." Thad's eyes darted about, doing a swift mental headcount.

Dacina followed his gaze. There were twelve of them, including Che, Garza, and Rin Zhou, plus three of her Junxun.

"Morrison, you take Garza and one of the Dagger's men and scout out the kitchens." The Marine shot Dacina a seeking look, and she nodded her agreement.

She knew what the Marine was doing; the kitchens were both the safest and least likely spot that Janus would choose, too far away for the doctor to bother. It was Thad's way of ensuring Garza's safety, just like her choices would protect Che.

Dacina motioned to one of her men. "We will go with the citizen minister to check out the hangar."

That seemed to please the Marine.

Dacina knew, like he did, that the most likely spot for Janus to hide was inside the laundry. That left the reclamation plant.

The man turned to Jonathan, an odd smile on his face.

The Alliance pilot straightened. "No."

The Marine's smile widened.

"Well, shit," Jonathan cursed.

"Literally, *ami*." The Marine clapped him on the shoulder. "Latrine duty falls to the new guy on the op."

"Buck up," said Ell, stepping forward. "I'll suffer alongside you."

Dacina had the oddest impression she had missed some subtext here, but had neither the time nor the inclination to suss it out.

"Well, then. It appears that leaves the laundry to us, Captain Severance." Rin Zhou stepped forward, weapon in hand. Beside her stood Dacina's final Junxun.

Thad inclined his head toward the woman. "After you, ma'am."

They separated into their teams, breaking into a jog as they headed for their respective destinations.

"Good hunting," the Marine called in a low voice.

"May your blade be swift."

Dacina thought she heard the man's soft, "Huh. I'll have to remember that one," as he walked away.

SHIT SHOW

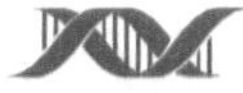

SHAR-KALI CORRECTIONAL FACILITY
AND REEDUCATION CENTER
AKSU DESERT

THE HUM OF the automated system and the mechanical sound of paddles churning liquid in the vats below masked Jonathan's ingress into the waste reclamation plant. He cleared the entrance quickly, as he'd been trained to do, his pistol tracking across the open expanse as he crossed from one side of the door to the other.

His quick slice-of-the-pie not revealing any immediate threat, Jonathan stepped cautiously inside. His gaze landed on the treatment pool, lit from within by the blue glow of ultraviolet light, but it was immediately drawn away when a clattering sound came on his left.

A lean, familiar form raced toward a set of metal stairs that led up to the plant's pulpit, where the SIs that controlled the waste facility were housed.

Ordering his drakeskin suit to flush a cloud of audio chaff, Jonathan sped after Janus. The chaff masked the clink and rattle of his footsteps on the grated metal walkway, while the plant's ambient sound covered the rest.

He motioned for Joule to swing around and approach from the other side, and the big cat obligingly turned down the walkway in the other direction.

{Found him,} he sent to the others as he closed in on the metal staircase.

{Coming up from below,} Ell replied. *{Be there in a few.}*

Jonathan took the steps two at a time, an idea forming.

Passing his pistol from his right hand to his left, he fumbled in his tactical vest for the flash-bang he knew was there. His attention on his pocket, he hit the top step and overshot, his foot coming down hard on the grated surface and causing a *clang* to reverberate loud enough to overcome the chaff.

A muffled exclamation sounded up ahead, and he saw the pulpit's door slide open. Then Janus leaned out, weapon in hand, and Jonathan was forced to duck when he saw the barrel spark.

He pivoted to the side, back flat against the control room's metal wall, feeling exposed as shots from the energy pistol scored the grating beneath his feet, and drilled heated divots into the metal wall above his head.

{Any time now would be good....}

Janus couldn't know precisely where he was—not with active stealth. The problem was the narrow gangway didn't leave him much maneuvering room, and if Ell didn't get here soon, he'd have to make a play for Janus before the man cut him down, drakeskin or no drakeskin.

He used his wire to manually trigger the SmartCarbyne lattice that ran throughout his body, reinforcing bones and strengthening muscles. He crept steadily forward, one eye on the sludge turning ponderously below, the other on the man taking potshots at the air around him as he gauged when to make his move.

When the doctor's gun hand swung to the left, Jonathan lunged. Picosensors that ran along the axons of his neural circuitry came online, functioning as supplemental nodes and signal boosters, propelling him forward with a speed and agility that far outpaced the human norm. He powered into the other man, driving him back into the pulpit.

Janus swung wildly, accidentally clocking Jonathan in the head with the butt of the pistol. They broke apart, and Janus scrambled to his feet, coming up with a metal pole in his hand that looked like it was from one of the paddles churning the contents of the vat below.

The doctor swung it like a bat, and Jonathan sprang away. With his enhanced reflexes, he could have easily evaded—if he'd had the space to retreat. As it was, he slammed into the pulpit's far wall, the end of the pole clipping him in the gut and knocking the wind from him.

Instinctively he curled into himself, gasping for air, just as the other man swung the pole down toward the top of his head. Jonathan jerked out of the way, grabbing at the pole with one hand. The ionic threads woven into the palm of his drakeskin suit fastened tight about the metal rod, and he twisted, the movement snapping the doctor's wrist with a sickening *crack*.

On a roar, Janus charged, bringing his pistol up once more. Jonathan backpedaled, reaching up to wrap his hand around the barrel, and knocking it upward as it discharged. At the same time, his heel hit the lip of the pulpit's entrance, knocking him off-balance.

He fell back, his head hanging over the side of the walkway. Blindly, Janus reached for Jonathan's neck, seeking a choke-hold—but then a ripping snarl sounded, echoing off the walls of the chamber.

With a startled yelp, the doctor released him, scrambling over his stealthed form in his haste to get away.

A low growl emitted over his wire. *{You owe me steak.}*

* * *

While Jonathan snuck into the waste reclamation plant through its main entrance, Ell circled around and came in from below and behind. That meant a quick jaunt through the prison's hangar bay.

The area held all the typical sights, sounds, and smells endemic to such places. She could hear the *ting-ting-ting* of cooling metal from a nearby shuttle that had recently landed. The floor she crossed was smeared with stains hinting at years of accumulated spills and hydraulic leaks.

On the other side of the cavernous bay, Ell saw shadowed figures limned on her overlay, her suit's IFF telling her where the Dagger and her entourage had begun their search. Her own destination was just ahead: a side entrance into the bowels of the reclamation plant.

As was typical of such areas, the edges bled shadows. Like with all vermin, it was just the sort of place Janus would gravitate toward.

Hearing Jonathan's call, she increased her pace. Slipping inside the plant, she was met by the sound of weapons fire, and then the clang of metal on metal as the two men sparred.

Catching sight of the stairs leading up from the vats to the walkways above, Ell raced toward them. If Janus managed to escape Jonathan's grasp, it was here she would intercept him.

{Sitrep,} Thad's voice rang in her head.

{It sounds like Jonathan's engaged Janus, and—} She paused at the foot of the stairs, head cocked.

{And...?}

{Wait one.} Ell listened. *{I think Jonathan's disarmed him. Going up.}*

{Entering from the second-floor hallway,} Thad informed her.

She sent him a mental nod. *{That should put you right above me. They're up at the pinnacle. Third level, small control center.}*

{Coming in from the other side, across from your Marine,} came Dacina's voice.

Ell smiled internally at Dacina's characterization of Thad as she began climbing, then scolded herself for her distraction.

Get your head in the game, Cyr.

She slowed when her head came even with the walkway, and shifted her grip on her rifle.

The events of the next few seconds unfolded rapidly.

Ell charged up the remainder of the steps just as Joule's angry snarl rang out above. Her forward momentum sent her crashing into Janus, the man fleeing the savage beast at his heels.

She reeled back, momentarily off-balance, and her rifle swung to one side as she freed a hand to grab at the railing and keep from pitching over the side.

In the next instant, she felt Janus's hand wrap around her neck, the barrel of a pistol pressed firmly against her temple.

SACRIFICES

SHAR-KALI CORRECTIONAL FACILITY
AND REEDUCATION CENTER
AKSU DESERT

"DROP YOUR WEAPON, or she dies!"

Janus's voice held an edge of panic that told Thad the man was operating from a place of great instability, his hindbrain in complete control.

He instinctively understood that to push the doctor at this moment would cause him to snap.

{Sitrep!} His own voice was laced with tension.

Somehow, he *knew* it was Ell that Janus had in his grasp.

{Guy's got the barrel of an energy pistol pressed to Ell's right temple, and I highly doubt it's dialed down,} Jonathan told him, his mental tone taut with rage.

They were both aware of what that meant. No one could survive a full-strength directed energy blast, shot at point-blank range.

Thad looked up to see the pilot's shadowed form, weapon drawn and pointed at an angle that placed Janus almost directly beneath where Thad stood.

{Got another problem,} Jonathan informed him. *{That pool's using accelerated forced degradation. The field it's emitting is interfering with my CUSP. My HUD's giving me a low-confidence error every time I try to draw a bead on him.}*

"Drop it!" Janus ordered.

{He thinks I'm the only one here,} said Jonathan. *{Gonna drop the CUSP. It's worthless right now, anyway.}* Aloud, the pilot called out, "Fine. Just don't shoot."

Thad heard the clang of the pistol hit the metal walkway.

"See? No weapon," Jonathan said calmly. "Now let her go."

Beneath him, Thad heard Janus scoff. "You think I'm a fool? I know you're carrying more than one."

{Keep him talking. I'm just inside the entrance, directly above them.} Thad stepped forward. *{Let me see if I can't —}*

He froze as the walkway creaked beneath his feet.

"You, up there! Move again, and she gets it!"

Thad's gaze shot to Jonathan. *{Tell me you have a clean shot, ami.}*

He saw Jonathan's silhouette shake its head. *{I don't, man. Guy's pulled her up right in front of him.}*

{He's taller than she is, dammit!}

{And he's lower on the set of stairs. Damn doctor's smart enough to have figured that one out.} He could hear the frustration in Jonathan's voice. *{I can't put a bullet in him without hitting her.}*

Thad abruptly realized the one person he hadn't heard from.

{Ell? Report!}

{I don't think she can, Captain.}

Dacina's voice told him she'd arrived, but when he scanned the walkway across from him, he couldn't pinpoint her position.

{Ziptie?} he asked.

{We call them shackles, but they are essentially the same.}

Thad heard shuffling sounds. The doctor was moving, and dragging Ell along with him.

"Let her go, Janus," he called out.

"Not a chance. She's my ticket out of here."

Across the pool, Rin Zhou stepped into view. Her eyes flicked up to Thad before settling down below. "You know we cannot allow you to leave, Doctor."

Janus's harsh laugh cut through the chamber. "Isn't that some irony. The prisoner telling the man who reports *directly to the premier* what he can and cannot do."

{Careful,} Thad cautioned. *{Don't push him.}*

It was difficult to see from this distance, but he thought he saw Rin Zhou's eyelids flicker in response. Otherwise, she did not react.

"Then listen to me," Che spoke from the shadows. "I'm the premier's right hand. And I am telling you to stand down."

Janus's laugh was tinged with hysteria. "His right hand? Oh, I don't think so. Know what I think?"

{Captain Case. Take the shot.}

Rin Zhou wasn't looking at Janus any longer; she was looking up at the walkway where Jonathan lay, stretched out, his P-SCAR rifle aimed at Janus's forehead.

The pilot shook his head. *{Can't. I'll hit Ell.}*

{I know. Do it anyway.}

{No!} Thad's head jerked from Jonathan to Rin Zhou. *{I don't give a good goddam who you are, lady, you do **not** give my people orders.}*

Rin Zhou stared dispassionately at him. *{Your emotions are engaged. You must recuse yourself.}* She turned to the room. *{Does anyone have a clear shot?}*

Below Thad, Janus continued to rant at Che. "You're about to become a puppet, Josza, no better than that poor bastard, Garza. You—"

Thad tuned out the doctor's diatribe and eased his way down the walkway, trying desperately to gain a vantage point from which he could sight on the man.

{Take the shot, Captain Case.}

{I can't...} Jonathan's voice faltered, and Thad saw his hand

waver.

Enlai pressed, *{The fate of the settled worlds—}*

*{**Fuck** the settled worlds!}* Thad growled. *{I'm ordering you, Case. Do **not** listen to her!}*

He saw a hole in the grating, and angled toward it. Carefully lowering himself, Thad eased his head through the opening—and cursed mentally.

The angle Janus held Ell was one that denied a clear shot, even from Thad's close position.

He saw Ell's eyes fix upon something or someone across the pool, then she nodded imperceptibly.

Thad whipped his head in the direction of her gaze just in time to see a weapon in Rin Zhou's hand.

With a roar, he rolled, bringing his own firearm to bear, but he was too late. He saw a muzzle flash, heard an echoing boom as the weapon discharged.

Twisting, he dove through the hole in the floor, landing hard on his hands and knees, but he ignored the pain. The hole in Ell's chest filled his vision as she sagged, dead weight in Janus's arms.

As if from a distance, Thad heard a bellow that sounded like it came from a wounded animal as he launched himself toward Ell's falling body. Some part of his brain recognized that the cry had come from him, yet he dismissed it, his focus entirely on the woman sinking to the floor. He caught her just as Janus reeled back against the railing.

The doctor's breathing was ragged, and his hand shook as it lifted the barrel of his weapon, but he brought his other hand up to steady his aim, his intent clear.

Thad reached for his pistol with one hand, still holding Ell with the other, but before he could draw on Janus, the flash of a dagger caught his eye as it came sailing across the pool of liquid waste to bury itself in Janus's neck.

The doctor's hand spasmed, his weapon discharging harmlessly above Thad's head before clattering to the steel platform. Janus staggered back, hands clutching at his neck.

A loud *crack* sounded, the discharge of Jonathan's rifle bouncing off the reclamation plant's metal walls.

The doctor's body jerked once more, his knees folding in an odd, disjointed way that told Thad the pilot had severed the man's brain stem, before the corpse tumbled over the railing and into the vat below.

With Janus no longer an immediate threat to him or Ell, Thad became aware of his surroundings, and of the blood seeping through his fingers from where they pressed against the wound in Ell's chest.

The sight caused his own heart to seize painfully.

"Ell-o-die," he whispered brokenly. "Don't you dare die on me, you hear?"

The smile she gave him was faint, and she whispered something he didn't catch.

He leaned closer as bodies crowded around him, ignoring hands that pushed insistently at him to try to get to her.

"Dacina has a medical kit," he heard Jonathan say. "Let her treat Ell."

Thad shook the pilot's hand from his shoulder and leaned closer. "What did you say?" he asked gently, squeezing Ell's hand in his.

Faint humor flickered briefly in her pain-filled eyes. "Joule says you owe me at least five steaks for that one...."

JOINT OPERATIONS

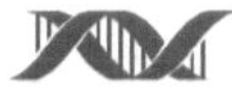

En route to Junxun Academy
Central Prefecture, Eridu

THE FLIGHT TO Central Prefecture occurred without further incident. Jonathan piloted the massive prison transport, with Dacina riding shotgun to give directions. Thad sat beside Ell, who was fast on her way to recovery, thanks to the syringe filled with CQDs that the assassin had injected into the sniper.

Carbon quantum dots were capable of molecular recognition and self-assembly, and were especially effective at reconstructing tissue and closing wounds. Thad spent a frantic few moments desperately searching his memory for whether or not CQDs were a medical therapy that worked with Ell's physiology.

"It's fine," she assured him, her voice already stronger as she struggled to sit up.

Thad shoved her gently back down to the bench where he'd laid her down when they boarded. "You sure 'bout that, *cher*?"

She smiled. "All good. No medical history of rejecting CQDs."

The dots were the backbone of field medicine, and if he'd been thinking clearly, he would have recalled that she wouldn't have been allowed on the teams if she'd been one of those rare individuals who didn't respond to the treatment.

He nodded and, once he was convinced she wouldn't do anything rash like try to sit up again, he gave her hand a quick squeeze. "We're going to have ourselves a little talk about this, that, and the third when we get home, *cher*. Just warning you about that now."

A smile lit Ell's eyes. "This, that, and the third, huh?"

With another squeeze, he stood. "Be back in a bit."

* * *

Jonathan looked up when Thad joined them at the front of the transport.

"All good?" he asked his friend.

"All good." The Marine turned and scowled over at Rin Zhou. "Not that I'll be forgetting any time soon what you did back there."

The former minister was seated behind the Dagger. Out of the side of his eye, Jonathan saw the woman incline her head.

"I would point out that the needs of the many—"

Thad jabbed a finger in her direction. "Don't even start with me, lady. We're here because of the needs of the many, but that does *not* give you the power of life and death over the few. *Especially* when they're not your own people."

"Your Ell gave me permission."

Jonathan's friend looked like he was about to go nova. "Want to run that by me one more time?" Thad's voice was dangerously low.

"She's right," Jonathan interjected quietly. "You and I both saw it."

Dacina cut in, redirecting their focus. "We approach."

An icon with a tag written in Aka'a appeared, identifying the building they were closing on as the Junxun Academy. It had a large, open expanse at its rear, and it was to this that Dacina directed him.

"The killing fields," Che murmured.

{Bloodthirsty lot, aren't they?} commented a member of the fireteams seated in the back.

Jonathan silently agreed.

The woman who met them when they disembarked didn't resemble the Dagger in any way, but her mannerisms somehow managed to convey a sense of family.

The other woman's gaze flickered over those assembled, her eyes coming to rest first on Che and then Rin Zhou. She dipped her head briefly in respect before her attention returned to the Dagger.

"Serae," murmured Dacina. "Stage one was a success?"

The smile that crossed Serae's face did not reach her eyes. "It was."

"And stage two?"

The female warrior held out a hand, a small pile of glittering disks in her palm. "Awaiting delivery."

Dacina turned and looked expectantly at Che.

Che, in turn, looked at Thad. "Are your people ready for this?"

"We are on this end. Let me confirm with those on the other end." Thad's head dipped, the man appearing to study his boots, his P-SCAR rifle cradled in his hands.

A moment later, the Marine's voice sounded inside Jonathan's head.

{Well, hoss? Wanna do that woo-woo thing you do, and see what's going on back home?}

SHELL GAME

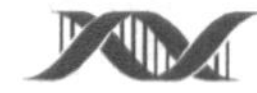

THE STARGLIDERS HAD taxied into position at the end of the runway, and Micah felt his palms grow slick with sweat.

This is it.

He surreptitiously slid his hands along the moisture-wicking fabric of his pant leg and then gripped the yoke once more.

He'd begun shadowing Garza's movements the moment the prime minister began taxiing from the Douglass-Washburn tent, toward the end of the runway. Now, he was about to take the place of the vessel's SI—without the man knowing.

As Garza rolled to a stop, Micah jiggled the yoke in the prearranged pattern that the prime minister would be expecting, the one that would tell him the SI was performing its safety check. He felt Garza's hold lighten, releasing the yoke into Micah's hands.

Exactly as the SI would do, Micah sent the starglider through a full range of control surfaces checks, moving the yoke forward and back, and side to side. He knew Isobel was doing much the same with the starglider on the tarmac outside the hangar doors, the one that would replace Garza's after the race's third lap.

Micah's eyes remained riveted to the countdown timer, and when it hit zero, he felt Garza push the throttle forward, adding back pressure to the yoke as he sent the vessel hurtling toward the end of the runway. When the ship hit eighty kilometers an hour, a slight pull of the yoke had the nose lifting as the vessel rotated.

So far, so good.

Now airborne, Micah kept one eye on the ship off Garza's right wingtip, piloted by Jiu Liam's body double—an accomplished pilot in his own right.

The race itself wouldn't truly begin until they crossed the starting flags, held aloft by drones at the aerial racetrack up ahead. Until then, the two stargliders would keep a careful pace.

As the starting line neared, Micah made a small correction, nosing the prime minister's vessel to the left and opening the space between the two ships. The vessel on his right waggled its wings once and did the same.

The moment the vessel's nose crossed between the two flags, Garza opened the throttle. The two stargliders leaped forward, racing down the straightaway, the first turn now half a kilometer ahead.

With one eye on the pylons and the other on the vessel beside him, Micah fought the urge to trim the ship to its fastest configuration, knowing that the SI that was supposed to be on board would not cut as many corners as he was willing to do.

He felt the little craft whip around the first curve in a tight, coordinated turn, and let out a low mental whistle.

The man's not half bad.

Garza eased out of the turn, righting the ship with almost painful care.

That earned him a mental chuckle from the test pilot.

{Student pilot, right there.}

Garza punched it on the straightaway, and Micah noted the man now led by about two lengths.

Jiu Liam's pilot was no slouch, though. He quickly made up the deficit, going into the next turn ahead of the prime minister.

The two ships continued to jockey for position, first one taking the lead and then the other, until they entered the final straightaway.

{Launching decoy ship now,} Micah heard Isobel say.

As the ships flew past the finish line, Micah saw the other man's vessel waggle its wings once more before the pilot pulled back on his stick and sent his ship into a flashy snap roll around Garza's starglider.

Micah could still hear the prime minister's startled inhale as the other vessel inscribed a loop around him, and then his own ship's 'SI' took control.

Micah nosed around, following the first ship's lead. He cut Garza's comms at the same time he flipped the starglider up into a knife-edge, crossing behind the mountain range and out of sight of the fairgrounds.

{You're clear. Cut loose and head home,} Isobel announced. *{I've got it from here.}*

{That's a good copy.}

Snapping the ship back into standard configuration, Micah began an immediate descent to the Proving Grounds airfield.

Isobel waggled the wings of her own ship as it crossed paths with his and joined up with the An-Yang ship. In moments, the two stargliders had popped back up above the mountain range, their noses pointed toward the fairgrounds.

Micah throttled back as the Proving Grounds runway grew larger in his forward screens. He landed with a slight bump, taxiing the ship directly to the Douglass-Washburn hangar. He could see the hangar doors open, saw a phalanx of guards, their weapons held at the ready.

Garza must be shitting his pants right about now, he thought. *Wish we'd been able to tell him our plans ahead of time, but the security they had around him was just too tight. Just a few more seconds....*

He maneuvered Garza's ship through the hangar doors and powered the ship down. His hangar console secure, Micah sprang to his feet and jogged toward the ship.

He saw the moment Garza realized that those who had abducted him this second time were the good guys.

"Captain Case," Garza said with some relief, "I understand you are the mysterious SI who hijacked me?"

Micah crooked a small grin his way. "Sorry about that. I would've told you if I could, but they had you covered pretty thoroughly."

The other man grimaced. "Raphael said, but I didn't dare hope. So it's true? He's being rescued?" Garza's gaze swung to Cutter. "You spoke with the governor-general?"

Cutter nodded. "You were right. Well, your mirror twin was, that is." His smile was a bit lopsided. "I gather you know I spoke with him and Rin Zhou."

Garza nodded. "He said as much to me, but we've both been a bit busy, and this mental communication thing is new. It's difficult to...." He groped for words.

"Keep all the plates spinning at one time?" Micah offered.

The prime minister nodded. "Exactly."

Admiral Toland stepped forward, gesturing to the man. "For your own protection, sir, we'd like to place you in stasis."

She began to lead him away, but the man balked.

"My wife—my kids—"

Cutter lifted a hand to forestall Garza. "All handled."

Still, Garza hesitated. "Let me at least let my... Raphael... know." He spared Micah a glance. "I'm sure you can understand how unsettling this is going to be for him."

Micah dipped his head in acknowledgment. "Don't worry, sir. We've got this."

The emotion in Garza's eyes defied description.

"Thank you," were the only words he said, but none other were needed.

The admiral's hand came down on his arm, and Garza turned wordlessly and walked away.

Micah heard Sam speak softly as she detailed why this measure was needed. He saw understanding cross the man's face, and was grateful when, as the unit opened, the prime minister climbed in without hesitation.

As the chamber slid shut and Sam brought the stasis pod online, Micah heard a commotion at the back end of the hangar.

"What's going on?" he heard one of the An-Yang officers ask.

A warning siren sounded, and Micah pivoted, seeking the source of the threat.

"Perimeter breach." The Douglass-Washburn manager's face looked pale as she said the words.

"What do you mean perimeter breach?" Cutter demanded.

"That tone's the general alert for the Proving Grounds," Isobel told them.

"That's a large area," Micah said. "The Grounds cover nearly four hundred thousand hectares."

"So how do they know we're *here*?" Sam asked, laying a hand protectively on the pod.

Micah shook his head, as stumped as the rest—until his gaze landed on the now-shut hangar doors. "*Shit.*"

His head swung over to Cutter and Toland. "Those doors weren't quite closed when the prime minister popped the fuselage on the starglider, were they?"

"No, they weren't," said the admiral. "Why?"

Micah swung around to face Isobel. "Is this hangar shielded?"

The test pilot's expression sharpened. "You're thinking they have a tracker somewhere on him?"

Sam's lips pressed firmly together. "Well, it's cut off now, there's no way a device like that can work in stasis. Do you think they're here for him?" Her gaze slid from her uncle to the stasis pod.

The woman shook her head. "There's no way to know for sure. I know it's a large area, but we have decent sensor coverage, starting at the surface and continuing a thousand meters up. Problem is, they're pretty basic. They'll let you know they've been tripped and that we have intruders, but not much more."

"They also sound if one of the drones goes offline," one of the techs standing nearby reminded her.

"Drones?" Micah looked over at the tech. "What make and model?"

It was Isobel who answered. "They're made from the same basic specs as the sphere of drones your Helios deploys when you go full stealth."

"So not likely to give a false reading, then."

She shook her head.

{Any way to pinpoint the breach, or at least narrow down its location?} Gabe's voice interjected.

Micah knew that there were two fireteams of Unit soldiers dressed in drakeskin suits and evenly spaced around the hangar. He could see their concealed forms projected on his overlay, thanks to the predictive systems upgrade the Navy had given his wire when he'd joined Shadow Recon.

"I can answer that." A figure decloaked, and Major Reid stepped forward.

Her gaze became distant, and Micah guessed that she was in communication with the Proving Grounds security team.

After a moment, she snapped her head around and motioned to the other shadowed figures, her response rapid-fire. "The alarm was tripped by a small invading force. They breached the perimeter two klicks away, and are closing fast."

Her voice took on a dispassionate tone as her gaze defocused once more. "Scrambling Unit forces to intercept."

The president of An-Yang motioned his security agents over to Reid. "My people will assist."

Cutter nodded a wordless thanks and then wheeled to face Micah, his expression grim. "I can guarantee you that this first force is acting as a diversion for a smaller strike force at the tip of their spear. I need you to take Sam and the stasis pod and get the hell out of here, now."

OOBLECK

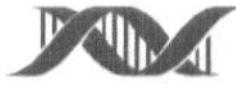

Douglass-Washburn Testing Facility
Beziér Proving Grounds

THERE WAS A loud thud and then a crash just outside the hangar doors, followed by the sounds of combat. The enemy had found them.

{I'll go with them,} Gabe sent, and Micah saw the shrouded figure with the former NCIC agent's ID label break away from his post and jog toward Sam and the stasis pod.

The click of claws on the ceramacrete floor told him that a shrouded Pascal accompanied the man.

Micah wondered briefly why, and then a thought flitted through his mind. *Probably sent by Cutter as extra insurance.*

Gabe's arm lifted. *{Our best chance is through there. We need to head deeper into the facility; find a way out the other side.}*

Sam pushed the stasis pod forward, and Micah and Gabe converged on either side of her.

Isobel appeared on Micah's left. "I can show you all the exits. This place doesn't have that many, but I know where they all are."

{You're with us, then,} Gabe replied. *{We just need to hang on*

a few more minutes. I have a transport on a fast intercept.}

"And several Novastrikes are scrambling now to engage," Reid called out from where she stood beside Cutter.

{Good. We'll take all the support we can get.}

They slipped inside the main building just as gunfire and the high-pitched whine of directed energy beams jumped in volume, signifying that the attacking force had breached the hangar.

"My uncle," Sam turned in a panic, but an invisible hand forced her back.

{He has plenty of people covering him,} Gabe assured her. *{Don't forget, the people attacking have no idea the An-Yang delegation is here with us. They're a force to be reckoned with and will come as a complete surprise. The enemy won't be able to get past them.}*

"They'd better not—" Sam stopped abruptly as the sound of directed energy fire reached them from up ahead.

Micah turned to Isobel. "We need a route, fast."

The woman spun in a circle, indecision painting her face.

Impatiently, Micah pointed to an intersection up ahead. "Where's that hallway lead?"

"It dead-ends at the testing pool."

{Testing pool? Is there an exit there?}

She nodded, and then shook her head.

Micah decided to let her explain along the way, and started forward as she talked.

"The pool's enormous, big enough to handle most ships that we design. We use it to run certain tests while the vessel's immersed."

"What's it filled with?" Sam asked, her breath coming in short gasps as she ran to keep up with Micah.

Isobel tried to shrug as she ran. "Right now, it's filled with water and some sort of colloid nanomixture. We'll never make it around before they catch up to us. It's a wide open space; we'd be sitting ducks—"

{What's on the other side?} interrupted Gabe.

"A service door that leads to the maintenance center for the pool. There is an exit beyond that, but there's no way—"

"Wait," Sam interrupted. "You said colloid mixture."

Isobel nodded.

"Any way you can get me patched into that maintenance system so I can take a peek at what's in that compound?"

Isobel nodded again, and a look of concentration crossed Sam's face as she accessed the data.

Suddenly, her face broke into a smile, and she took off running, shoving the stasis pod ahead of her.

"Wait, what the hell?" Micah called out, following her down the corridor and into the passage that led to the pool.

Gabe matched his pace, and when they caught up to her, asked, *{I take it you have a plan?}*

Sam shot them a mysterious smile as they rushed down the hallway toward the double doors at the end.

The sound of battle was increasing in volume, and Micah knew they were running out of time. He palmed the door open when they reached it, and drew in a ragged breath as they opened and revealed the size of the pool.

Isobel was right; there was no way they'd make it to the other side before the enemy caught up with them. They'd be picked off one by one, with Gabe their sole defense.

"This won't work," Micah objected. "We'll never be able to get around this."

"That's good, because we're not going around."

Sam laughed at the shocked expression that must've played on his face.

"We can't swim it," he protested. "Not with Pascal along."

Inside his head, the big cat made a chuffing sound of agreement.

{Water disgusting. That's what tongues are for.}

Ordinarily the panther-like animal's comments would've elicited a laugh, but Micah was a bit too busy freaking out over their situation. Sam legitimately appeared to consider crossing the pool a viable alternative.

"We won't be swimming," she assured them. "But I do need you all to trust me. Back up a few steps, because you need to be running at full speed when you hit the surface of that water."

Micah shook his head, unable to fully process what she was telling him to do. "You expect us to... walk on water? Are you nuts?"

"It's not nuts. It's *science*." Sam shot him a grin. "Trust me, flyboy. You're in my wheelhouse now. And don't stop when you reach the other side, either. Aim for the door, and I'll trigger it open for you from the control booth. Just keep going."

"Just keep swimming," Isobel said in an odd tone.

Micah shot her a glance but didn't ask what about the phrase amused the pilot.

{Well, whatever you're going to do, we'd better do it now. I estimate they'll be on us in less than two minutes.}

Sam nodded, backing up. "Remember, don't stop, whatever happens."

Every instinct Micah had told him to stop her. Instead, he backed up alongside her, and when she raced for the water, he sprinted beside her.

The physicist didn't break stride, she just kept going... right over the surface of the water. Then he was there, too, his feet pounding on what he could swear was a hard surface, and yet the view of the pool in front of him belied the sensation.

Holy hell! I'm frickin' walking on water!

The mental disconnect was nearly more than he could handle, and he felt the stirrings of Jonathan's mind inside his head, but shoved them away, needing every bit of his brain to concentrate on propelling himself forward.

{Not natural,} Pascal grumbled, eliciting a choked laugh from Gabe, whose invisible form kept pace with Sam on the other side.

{Says the cat who can talk.}

"Just think of it as an illusion. Something that's not really there. But whatever you do, Pascal, don't stop," Sam repeated. "Do you understand me?"

The cat paced left and right along the side of the pool, initially unwilling to commit himself to such an act, his feline hindbrain refusing to allow him to get wet. It was finally overcome by the evidence before him, of three humans pushing a stasis pod across the surface of the testing pool.

Finally, Pascal launched himself forward, yelping once when his feet touched the surface of the water, only to find that it did indeed push back at him, though not as firmly, since the cat hadn't built up the speed the humans had.

Micah nearly laughed when he glanced back at the large feline trying to high-step his way across the pool.

{You're going to have to explain this to us when we get out of here.} Gabe sounded fascinated by the entire experience.

"How about I explain it to you once we get into that transport and we're safely out of here without bullets flying overhead," she retorted.

{Deal.}

As promised, Sam keyed the door open just as they reached the other side. They rushed through into the control room, Micah turning when he heard a second yelp from Pascal.

The cat had slowed too much and had begun to sink.

Micah and Gabe leapt for the pool's edge, dragging the now-wet feline from the water.

{You said wouldn't get wet,} Pascal growled.

"I said not to slow down, too," Sam scolded, glancing around.

Micah followed her line of sight to a pile of towels on a nearby shelf.

"Hurry, grab a towel to cover our trail," she urged.

They mopped up the evidence of Pascal's dunking, their movements hurried as the sound of gunfire increased in volume, signifying that the fight had spilled into the dead-end corridor that led to the pool.

"Where's our transport?" asked Micah as they retreated into the control room and Sam triggered the door closed, shutting them inside. "And where's the exit from here?"

Isobel pointed to an emergency exit door beside a shelving unit of supplies.

{Transport's pulling up now.} Gabe stepped up to one of the consoles in the control room. *{Isobel, can you bring up a diagram of this facility?}*

Nodding, the pilot stepped up, and in seconds, had it displayed.

{Show me where we are. I need to tell the transport where to land.}

* * *

Sam didn't take an easy breath until after the shuttle had lifted off and she could see the twin pair of Novastrike ships escorting their vessel back to the base.

Isobel had opted to stay behind when a pair of Unit soldiers showed up beside the doors as backup for their departure.

"I believe you owe us an explanation for what happened back there, doc," Gabe prompted, unsealing his drakeskin and pulling his hood back. "You said it was science. What kind of science, exactly?"

"Have you ever heard of oobleck?"

"Nope, but I'd be willing to lay odds it means something like 'liquid that hardens on impact,'" Micah quipped from where he sat beside her, one arm thrown casually behind the back of the transport's bench seat.

She sank back into its cushions, willing her heart to slow as she thought about how to word her explanation. "That pool was filled with a mixture of water and a non-newtonian substance."

"Non...?" Gabe quirked a brow at her.

"The substance is a colloid held in a nanoparticle shell. When activated, it turns the water in that pool into a material with shear-thickening properties."

"In simple, non-science-y words, that means...?"

" 'Liquid that hardens on impact.'"

*{**Not** hard. I sank. Got wet. Cost you three steaks.}*

CHECK

VARIOUS SIMULTANEOUS LOCATIONS
CERIBA AND ERIDU

AT THE ALPHA Centauri heliopause, a Calabi-Yau gate flared. Its extra-dimensional energies danced in a coruscating display against a glittering backdrop of stars, heralding the arrival of wave after wave of battle groups, each led by a capital ship.

With military precision, the formation disappeared one by one, as suddenly as they had arrived—each individual ship enveloped in its own brilliant blue Casimir bubble.

Though close study would show their configurations to match those of the Geminate Navy, all ships broadcast Akkadian idents.

Signals Intelligence would also later confirm that, at the exact same moment, an An-Yang strike unit jumped from their orbit around Proxima's star into Scharnhost space. Curiously, they, too, transmitted Akkadian transponder codes.

Simultaneously, several highly trained tactical groups converged on their targets: both on Ceriba and on Eridu.

The Ceriba teams had two destinations. The first silently infiltrated the ICU ward at St. Clair Township's Memorial

Hospital. A second arrived at the preschool where the prime minister's twin daughters attended.

The teams on Eridu dispersed, each to deliver a data chip to a high-ranking minister, detailing the extent of Project Obelus—and identifying Asher Dent as its author.

* * *

Thad waited as Jonathan reached out to Micah.

After a second, the pilot sent Thad a mental nod. *{A Navy battle group just jumped through the gate. A small force from An-Yang jumped to Scharnhorst space at the same time. They've coordinated their arrivals.}*

{What's our window to get this done?}

{They should be popping out half a million klicks from Eridu in an hour. Shadow Recon ships are already here. They're lurking overhead, ready to put on a show. Cutter says we're cleared to proceed.}

Thad's attention returned to Che. "We're green." One side of the Marine's mouth kicked up in an ironic half smile. "You're about to have two pretty big military ship formations appear right in front of your home fleet."

An answering twinkle appeared in Che's eyes. "I trust they're friendlies?"

"Not to Asher Dent they aren't," Ell murmured.

Che turned and gave her a predatory smile. "Excellent. Neither are we."

* * *

Asher Dent had just closed the latest report from Clint Janus when Citizen General Warren Hatami, Akkadia's minister of defense, sent him a priority ping.

{Sensors from our advanced listening platforms have detected two large footprints at the Geminate gate. They've since disappeared.}

Dent had expected a response such as this from the Alliance Navy. It wouldn't do them any good.

{I'll take care of this personally.}

He cut the connection and then reached out to his secretary, ordering the man to get the Shar-Kali prison warden on a secured channel.

If Garza couldn't persuade the puppet functioning as his stand-in, Asher would have Janus turn the persuasion up a notch.

He stood and began to pace when the seconds turned into minutes and still the man had not connected them. His assistant was usually so efficient; it was highly irregular for Dent to be left waiting while his request was fulfilled.

He resisted the urge to prod the man, though he knew in his gut something had gone wrong.

As the minutes stretched out, his suspicion crystallized into certainty, so bypassing protocol, Dent reached out to Shar-Kali himself—only to have the connection rebuffed.

CHECKMATE

Premier's Briefing, State Assembly House
Central Prefecture, Eridu

IT HAD BEEN half an hour, and still Asher Dent could not reach the Shar-Kali prison facility. He knew it was quite possible that Rin Zhou had managed to take it. That outcome had been low on his list of probabilities, and yet he had a contingency plan in place for just such a thing.

He reached out to his minister of defense, and when Hatami's image appeared on his holo, Asher's agitation was such that he didn't notice the other man's cool greeting.

"I need you to send a platoon of Junxun to Shar-Kali immediately. There is an uprising. Rin Zhou Enlai is to be dispatched with extreme prejudice."

"Is she, Premier Dent?"

The man's odd tone finally registered.

Asher frowned. Voice sharp, he demanded, "Are you questioning my orders?"

"What of the ships that transitioned through the gate?" the other man asked.

Asher reared his head back, nonplussed by the sudden topic

change. "Ships transition through the gate continuously. What is unusual about these?"

"The energy footprint recorded by our listening platforms suggests the ships are military," Hatami said, his tone sounding detached, almost bored. "The EM waveform matches the Geminate Alliance Navy."

"When did this happen?"

The man looked up and to the right, apparently accessing the information via his wire. "Ah, that would be... about an hour ago."

Asher could barely contain his rage. "Why am I just now hearing of this?"

"Other things that came up that took priority." He shrugged. "Besides, there was some confusion between the advanced signature analysis and the IFF they were broadcasting."

Again with the odd tenor in the man's voice.

The urge to rip the defense minister a new one nearly overpowered the sudden unease Asher felt at the mention of the odd IFF signal.

Silently vowing to address the man's insolence at a later date—*Hatami has just been ushered to the top of the Project Obelus line*—Asher opted for information over respect. "What about an IFF ident could *possibly* be confusing?"

The man looked him dead in the eye. "They're using Akkadian transponder codes. The kind that Home Fleet won't question."

Disquiet filled Dent, and he signed off, hardly noticing that the man on the other end had been less than obsequious.

Ten minutes later, Asher's office door slid open—an action that temporarily stunned him into silence.

No one had ever had the audacity to enter without receiving permission first. The breach of protocol was unheard of in the Akkadian Empire.

Every one of the Imperial cabinet members filed in, the expressions on their faces ranging from suspicion to rage to the cold mask of death.

Dent pushed his chair away from his desk and stood. "What is the meaning of this?" he demanded.

The ministers fanned out.

"Oh, I think you know what this is." Warren Hatami's voice was harsh.

"We don't have time for this nonsense," Asher snarled. "There is an uprising going on within the Shar-Kali prison. There is a fleet above our skies that somehow managed to obtain clearance codes which allowed them past our screening forces. I will have your head for this!"

Arms crossed, Warren Hatami shot Asher a sardonic look. "An interesting development, wouldn't you say?" He examined his fingernails, adding in an offhand manner, "Their EM signature's quite interesting, too."

Asher narrowed his eyes. "*What* signature?"

"I believe I can answer that," a new voice stated from the entrance.

Rin Zhou Enlai stepped through, flanked on one side by Che Josza, the other by a Junxun assassin. It was the woman known as the Dagger, Che Josza's infamous shadow.

To his utter shock, behind them entered three people he'd never expected to see. Two weren't Akkadians at all; they were from the Geminate Alliance.

"So, you're in bed with the Alliance now? Traitors to the empire?"

"Interesting that *you* would use that word," the minister of the exchequer mused. "Let's discuss that term, shall we?"

"Yes, who is the real traitor here?" the minister of defense added.

Asher saw the assassin send a hand signal to someone out in the hall. A slumped body appeared in the doorway, supported between two Junxun warriors.

They dragged Clint Janus's body toward him, and unceremoniously dumped the dead man at Asher's feet.

"Whatever he told you," he began, but a sharp gesture from Rin Zhou cut him off.

"You would enslave your own people? That is *not* what the leader of the Akkadians does to his own," she growled.

"And you would be the better choice?" Asher scoffed and pointed skyward. "The leader of the Akkadian Empire wouldn't willingly invite outsiders into our own skies. You would give Akkadian transponder codes to our enemies!"

"Oh, it's not just the Alliance above us." Che Josza sounded bored, his stance casual and nonchalant, but his eyes blazed with anger. "The Shang Dynasty of An-Yang is represented as well. And the Coalition of Worlds *would have* sent their own representatives, but they couldn't scramble the ships fast enough.

"You're going down, Asher Dent, and there is no world anywhere that will harbor you."

One month later....

A FOND GOODBYE

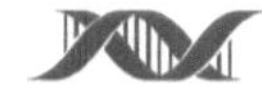

Governor-General's Mansion
St. Clair Township
Ceriba

The setting for today's debrief wasn't anything like what Micah had expected. His gaze wandered past the industrial-sized chiller to the carbyne-reinforced clearsteel windows, inset behind the governor-general's kitchen sink.

He, Sam, Thad, and Ell were seated around the biggest damn polished stone countertop, smack in the middle of the biggest damn kitchen he'd ever seen in his life.

You're doing it again, an amused voice sounded in his head—the one voice that security surrounding the governor-general could not jam or block.

You should be here, not me.

Jonathan's voice took on an impatient tone. *We've been over this. Showing up together wouldn't be the kindest thing to do to the prime minister right now. Besides,* he added, *you were the one who spent the most time with José—other than the prime minister, of course.*

Micah's attention was brought abruptly back to his

surroundings when he realized the governor-general was patiently holding a plate out to him, two slices of a flaky dessert piled atop it.

"Sorry, ma'am," he murmured, accepting the povitica.

Laura Castro nodded, a sympathetic awareness in her eyes as she returned to the task of slicing the pastry to serve to her guests.

{What was that all about, hoss?} Thad nudged Micah with his elbow.

{Jonathan,} was all he said, but it was enough.

Thad straightened and smiled his brilliant white smile when the governor-general served him next.

"I can tell by the look in your eyes that you all are wondering why we asked you to meet here," Raphael Garza said from his seat beside Castro, on the other side of the countertop.

Duncan Cutter paused, povitica halfway to his mouth, and broke into a grin. He pointed the piece of pastry at the governor-general, and then waved it around.

"I told you they wouldn't know what to think about a casual audience like this. Just look at them."

With a chuckle, he sank his teeth into the sweet dessert.

Laura Castro paused, plate in hand, as she regarded those gathered with a half-smile.

Colonel Valenti and Admiral Toland were there, as were Gabe, Harper, and a very wide-eyed Katie Hyer. The latter sat on her stool, her back ramrod-straight, holding herself perfectly still, as if afraid to move.

I'll bet Gabe had a talk with her.

Of the 'Chief warrants should be seen and not heard' kind? snarked Jonathan.

Micah bit off a chuckle, ducking his head to hide his amusement. *Stop it.*

"Please eat," Castro said to those who had politely abstained, as she handed Gabe the final plate. "In this kitchen, we don't stand on ceremony." The governor-general's cheek dimpled as she confessed, "That's why it's my favorite room in this beast of a house."

They dug in. After a few quiet moments had passed, Garza pushed his plate aside. Crossing his arms atop the polished stone, he gave Castro a solemn, expectant look.

In response, the governor-general sat back, a contemplative look touching her eyes as she considered them all.

"You know, it's not every day that a group of people are tasked with the impossible and somehow manage to pull it off."

Garza nodded his agreement. With a faint smile, he gestured around the island. "That's why we invited you here today—to say thank you, and to ask you to help us better understand what went down this past month." He shot a quick glance at Cutter. "A last debrief, if you will."

Beside him, Micah saw Sam carefully brush her fingers off before folding them in her lap.

"I'm... so very sorry, Mister Prime Minister."

Raphael held up a hand. Eyes earnest, he leaned toward Sam. "I wanted to thank you, and Admiral Toland, for everything you did to try and save José. You went to great lengths, and I appreciate that—more than you can know."

A somber quiet descended upon the room at his declaration. Sam nodded and looked down at her plate, clearly uncomfortable.

Micah reached over and squeezed her hand.

"Doctor Travis," Raphael's tone was reflective, curious. "How was it possible that José shared the same memories with me when he didn't live them, like I did?"

Sam's mouth twisted into a wry smile. "There's a lot we still don't understand about the human mind, even after centuries of study. But we do know memory is encoded in the nucleus of the neuron through epigenetic changes. That same encoding would have shown up in your twin."

Her gaze turned thoughtful. "However, it's the synapses firing that activate that memory, so when you thought of it—or he did—it...well, it made it real for him, if that makes any sense."

The prime minister looked down at his plate. "Oh, it was very real. *He* was very real. And I want to thank each of you for coming to his funeral. His life might not have been one that we could either celebrate or ever acknowledge publicly, but it was one lived courageously, and with great sacrifice."

Raphael's head came up again after a moment. "Can you tell me what it was that ultimately killed my twin?"

Sam glanced over at Toland, who answered the silent plea in her eyes with a slight nod.

"We told you upon your return that we had discovered that your mirror twin suffered from something we call cell senescence," the admiral began.

At Garza's nod, she continued.

"No matter what we tried, we couldn't reverse it, so we attempted to clone tissue samples—*not* another Garza," she clarified quickly, "but a critical mass, if you will, of enough DNA to try to transfer the quantum connection."

"It worked." Garza's words were clipped.

From grief, Micah realized.

He misses the connection. They didn't have much time together, but they were close, Jonathan murmured.

Hard not to be.

Micah caught a hand signal Cutter sent to Valenti, and the colonel stepped in.

"The team we left behind on Eridu went over Janus's research with the task force Rin Zhou Enlai assigned to investigate. This arrived yesterday."

She palmed a portable holoprojector, and a report, clinical and concise, appeared.

A single line jumped out at Micah.

"Janus *knew* the clones didn't have long to live?" Ell's tone held a mix of incredulity and horror.

Valenti nodded. "He did."

"It's likely he hid it from Dent, thinking he could perfect the process as the plan for Obelus progressed," Gabe contributed in a musing voice.

"Profiling, are you, Agent Alvarez?" Cutter's voice held just a trace of joviality, the right amount to snap the conversation away from morbid thoughts and back along more productive lines.

One side of Gabe's mouth ticked up, but he refused to take the bait.

"What is Premier Enlai planning to do with the research now?" It was the first time Katie had spoken, and by the slight tremor in her voice, she half expected to be shot down for her temerity.

The prime minister shot her an *atta boy* look of approval. "Very good question, Chief." He turned to Cutter. "I assume you have an answer?"

Cutter motioned to the analyst at his left hand.

Harper responded, "Rin Zhou realizes that pursuing Obelus is an exercise in futility. From the research they recovered, our people gleaned that the telomeres unravel completely at around the one-month mark, and there is no indication that chiral research can overcome this problem."

She shot a quick glance at Micah, and amended, "Excepting what Stinton did to you and the animals on deGrasse, which no one has yet been able to figure out or replicate."

The analyst cleared her throat uncomfortably, shooting Garza an apologetic look. "From the point of view of a megalomaniac like Asher Dent, that's... ineffective. Who wants to create a pawn, only to have to turn around and create a new one again and again? And that's not even considering the suspicion it would raise, if every leader in every star nation began turning up dead after a matter of weeks."

Laura Castro made a sound of agreement deep in her throat that sounded suspiciously like a growl. "Speaking of Dent...." The governor-general turned first to Harper and then to Cutter. "I'm shocked to hear myself say this, but for once, I don't think the Akkadians were bloodthirsty enough. They didn't cut him down where he stood?"

Something passed between Cutter and Valenti. Valenti shook her head.

"They did not."

Micah saw Garza's hand fist at those words.

"And he's escaped," Castro stated in a flat tone.

"Yes, but we have a joint operations team of Akkadian, An-Yang, and Alliance personnel working on it. They'll find him," Cutter assured her.

He leaned forward, looking past Micah and Thad to catch Ell's eye. "It's being led by a friend of yours, Agent Cyr. And I hear that the Dagger never misses."

Micah felt a tremor pass through Thad at those words, but all the man said was a low, "Ooh-rah."

"A toast, then." Castro motioned to one of the agents, and the woman obligingly picked up a tray from the sideboard and set it between Castro and Garza. On it were small shot glasses, filled with a light amber liquid.

Once they were passed out, the governor-general lifted hers, and Micah swore he could see the light of battle in her eyes.

"To the team whose journey began at the genesis of a novel biological discovery, four years ago in Luyten's Star. Some might call it the Alliance's own Pandora's box.

"The secret of chiral life has escaped the confines of that box, and it can never be put back. But, like Pandora's box, what remains is hope.

"Your team, Task Force Blue, the chiral project and its chiral members, have just saved literally every government in the settled worlds from enslavement, and for this, you have the thanks of not one, but many a grateful nation."

Castro lifted her glass higher. "Here's to you. And to finding Asher Dent. May there be no asteroid he can hide behind that will shield him from your fury."

A word from LL Richman

Thank you for reading *Chiral Justice*. I hope you enjoyed the ride. Turn the page to read an excerpt from a new series, set at the dawn of the Biogenesis War. The Early Years series begins with **Operation Cobalt** and continues in **The Chiral Conspiracy.**

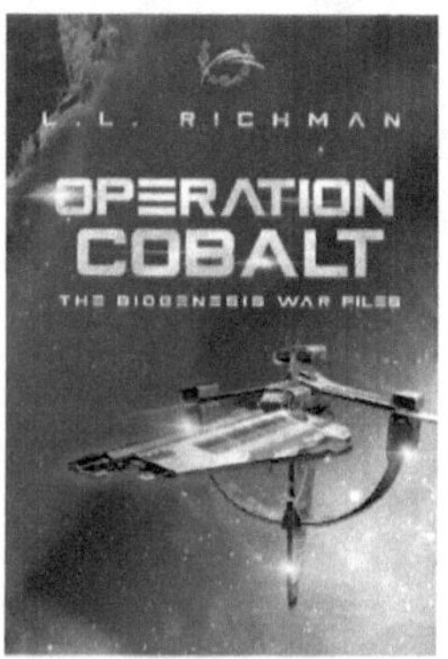

If you don't mind, please take a minute to leave a short review. Not only would it make this writer a very happy person, but also your review makes a real difference. It's an effective way you can help keep this series going. The more reviews, the easier it is for new readers to find these tales!

Connecting with you as a reader is also one of the most rewarding things about writing. I'd like to invite you to join my VIP Reader's Group at bit.ly/biogenesiswar. There, you'll receive the latest news about new books and deals, plus receive free content and exclusive excerpts from upcoming books.

PREVIEW: OPERATION COBALT

They want a fight? She'll give it to them.

Katie Hyer is minding her own business, hauling ore for Cobalt Mining, when a mysterious ship appears suddenly out of the black. It soon becomes clear that same ship is inbound for the mining platform she calls home.

When the secessionists on board take Sierra Twelve hostage, Katie will go to any lengths to free her friends and family—even if it means waging her own personal war of attrition.

And when Katie goes to war... people die.

— BOOK 1 —

THE BIOGENESIS WAR FILES

OPERATION COBALT

"Victorious warriors win first and then go to war, while defeated warriors go to war first and then seek to win."
~ Sun Tzu

"The way to win in a battle ... is to know the rhythms of the specific opponents, and use rhythms that your opponents do not expect."
~ Miyamoto Musashi, *The Book of Five Rings*

ONE

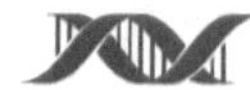

CMS *GOBLIN*

COBALT MINING SECTOR TWELVE

BIG BLUE (SIRIUS A)

"FRED, NO! THAT'S not a chew toy!"

Katie Hyer planted her boots against the hatch she'd just sealed and pushed away from the surface. The action sent her shooting across the cramped space toward the mining tug's cockpit.

The strains of a catchy, old-Earth tune filtered from the ship's audio system as she snagged the pilot's seat with one hand to arrest her forward motion. A reluctant smile tugged at her lips when she heard Carrie Underwood's voice belt out something about the more men she's around, the more she loves her hound.

Jeremy's timing, as usual, was impeccable. The traffic controller who worked Cobalt Mining's first shift liked to spin the tunes during times when there weren't any ships coming or going from the Sierra Twelve platform. Tuesdays were what he called 'country music day'—whatever that meant. Katie had yet to figure out which country the music represented.

"Betcha Underwood's dog never tried eating his own safety net," she muttered as she reached for her pet.

The dog was floating butt-first just above the co-pilot's seat, net clamped firmly between his jaws. The remainder waved in the null-*g* environment as he yanked the material back and forth.

She reached for a corner when it floated her way, but Fred intuited her intent. The basset puppy kicked against the copilot's chair and went flying toward the back of the ship. Katie sighed and followed.

The netting wasn't hers; it belonged to Cobalt Mining. She'd intended to return it to the dock earlier in the week, but Fred's baby seat hadn't yet arrived, so she needed it to keep him secure when she was maneuvering the ship.

Fred thought this was a fun, new game; she could see it in his eyes. His floppy ears haloed around him as he sailed across the small cabin. They flattened against the aft bulkhead when he bumped against it with a muffled *oof.*

Or was that a woof? she wondered.

She caught up to him and tugged at the drool-slicked material clamped between his jaws. Fred doubled down, emitting a cute baby growl.

"No!" she scolded. "You can't eat your seat belt. Now, gimme!"

He let out another growl as a great gob of slobber went floating through the cabin.

Katie sighed once more and called out to the ship's Synthetic Intelligence. "*Goblin*, release containment nano, please. Cabin bulkhead, aft."

From the corner of her eye, Katie caught a flicker of light as a haze of glittering specks leached from the bulkhead to envelop the floating droplets. A slight breeze grazed her cheek, and she knew the ship was directing the airflow to recall the nano back into the fabric of the bulkhead.

She eyed her recalcitrant pet. "Well, at least you left your diaper alone this time."

Intellectually, she knew that *Goblin*'s containment nano could just as easily herd any errant puppy pee into the ActiveFiber coating that layered the ship's bulkheads, but the thought kind of grossed her out.

Katie gave the cargo netting one last sharp tug, her feet planted against the aft bulkhead. It came suddenly free, which sent her rocketing back the way she'd come, her head rapping sharply against the short span of bulkhead that separated the cockpit from the tiny cabin.

With a small groan, she dragged her hand through her shock of maroon curls, fingers poking at the tender spot the medical nano in her body was already in the process of healing.

Schooling her face into stern lines, she shook the liberated material at him in mock-threat.

"Bad boy, Fred! Bad! This is *not* a toy!"

Fred looked back at her with large, sad, brown eyes. She relented, gathering him up in her arms and placing a kiss on his forehead.

Her thoughts snapped back to her surroundings when the music cut out and *Goblin*'s SI announced, *{Warning! Unknown vessel approaching on an intercept heading.}*

Katie's training automatically kicked in.

"Show me that ship," she ordered as she shoved Fred into the co-pilot's chair, securing him with quick, practiced motions.

The view on *Goblin*'s main holoscreen shifted to show the incoming vessel. With a muttered curse, Katie slammed herself into her own seat.

Fingers flew over the pilot's board as she brought the drives online and sent the tug into a steep dive. Far from the nimble response she would have liked, the ship turned exactly as expected: like a bloated whale.

She saw instantly that *Goblin* lacked the control authority to evade—not with the load of metal ores tied to its back end. She triggered the quick-release, and the jackscrew-controlled tow hook assembly floated free.

Now significantly lighter, the tug leapt forward like a thoroughbred released from the starting gate. Freed from its encumbrance, *Goblin*'s massive fusion drives dodged the approaching vessel with enviable agility.

Katie switched the forward viewscreen to the aft sensor feed, mentally bracing for a collision between the newcomer and the asteroid chunks she'd just ejected—but it never came.

The ship, still flying dark, jinked out of the way, thrusters firing in a complex dance. Katie was reluctantly impressed. Whoever was handling that vessel knew what they were doing.

She let out an annoyed grunt when the near-impact bestowed a spin to the netted ores—a spin she'd now have to match in order to reacquire her load.

With one last twitch, the ship raced away, on a course that led right to Sierra Twelve.

"Jerks. Ever heard of karma?" Katie addressed the departing spacecraft. "Hope yours ends up biting you in the ass."

TWO

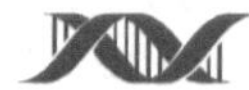

DAP Helios, GNS *Scimitar*

Decommissioned mining platform

0.9 AU from Sierra Twelve

Twenty-eight hours earlier....

THE MYSTERIOUS SHIP that had nearly sideswiped *Goblin* was flying dark for a reason. Its frantic pace was the result of a run-in with an Alliance Navy vessel.

GNS *Scimitar* was a fast-action Helios, the stealthed version of one of the most ubiquitous utility ships in the Geminate Navy. Though the Helios was a familiar enough sight in the Alliance military, one look at *Scimitar*'s unique profile and adaptive coatings was enough to make any criminal turn tail and run.

Scimitar's flight crew should have been on their way home after having retrieved a Tier One team from an operation deep within the Sirius system—but just as Rafe, the ship's pilot, set course for the star's heliopause, an invitation arrived.

Micah Case, *Scimitar*'s co-pilot, was the first to see the

incoming message. He lifted a brow as he read its contents, silently passing it on to Rafe. Rafe, in turn, sent it on to Team Five, the Special Recon unit that now occupied *Scimitar*'s aft cabin.

The invitation was simply worded:

From: James Bridgetree, Commander, 76th Coast Guard Regiment.
To: Lane Reid, Captain, SRU Team Five.
The 76th invites you to an impromptu war game...

The message then spat out a string of coordinates.

No words needed to be said; Micah and Rafe were both certain it would be turned down. To the surprise of both men, Reid accepted. The two men exchanged a bemused look, and then both set themselves to the task of turning the ship around.

{Flip and burn in five seconds,} Rafe announced over the shipnet.

{What the hell, Cap?} The voice of Dana, the crew's gunner broke in on the flight crew's private channel. *{The gate's in the other direction.}*

A quick glance over at Rafe told Micah the pilot was engaged in conversation with someone—Reid, most likely.

{Looks like Reid's team is going to play war games with the coast guard,} Micah supplied.

{Coasties?} Cass DeWitt echoed from her flight engineer's position behind Rafe.

{Sounds like,} Micah agreed.

{Huh. War games?} asked Dana.

{That's what the message that came in said,} he told her. *{It was in the clear, so I'm taking it at face value.}*

{Huh,} she repeated.

Micah couldn't tell if Dana's *huh* meant she was surprised that Team Five would accept, or that she expected the coasties to be handed their asses in short order.

Probably both.

Additional telemetry came in from the 76th, directing them to their rendezvous. While Rafe set *Scimitar* on that heading, Micah deployed the sphere of surveillance and reconnaissance drones that were his responsibility as co-pilot. Not that the maps indicated anything other than micrometeorite dust between here and there, but a Shadow Recon pilot left nothing to chance.

A few hours later, the crew found themselves closing on an abandoned mining platform in the middle of the black. As Rafe brought the Helios in on a smooth arc, Micah considered just how asymmetrical a mock skirmish would be between the 76th and the special forces operators seated in the back of the ship. Over the flight crew's private comm channel, he voiced his thoughts to Rafe.

{Turns out the 76th's garrison commander is an old friend of Reid's and heard through the grapevine they were in the area,} Rafe replied. *{Apparently, she owes him one and he just called in the favor. Guess he feels his coasties need to be shaken up a bit.}*

Dana's sarcastic *{Ya think?}* brought a grin to Micah's face. Then a warning chime sounded, and he gave the approaching platform his full attention.

According to the automated signal of a stationary buoy floating a hundred thousand klicks spinward, the mining platform belonged to the Cobalt Mining Consortium. The buoy's broadcast informed any comers that the platform was now closed.

A follow-up transmission from the 76th filled in the rest: the mining platform had reached the end of its useful life, and so Cobalt had it decommissioned six months ago. It was scheduled for demolition in the coming year, but in the interim, the coast guard had gained Cobalt's permission to conduct exercises aboard the abandoned structure.

Scimitar approached from stellar north, and as they neared, Rafe dropped an icon onto an access hatch.

{That's where the team will insert.}

Micah nodded. *{Copy that.}*

{Keep monitoring nearspace, in case the coasties decide to get clever and sneak a second wave of sailors aboard, to flank Reid's team,} Rafe added.

{That'd liven things up,} said Dana.

Cass snorted. *{Yeah, it'd take 'em a good ten minutes longer to ferret them out.}*

{Cass,} Rafe called warningly, and the flight engineer responded by giving his pilot's seat a shove with her booted foot.

{Fine. I'll behave.}

None of *Scimitar*'s crew had any doubts about the outcome of today's exercise, though Cass and Dana had begun placing bets on how long it would take the Unit men and women to sort the coasties and call for an extraction.

Micah tuned them out, opting to listen in on the team's combat channel as they geared up instead.

His lips twitched when he heard, *{**Paintballs**? Are you fucking kidding me, hoss?}*

The voice belonged to Thad Severance, Team Five's second-in-command. A hulking Marine with dark skin and an easy smile, the man had the mind of a brilliant tactician and could give intimidation lessons to an apex predator.

Micah's smile widened as Thad continued to rant, his tone dripping with disgust. Clearly, he thought a paintball gun was a wuss thing for a Marine to carry.

{Dude. These are coasties,} came an exasperated reply. *{You can't play with your usual toys, capiche? Plus, I spiked it with a little something extra.}* That was Jack Campbell, the team's intel officer and hacker extraordinaire.

He was also a licensed pilot, the only one on Team Five. That skill come in handy more than once in recent years. When the team couldn't make it to the prearranged extraction point, Jack had commandeered whatever local skiff he could get his hands on, while the flight crew aboard *Scimitar* reconfigured, navigating to the fallback site instead.

Apparently, Jack had just added to his skill set, branching

out into weapons design by modifying a child's toy into an offensive weapon.

Through the ship's aft feed, Micah saw Thad pick up the plastic-handled weapon to examine it more closely. His hands dwarfed the thing.

{You spiked it,} the big Marine repeated. *{You mean you integrated a Spike into the paintball itself?}*

{Yep.} Jack sounded smug. *{Tag one of 'em and they're going to be wearing more than a bright blue spot. With the Spike's electronic breadcrumb trail, you'll be able to track them anywhere they go.}*

{That's an unfair advantage, Lieutenant.} Lane Reid looked up from where she'd been cleaning her knife to level a hard look at Jack.

*{Aw, c'mon, Cap, **we're** an unfair advantage,}* he protested. *{Besides, it gives us a chance to test out a new piece of gear in a semi real-world application, with none of the risk. How often do we get that?}*

*{You can't be serious. You plan to add blue **paintballs** to our arsenal?}* Elodie Cyr pulled to a stop in front of the intelligence officer, one hand wrapped around her sniper's rifle. The other held a blue ball between thumb and finger as if it were a deadly contagion. She looked as incredulous as she sounded.

{This is just a prototype,} Jack assured her. *{And no, the end product won't be embedded in a ball of blue paint.}*

Ell grunted and palmed the ball as she turned away, but otherwise refused to respond.

Undaunted, Jack continued handing out his modified paintball guns. They joined the team's standard loadout of carbyne blades, flash-bang grenades, pulse pistols, and flechettes.

By the time they were done, *Scimitar* had come to rest alongside the maintenance hatch. Rafe deployed the umbilical; from that point, it took the team less than five minutes to enter the platform and seal the hatch behind them.

As Rafe focused on the delicate dance of holding station a

scant few meters from the platform's skin, Micah returned his attention to the sphere of drones that encased the Helios in a protective sphere.

Apart from the two teams playing an elaborate game of capture-the-flag, and a decent-sized coast guard cutter on the platform's opposing side, the area *should* have been abandoned. And it was… for about half an hour.

The flight crew kept an open channel with *Scimitar*'s end muted, while Reid met with Bridgetree and they hammered out the rules of engagement and then dispersed. Twenty minutes later, the teams' HUDs flashed green, and the hunt was on.

Micah's attention was split between the team's feed and the constellation of drones deployed in nearspace, around the section of mining platform where *Scimitar* hovered. Fifteen minutes into the exercise, a blip caught Micah's eye.

He waited for it to repeat, and when it didn't, he sent a quick mental command to the swarm of drones he controlled. The tiny vessels turned in a tight curve, angling back toward the EM signature that had disappeared just as quickly as it had shown up. Moments later, he had a visual.

{Contact!} he sang out, sending the feed to Cass to verify. *{Two ships, just cresting the top of the platform.}*

{Are they coasties?} asked Rafe.

{Checking,} Cass replied. Then, a beat later, *{Nope, the cutter says they're not.}*

Dana interrupted, her voice taut. *{Hey, Cap? Their signature indicates they're weapons hot.}*

That caused Micah to straighten. He'd been sure the ships were part of the 76th's assault plan.

The initial blip morphed into a more detailed visual of the approaching vessels as Micah's drones filled in the missing information. He sent it to *Scimitar*'s forward holoscreens.

That drew a grunt of displeasure from the man seated to Micah's right. Rafe's hands danced over his controls, and in the next instant, the slightest tremor shuddered through the ship.

An alert accompanied the action, appearing on Micah's overlay. It informed him Rafe had just jettisoned the umbilical that tethered them to the platform's hatch. A second telltale followed the first, this one indicating the airlock had just cycled shut.

Scimitar was on the move.

{Noble One, this is Spartan.} Rafe's voice cut in over Team Five's combat net. *{We have two unidentified ships, armed and assumed hostile. I say again, armed ships, assumed hostile. Breaking away to engage.}*

Rafe's brief comm was met with silence, but that didn't worry Micah overmuch. If the hostiles' presence extended to the platform, it was possible they'd made contact and were already engaging.

Micah almost felt sorry for their surprise guests. If there was criminal intent, no team was better equipped to take them out than SRU Team Five.

The Helios drifted silently away, Rafe's deft hand at the controls seamlessly reconfiguring the ship's tunable outer layer from a reflectance that matched the platform to one that emulated the blackness of space.

Scimitar was now effectively a ghost, with full stray-light suppression on all EM bands. The chances of the two unmarked hostiles finding the Shadow Recon ship were next to none, but that didn't mean its flight crew were going to sit on their hands while a threat lurked nearby.

* * *

Thad had taken a knee and was looking at a pile of rubble through the reticle of his P-SCAR rifle, debating whether he was looking at a trap set by the coasties, when the call from *Scimitar* came through.

{Noble Two, this is Spartan. Do you copy?}

Thad did a slow visual sweep of the area. He sent a brief, two-click acknowledgment as he slid back toward the concealment provided by the passageway.

{Unable to reach Noble One,} the voice continued. *{We have a situation.}*

Rafe's update was delivered in the preternaturally calm voice all Shadow Recon pilots seemed to have, no matter how tense things got. As he listened, Thad turned the news over in his tactician's mind.

{You sure they're not coasties?}

{They don't fit the profi—} Thad heard Micah swear as he abruptly cut off, only to come back in the next instant with an update. *{Negative, Tango One is now closing on the coastie ship.}*

Thad scrubbed the stubble on the side of his face. *Well, ain't that just a fine kettle of fish.*

He turned and motioned the two team members on his six to come forward. When they were within range, he reached out to establish an untraceable, peer-to-peer connection.

{We have a new player, not connected to the 76th. Assume active hostiles.}

The woman facing him remained impassive, but the demolitions man crouching beside her lifted a brow, and his gaze slid sideways. *{And here you thought this exercise would be boring, Sarge.}*

He elbowed the sniper lightly—or would have, had Ell's hand not whipped out and twisted the man's arm behind his back.

{Ow, dammit!}

{You were saying, sir?}

Thad buried a smile as he glanced back toward the intersection.

{We need to contact the coasties. Let them know we have company, and the exercise is off.}

Ell released Mike's arm and then shot Thad a considering look. *{I can climb overhead, drop behind them and deliver the message.}*

Thad nodded. *{Go.}*

She slung her P-SCAR rifle over her shoulder, crossed on light feet to the bulkhead, and then began her silent ascent.

Spars ridged the bulkhead's surface in regular intervals, making it easy for the sniper to find purchase. The sticky organogel threads lining the palms of her drakeskin suit would enable her to remain there indefinitely.

Halfway up the wall, Ell engaged her suit's active stealth and faded from sight. Thad's suit kept track of her, its predictive systems using the team's connection to track her telemetry, her position showing as a ghostly outline over his HUD.

That part of his plan in place, Thad glanced over at Mike. *{Rafe couldn't raise the captain. Find her and give her a sitrep.}*

He brought up a schematic of the platform and dropped a pin on its control center *{We know she was headed here. If she's not responding, chances are that she, Jack, and Asha have already had a run-in with whoever's out there badgering* Scimitar. *Round up any coasties you find along the way.}*

Mike nodded. *{Yessir.}*

Thad squinted at the pile of rubble. *{Stay frosty and don't get yourself caught. In the meantime, I think I'll do a little tracking myself.}*

{Good hunting, LT.} The demolitions man rose and crept silently down the passageway, the platform's emergency lighting lending an eerie cast to his form before he faded from view.

* * *

Rafe had brought *Scimitar* around on the same heading as the ship bearing down on the coast guard cutter, kicking thrusters to maximum to gain on the unmarked vessel.

{ECM, Lieutenant,} ordered the captain. *{Cass, warn the 76th they're about to have company.}*

Micah was already in motion, having anticipated the order for electronic countermeasures. His right hand pushed outward, his left simultaneously curving inward, even as Rafe spoke.

The movements weren't physical actions; as deeply

enmeshed as Micah was with the ship's SyntheticVision system, they were more of a visual manifestation of his thoughts. They also resulted in immediate motion within the swarm of drones under his command.

{*ECM away.*}

The drones he recalled with his left hand docked silently with the ship, while the ones released by his right were flushed from several ports along *Scimitar*'s flank. Clad in the same stealth coating that enveloped the Helios, the drones were nearly impossible to detect.

Micah separated them into two swarms. One went speeding back toward the ship that was skimming across the platform's surface in its hunt for *Scimitar*. The other inserted itself between the cutter and the enemy vessel.

{*Dazzlers en route, Banshees on hold,*} announced Micah.

{*Good. Coordinate with the coastie defense grid to avoid crossfire,*} Rafc instructed.

The Dazzlers Micah had unleashed were tiny yet powerful tools in the ship's arsenal. When activated, they emitted strong electronic jamming that would deny targeting information to the enemy. The drones also blocked communication, making it impossible to coordinate an attack—and, in this case, to contact anyone who might be on the platform.

While the Dazzlers were defensive, the drones Micah held in reserve were not. Where the Dazzlers' purpose was to confuse and confound, the Banshees were built to pack a powerful punch. Their payload of missiles varied by class, and all of them mounted five-centimeter lasers that could deliver pulsed bursts of weapons fire on Micah's mental command.

{*Any guesses as to who our friends out there might be?*} the mental voice of *Scimitar*'s gunner tickled Micah's ear as he watched her target the tangos. The twin large-bore, RAU-19 railguns under Dana's control tracked the vessels the ship's IFF had identified as 'Foe'.

{*My credit's on pirates,*} Cass volunteered. {*It's no secret this platform's being decommissioned. Makes a perfect hideout—or a place to offload goods.}*

Dana scoffed. *{Well, we know one thing for sure. Whoever they are, they don't have the brains God gave a gnat. Who'd be dumb enough to go up against a Shadow Recon ship?}*

{Let's find out.} At Rafe's words, a highlight appeared on Micah's overlay. In the next instant, Rafe enlarged the image until the 'SS' icon emblazoned on the ship's ventral fin could be clearly seen.

Micah unleashed a few choice words. *{Aw, that's just great. Don't waste your time trying to persuade them to surrender. Those secessionists would rather die than give in.}*

Rafe grunted his agreement. *{Better warn the team.}*

A beat later, his voice came over the combat net. *{Noble, this is Spartan. Tangos are SS. I say again, tangos are SS. Assume you have company, over.}*

{Copy, Spartan.} Thad's voice sounded gruff, as if he were already in the thick of battle. His next words confirmed Micah's suspicions. *{Engaging.}*

The SS in the logo stood for 'Secede Sirius'. They were a separatist group that had been trying unsuccessfully for more than a century to persuade the citizens of the Sirius binary system to secede from the Geminate Alliance.

Highly nationalistic, the group's chief complaint was the imbalance of power between the two star systems of Procyon and Sirius. Their platform promised to rectify that.

The organization regularly attempted to place themselves on ballots. Sometimes it worked; most times, it didn't. They'd been around so long, few took them seriously.

That had recently changed. The SS, as they now called themselves, was under new management—one willing to use violence to make its point.

Rafe sent the Helios breaking north of the stellar plane, giving them a clear shot as the ship entered weapons range.

{Free to engage,} he said, *{but try for disabling shots if you can.}*

Micah heard Dana's reply as if from a distance. The merge

he shared with the ship rendered the cockpit invisible, transmuting his perception into a different reality altogether. It was as if he floated freely in the black, his view unimpeded by something as mundane as bulkhead and hull.

Over comms, he heard Cass coordinating with the coastie defense grid, updating them in real-time of *Scimitar*'s intentions.

Scimitar surged forward. The next few minutes passed by in a blur, yet held that quality of time slowing that so often happened when senses were acute.

Although *Scimitar* was invisible to EM scans, Dana's railgun fire easily marked the Helios' location. The SS vessel returned fire, and Rafe slewed to port, tracer rounds from the enemy ship flashing by.

Micah swiveled his head to follow the other spacecraft as it began evasive maneuvers, the reticle of his Banshee's targeting app locking onto the enemy ship with smooth precision. With a thought, the drone under his command spat out a series of two-second bursts, pulsed light from its five-centimeter laser hitting the seam where the fusion drive met its powerplant.

The Banshee's initial assault weakened the area just enough that the follow-up missile Micah unleashed punched through the outer hull, severing its drive train. The other craft disintegrated instantly.

Even as the debris field expanded, Rafe was already banking *Scimitar* into a tight curve.

*{What part of **disabling** shots did you not understand, Lieutenant?}*

{That ship shouldn't have blown like it did.} Micah spared a swift glance at the man seated to his right. *{It's almost as if they had some sort of dead-man's switch wired in to ensure no prisoners were taken.}*

{Survivors?} Rafe barked the question at Cass as the ship carved an arc that took them below the plane of the system, neatly avoiding the debris field.

Out of the corner of his eye, Micah saw the crew chief shake her head. *{It must have been remotely piloted, I'm not reading any biological material in the field at all.}*

{Huh. Anyone else think this was a bit too easy?} Dana spoke into the silence.

A quick blip caught Micah's eye. At the same time, Cass let out a string of curses. *{Dana, next time, keep your damn mouth shut.}*

Three more ships swept out from behind a well-positioned asteroid whose metal content had effectively blocked their ship's scan from reading them.

{Brace for maneuvers!}

The story continues, in *Operation Cobalt,* available now.

AFTERWORD

I always love including at least one cool, new emerging tech in each book. In *The Chiral Conspiracy*, it was MXene (pronounced 'Maxine'), a 2-D material first developed in 2011. In 2018, chemical engineers created a MXene membrane that functioned as a hydrogen sieve, separating gases at a molecular level.

The ships in The Biogenesis War have MXene incorporated into their external surfaces as a way to 'background harvest' fuel from the interstellar medium. While it's not a primary fuel source, it never hurts to harvest hydrogen wherever you can.

(H2 is slightly more plentiful in Alpha Centauri than it is in Sirius and Procyon, but it's not too terribly concentrated, with electron density only ~ 0.07 cm^-3.)

Besides, it's cool.

In this book, I employed an emerging piece of tech that, as of this publication, is less than a month old: they are the CQDs that Dacina injected Ell with after she was shot, in order to speed her healing.

Quantum dots (QDs) are man-made nanoscale crystals that can transport electrons. But QDs aren't new; they were theorized in the 1970s, and have been in use in research for many years.

Quantum dots are sometimes referred to as artificial atoms, because their structure so closely resembles naturally occurring atoms.

Carbon quantum dots (CQDs), on the other hand, were accidentally discovered in 2004. They differ from your basic QD in one critical respect: carbon QDs aren't toxic to the human body. CQDs are capable of molecular recognition and self-assembly, which opens up a whole world of possibilities.

A January 2021 study, published in *Biopolymers for Biomedical Applications* indicates that they are especially effective at reconstructing tissue and closing wounds, which was the basis for my extrapolation of how it was used in this book.

Finally, I wanted to end with a bit of science. In case you had never come across the word before, oobleck is real.

Oddly, its name is borrowed from a classic book written by Dr. Seuss. Classic oobleck is made from a simple mixture of cornstarch and water. When combined, it transforms into a material classified as a non-newtonian fluid. Non-newtonian fluids don't obey Newton's law of viscosity.

Viscosity is the amount of internal friction a fluid has. The higher the viscosity, the greater the friction, and the slower the fluid flows. Some liquids become less viscous when heated— maple syrup, for example. It's something we've intuitively experienced all our lives to the point we hardly notice it, unless we're soft-matter physicists, or mechanics, or engineers.

One thing all standard fluids have in common is that this viscosity is something that is constant, unchanging. Always the same, under a given temperature and pressure.

Not so with some fluids. These non-newtonian fluids behave in very counterintuitive ways. Take ketchup, for instance. Who hasn't smacked the bottom of a ketchup bottle, only to have it gush out in a great gob all over their fries?

Ketchup should flow at exactly the same rate, regardless of how hard you shake the bottle. That's what any other liquid, like motor oil, your favorite shampoo, or even cough syrup would do. But with ketchup, when you smack the bottom of that bottle, the force of the impact actually causes the fluid to flow faster.

It's non-newtonian.

Oobleck, like you read in the story, is the opposite. It's shear-thickening, which means when you strike it, it seizes up, flows slower. It hardens.

And hundreds of years in the future, testing facilities like the one at Douglass-Washburn just might have a use for a material that, with a single command, can change from liquid to oobleck.

You never know, right?

TERMINOLOGY

ActiveFiber Coating – a coating used to layer the bulkheads of ships and space stations. It has self-healing properties, similar to self-cleaning fabrics used for shipsuits. The fiber is infused with nanobots, which can absorb contaminants within an area, break it down into its constituent parts, and reuse the material.

Branes – can be envisioned as a type of indentation within the Bulk. The universe in which we live is an example of a brane.

The Bulk – the many layers, or branes, that comprise hyperspace, the area of extradimensional space outside the dimension our universe inhabits.

Calabi-Yau Gate – This method of folding space is powered by siphoning dark matter out of a Ricci-flat manifold. The manifold, a special curvature within the Bulk, is a place where the vacuum energy of space can be accessed. Once converted to Casimir energy, it is then used to bend the Bulk, allowing for instantaneous travel from one location in normal spacetime to another, regardless of distance. The amount of Casimir energy differs, based on the amount and direction of the bend.

Coalition of Worlds – The Coalition isn't a governing body, but rather an alliance of independent star nations, for the advancement of peace and collaboration between the settled worlds. Its members include the Sol, Alpha Centauri, and Proxima Centauri star systems.

Sol's member nations are Terra, Mars, Venus, and the Ganymede and Europa colonies. Alpha Centauri B's star nation is Zoser. Alpha Centauri A (Rigel Kentaurus) is the Akkadian Empire. Proxima Centauri's member nation is the Shang dynasty.

The Coalition's articles state that all eight governmental bodies are equally represented, however, some are unofficially regarded as more equal than others.

The star nations within the Sol System hold the lion's share of influence.

Colloid Nano – Colloids are extremely tiny insoluble particles that are so light, they remain suspended in air. When grafted onto nano, colloid nano clouds can be released.

Thanks to brownian motion, the force of the particles in the air around them is greater than the force of gravity attempting to pull them down, therefore they float and are susceptible to the activity of air currents.

Colloidene Nano – A colloidene is made from a colloid particle, but formed just like single-layer graphene. Patterned in a honeycomb lattice, it employs some of the click-assembly techniques used in chemistry.

Pre-loaded common codes, or 'bricks', give nano creation a jump-start. The result is a nanobot, programmed to rapidly alter existing nano to whatever the person controlling it needs it to be.

Crowbars and LockPiks – Both are lock-picking programs, although LockPiks are covert where Crowbars are overt.

A Crowbar is a brute-force version that borrows click-assembly techniques used in chemistry to rapidly alter the properties of existing nanolocks. Pre-loaded common codes, or 'bricks', give the Crowbar a jump-start, pushing a cascade failure into the lock that cracks it wide open. In the process, it rendered the lock useless.

In contrast, a LockPik is a slower and more subtle program that works to subvert a lock's program while maintaining its program integrity so that it can be reset back to original specs after the LockPik's use.

DBCs – A digital-to-biological converter capable of printing complex, synthetic biological material from detailed molecular diagrams transmitted to it.

DUET Wires (aka "the wire") – DUET is a little-used acronym for communication nanocircuitry implanted in the brain.

DUET stands for Direct Uplink Evanescent Telecom. Much to the dismay of the corporation that invented the tech, that name never took hold. Commonly known simply as 'the wire,' a DUET implant must wait until the brain has reached a certain development level.

A web of nanoscale tendrils is deployed at critical spaces within the brain: information inputs at dendrites, and data outputs at synaptic terminals.

Evanescent (E-V) Nanocircuitry – E-V nanocircuitry is the foundation upon which the DUET system was launched. The core communication unit embedded in the brain makes use of the optical phenomenon of evanescent modes with imaginary wave numbers and a poynting vector of zero to achieve the mathematical equivalent of quantum tunneling for the instantaneous transmission of information.

Ford-Svaiter nodes – F-S nodes use the concept of focusing vacuum fluctuations with parabolic mirrors to induce a quantized field wherein evanescent nanocircuitry can be used to establish instantaneous communication. An F-S node is encased inside a Starshot Buoy. Buoys are seeded throughout a star system in a pattern known as the Starshot Constellation. All inhabited star systems have deployed Constellations.

INS, Interstellar Navigation System – The INS uses pulsars as navigation beacons to generate an interstellar positioning system.

Junxun Tèzhǒng – Akkadia's elite intelligence branch of the State Army, those chosen as Tèzhǒng are sent through a crucible of deep indoctrination that refines its members into surgically efficient killing machines. Most Tèzhǒng operatives focus on a specialty, with the most elite being its assassins.

MAC –Magic-Angle Carbyne is the strongest material known in the 25th century. It is fashioned from two single-layer, honeycomb lattices of carbyne, twisted so that they sit at a specific angle relative to one another. MAC is two times stronger than graphene or carbon nanotubes.

MXene – A high-temperature 2-D laminar molybdenum carbide material that functions as an ultrafast sieve. Alliance Navy ships are coated in the material. When in motion, the material pulls $H(0)$, ultra-dense hydrogen that dark matter is made of, from the interstellar medium for use as fuel. The $H(0)$ is stored in CNT-reinforced receptacles lining the ship's hull.

No-wake zones – The biggest reason for a no-wake-zone around a space station is because of the amount of neutron radiation generated by a ship's fission drive. A minimal dose of 4.4 GW of neutrons will deliver a lethal dose at half a kilometer in 1/5 of a second. As a result, all ships are manufactured with very thick, effective anti-radiation shadow shields. As a precaution, all ships must maintain mandatory separation when operating fusion drives.

Ricci-flat manifold – a special curvature of space found in the Bulk, also known as hyperspace.

Scharnhorst Drive – Interstellar drive that generates a Casimir bubble. This allows the drive to both harness and magnify the Scharnhorst effect, a phenomenon in which light travels faster than c. The drive allows a ship inside its bubble to travel at triple the speed of light.

SmartCarbyne – A self-repairing version of MAC, used as the building material for space elevators.

SmartCarbyne Nanofloss – This adaptation of SmartCarbyne is a lattice of ultrafine SC filaments, implanted to reinforce bone, muscle, and sinew. This
military augmentation is usually given to fighter pilots and special operations soldiers.

It was originally adapted for military use to protect pilots in high-*g* maneuvers. An accelerometer embedded in the pilot's wire controls the deployment of an SC lattice, woven into the soft tissues of vital organs. When experiencing acceleration greater than what the human body can withstand, the SC lattice automatically hardens, protecting the pilot.

Spike – Special operations electronic breadcrumb trail, only useful at short range. Each spike has a unique geometric signature. That signature is contained in the Alliance military database. An app registers the negative space created by each spike on whatever surface it resides. Once a person or item has been spiked, the search app keeps track of the void that particular spike makes, pinpointing its location while it remains in range.

Tau-Neu Chambers – Stasis chambers where all atomic function is held in suspension. The term comes from the Latin symbol, tau, [τ] which in physics and engineering represents the time constant. Neu, or the Latin 'nu', represents the molecular vibration mode, v_x which, in stasis, is zero.

TENGs and PENGs – Triboelectric nanogenerator batteries are power-harvesting batteries that capture the electric current generated through contact of two materials, converting movement to stored energy. PENGs are piezoelectric nanogenerators that charge using ambient sound in the atmosphere around them.

Ziptie – a nano breach application for use in restraining people. Once placed onto exposed flesh the app immediately unpacks itself, blocking an individual's wire from transmitting a call for help, and rendering the victim temporarily immobile.

PRINCIPAL CHARACTERS

GEMINATE ALLIANCE

Jonathan Case: Captain, Geminate Navy. Former Shadow Recon pilot, now attached to Task Force Blue, a special forces team created by the National Security Agency in response to threats to the Alliance.

Micah Case: Jonathan Case's chiral clone. The process created an untraceable, unhackable mental link. As far as the settled worlds know, there is only one Jonathan Micah Case. The two men share the same identity outside the Task Force, their unique abilities hidden and employed on behalf of the Geminate Alliance.

Samantha Travis: Radiation physicist and medical doctor, Sam rescued Micah and saved Jonathan's life. She is read into Task Force Blue and works for the Alliance in chiral research. Duncan Cutter's niece.

Duncan Cutter: Director, National Security Agency, Geminate Alliance.

Thaddeus Severance III: Marine captain, former head of Special Reconnaissance Team Five, now leader of Task Force Blue.

Elodie Cyr: A former sniper and member of SRU Team Five, Ell is now an NCIC Special Agent, in charge of the Navy's Criminal Investigation Command office on Hawking Habitat. She has been read into Task Force

Blue and has assisted on previous team deployments.

Colonel Tala Valenti: Leader of the Special Reconnaissance Units, and of Task Force Blue.

Harris Carlisle: A three-star general from the Geminate Marines, and Vice Chief of Joint Operations Command.

Raphael Garza: Newly appointed prime minister of the Geminate Alliance.

TASK FORCE BLUE

Unit Team:

Captain Thad Severance: team leader.

NCIC Special Agent Gabriel Alvarez: team second-in-command.

Sergeant Boone Brady: Sniper and ordnance specialist.

Sergeant Asha Holt: operations and team medic.

Flight Crew:

Jonathan/Micah Case: Captain and pilot.

Yuki O'Connell: Lieutenant and co-pilot.

Nina Vandiver: Chief Warrant Officer and 'backender'; the crew's gunner.

Will Morris: Specialist and flight engineer.

Katie Hyer: Chief Warrant, currently cross-training with both Yuki and Will.

THE AKKADIAN EMPIRE

Asher Dent: Former Minority Leader of the Coalition of World's General Assembly. Recently assumed the title of Premier of the Akkadian Empire.

Che Josza: Former Citizen General First-Class, demoted from Third-Class after failed attempt to seize chiral material. Recently appointed as Minister of State Security.

Dacina Zian ("Fierce Dagger"): Akkadian assassin and member of the Junxun Tèzhǒng. Self-appointed protector of Che Josza.

Rin Zhou Enlai: Former Minister of State Security under previous administration.

Clint Janus: Akkadian sleeper agent, born and raised in Geminate Alliance. Biochemist who recently disappeared from the Alliance, resurfacing in Akkadia.

WEAPONRY & ARMOR

CUSP – Compact Ultra-Short Pulse pistol uses a pulsed, laser-induced plasma to either paralyze, flash-bang, flash-blind, or deliver searing pain, depending on the weapon's setting.

P-SCAR – Pulsed Special Combat Assault Rifle.

RAU-19 – Railgun mounted on DAP Helios attack craft.

Banshees – Each Banshee fighter-bomber mounts a five-centimeter laser, and is capable of strafing runs. In addition, each USV carries a pair of missiles, their yields varying by Banshee model type.

Dazzlers – Dazzlers emit decoy ECM and jam signals, robbing enemy vessels of their ability to coordinate their attack.

Drakeskin armor – A carbyne-reinforced synthsilk skinsuit, used by special operations forces when infiltrating hostile territory.

Drakeskin stealth suit – A drakeskin suit with a nanoweave embedded into the topmost layer of fabric that is tunable to the environment, providing visible-spectrum stealth. The underlayers are made of metamaterials, which use transformation optics to shield the wearer from view by controlling electromagnetic radiation and guiding incident waves around the wearer.

About the Biogenesis War™ Universe

In the twenty-second century, humanity reached the stars.

With colonies established throughout the Sol system, pioneers hungry for new ventures traveled beyond its borders to nearby Alpha Centauri. There, they planted the first seeds of what would become three independent star nations—two around its binary stars, a third orbiting nearby Proxima Centauri.

Not long after, a theoretical form of propulsion became a reality. The experimental new drive's Casimir bubble magnified the Scharnhorst effect, allowing velocities up to three times the speed of light.

A brave band of explorers took a chance on the new tech and launched a pair of colony ships toward the binary stars of Procyon and Sirius. Their descendants flourished, forming the Geminate Alliance.

While the Scharnhorst drive made it possible to reach stars as distant as Sirius and Procyon, travel between the fledgling colonies and their parent star was still measured in years. The Geminate settlers were on their own, and they knew it.

Three hundred years passed. In the mid-twenty-fifth century, a pair of Alliance scientists discovered a way to fold spacetime, bending the compactified branes that were stacked within the Bulk of extradimensional space. Thus, the Calabi-Yau gates were born.

These specially-tuned, 'pair-partnered' gates provided instantaneous travel between star systems, regardless of distance. For the first time, far-flung civilizations reconnected in real time, and true interstellar commerce became a reality.

Those back in Sol had formed a loose association known as the Coalition of Worlds. The Coalition eagerly embraced the Alliance's gate tech. Treaties were signed, leases granted, and soon the Geminate government had gates at each heliopause.

A robust and vigorous trade developed between the settled worlds, ushering in a prosperous new era for every star nation involved—with one exception: Akkadia.

The star nation orbiting Rigel Kentaurus had built an export economy around handcrafted materials whose value was based on scarcity, forced by Scharnhorst limitations and slow trade routes. This was utterly disrupted by the gates.

Akkadia plunged into a recession. Desperate circumstances allowed an oppressive regime to wrest power from its premier. The planet went from an artisan's enclave to a totalitarian government.

The current Ministry of State Security was rumored to have its hooks in every star nation from Terra to Sirius. It stole tech where it could, sabotaged when it couldn't. Such actions propelled Akkadia into a state of cold war with the rest of the settled worlds.

And then the Akkadian Premier set his sights on the Geminate gate tech.

The Alliance has no idea how far Akkadia is willing to go to achieve this goal. They're also unaware how thoroughly they've been compromised, but they're about to find out....

ACKNOWLEDGMENTS

This particular book became challenging to write midstream, not because the words wouldn't flow, but because I suddenly found myself without a means to type them.

Mid-December, I landed in the ER with a boxer's fracture in my left hand. I ended up dictating more than 80,000 words—a good two-thirds of this book—instead of typing in the conventional manner.

Special thanks go out to a cadre of incredibly talented people who helped bring this to you in a timely fashion, a mere four weeks after its original release date.

These beta readers helped me spot inconsistencies and catch errors where dictation software rendered 'hangar' as 'hanger' (anathema to a pilot like me!).

John, as always, thank you for being my science sounding board. Steve and Dawn, thank you, not only for the years of military service you gave to our country, but also for lending me your expertise. Any mistakes readers may find are entirely my own.

Manie and Charlie, your keen sense of story helped catch places where the spoken word had veered slightly off course. I have Crystal and Marti to thank for that, too. Your eagle eyes caught a plethora of misspellings that invariably crop up in a manuscript of this length.

Above and beyond all this is the incredible work of an editor who not only gets me, she gets the characters, and the story. Thank you, Jen, for helping me to stay true to Thad, Ell, Micah, and the rest. You're an angel.

Lastly, I want to thank Marty for picking up the slack these past seven weeks while my hand was in a cast—especially when 2021 told 2020, "hold my beer," and then proceeded to dump us into extraordinarily cold temperatures that resulted in broken pipes and a flooded home. To say you're the best is an understatement.

ALSO BY LL RICHMAN

The Biogenesis War Series

The Chiral Agent

The Chiral Protocol

Chiral Justice

Chiral Agent/Chiral Conspiracy audiobook set

Chiral Protocol/Ambush in the Sargon Straits audio set

The Biogenesis War Files: The Early Years

Operation Cobalt

Ambush in the Sargon Straits

The Chiral Conspiracy

ABOUT THE AUTHOR

L.L. Richman has a diverse background, balancing a career as a film director with evenings spent running a linear accelerator.

Physics is a big part of Richman's life—particularly radiation physics. Whereas most people keep plates and cups in their kitchen cabinets, Richman's are filled with radioactive materials, lead-lined gloves, and a Geiger counter.

A self-proclaimed 'NASA brat,' some of Richman's earliest memories are of following her father through the Johnson Space Center, of being inside Mission Control (but not while it was active), of fast planes and astronauts.

Richman went on to become a pilot, and can often be found flying a Piper Cherokee, or photographing Deep Sky Objects (DSOs) late at night.

She shares her home with a physicist and three cats, two of whom are appropriately named Maxwell and Faraday.

For more information on upcoming releases or the latest news on space science and technology, like LL Richman's Facebook page, or join the Biogenesis War Facebook group.